For Eric, for all the roads we've travelled and the adventures ahead. May our journey together always be filled with love, laughter and endless discoveries.

About the Author

Caroline James always wanted to write but instead of taking a literary route, she followed a career in the hospitality industry, which included owning a pub and a beautiful country house hotel. She was also a media agent representing many celebrity chefs.

When she's not writing, Caroline likes to go wild water swimming or walk with Fred, her Westie.

www.carolinejamesauthor.co.uk

facebook.com/AuthorCarolineJames

x.com/CarolineJames12

instagram.com/carolinejamesauthor

bsky.app/profile/carolinejames1.bsky.social

Chapter One

'D*on't let the old man in...'*

Atticus Arnott didn't want to let the old man in but had no idea how to stop him. After almost forty years of marriage, life without Clara seemed pointless.

'What would you make of it now, eh, Clara?' Atticus looked towards the sky. 'I don't know what's going on up there, but the world seems to have gone mad down here.'

Perched on a drystone wall, Atticus adjusted the brim of his weathered cowboy hat and gazed out over his property. Below, a cluster of stone buildings nestled in the valley, blending seamlessly with the patchwork of fields surrounding his farm. With a quiet grunt, he leaned on his crook and dug into his overcoat pocket to pull out a treat. 'There you go, girl,' he said softly as Ness, his scruffy Collie, wagged her tail.

His thoughts ran to the countless miles he'd tramped across the fells surrounding the farm. Happy days with Ness bounding along at his side, her eyes bright with anticipation, ready to spring into action and skilfully herd. But now the fields stood silent, and the gentle bleat of his Herdwick sheep faded into memory, their echoes as faint and ghostly as Clara's voice.

Atticus had a deep connection to the land, having farmed it all his life. His respect for the heritage of his Herdwick sheep had been passed down through generations of the Arnott family, and as a young boy, he'd learnt the skills specific to Cumbria's farming challenges from his father and grandfather. The rural lifestyle suited him and Clara as young newlyweds, especially when they inherited the farm.

'We did alright,' Atticus murmured as he plodded along.

The modest income from breeding and selling his sheep enabled them to raise a family, though neither Mungo, his son, nor Mary, his twin, showed any interest in continuing the shepherding life.

Reaching an old wooden kissing gate, Atticus paused, his gaze lingering over the weathered slats he'd replaced countless times over the years. This was the place where he'd proposed to Clara, just eighteen years old, during a Sunday afternoon walk.

'You were as beautiful as the sunrise over the fells,' he said softly to the sky streaked with rhubarb hues, recalling Clara's fiery red hair, sparkling emerald eyes, and the freckles that danced across her cheeks. When he first kissed her, her lips were as soft as freshly fallen snow.

Atticus stroked the smooth, familiar gate and let out a long, wistful sigh. Five years ago, at sixty-five, Clara's heart attack had been sudden and fatal. One moment, she was busy on the farm; the next, she was at the kitchen table clutching her chest.

'*Don't let the old man in...*' she'd whispered with her final breath to her heartbroken husband. Words borrowed from her favourite actor, Clint Eastwood, in a film they'd watched countless times together.

Atticus pushed open the gate, and Ness darted ahead.

'Ah, Clara, we never did get to take that dream holiday, did we?' Atticus murmured, his gaze drifting skyward. 'Spain seems like another world now.'

He remembered how they'd planned to celebrate a wedding anniversary with a month-long escape to Spain, and studied countless brochures, imagining their days on the sunlit shores of the Costa Blanca. Now, that dream lay shattered, nothing more than a memory of what might have been.

After Clara's death, Mungo pieced together the fragments of his father's shattered life. Watching Atticus decline, Mungo made the difficult decision to leave his thriving career with an IT company and relocate his family to Barn Hill Farm.

'So many changes,' Atticus mumbled as he looked down at the valley.

In the distance, he could see the market town of Eden, where the spire of the Church of St. Lawrence reached into the clear blue sky. On the gentle slope, the converted farm buildings clustered around a main house. As he studied his farm, Atticus thought of Mungo's wildly ambitious plans for Barn Hill Farm's future.

To Atticus's horror, they didn't include breeding and raising sheep.

Mungo's vision of a café and farm shop, followed by a caravan site and glamping area, was, in his opinion, the only way forward if the farm was to support everyone.

'But what about the sheep?' Atticus had argued.

'They must go. We can't survive if things stay the same,' Mungo reasoned. 'The location of Barn Hill Farm is perfect. There's a main road on our doorstep, which is a thoroughfare to the Lakes, and we'll be a destination for locals and holidaymakers, who pour into the area all year round.'

In his heart, Atticus knew that Mungo had been right. If changes didn't happen, the farm couldn't sustain them all. Atticus wasn't getting any younger, and Mungo wasn't prepared to miss out on an enterprising opportunity and see his inheritance go to waste.

But losing his beloved Herdwick sheep had been painful for Atticus.

Mungo's progressive strategy was quickly passed by the local planning department, which supported his ideas and welcomed opportunities for employment and tourism. The Department for Environment, Food, and Rural Affairs secured him a large grant. Atticus's sheep stock had been reduced to a mere handful of cute-looking animals, penned for children to feed and pet. The black lambs were endearing to the visitors, but they didn't quite quell Atticus's sadness about losing most of his flock.

As Atticus trudged on, Ness ran ahead, tail wagging, nose glued to the ground. At seventy, Atticus had lost his get-up-and-go. It had 'gotten up and gone' with Clara's death, and he had neither the will nor the need to find it.

Reaching a rocky outcrop, Atticus paused, his eyes fixed on the bustling car park surrounding his home. It was packed with visitors eager to enjoy a hearty breakfast in the café before stocking up on provisions at the farm shop. His eyes scanned the yard, landing on Mungo's wife, Helen, as she emerged from the farmhouse. Crossing the yard to the café, she deftly tied on an apron and gathered her dark hair into a ponytail. He thought of her scones – plump, fluffy, and as delicious as her cakes. Renowned throughout the region, they earned top awards at the county show.

As his granddaughter came into sight, Atticus gave a half-smile, watching Eliza bounce alongside her mum. At thirteen, Eliza was younger than her brother Jake, all gangly limbs and a mop of curly black hair. Her freckled face bore a striking resemblance to her Grandma Clara's, and Atticus felt a swell of pride for the girl, who pot-washed and cleared tables at weekends to add to her pocket money – funds she spent on newfangled gadgets that left Atticus baffled. He cherished the time they shared when Eliza came home from school; those moments were a bright spot in his day.

'Grandad, you need to get with it,' Eliza told Atticus as she shrugged off her blazer and threw her bag onto the floor. 'If you had a laptop, you could be searching the internet. It's like having an encyclopaedia at your fingertips.'

'And what would I want with one of those?' Atticus asked as he made a drink for Eliza, and they sat companionably in his kitchen.

'Jake says you should join a dating site.' Eliza nibbled a chocolate biscuit. 'He googled "Farmer's Friends" and says there are lots of old ladies looking for love.'

Atticus almost spat out his tea.

Eliza, ignoring her grandad's horror, ploughed on. 'You're quite good-looking for an old person.' She studied his face. 'And you've still got all your hair.' She licked chocolate from her fingers and reached for another biscuit. 'But it would have to be someone who likes smelly dogs and shaggy sheep, and Jake says she'd need a sense of humour to put up with your grumps and moans.'

'Does he, indeed?' Atticus shook his head. 'Well, you needn't worry your pretty little head as grandad has no intention of looking for a dog-loving, sheep-friendly companion.'

Atticus wished that Jake would mind his own business and attend to other matters. His grandson showed little interest towards academia, preferring to spend his free time tinkering with engines and helping at the caravan site. Jake took pride in keeping the grounds immaculate and ensuring all the utilities were in perfect order. If something needed fixing, Jake was always first on the scene with a friendly smile and his toolbox in hand.

Ness began to bark, and Atticus frowned as he raised the brim of his hat and saw smoke puffing from a tractor. 'What's Jake up to now?'

His grandson was headed towards the glamping area, steering the vehicle confidently. Clad in a bright red shirt, quilted gilet, jeans, and wellingtons, Jake was a mini-

Mungo. At sixteen, tall and handsome, he carried himself with the same self-assured air.

Atticus stretched his fingers as a familiar ache of longing settled in. How he wished Clara could slip her warm hand into his. 'Aye,' he murmured softly, 'what would you make of it all now?'

Mungo Arnott paused as he crossed the yard from the farmhouse. The morning mist was rising, curling above the fells where golden sunlight danced across the landscape, casting shifting shadows like a game of hide-and-seek. It was a sight he'd cherished since childhood, and one that never lost its magic. Silhouetted in the distance, Mungo could see a man trudging over the rugged terrain, while a dog bounded ahead, tail held high.

'The old man's out and about,' Mungo said to himself, then turned and headed to his office, a converted outbuilding.

With his hands thrust deep into the pockets of his gilet, Mungo couldn't help but wonder about his father's solitary habits. Since his mother's death, Atticus had withdrawn, and when Mungo had proposed leaving his job and moving his family to Barn Hill Farm, Atticus had barely reacted.

'Whatever you think best,' Atticus had said. It was the same response he gave to every suggestion, even as the farm underwent sweeping changes. Despite Mungo's efforts, Atticus remained uninvolved. If Mungo asked for an opinion, or even about his well-being, his father would repeat his familiar refrain: 'Whatever you think best, and I'm fine – perfectly happy.'

Reaching his office door, Mungo stepped into the welcoming space where sunlight streamed through the windows overlooking the café and rolling fells. A wall of framed photos of before and after the renovations documented the farm's transformation, while the quiet click of a keyboard filled the room, and a familiar face peeked over a computer screen.

'Morning, Mungo,' Ali greeted him, her eyes flicking towards the window. 'I see your dad's out for a walk.' Running her fingers through a crop of blonde hair, Ali pushed back her chair and stood. 'Coffee?' she offered.

'Just the job,' Mungo replied.

Moments later Ali placed a steaming mug of frothy coffee on the desk beside him. 'You looked worried,' she said. 'What's up?'

'Mary arrives today,' Mungo sighed. 'I know that as soon as she gets settled, she'll start on about Dad's listlessness, and how he's not involved in the farm.'

Mary, Mungo's twin, lived in Ireland and was coming to spend the school holidays in Cumbria with her four children, leaving her high-flying husband behind.

'She's worried about your dad, naturally. He's not the same man he used to be.'

'Aye, and twice as grumpy,' Mungo replied with a half-smile. 'But I'm concerned for him too, Mum's death still lingers heavily.'

Ali perched on the edge of her desk, her tone softening.

'He never really got over your mam. Clara was a wonderful woman.'

'It's been five years, Ali.' Mungo sipped his coffee. 'He should have moved on by now.'

Mungo understood the grief of losing Clara; they'd all felt it deeply. Although the passing of time had blunted the edges, the memories stayed a bittersweet comfort. Yet Mungo struggled to accept how quickly his father had retreated, handing over the farm without protest. Mungo had been braced for a battle, but Atticus had simply stepped aside. He was as docile as one of his beloved lambs when they moved him out of the grand house and into the small, charming cottage, which was far too cramped for Mungo's family.

'It's a shame he can't have a little job,' Ali remarked. 'Something to give him a sense of purpose, maybe helping with the caravans or looking after the grounds.'

Mungo nodded. 'He says he doesn't want to interfere.'

'Your dad must see how successful you've made the place,' Ali said, glancing at her spreadsheet of the farm's accounts. 'The farm shop and café are always busy, and the caravan pitches are booked months in advance.'

'I've no idea if he even thinks about it,' Mungo sighed. 'But I know he'd be lost if I hadn't stepped in.'

'Couldn't he have sold up and moved somewhere small and manageable?' she replied.

Mungo stared at Ali in disbelief.

'Alright,' Ali laughed. 'Maybe the cow will jump over the moon before your dad leaves his land.'

'He'll only leave in the back of a hearse and return to be scattered over the hills,' Mungo added.

'Don't dwell on the past,' Ali said with a reassuring smile. 'Barn Hill Farm is thriving, and it's all thanks to you. The local community is grateful for all the jobs you've created.'

Mungo looked at Ali and couldn't imagine what he'd have done without her. Atticus refused to get involved in the business and the responsibility for Mungo weighed heavily.

In her fifties, Ali had retired from a successful career as a finance director at a London bank after the sudden passing of her husband, a lawyer. Needing a complete change, she moved to Cumbria, but living on the land wasn't the country dream Ali envisaged, and bored with gardening and coffee mornings, she'd jumped at the chance when Mungo offered her a job. She missed the pace of business and told friends, '*My job keeps me young and my mind sharp.*' Relishing the opportunity to keep the farm's finances in check, Ali ran everything smoothly.

'I'm looking forward to seeing Mary again,' Ali said, glancing up from her computer. 'What time does she arrive?'

'Late afternoon.'

'Is she driving?' she asked.

'Aye, she has more baggage than any airline can handle,' Mungo replied.

'Four kids for a month takes a lot of juggling,' Ali said with a grin. 'But Mary landed on her feet when she crossed the Irish Sea.'

'I don't think a weekend at a gourmet food festival in Kindale was meant to include marriage, but she certainly did well,' Mungo agreed.

He remembered how upset he'd been when his sister finished her studies in business management, went off for a girls' weekend, and never returned. They'd been close growing up, but once Mary left home and Mungo went off to pursue his career in computing, the pair became distant. When Mary fell in love with her husband, Conor, at the food festival, it led to her working with him. As their love blossomed, so did Conor's estate agency business.

'Good for her,' Ali added. 'It's great that she returns to Cumbria each summer, so you'll all be together.'

Mungo nodded. Ali was right. Having Mary back *was* good, and the kids loved having their cousins around. Mary and Helen were the best of friends, too.

If only his dad could summon the same enthusiasm when the family reunited.

Mungo spotted Atticus crossing the yard and tapped on the window, waving to get his attention. Ness wagged her tail, but Atticus stomped his boots on the cobbles, oblivious to everything around him. Pushing open the door to his cottage, he disappeared inside.

Mungo sighed, picked up a pen, and turned to Ali. 'Before we are overwhelmed with visitors from across the sea, shall we get on with the day?'

Chapter Two

'Kids, get in the car!' Mary Murphy yelled at her brood, shoving the last suitcase into the back of her Range Rover before leaning on the door with a sigh. She patted the pocket of her faded blue jeans to check for her phone, then headed to the driver's side, where Finn was slouched.

'Back seat, pal,' she said, gesturing with her thumb and gently nudging her son.

Finn, bleary-eyed, let out a long yawn. 'I wanna ride upfront,' the nine-year-old grumbled.

'Not happening,' Mary replied. 'Caitlin's already claimed the passenger seat, and she's helping me with directions.'

Finn scowled at his older sister as he climbed in beside Maeve and Declan, who were fighting over a bag of sweets. Caitlin, as smug as only a sixteen-year-old can be when winning a war over a younger sibling, stuck out her tongue. But Finn was irritable and, wrenching five-year-old Declan out of the way, punched Caitlin on the shoulder. Declan began to howl and kicked out at Finn, who returned the assault with an elbow in Declan's tummy.

'Mam! Mam!' Declan shrieked, squeezing tears from his blotchy eyes.

'Belt up, all of you, now!' Mary yelled. 'Maeve, hand out those sweets.'

Maeve tossed the sweets to Finn. 'You'll all get fat,' she remarked, flipping open her phone to examine her pouting reflection. At thirteen, Maeve was always aware of her appearance and glued to social media, where her dream of becoming an influencer consumed most of her thoughts.

'All set?' Mary asked, straightening the collar of her cream silk blouse. She turned her head to check that the seatbelts were fastened as her children settled in for the journey ahead. Satisfied, she started the engine and eased the Range Rover slowly out of the driveway of Belvedere House.

'Why can't Daddy come?' Declan whined, clutching his teddy as he gazed out of the window. He waved the stuffed animal at his father, who stood in his pyjamas, bleary-eyed on the front steps, watching them leave.

'Because your daddy needs more sleep and has to go to work.' Mary raised her hand and blew a kiss to Conor, her husband.

'I wish Daddy was coming too,' Caitlin griped, wriggling further into her seat as she folded her arms.

Mary sighed, the memory of her conversation with Conor playing in her mind. For the umpteenth time, she had suggested that he might enjoy a break from work by joining them in Cumbria. Instead, Conor had wrapped her in his arms and kissed the top of her head.

'Happiness for me,' he teased, 'is having my large, loving, close-knit family...' He paused for effect. '...in another country for the summer holiday.'

Mary told herself that Conor was joking, but deep down, she suspected there was truth in his words. Her workaholic husband rarely prioritised time away from the office. As she reached out to lightly stroke Caitlin's track-suited leg, she said, 'Your dad's far too busy to take time off, and you kids are lucky to have so many holidays. He always makes it up to us at Christmas.'

Mary thought of Conor's extravagances during the festive period. Closing the real estate business for two weeks, her husband spent every moment treating his family to a lavish pantomime at Cork's grand Opera House, gourmet meals at the best restaurants, and all the latest gadgets. None of them could complain. Life in Kindale was perfect.

'Now, settle down, the lot of you, and let me concentrate on driving.'

Mary hoped the kids would soon be asleep, leaving her to enjoy the drive. As she'd anticipated, before the signs for Cork came into view, her brood was snoozing. Even Caitlin's eyes had closed. Usually keen to help with the route, she now had an inflatable pillow tucked behind her neck, her long, dark hair falling softly over her dipped head.

Mary glimpsed her reflection in the rear-view mirror. She knew that her rich brown curls showed the first signs of grey, and there were fresh wrinkles around her eyes. But regular visits to Gaelic Glow, a posh Kindale beauty salon, helped maintain her fresh-faced look, unlike her waistline, which seemed to be on a journey of its own. Weight-loss injections had been suggested at the salon, but Mary refused. Nor would she plump her lips or join the cosmetic surgery club, where the only membership required was the willingness to part with a large chunk of cash.

Mary saw that Declan, clutching his teddy bear, was sucking his thumb. Finn held onto a football and nestled beside Declan while Maeve reached out her arm to encase her younger brothers.

'My raven-haired babies,' Mary breathed, and her heart lurched as she thought of their innocence. Free from cares and untouched by the world's harsh realities.

Her children had inherited Conor's dark hair, long lashes, and flawless skin that tanned easily and glowed in the summer sun. Conor believed there was Spanish blood in his ancestry, while Mary sometimes mused over her Cumbrian roots, possibly Roman. She often thought of her father's name, Atticus, named after Titus Pomponius Atticus, a Roman literary figure.

Thank goodness Dad isn't called Pomponius, she thought to herself, smiling as she navigated the motorway toward Dublin port. Her grandparents, long gone, must have had a mischievous sense of humour when they christened their son. At least Mary had a simple name. She thought of Mungo, her brother, who'd endured relentless teasing during his school years. The story behind his name was straightforward: Clara, their mother, had been obsessed with the pop group Mungo Jerry. She often sang their hit *In the Summertime*. It was easy for Clara to name her son, with the tune playing in the background, when the twins were born on a sunny July morning.

Mary chuckled to herself. *At least she hadn't been christened Jerry!*

The miles whizzed by, and by lunchtime, the kids were awake.

'I'm hungry,' Finn announced as they drove into the port.

'Then we'll have a meal on the ferry.' Mary stared out to the sea, where the water was as still as a millpond. 'It's going to be a calm crossing to Holyhead,' she smiled.

The drive from Holyhead to Cumbria, mostly along motorways, took about four hours. As they neared Cumbria and the last few miles lay ahead, they passed a service station.

Caitlin stirred. 'Can we stop? They have a great farm shop here.' She gazed at a cluster of trees surrounding a small lake, where travellers relaxed at picnic tables.

'No,' Mary replied firmly. 'We're almost there, and you know that your granddad has the best farm shop in the area.'

Mary bit her lip. Barn Hill Farm had grown far beyond the humble sheep farm of her childhood, and its recent success was entirely down to Mungo. Atticus, on the other hand, couldn't be credited.

'Hey, look, Mam,' Caitlin said as she sat up. 'Here's our turn.'

As the Range Rover glided through the last stretch of road, Mary lowered her window, breathing in the rich, heather-scented air that drifted from the fells. 'Ah,' she exhaled with pleasure. 'I'm home.'

Returning to Cumbria in the warm, dry days of late July and August always filled her with joy. The fells, dotted with wildflowers, were lush and green, and with the Lake District National Park nearby, the kids loved exploring.

Mary thought about her father, wondering if Atticus would feel any different about their visit this time. Since Clara's passing, he'd shown little enthusiasm for family gatherings, and Mary yearned for that to change. Despite her efforts to involve him with his grandchildren, Atticus remained distant, generally preferring his own company.

Mary yearned for the days when her dad had been happy. Back then, the farmhouse kitchen buzzed with life, its warmth radiating from the AGA cooker as Clara created her treats. The rich aroma of freshly baked cakes and bread would fill the air, while Atticus pinched a slice of cake as it cooled, teasing Clara with a playful slap on her rear. The kitchen table was the heart of the home, always surrounded by family and friends.

'This year, Dad,' Mary said as she pulled off the main road and turned onto the driveway of Barn Hill Farm, 'you're not going to be a miserable grump.'

Mary noticed the farm shop and café were bustling with visitors as her childhood home appeared. Barn Hill House, constructed generations ago from weathered local stone, was nestled into the landscape. The garden was a riot of colour, thanks to her sister-in-law Helen's meticulous care, with overflowing hanging baskets and pots on the front porch. The contrast with her futuristic, glass-fronted, modern pile back in Kindale struck her, and Mary yearned for the cosy simplicity of wooden beams, vintage furnishings, and Helen's touches that brought warmth to every corner.

Mary parked her vehicle next to Mungo's Land Rover and sighed. Her dad had everything: a lovely cottage, financial stability, and a family that loved him. Surely, there was a way to ignite his passion for life again. Mary remembered that Atticus had always been industrious. If he wasn't happily herding sheep, he was tinkering about in his workshop repairing an old engine, crafting toys, or inventing a new game for them all to play. He always found time for their annual holiday to Wales, not forgetting his regular pint in the pub with his best friend, Arthur.

She cut the engine and stepped onto the cobbled yard, making a vow that during this holiday, she'd bring her father back to life to enjoy whatever years he had left.

'Mam,' Caitlin's excited voice called out, 'Jake's driving Grandad's tractor!'

Mary turned just in time to see Caitlin leap from the car and slam the door as her sleeping siblings woke and scrambled out with equal enthusiasm.

'Will he let me ride too?' Declan bounced on his toes, wide-eyed and still clutching his teddy as Jake chugged towards them.

Caitlin ran ahead, hopping onto the tractor's running board, her hair whipping behind her as she held on tightly.

'Welcome!' Jake called out, pulling Finn into the front seat beside him, while Maeve joined Caitlin, balancing precariously but laughing in delight.

'Me too! Me too!' Declan cried out.

But before Jake could disappear with his cousins, Mary swept her five-year-old into her arms. 'Not on your life,' she said firmly. Her tone softened as Jake caught her eye. 'Jake, you know better than to drive that tractor with passengers!'

Jake's grin widened, and the playfulness in his eyes was difficult for Mary to resist. 'Maybe later,' Mary relented to Declan, 'but only if Grandad supervises.'

Jake revved the engine, and Caitlin and Maeve screamed as Finn clung on.

'Welcome home, Aunty Mary,' Jake called out to the whoops and cheers of his cousins.

Mary smiled and watched them disappear into the distance, her heart full. She was home, and despite the challenges ahead, she was ready to tackle Atticus and bring back the joy to her dad that she felt herself.

Chapter Three

In the kitchen of his cottage, Atticus woke from an afternoon nap and placed the kettle on the hob of the AGA cooker. He then turned to the sink, where plates were piled on the draining board. Once carefully dried, he walked across the quarry-tiled floor and positioned the crockery in exact order on the shelf of an old pine dresser, beside a weathered wooden box.

'Just as you like it, Clara,' Atticus said, inching a plate into perfect position.

He stirred milk into his freshly made brew and watched as the liquid turned a deep muddy brown, then tossed the bag into a bin under the deep stone sink. As he sipped his tea, Atticus stared fondly at the box on the dresser. Worn smooth by years of handling, the dark wood had faint cracks along the grain. Clara kept her embroidery needles, thimbles, and scissors in the box, but now, nestled on the faded velvet lining, a glass vial was sealed tight.

Inside the vial, Atticus had kept back a small quantity of Clara's ashes, a keepsake of his love and loss.

Ness lay nearby on a rug, but as Atticus reached down to stroke her, she raised her head, her tail beginning to thump. 'What is it, old girl?' he asked as he heard an engine chugging past the cottage. Resting a hand on the wooden draining board, he peered through the open kitchen window.

Outside, a vintage tractor came into view, and Atticus smiled. 'Ah, my Little Grey Fergie,' he whispered, admiring the clean lines and innovative engineering of a vehicle he'd lovingly restored many years ago.

Perched behind the wheel, Jake waved to his granddad.

'Be careful!' Atticus called out.

'Hi, Granddad!' the children yelled and balanced perilously as Jake revved the engine.

'Watch the paintwork!' Atticus shouted.

Caitlin and Maeve wobbled unsteadily, perched on the running boards, and Atticus winced as their trainers bounced up and down. Jake, with Finn still beside him, revved the engine again, tooted a horn and roared away across the yard towards the fells.

Atticus wondered why Mary allowed her offspring so much freedom. Scraping a chair across the tiles, he sat down and murmured that his grandkids should show more respect for his vintage vehicle.

'Mary has arrived,' Atticus said to Ness, stroking her head. 'Now there'll be a commotion.'

Sipping his tea, Atticus knew that at any moment, the cottage door would burst open, and Mary would surge in.

He glanced at the wall clock and decided to head off to the pub for a quick pint before the whirlwind that was Mary built pace, and his peaceful day was over.

Atticus reached for his hat and slipped out of the kitchen.

With Ness by his side, the pair hurried across the yard, blending in with visitors who were buying last-minute provisions in the shop. Slipping through a gate, he began to walk along a path that led to the pub.

The Black Bull stood proudly at the heart of the village green in the quaint village of Eden. It offered craft beers and, more recently, a menu of local dishes. As Atticus and Ness wandered through the pub garden, they passed holidaymakers and hikers, enjoying a thirst-quenching drink as they reflected on their day out on the fells. Nearby, a family of ducks waddled through a cluster of wildflowers beneath the sweeping branches of a willow tree before gracefully gliding into the pond.

Ness tugged on her lead, and Atticus shook his head. 'Never mind the ducks,' he said, 'a pint is more important.' Keeping his dog by his heel, he wandered into the pub where his best friend, Arthur, sat in a cosy corner of the snug, munching on pork scratchings.

'A pub should be a pub, not a fancy restaurant,' Atticus complained.

'It's true.' Arthur nodded and lifted a pint to his lips, leaving a frothy moustache. 'It's a place to sup. Half these folks don't even talk to each other,' he chuntered and offered his friend a pork scratching.

The two men looked beyond the snug where families were dining. Many youngsters had their eyes focused on a screen, engrossed in online activity, oblivious to the interesting memorabilia covering uneven walls beneath low-beamed ceilings. Old photographs of local landmarks hung beside antique farming tools and vintage advertisements for the pub from days gone by.

'Mary has landed, eh?' Arthur asked.

Atticus licked the salt from his lips and rubbed his hands along the rough fabric of his moleskin trousers. 'Just arrived, and Jake is driving around the yard like Lewis Hamilton.'

'No wonder you needed a pint.' Arthur nodded.

The snug, with its small windows and worn wooden benches, was dimly lit and offered the perfect retreat from the noisy chatter in the main bar. Here, Atticus and Arthur played dominoes every week, representing the pub in the local league.

Arthur leaned back and cradled his pint. The owner of a nearby smallholding, Arthur's weathered face was etched with lines of experience, and his eyes sparkled with memories. The air was thick with camaraderie, born of years spent together in this very spot.

When Clara was alive, Arthur and his wife, Shirley, joined the couple for quiz nights. Now, as the two men raised their glasses in a silent toast, they were simply two old friends enjoying each other's company in their favourite haunt.

'Shirley says she'll be over to see Mary,' Arthur commented.

'That'll be grand.' Atticus reached into his pocket for a treat for Ness and rubbed her head as she ate it.

'Will Mary be expecting you to spend time with the grandkids?' Arthur asked.

'Aye, like every year.'

'They're a bit too lively for the likes of us, if I remember them all correctly,' Arthur replied.

'Kids today want entertaining,' Atticus grumbled. 'Mary is constantly on the go, finding things for them to do.'

'Not like our day, eh?' Arthur nodded. 'The fells were our playground when we weren't helping out on the farm.'

'It's true.' Atticus thought of the hours he roamed over the hills with Arthur, building dens in ditches. 'Another pint?'

Suddenly, the door to the snug flew open, and Mary burst in. 'I thought you'd be in here,' she said, giving Atticus a hug.

'Hello, Mary love.' Atticus smiled and reached out to wrap an arm around his daughter. Stroking the soft skin of her face, he felt his heart tug. She was so like her mother, beautiful in every way.

Seeing tears in the corner of her dad's eyes, Mary patted his arm. 'Don't waste a stand-up,' she said, swinging a leather tote from her shoulder. 'I'll have a white wine, please Dad.' She turned and grinned at Arthur, then pecked him on the cheek. 'What are you two up to? Putting the world to rights over a pint?'

'It's good to see you, Mary.' Arthur smiled. 'And you're looking well. Must be all that fresh Irish air.'

'And rich country living,' Atticus added as he placed the drinks down. 'Is Conor still making millions?'

'Probably as many as Mungo.' Mary picked up her glass. 'Cheers to you both, it's good to be here.' She grinned, before taking a slug of her wine. 'Now, Dad, tell me all the news from the village and Barn Hill Farm.'

After another round and bidding goodbye to Arthur, Mary took Atticus's arm. Reg, the landlord, said it was good to see Mary again and hoped she'd be a regular during her holiday. Several locals acknowledged father and daughter arm-in-arm, and Atticus replied with a grunt as he tipped his hat.

'Still as unsociable as ever,' Mary said as they crossed the road. 'Do you never stop to have a chat?'

'I've nothing to talk about.'

'Dad, you've a zillion things that you could pass the time of day with,' Mary sighed. 'When Mum was alive, she couldn't shut you up.'

It was true. Atticus had loved keeping up to date with life in the locality. He knew every farmer for miles around, and together with Clara, they'd had a pleasant life in the community.

'Why don't you join in with village events anymore?' Mary asked as they walked along the path to the farm.

'It's not the same without your mum, I'm no more than a spare part. No one wants an old man getting in the way.'

Mary sighed. *What had happened to the funny, happy dad she'd grown up with?*

'You're not old,' she said firmly. 'Seventy is nothing these days, and you're still as fit as a fiddle and as handsome as a prince.'

It was true. Despite his sadness, her dad was still the good-looking man he'd always been. His thick black hair, greying at the sides, and dark amber eyes, softened by time, still gleamed. Lines around his eyes told a story of resilience, and he had a rugged attractiveness. Tall, fit, and energetic, Atticus carried himself with an easy grace.

'Aye, well, the bones are beginning to creak, and my back is starting to play up.' Atticus stopped and grimaced as he stretched his neck, confirming his point.

'Use it or lose it!' Mary was emphatic. 'Some warm sunshine on your bones might ease that. Why don't you take that trip to Spain you always planned with Mum?'

Atticus wished that Mary would stop nagging. She'd only been back five minutes and was already telling him what to do. 'I'm fine as I am, don't worry about me,' he said.

As they passed the café, the last diners were making their way to their cars. Mary and Atticus stood back as a four-by-four cruiser, towing a twin-axle tourer, slowly drove past, heading to the caravan park. Close behind, a motorhome with foreign number plates appeared. The vehicle's rear was covered in international stickers, each telling the story of the owner's journey around Europe.

'It's like a motorway junction these days,' Atticus tutted. 'You're not safe to walk about on your own land.' He scowled as the motorhome driver leaned out his window and held up a hand.

'*Groeten aan jou*!' the mature driver smiled.

'Greetings to you too,' Mary replied, recognising the Dutch plates.

'Aye, greetings,' Atticus mumbled.

When they reached the farmhouse, she saw Helen standing on the porch with Declan in her arms.

'Here's my gorgeous boy,' Mary said. 'Say hello to your grumpy grandad.' She ruffled Declan's hair and deposited the toddler in Atticus's arms.

Atticus held the wriggling toddler as Declan tugged on the brim of his hat.

'Where are the kids?' Mary asked Helen.

'Glued to the kitchen table, gobbling food like they haven't been fed for days,' Helen replied. 'Come in and join us.'

Sensing his reluctance, Mary grabbed her father's arm and steered him into the farmhouse. 'Don't you want to say hello to your grandchildren?'

'Aye.' Atticus winced as Declan grabbed his hat and pulled it from Atticus's head to make a bed for his teddy. 'Of course I do.'

In the kitchen, seven raucous children sat around a large oak table. In the centre, plates were piled high with savouries and cakes.

'Grandad,' Jake called out, 'come and sit here.'

Atticus sat down, and Jake held a plate of warm sausage rolls. 'These are delicious,' he said, handing one to Ness, who gobbled it down in seconds.

'I hope you're looking after that tractor, it's nearly as old as I am and needs lots of care.'

'Don't worry,' Jake replied, 'I love the Little Grey Fergie as much as you do.'

'You shouldn't have bodies sprawled all over it. It's not right. Vehicles like that need respect,' Atticus grumbled.

Mary listened to her father and Jake discuss the merits of owning and running a vintage utility tractor. They discussed in depth the four-speed, unsynchronised transmission that had been manufactured by Ferguson in Coventry in 1951. Taking a slice of gingerbread, she felt pleased that Jake had something in common with her father. Their love of engines and anything mechanical was a shared pastime.

As Helen poured more drinks and restocked plates with quiche and pork pies topped with apple sauce, Mungo appeared.

Pulling out a chair, he took a pie and sat beside Jake and Atticus.

As the trio ate, Mary, keeping one eye on the children, listened to their conversation. Atticus explained to Jake the merits of entering an antiquated vehicle into the county shows held annually in Cumbria.

'Your Grandma Clara and I used to enjoy a day out at a show,' Atticus said.

'Why don't you do it again?' Mungo asked.

'Ah, it's not for me,' Atticus tutted. 'Too much work and fierce competition.'

'But Grandad, I can help,' Jake said. 'I love working on an engine and doing up a vehicle. We could do it together.'

'He has a point,' Mungo sat forward, his head on one side as he waited for his father to respond. 'Jake can learn from you.'

'Oh, I'm too old for all that,' Atticus said, rising and pushing back his chair. 'I'll be getting off now.' He walked over to Declan and removed Teddy from his temporary 'bed', prising Declan's sticky fingers from his hat.

Declan pouted, gripping Teddy tightly.

'Your Mam will find another hat for Teddy,' Atticus said as he brushed crumbs from its brim.

Mary watched her father leave and heard Jake complain to Mungo that he wished his grandad had more time to spend with him. His expertise with vehicles was better than anything Jake could learn at college.

Suddenly, with all the talk of the tractor, Mary's mind was racing. A memory of childhood came back to her as she thought of the old barn where the Little Grey Fergie used to be stored. With the children's chatter in the background, an idea began to form.

Could a remnant of those holidays still be in the barn?

Might there be a way to wake Atticus up and help him embrace the golden years?

An idea sparked, but her plan would require careful scheming and hinge entirely on her father's love of hoarding anything remotely tied to the farm.

Crossing her fingers, Mary felt a surge of determination. Reaching for another piece of gingerbread, she chewed thoughtfully, her mind spinning. She knew her father well enough to understand one crucial detail. He must believe the idea was entirely his own. Licking crumbs from her fingers, she gave a decisive nod.

It was bold but worth a shot, and her idea might just work!

Chapter Four

The following morning, during his tour of the business, Mungo watched caravan guests in the shop loading baskets with farm-fresh eggs, pantry staples, and regional treats. The butcher's counter showcased prime cuts and tender lamb, and the cake display tempted him with fluffy scones. Mungo's stomach rumbled. It was time for breakfast.

At the farmhouse, Eliza greeted him, 'Hi, Dad.' She wrestled a scrunchie around her wild hair in readiness for her stint in the café. 'You'd better be quick if you want something to eat.'

'Thanks for the heads up, I'm starving. Have a good shift, the café is full already.'

'That means I'll be knee-deep in pots.' Eliza grinned and, tying an apron, dashed away.

In the kitchen, Finn was dribbling a football. 'Uncle Mungo! Play football with me?'

'I'll certainly have a kickabout later,' Mungo ruffled Finn's thick curls as he shot the ball into the hallway.

Mary was fussing around the table, and Mungo thought how well she looked. Irish life suited her, despite the hectic lifestyle. Her chestnut hair cascaded in waves, and her peachy complexion was as fresh as the day she'd left for Kindale.

'Conor couldn't make it?' Mungo asked.

'He's swamped with a big land deal,' Mary said, peeling a banana. 'He's barely been home.'

'I thought summer was a quieter period?'

'Not for property deals,' she sighed. 'It's cutthroat, and Conor must stay competitive.'

'Well, I'm just a humble shop manager.'

'With a booming business,' Mary countered.

Mungo shrugged. Business *was* booming, but borrowings were high to cover their rapid expansion, and repayments were a constant worry.

'It's good to have you here,' Mungo said, biting back the thought that Conor should have made time to be with his family, though the two men had never been close.

Turning to Helen, he asked, 'What are your plans for the day?'

'I'm taking Maeve and Caitlin to a craft fair in Eden this morning,' Helen said and sipped her coffee. 'I've baked scones for the cake stall.'

Maeve gave a thumbs-up while Caitlin frowned, glued to her phone.

Mary began to clear the table and wiped sticky fingers and jam-smudged faces. 'I'll take the boys to see Dad.'

'I'm sure he'll enjoy your company,' Mungo smiled. 'You'll find him up on the fells.' Reaching out, he grabbed Helen's coffee and drained it. Dodging her playful slap, he winked. 'Enjoy the fair,' he said, kissing her cheek. 'See you all later.'

Seconds later, Mungo was out of the door.

Up on the fells, the morning sunshine softened the craggy peaks of the rugged landscape, creating ever-changing patterns on the sloping hills. Atticus sat in his usual spot on the drystone wall and, as he did every morning, felt the magical spell of Cumbria embrace him. How he longed for the days when, together with Clara, he'd led a simple, unhurried life of caring for their sheep, raising their children, and enjoying the gentle goings-on in the village.

Atticus sighed, feeling like a stranger on his own land.

Reaching down, he stroked Ness's soft, silky fur. The dog nudged his hand and began to thump her tail. Her imploring eyes told him that it was time to move on. Morning walks were not meant to be spent sitting still while rabbits and hares darted among rocks and heather, teasing the Collie, who longed to be in hot pursuit.

Returning his gaze to the farmhouse, Atticus wasn't surprised to see Mary heading his way with Declan hanging off her hand, and Finn bouncing a ball alongside.

His peaceful morning had ended.

'Come on,' he said, cuffing the dog. As he stirred Ness into motion, Atticus straightened the brim of his hat, then stood upright, leaning on his crook. 'It's time to face the music.'

Mary had been unable to find her father in his cottage but knew he must be up and about. An empty cup with the dregs of tea sat beside a crumb-filled plate, but elsewhere, the place was tidy. *At least he's looking after himself*, she thought, as she wandered over to the pine dresser and fondly stroked Clara's plates, so lovingly collected over the years.

Her fingers touched an old wooden needle box, and she traced the edges of the lid. 'Dear Lord, he's still got some of Mum's ashes,' Mary whispered as she peered inside.

It had been years since they'd scattered most of her mother's remains over the fells, a gentle wind carrying Clara away into the endless sky, just as her mother had wanted. But Atticus had kept a little back. Mary swallowed hard and glanced at her mother's empty chair by the stove. 'I understand, Dad,' she murmured. 'I really do.'

In the yard, Mary walked past a pen where half a dozen Herdwick sheep were being petted by a group of children. *No wonder Dad felt so sad*, she thought, remembering the vast flock that had been her father's pride and joy. But after her mother's death, Atticus's grief, which appeared to have no end, had led to his lethargy, and it never seemed to change.

But could Mary change her father? There was only one way to find out.

Wandering along the trodden earth that formed a pathway from the farm to the fells, Mary felt Declan pulling on her hand. His weight was heavy, and with the exertion of the climb, she wished she'd put more effort into her gym sessions. Her occasional visits to Kindale Golf and Wellness Retreat hardly warranted the expensive membership. As Mary felt a shortness of breath, she determined that she would indulge in her fitness when she got home. Sitting in the restaurant with the Ladies' Lunch Club did nothing to improve her stamina or waistline. Unlike Conor, who was as fit as a fiddle and insisted on spending time there most days, assuring Mary that most of his deals were done on the golf course and in the bar, and justified the expense.

'Where's Grandad?' Declan asked, gripping his teddy.

'Probably hiding beside the long wall.' Mary pointed as she steadied her youngest son.

'Will he play football with me?' Finn kicked the ball as they reached the summit.

'You can ask him.'

'How much further?' Declan began to whine.

'We're nearly there. Look, here's Ness.'

Mary saw the Collie race along the grass and, with a natural herding instinct, manoeuvre around Finn to dribble the ball between her paws and intercept his pass.

Declan thrust his teddy into Mary's arms and ran ahead to join in.

As the game got underway, Mary turned to look for Atticus and found him, as she expected, by the long wall.

'There you are,' Mary called out. 'We've been looking for you.'

'Aye, well, you've found me.' Atticus smiled as Mary kissed his cheek.

'I need to sit down. The climb up here has me gasping.'

'Finn has some fancy footwork,' Atticus commented as he watched his grandson circle the ball around Ness with lightning speed.

'He's on the school team and plays for Kindale in the Under Twelves.'

'It was rugby in my day.'

'Ours too.' Mary looked thoughtful. 'I remember Mungo being a great prop-forward when he played for the school.'

'He was built for it,' Atticus nodded.

'Finn is like his father; he is lean and athletic and scores every time he plays.'

Mary turned her head a fraction to study her father's face. He was chatty today, which was a good sign. 'So,' Mary began, 'how are you feeling?'

'You sound like your brother. I get asked that question every day.'

'And what's your answer?'

'The same as it always is. I'm fine, perfectly happy.'

'But Dad, you don't *do* anything. You used to be so active, but now, it's just dog walking and playing dominoes.'

'And what's wrong with that?'

'It's not what Mum would have wanted.'

'Here we go...' Atticus began to tap his foot. 'If your

mum isn't nagging me from above, you chip in with your pestering from below.'

Mary's eyes widened. 'Mum talks to you?'

'All the time.'

'What does she say?'

Atticus gripped his crook and stared out at the hills. His eyes, amber depths that twinkled when he laughed, were wet. 'She tells me not to let the old man in.'

'Clint Eastwood.' Mary smiled, recognising the words. *How many times had Mum enjoyed the actor's films!* But realising that Atticus had let old age come romping in, Mary suddenly felt annoyed.

'Listen,' she said and eased off the wall. 'It's time to stop living in the past! If Mum is still with you in spirit, don't you think she'd be getting fed up with you?'

'Eh?' Atticus raised his eyebrows.

'Make some more memories. Take Mum on a new journey.' Mary stood with her hands on her hips. 'Look out your window, Dad, and smile more because you're fit and healthy, and age is just a number.'

Atticus shook his head. 'I'm getting on, Mary. My get-up-and-go has gone.'

'You're NOT old,' Mary's voice rose. 'Seventy is nothing these days. It's all a state of mind.' Seeing Finn and Declan pause their game to stare, she smiled and waved before carrying on. 'We're going to be productive today and make a start on clearing out the old barn, where you're hoarding stuff that should have been rehomed years ago.'

Atticus banged his crook on the ground to shake off debris then nodded towards Declan's abandoned teddy.

'Are you bringing that with you or leaving it here?' he asked.

Mary snatched the bear while Atticus marched ahead. As he passed the children, he whistled for Ness. The dog, reluctant to stop playing but conditioned to her owner's commands, trotted obediently behind him.

'Aw, Grandad!' Finn's face creased in frustration as the game abruptly ended.

'Is Grandad grumpy?' Declan asked.

Mary scooped Declan into her arms and hurried behind Atticus to return to the farm. 'Grandad has a job to do,' she said, marching everyone down the hill.

The barn door creaked as Mary wrestled with the closure. With a sigh, Atticus nudged her out of the way and opened the door. As they stepped in, dust motes swirled in the streaks of sunlight that sliced through gaps in the weathered wooden planks, their rough surfaces bearing the scars of decades of use.

'When did you last come in here?' Mary asked. She was conscious of the rusting nails jutting out at odd angles and held Declan's hand tightly.

'Years ago,' Atticus replied. He stared at the shelves sagging under the weight of glass jars filled with nails, screws, and bolts. A dull-bladed sickle lay propped against the wall. 'Your brother let me keep this barn to store anything I wanted to hold on to when he made all the changes to the farm.'

'Well, don't you think it's about time you had a sort out?'

'I wouldn't know where to begin,' he said and kicked an ancient wheelbarrow.

'I'll help you,' Finn said excitedly. Fascinated, he stared at a child's wooden chair, its paint chipped and peeling.

'That was mine,' Mary said, her voice full of nostalgia. 'Grandad painted it pink for me. Do you remember Dad?'

'Aye.' Atticus began to chuckle. 'You thought you were a princess on a throne.'

The door creaked, and they turned to see Jake.

'Grandad!' Jake shouted. 'What's going on in here?'

'We're having a sort out,' Mary said, brushing dust off Declan's hands. 'Can you help?'

Jake beamed. 'I've been dying to get in here, but Dad has forbidden me.' His eyes gleamed as he saw the old tools. 'It's like a time capsule. What's first?' he asked, rubbing his hands together.

Mary smiled. 'Shall we see what's at the back of the barn?'

They made their way past a pile of sheep shearing gear, and Atticus paused to study a pile of old combs, cutters, and weighing scales.

'Did you use all this?' Jake asked, frowning as he picked up a tin of raddle powder.

'Aye, and I used this marking harness to brand the sheep.' Atticus stroked the aged equipment.

'What's behind all this big stuff?' Mary asked, gesturing for Jake to help lift and move a stack of wooden posts and several reams of mesh and fencing material to one side.

Mary felt almost giddy as the shape of something familiar began to appear in the barn's shadowy rear. Her heart was thumping as she moved toward the heavily draped canvas, covered in decades of dust and cobwebs.

'What is it?' Finn asked nervously.

'Well, I never...' Atticus was motionless as he stared at the object. 'I'd completely forgotten...'

Everyone was silent and the old barn seemed to hold its breath.

Then Mary nodded to Jake, and suddenly, they took hold of the canvas and pulled it away with one dramatic sweep. Clasping her hands to her mouth, Mary gasped.

There she was! The Westfalia camping van!

A relic of past family holidays, once a bright yellow but now dulled by time, it was unmistakable. The round headlights stared like eyes, and the front grille seemed to smile as the old van was reunited with its owner.

Atticus was frozen, unable to move. 'Hello, Winnie,' he whispered.

'Grandad!' Jake breathed. 'She's amazing...' He stepped forward and slowly began to caress the paintwork, assessing her condition with awe.

'Do you remember?' Mary asked, her voice soft as though afraid to break the spell.

A smile broke across Atticus's face. 'How could I forget?' he murmured, his voice full of emotion. 'Winnie took us everywhere.'

'I wondered if you might get her going again,' Mary said and glanced at Jake. 'With your grandson's help, of course.'

'Oh, yes, Grandad, we have to!' Jake said excitedly.

'Well, she's going to be in a state,' Atticus finally replied. 'It would be a big job to bring her back to life.'

Mary looked at her father, and a flicker of hope stirred in her chest. Maybe, just maybe, she'd found the key to unlock his lethargy, and Winnie – the camper that had once carried so many memories – could bring Atticus back to life, too.

The old van sat in its fading glory, patiently waiting, as if it knew it had another story to tell. And perhaps, Mary prayed, with Jake's hard work and Atticus's enthusiasm, the best chapters for Winnie and her dad were yet to come.

Chapter Five

In the warmth of the lazy summer evening, laughter and chatter filled the garden of The Black Bull. Customers gathered around picnic tables to enjoy alfresco dining, tucking into hearty food and sipping on locally brewed beer. Hanging baskets, bursting with flowers, nestled beneath the thick thatched roof.

Inside the packed pub, tantalising cooking smells wafted from the kitchen, while a local musician strummed a guitar. He sang familiar folk songs, and locals joined visitors to sing along. In the snug, dressed alike in plaid cotton shirts and corduroy trousers, Atticus sat next to Arthur in their favourite corner by the bar.

'It's busy here tonight,' Atticus complained as he tipped his hat back.

'It's like this most nights when Reg has the music on,' Arthur agreed.

'I can hardly hear myself think,' Atticus grumbled.

At that moment, the song ended, and the singer announced that he would take a short break.

'That's better,' Arthur said. 'Now you can tell me what you've been up to today. Has Mary been mithering?'

Atticus held his empty glass up to Reg, the landlord, who slid two fresh pints towards them. 'Mary has made it her mission to enhance my life.'

Arthur looked puzzled, but Atticus continued, 'She says I should look out of my window and smile.'

'They'll be locking you up if you do too much of that.' Arthur chuckled.

'I've spent all afternoon with her and Jake, going through stuff in an old barn that I wouldn't let Mungo clear out.'

'Is there much in there?'

'Well, I used to store the Little Grey Fergie in one section, but Jake has her in his own workshop now.'

'Anything else?'

'Oh, you know, bits and pieces that I didn't want to get rid of.' Atticus was enjoying building the suspense. 'And some of my own things that I'd forgotten about.'

'Like what?'

'There's a pile of shearing gear, some old combs and cutters and weighing scales.' Atticus stared wistfully into his pint.

'Not much use to you now.' Arthur nodded.

'Aye, I know.'

For a moment, the pair sat with folded arms, a far-off look in their eyes.

'Was that it?' Arthur asked impatiently. 'No pot of gold that you'd forgotten about?'

'Well, Mary insisted that I go through everything, and there *was* something...'

Arthur sat up, his curiosity piqued.

'Do you remember that camper Clara and I used to take on holidays when the twins were small?'

'The bright yellow 1985 VW Westfalia?' Arthur almost dropped his pint. He recalled the vehicle with fondness and, reaching out, grabbed his friend's arm.

'Aye, that's the one.'

'I remember it well. Today, it would be a prized vintage vehicle.' Arthur nodded enthusiastically. 'Don't tell me you've still got it?'

'Jake found her tucked away behind a tall stack of handling pens. I couldn't believe it because I'd forgotten all about her.'

'Good grief.' Arthur rubbed his hands together, then paused. 'But I expect she's falling apart?'

'On the contrary, her bodywork looks good, and once we'd got the bonnet up, Jake felt sure he'd be able to get the engine going.' Atticus grinned. 'She was mucky though. Her colour looked grey, not yellow.'

'So, what are your plans?'

'I'll let Jake tinker around and see if he can get the old girl to start. Then I'll probably sell her, not that she'd be worth much.'

'You might be surprised. A vintage vehicle like that might be a collectable,' Arthur said, his eyes glowing. 'Well, I never... Who would have thought it?'

The following morning, Atticus, as usual, woke early and crept out of the cottage as dawn rose and his family slept. The sun began its gentle ascent, and as birdsong filled the air, the rolling hills emerged from the darkness. Atticus, crook in hand, made his way to his favourite spot while Ness ran ahead, casting dancing shadows on the dew-kissed grass.

Atticus settled himself on the long wall. This was the best part of his day and from his viewpoint, he could watch the familiar world below. He remembered the days when his sheep, like fluffy clouds, moved in unison over the fells, and he could almost hear their gentle bleat and contented munching as they grazed.

In his mind, he saw Clara, her hair like a golden red ribbon fluttering in the breeze as she wound her way along the path with a basket in her hand. So often, she would join him for a picnic while enjoying the happy rhythm of their life in the countryside.

'Hey, Clara,' Atticus suddenly called out. 'I've found Winnie! What do you think?'

Slowly, her ethereal vision shimmered, and she turned to face him. 'I think it's time you made that trip to Spain...' And then, her ghostly image was gone, fading like a distant puff of cloud.

The countryside was quiet, save for the beating of Atticus's heart. Ness placed her head on his knee, and with a thoughtful expression, he began to stroke the old dog.

Atticus had fallen asleep. His eyes were closed and his head drooped when the sound of an engine suddenly disturbed the peace.

'Wake up, old lass,' Atticus said, gently prodding a drowsy Ness with the toe of his sturdy boot. He stared down at the farm and squinted.

The Little Grey Fergie was chugging along the yard, smoke puffing from her chimney. Attached to the bar behind the tractor, Winnie was being towed. When it came to a stop, Atticus saw Jake leap from the driver's seat.

'What on earth!' Atticus called out.

Jake released the vehicle, and Atticus could see that his grandson, dressed in overalls, had moved the tractor away and wheeled a workbox into the yard.

'Jake's got Winnie out!' Atticus crossly said to Ness.

Cursing, he moved swiftly down the path. As the pair got closer, Atticus saw Mary. With Declan in her arms and Finn bouncing a ball alongside, she stood beside the camper, staring towards the fells.

'Morning, Dad,' she called out. 'It's a perfect day to do something useful.'

Atticus reached the yard and was about to forbid Jake from going under the bonnet when a jet of water from a hose almost knocked him back. 'Look out!' Atticus yelled.

'I thought I'd clean her up before we start work on the engine,' Jake called out. Taking a sponge from a bucket of soapy water, he handed the hose to Finn and began to wash the camper. 'Hold it steady while I ease layers of muck off her bodywork,' Jake instructed his cousin. Taking great care, he lathered the sponge and began to rub the paintwork in gentle circular movements.

'I didn't give him permission to do this.' Atticus turned to Mary, frustration in his voice. 'A vintage vehicle needs to be carefully handled.'

'Well, someone had to make a start,' Mary said as Declan wriggled free from her arms. 'You've let it sit in the barn for decades.'

'Mummy, what is it?' Declan asked. His little face was puzzled as he gripped his teddy and watched Finn and Jake move around with the bucket and hose.

'It's Grandad's special van,' Mary replied. 'A little house on wheels.'

'Has it got a bed?'

'Yes, and a kitchen.'

Declan moved over to Atticus. 'Grandad, what's your house called?'

Atticus felt little fingers reach out and curl themselves into his palm. Declan's soft skin was warm against the rough calluses on his hand, and for a moment, Atticus felt a stab in his chest as the little boy, still gripping his teddy, cuddled against his legs. His heart began to melt, and a stirring emotion took Atticus by surprise. 'We used to call her Winnie,' he said.

For a moment, the years dissolved, and a young Mungo was beside him.

Atticus closed his eyes and heard happy chatter as Clara and little Mary climbed into the camper. '*We're all going on a summer holiday...*' they'd sang.

What fun they'd had on their outings!

'Are you alright, Dad?' Mary asked, touching his arm. 'Dad?' she repeated. 'You're miles away.'

'I'm fine.' Atticus held onto Declan and watched years of grime dissolve as Finn and Jake worked methodically. A smile tugged at him as the yellow paintwork slowly emerged.

Maeve and Caitlin came into the yard, and as Maeve raised her eyes from her phone, she asked, 'What's going on?'

'We're working on Grandad's old camper,' Mary said, linking her arm through Caitlin's. 'It's called Winnie.'

'It looks like a wreck to me,' Maeve mumbled.

'It's far from a wreck,' Jake said, studying his handiwork. 'We'll have to re-chrome' – he softly stroked the trim – 'but the paintwork is amazing. I'll get to work with polymer wax. It will bring this up like new.'

'Can you fix the engine?' Mary asked.

Atticus felt a shiver as Clara whispered in his ear, '*Of course, you can! You'll have the old girl fixed up in no time.*'

'Well, it will need stripping down...' Atticus began. Staring in at the dust-covered engine, he pointed out details to Jake. 'It's a fuel-injection system, known as a DigiJet,' Atticus explained. 'And this model, built in 1985, is a 1.9 litre, water-cooled.'

Finn joined Jake with the engine inspection. Their heads dipped as they listened to their grandad enthuse.

'You can see that it's a manual transmission,' Atticus adjusted Declan's weight on his hip.

'So, she's heavy on gas.' Jake nodded.

'There's a lot to do to get her back on the road.' Atticus pursed his lips.

'All the usual checks – spark plugs, air, fuel, and oil filters.' Jake began to poke about. 'The brake fluid will need flushing and replacing,' he added.

'If there's any left after all this time. It's a big task.'

'Can me and Teddy sleep in it?' Declan asked, rubbing his cheek against Atticus's face.

'And me?' Finn turned to his grandad.

'The inside will be in a state and need fixing up. The mice will have had their way over the years, and everything will be in tatters.'

Atticus moved around the vehicle and, still holding onto Declan, slowly slid back the side door. The mechanism was rusty and reluctant to move, but with Jake's help, the inside of the camper was soon revealed.

'Well, that's a surprise...' Atticus shook his head as though to clear his vision.

'Grandad, I can't believe it!' Jake's jaw dropped as he took it all in.

'Goodness me,' Mary whispered.

'Wow!' Maeve exclaimed, pointing her phone as she began to take photos.

Atticus stared wide-eyed as the decades fell away.

'Well, would you take a look at that...'

Chapter Six

As July rolled into August, a month passed quickly at Barn Hill Farm, and as another warm summer evening stretched ahead, the garden at The Black Bull was full. Reg moved methodically through the maze of tables, eagle-eyed for abandoned glasses.

At a table overlooking the village green, Mungo sat with Mary.

'I can't believe the change in Dad,' Mungo said. 'It's as though his batteries have been charged, and he's suddenly come back to life.'

Mary reached for her wine. 'It's only taken five years but finding that run-down old camper seems to have reinstated his get-up-and-go.'

'It's hardly run-down now; he's worked miracles with Jake. The camper is a showpiece. Have you noticed how guests at the caravan site always wander over to check it out?'

'Yes, visitors to the café and farm shop stop and stare, too.' Mary smiled.

'Your Maeve has been posting it on her Instagram account, hashtagging "#VWCamper" and "#Winniethe-Westie".' Mungo shook his head.

The bright yellow Westfalia camper van was now a collector's dream – a timeless icon of adventure and freedom – standing proudly in the yard. Atticus and Jake had worked tirelessly on the engine, spending every spare moment on it. They'd stripped it back and replaced worn parts that they'd found on the internet, after endless searches that introduced Atticus to the wonders of the World Wide Web. The chrome shone on the bumpers and grilles, and the paintwork gleamed. With its classic design and sturdy construction, Winnie's smooth curves and rounded edges gave a distinctive vintage appeal.

The siblings sipped their drinks, and Mungo thought back to the day he'd wandered into the yard to find the family gathered around the camper.

Expecting the worst, Atticus had slid back the vehicle's door. '*Would you take a look at that...*' he'd said in astonishment.

They all gasped as they stared inside, where time had stood still since Winnie's last outing. As though Clara had just stepped away after flicking a duster over the interior.

Mungo watched as Atticus reached in and, pulling back the neatly drawn curtains, revealed a spacious interior. A sofa that converted into a bed was upholstered in fabric Mungo recognised from the couch in Atticus's cottage, and it looked as good as new. Two identically covered seats swung away from the dashboard, curving around a fold-down table. Along one side, a refrigerator, sink, and stove were integrated with rich wood panelling into cupboards, providing storage for clothes and camping accessories.

Mungo stepped into the camper and flipped a hinge to create a pop-up roof. Standing upright, he opened drawers to see his mother's neat utensils lined up in perfect rows beside carefully stored plates and mugs.

Bringing himself back to the present, Mungo drained his pint and turned to Mary. 'I was shocked when I saw the camper, after being abandoned in the barn for decades.'

'Me too,' Mary agreed. 'It was like a time-warp. Mum had sealed her memories inside, keeping them safe for the next journey.'

'But she couldn't have known it would stand unused for decades.'

'I agree, but all these years later, it's as though she's sent Dad a message.'

Mungo nodded.

'Have you seen the add-on awning?' Mary asked.

'Yes, very colourful – like a separate room. Dad found it on the internet and adapted it to fit.'

Mary shook her head. 'I still can't quite believe that Dad uses the internet now. Wonders never cease.'

'I thought Jake had done all the searching, but he tells me he's been giving Dad lessons, and he's taken to Google like a duck to water.'

'No surprise there. Dad is good with engineering, so

why not technology?' Mary shrugged. 'What do you think he'll do with Winnie?'

'Sell it, I suppose. There's plenty of offers,' Mungo replied. 'Or, because of the memories of Mum, he'll pack it back into storage.'

'I've told him he should take a holiday, head off to Wales again like we used to.'

'That's a good idea. I wouldn't want him going any further at his age, especially in such an old vehicle.'

'Come off it, Mungo, he's hardly ancient and Dad is more than capable of fixing an engine if anything goes wrong.'

'What if he was ill? Or if Winnie broke down in a remote spot?'

Mary shook her head. Mungo was surprisingly protective of Atticus, and now that their father had a new interest, Mungo seemed reluctant to let it play out.

'You're heading home in a few days,' Mungo said. 'We're going to miss you all.'

'It's been a lovely break, but I've a husband who spends far too much time at the country club, and I need to get back.' Mary finished her wine.

'Too busy making money, you can't deny him that.'

'No, but he will have forgotten what we look like,' she said, grinning. 'And I have to get the kids ready for the new school term.'

Mary checked her watch. She'd been trying to call Conor all day, but his phone went to voicemail. *He must be run off his feet*, she thought, imagining the complexities of the land deal he was trying to secure.

They both looked up as they saw Reg heading towards them. 'All done with these?' Reg asked and removed the empty glasses.

Heading back to the farm, they fell into step. 'Don't worry about Dad,' Mungo said. 'He'll settle back into his routine, and we'll keep an eye on him.'

'But I do worry. Without an interest, he might fade away.'

'I know, but to have a life, you have to *want* a life,' Mungo said, 'and only Dad can decide how he chooses to spend his time.'

In the snug of The Black Bull, Atticus knew *exactly* how he'd chosen to spend his time. But as he pondered the decision with Arthur in their favourite corner, he felt certain that Mungo wasn't going to like it.

Atticus's hands, the nails dark with oil, were wrapped around a pint glass, and his amber eyes wide with a twinkle of mischief. 'So, what do you think?' he asked his friend.

Arthur, his grey hair neatly combed, removed the spectacles perched on the bridge of his nose and placed them down on a printed paper on the table. 'I think you might have lost your marbles,' he replied.

'But what do you *really* think?' Atticus insisted.

'Well, you've definitely lost the plot, but... if Shirley would give *me* leave of absence, I'd be coming with you,' Arthur sighed. 'The moon will turn blue before that happens,' he added. 'I thought you'd place Winnie back in storage and bring her out for a little holiday to Wales now and again. What's put this idea in your head?'

'I've been talking to Jake, and the lad has given me things to think about,' Atticus began. 'He's opened my eyes and shown me how to use the internet and Arthur...' – he paused, a smile creeping across his face – '...it's brilliant! There's an entire world out there that I've been too stuck in my grief to see. Rediscovering Winnie, well, it's like she's shaken me awake after years of being stuck.'

'Your Clara would be pleased to hear you talk like this.' Arthur nodded.

'So, do you think it's a good idea?'

'I think it's your best idea in years.'

Atticus picked up the piece of paper Jake had printed off the internet. 'Solma Vacaciones Camping welcomes visitors all year round,' he read aloud. 'It says the low season is the perfect time for those of advanced years to relax and enjoy the climate, and special rates apply for motorhomes and caravans.'

'Are you sure about camping?' Arthur thought of the site at Barn Hill Farm that Atticus refused to have anything to do with.

'Clara and I took Winnie away when the kids were young, and I managed then,' Atticus reasoned.

'But that was to Wales, and the furthest you got was Bangor.' Arthur shook his head. 'Now you're proposing to set off for the Costas and drive thousands of miles in a forty-year-old camper?'

'Aye, it's amazing how the internet opens your mind to

possibilities,' Atticus said, taking a sip of his beer. 'Many retired Continentals do it, and lots of Brits too.'

'But why that site?' Arthur asked.

'Clara always wanted to go to Alicante and discover the Costa Blanca. We'd even planned a holiday,' Atticus explained. 'The site is situated in an area she wanted to visit. I thought I might scatter her ashes.'

'So, you're honouring her memory by making the trip?'

'Exactly. It's what she'd want me to do.'

Atticus thought of the hours he'd spent over the last month, silver-surfing through sites Jake had guided him to. It was as though he'd suddenly woken up and the spirit of Clara was urging him to embrace a new chapter.

'Jake will have much to answer for when Mungo and Mary find out,' Arthur chuckled.

'Mary will be pleased. Its Mungo that's the problem,' Atticus replied with a shrug. 'He thinks a few days in Wales is as far as I should go, and that's probably too far for an old dodderer like me.'

'I think I agree with Mungo, but if you're determined to go ahead with this trip, research as much as you can with Jake.'

'Aye, Jake's been an inspiration.' Atticus reached into a pocket. 'Look, he's even fixed me up with a mobile.'

Arthur stared at the latest version of the iPhone that Atticus held in his hand. 'That must have cost you. Can you use it?' he asked.

'It cost an arm and a leg, but I like it, and Jake says you can't travel without one. He's shown me how to use the camera too, so I can keep a memory of where I go. Plus, he's programmed everyone's details into it.'

Arthur drained his glass and nodded to Reg for a refill. 'Better add two large whiskies,' he said, 'I think we're going to need them.'

He stared at Atticus, amazed by the transformation in his friend. In the last week or so, Atticus had lost his weariness and gained a zest for life.

'It says here that the site is a ten-minute walk from the Costa Blanca seafront and a five-minute drive from the town of Guardamar,' Atticus continued. 'With a varied entertainment programme, a restaurant serving international food, and a café and bar beside a poolside terrace.'

'That's all well and good, but how will you get there?'

'Jake and I are planning a route. I can either drive through France, cross the border into Spain, and head south along the coast, or take a ferry to Santander and drive across the country.'

'And you're confident Winnie will make such a long journey?'

'Jake says I need to get international breakdown cover and European vehicle insurance in case Winnie has problems.'

'Have you got health insurance?'

'I need something called a EHIC health card, which I've applied for, and Jake reckons the Caravan and Motorhome Club will cover all the insurance for me.'

'Have you joined?'

Atticus reached for his whisky. 'I'm a fully paid-up member as of today,' he grinned.

'But what about the dog?'

The men glanced down where Ness lay sound asleep.

'I'll take her with me.'

'Eh?' Arthur's jaw dropped open. 'Isn't she a bit too old for gadding about and eating foreign food?'

'It'll do her good. I can hardly leave her behind.'

'Does she need a passport?'

'Aye, we both do. It's a right rigmarole sorting all the paperwork out, but Jake is on it.'

'Sounds to me like Jake should be going with you.' Arthur reached for his whisky.

'The lad has school, and as much as he wants an adventure in Winnie, Mungo would kill me if I took Jake away.'

'So, you are comrades in arms with your grandson?'

'Yes, Jake is sworn to secrecy until I set off.'

'Do you think Mungo will kick up a fuss?'

'Aye, I do. He doesn't think I can get to the end of the road on my own anymore, let alone set off on a long journey.'

'Then all Jake's hard work is a fait accompli.'

'Aye, something like that, but the lad's no fool. I'm making his time financially worthwhile and have promised him the Little Grey Fergie when I've passed over.'

'But can you afford all this?' Arthur asked.

'Have you forgotten about that patch of land I sold?'

'Ah, yes.' Arthur nodded. He remembered that when Mungo had taken over the farm, he'd suggested that Atticus keep hold of three acres of land running parallel to the road on the edge of the village.

'I got far more for it than I ever could have dreamt.'

'There are four luxury houses on it now,' Arthur said. 'Eden is a desirable village.'

'It gave me a nest egg – one I'd planned to leave to the grandchildren.'

'If I was you, I'd blow the lot.'

'I've no intention of doing that, but money is hardly a worry, and my name is still on the farm. It will all go to the family, of course, so they'll be well provided for.'

'When do you plan to set off?'

'As soon as my passport is sorted and the paperwork for the dog in order.'

'She'll need to visit the vet for a rabies injection too, I imagine?' Arthur asked.

'Aye, up-to-date boosters and tapeworm treatment too.' Atticus looked at Ness, who'd raised her head and growled at the mention of the vet. 'The old girl has a sixth sense,' he chuckled, recalling the dog baring her teeth at Mr Herriot the last time she'd been for her boosters.

'Where will you stay while you travel?' Arthur asked.

Atticus did a double-take and stared at his friend. 'Where do you think? In Winnie, of course.'

'But what if you get stuck somewhere without electricity, water, or conveniences?'

'This isn't the last century; folk travel like this all the time and manage,' Atticus said. 'Besides, once I get to the camping site, there will be all the facilities I could possibly need.'

'The domino team will miss you,' Arthur said.

'I'm sure you can hold the fort while I'm gone.'

'Well, all I can say is good luck and I wish I was riding shotgun beside you.' Arthur raised his glass. 'You're growing older with Europe at your feet – let your age be your guide.'

They both clinked glasses and stared fondly at each other.

Atticus looked thoughtful. 'Jake always says, "Travel is the fountain of youth".'

'That lad has a vivid imagination,' Arthur grinned. 'But when you return, I expect you to look twenty years younger.'

As Atticus sipped his whisky and Arthur ordered another, a thought ran through his mind.

If I return!

Chapter Seven

Mungo sat in his office and stared at the screen on his desktop. Halfway through October already, and the farm's finances were worrying. Buying in stock for Christmas had drained their accounts, and it was essential that they sold out to get through the quiet months at the start of the new year.

'Coffee?' Ali called out. She stood beside a machine where a grinder whirred, pulverising coffee beans into a fine powder. Taking a mug, she handed Mungo a rich, velvety brew.

'Your dad is busy,' Ali said and moved to the window. 'He's back and forth from the cottage to the barn. What do you think he's up to?'

Mungo didn't look up. Figures on a spreadsheet were dancing before his eyes. 'It's the camper van,' Mungo replied. 'He's been fixing it up.'

'Is he going on a holiday?'

'I hope not,' Mungo sighed. 'I've got enough to worry

about with the business without having to deal with Dad setting off anywhere on his own.'

'I think it's great that he's got an interest,' Ali said, watching Atticus walk purposefully across the yard.

'It won't last,' Mungo murmured, reaching for a calculator. 'He never goes anywhere other than a drive around the village with Jake beside him, which, at seventy, is far enough. I don't want him going any further.'

Ali glanced sideways at Mungo. She thought his comment ageist and rather controlling. She considered Atticus to have more life in him than most people his age.

'Well, your dad has perked up. He's walking tall and even wearing that crazy old Stetson cowboy hat at a jaunty angle,' Ali said, stretching her neck to watch Atticus. 'You know he's a good-looking man. I could easily fancy him.'

Mungo looked up, shocked by Ali's words. Pushing the calculator aside, he grabbed his coffee to join Ali.

They watched as Atticus disappeared into the barn.

Ali was right, Mungo thought. Atticus *had* perked up in the last few weeks, even joining the family for meals and sitting next to Jake to discuss engines and the internet. Instead of spending hours on the fells each day, Atticus now rose early to disappear into the barn to work on Winnie, only appearing for a brisk walk with Ness.

'Have you asked him what he will do with the camper?' Ali asked.

'He says he will probably give it to Jake in time. Before that, he needs to check that it runs well and is in good working order.'

'I expect Jake will take a gap year and set off as soon as

he passes his driving test. A vehicle like that will be irresistible for a young person.'

'Not a chance,' Mungo scoffed. 'Jake's grades are terrible, and he has his education to finish. It's hard enough getting him to study without his grandad distracting him.'

Mungo turned from the window and went back to his desk. Turning to his laptop, he studied the screen. 'Let's crack on,' he said. 'We've got a business to run, and unless I keep on top of everything, it will soon be running me.'

Five hundred miles away, across the Irish Sea, Mary stood in the utility room at Belvedere House and stared at her washing machine. Leaning on a granite countertop, her eyes fixated on the colourful garments that danced behind the glass window. A pile of soiled clothes lay at her feet, waiting to be sorted. The mundane chore of laundry had, for the moment, ceased, as Mary found herself in a trance, watching the machine's back-and-forth motion.

In her hand, she clutched a cotton Oxford shirt.

Mary slowly raised the shirt to her nose, catching a trace of Conor's aftershave on the fabric. But overpowering that scent was something much stronger – a potent aroma of patchouli, vanilla, and caramel. *Angel by Thierry Mugler*. A memorable perfume that Mary recognised from lingering traces in the changing room at Kindale Golf and Wellness Retreat and at the table where she dined each week at the Ladies' Lunch Club. Choosing the much lighter, floral tones of Dior Diorissimo for herself, Mary knew of only one woman in her circle who wore that identifiable scent.

Lucinda Darby. Conor's business rival.

Darby Auctioneers, a family concern, had been handed down to Lucinda, the only child, following her inheritance, and she continued to run it to this day. Intelligent, witty, rake-thin, and stunningly beautiful, Lucinda was twice divorced and went through lovers quicker than the blink of an eye.

Surely not!

Mary gripped the shirt and willed herself to ignore the scent, but her mind was whirring.

No wonder Conor hadn't wanted to join his family on their holiday!

She remembered his words as he stood on the steps of Belvedere House, waving his family goodbye as they set off for Cumbria.

'*Happiness to me is having my large, loving, and close-knit family in another country for the summer holidays,*' Conor had said.

Mary thought he was being playful, joking about his family demands when his summer workload was heavy. Now, Mary imagined Lucinda pressing herself against Conor.

She must be mistaken! Conor couldn't possibly be having an affair.

Questions flooded her mind, and Mary remembered the umpteen times she'd tried to call him during the holiday, speaking only infrequently. Conor had assured Mary that business was taking up every moment of his time, and he was exhausted by the time he fell into bed.

No wonder he was exhausted if he was falling into bed with bloody Lucinda Darby!

How could he?

Why would he?

At the Ladies' Lunch Club, Lucinda often joked that she insisted husbands and lovers be precluded by written formalities from any part of her business or wealth. Mary thought of the property Lucinda called home. Palatial and sprawling, Creek House was situated on the banks of the Brandon River, which ran into the estuary in Kindale. For as long as she'd known him, Conor repeatedly said that he'd give anything to own such an estate. With indoor and outdoor swimming pools, a stunning topiary garden, salmon fishing rights, and gorgeous grounds, it was highly sought after. Once belonging to a celebrity chef, Lucinda had pipped Conor to the post and purchased the property. She'd snapped it up for a pittance when the chef was going through yet another insolvency.

Had Conor lost his heart – and his mind – in pursuit of Creek House Estate?

Mary's stomach clenched in a gut-wrenching sensation as the reality of her husband's possible betrayal sank in. The faces of their four beautiful children swam in her mind. She had to be mistaken. Conor loved his kids, and she was certain he loved her, too.

Taking a deep breath, Mary released it slowly, willing herself to become composed. She thrust Conor's shirt to one side. She must have time to think before she endangered her world and shattered it into a million irreparable pieces.

The washing machine had completed its cycle. Opening the door, Mary removed the clean contents and placed them into the tumble dryer. Leaning down, she gathered the soiled clothes, grabbed Conor's shirt, and thrust it in too. Flicking the dial, Mary set it to a hot wash.

'Don't be ridiculous!' she angrily told herself. 'There has to be an explanation.'

A furrow creased her brow, and Mary's mind was a whirlwind as she took a last glance at the shirt being tossed in the machine.

If only her thoughts could so easily be washed clean.

Chapter Eight

Atticus stood in the old barn's workshop and rocked on the balls of his feet. His body was tense as he dug his hands into the pockets of his moleskin trousers and stared at his little house on wheels. Beside him, Jake, on an Inset Day from school, stood back to admire the newly refurbished Winnie. He held a cloth and leaned in to give the bright yellow paintwork a final polish.

'Grandad, I reckon that you are all set.' Jake folded his arms. 'There's nothing left for us to check. Winnie is ready, so you need to decide if you *are* going to be on tomorrow night's ferry.' He turned to face him. 'It's now or never.'

'Aye lad, I know,' Atticus replied, one hand subconsciously stroking Ness.

Ness sat between the two on a blanket in her box. The dog cocked her ears, as though determined to hear Atticus's decision too.

'Arthur reckons that if I go, I should set off in the early

hours to avoid heavy traffic on the motorway,' Atticus said, his voice hesitant.

'That would make sense,' Jake said. 'The ferry doesn't leave till nine at night, so it gives time for you to wander around and have a look at Portsmouth.'

Atticus nodded, still uncertain of his decision.

'I've put everything in a file for you,' Jake said. 'All in the correct order as you travel. It's on the passenger seat.'

'Are you sure everything's in there?'

'Yes.' Jake rolled his eyes. 'My dad might think I'm hopeless with learning and schoolwork, but when something matters, I make sure I'm organised.' He turned to Winnie and opened the driver's door, and reached in to grab it. 'Look, we can go through all of this before you set off,' he said, holding up the thick file. 'We'll also have another lesson on your mobile.'

Atticus stared at the file containing everything he would need for his journey.

Suddenly, his shoulders visibly relaxed. Rubbing his hands together, he gave a nod of his head and smiled at his grandson. *Finally, he'd made his decision!* The crossroads had been reached, and it was now or never. With determination, Atticus slapped Jake on the back.

'Well, I suppose it wouldn't make sense to waste that ferry ticket,' Atticus said. 'And all the money paid out for Ness.'

Hearing her name, Ness leapt from her bed and began to paw at Atticus's leg, her tail thumping excitedly.

'Brilliant! You'll be like the oldest hippy in town!' Jake's eyes shone. 'Just wait till I tell all my mates that my grandad is driving across Europe to the beat of his own drum.'

Atticus raised his eyebrows. Jake may be falling short in most subjects, but he'd get an A-star in English if he continued to be so profound.

'When will you tell Dad?' Jake asked.

'Better get it over and done with at lunchtime,' Atticus replied.

'Will you let Aunty Mary know too?'

'Aye, I'll do that.' Atticus nodded as he reached down to swing Ness's box into the back of the camper.

Inexplicably, an inner voice told him that his daughter already knew. Atticus remembered Mary's departure from the farm. With her luggage and kids packed up in the Range Rover, she'd stood in the yard and embraced him. As he felt Mary's silky head against his cheek, Atticus heard her whisper, '*The road less travelled is the one that leads to the most exciting adventures. Remember Mum's words and don't let the old man in.*'

'You'll need a sleep this afternoon before you set off,' Jake said.

'Alright, I know.' Atticus was acutely aware of youth over age, reminding him that a four-hundred-mile journey in the middle of the night required an alert pensioner behind the wheel.

'I can't wait to see Dad's reaction,' Jake grinned. 'He's going to blow a fuse.'

Atticus sighed. He didn't want to encounter Mungo's reaction and knew his grandson was undoubtedly right.

'Oh well, I'd best get it done,' Atticus carefully closed

Winne's sliding door. 'But in the meantime, let's go over to the cottage and review that file of yours together.'

Lunchtime in the family farmhouse didn't go as Atticus had planned. As Helen served soup and sandwiches, Eliza dragged a chair noisily across the kitchen floor before throwing herself down at the table. She moaned about how an Inset Day from school shouldn't be spent doing homework.

'Why can't I go into the village with my friends?' Eliza complained.

Atticus kept his head down as Mungo berated his offspring, telling both Eliza and Jake to sit in his office that afternoon so he could supervise them while they did their homework.

'But that's not fair!' Eliza yelled, banging her spoon on the table.

As Mungo held firm, Atticus ate silently. There was no appropriate pause in the conversation for him to announce his news, and it was with relief that he finished his meal and could hurry out of the kitchen to return to his cottage.

A little while later, as Atticus relaxed in his armchair with Ness beside him, his mobile rang. He stared at the device before sliding his finger across the screen to answer, just as Jake had shown him.

'You bottled it!' Jake whispered as Attius held the phone to his ear.

'I'll tell him later.'

'Well, I won't be around. I'm playing football for the village tonight in a friendly.'

Jake sounded grumpy, and Atticus wondered if the lad had been looking forward to the family confrontation. They both knew that fish would climb trees before Mungo approved of his father setting off to Spain in a forty-year-old vehicle.

'I'll call you when I get to Portsmouth tomorrow morning,' Atticus said. 'Now, get your homework done and make sure you win your match tonight.'

Atticus knew he needed to speak to Mungo, but, unsure of the best time to take his son aside and tell him of the journey he was about to embark upon, he dithered. The longer he took, the less inclined he felt to break the news. Wouldn't it be better to let Mungo know when he was well on his way, ensuring there was no possibility of being talked out of his decision? He needed advice from an adult, and, reaching for his mobile again, Atticus decided to call his best friend.

Arthur would know what to do.

'Are you absolutely sure I'm doing the right thing?' Atticus asked as he sat behind Winnie's wheel in the early hours of the morning, under the cloak of darkness, staring at Arthur.

Sitting alongside Atticus, dressed in a woolly bob hat and a fleecy dressing gown, Arthur wore cycle clips over his pyjama bottoms, which gripped the flannel fabric around his spindly legs.

'Absolutely,' Arthur said firmly. 'But Mungo will string you up if he finds out that you're off galivanting for the first time abroad, on your own at your time of life, in this old camper. He won't think it safe.'

With Ness sitting upright between them, Arthur had his arm around the Collie dog.

'I'm not so sure I am doing the right thing. Perhaps I should have told him,' Atticus said as he inched Winnie out of the barn.

Moonlight peeked beyond the night cloud and an eerie glow illuminated the camper's bright paintwork. Awakened from the confines of years in the barn, Winnie's newly rebuilt engine, precisely tuned, purred perfectly.

Atticus drove slowly across the yard. As he passed the farmhouse, both men simultaneously lowered their heads, hoping their crouched position would shield them. Conscious that any engine noise might alert the sleeping family, both held their breath.

With each passing second, Atticus felt like a phantom on the run.

Suddenly, a figure leapt out and threw itself into the headlights. Atticus slammed on the brakes, and as the front-seat trio plunged forward, Arthur's bob hat slipped over his eyes. Arthur gripped the dashboard and shouted, 'What the hell?'

Atticus blew out his breath. 'It's only Jake, don't panic.' Winding down the driver's window, Atticus hissed, 'What on earth are you playing at? I could have killed you.'

'I wanted to say goodbye and give you this,' Jake replied, thrusting out a plastic figure.

'What is it?' Atticus asked, puzzled, as he took the eight-inch object and tilted it towards the light.

'It's a lucky travelling gnome, symbolising an intrepid spirit and a determination to discover the unknown.'

Arthur, who appeared from under the brim of his bob hat, perched his spectacles on his nose. 'It looks like something the dog might chew,' he said. 'You won't see many of those in Spain.'

Ness jabbed her nose at the gnome's chubby cheeks and long white beard. She sniffed its patched-up jacket and scuffed leather boots. The gnome's blue eyes sparkled with mischief as it held up a walking stick adorned with ribbons and a flag that read, 'Adventure Awaits'.

'Aye, well, that's very kind, but there'll be no adventure if I don't get going,' Atticus said, tucking the gnome into his pocket. Time was ticking on.

'I wish I was coming with you, Grandad,' Jake said. His face was beginning to crumple, and Atticus could tell his grandson might burst into tears at any moment.

'There'll be another adventure with your name on it,' he said softly. 'But for now, get your schooling under your belt and keep out of trouble.'

'Send me lots of photos.'

'Aye, you can rest assured I'll use that fancy phone.' Atticus reached out and ruffled Jake's thick, dark hair. 'Now be a good lad and get back to bed.'

'I love you,' Jake said, and with sluggish feet, he backed away from Winnie.

'And I love you too,' Atticus replied, feeling a lump in his throat as he waved and watched Jake's figure recede.

Still mindful of waking Mungo, he slowly drove Winnie out of the driveway, across the main road, and through the village.

'You can drop me off anywhere,' Arthur said as his smallholding came into view. Tucked neatly in fields adjoining the village and named by Shirley when they married, Shirlarth Cottage had been their home for more than forty years.

'I'll take you to your door,' Atticus replied as Winnie cruised along.

'And wake Shirley?' Arthur's eyes widened. The gate to his home was open, and a long driveway lay ahead. 'And what do you think she'll say when I tell her that I crept out like a thief in the night to cycle to Barn Hill Farm to say goodbye to my foolish old mate, who hasn't the balls to tell his family he's leaving?'

Arthur's eyes scanned the entrance for signs of a raging wife, but the only eyes that stared back were from Shirley's collection of garden gnomes. The whimsical little guardians of the flowerbeds had pointy hats and cheery smiles, and Shirley's sentinels of suburban life scared the life out of Arthur, who was sure they came to life when no one was looking.

'Well, when you put it like that...' Atticus agreed.

Moments later, he helped Arthur lift his cycle from Winnie's interior. The friends shook hands as they stood in the moonlight on damp grass.

'Thanks. F...for all your help in planning this adventure and seeing me off to say goodbye,' Atticus muttered, his voice cracking with emotion.

'Aw, getaway. I wish I was coming with you.' Arthur stared down at his hands. 'Keep in touch, and make sure you put away some memories in your memory bank for the days when you no longer can,' he said.

'Aye, my old mate, you can be sure.'

They shook hands again, then Arthur reached for his bike.

'I'll have to go, my slippers are getting wet,' he said, and with a wobble and a wave, he gripped the handlebars.

'Farewell for now,' Atticus whispered as Arthur disappeared into the darkness. 'Till we meet again.'

Chapter Nine

Atticus and Ness enjoyed a smooth and trouble-free journey as they headed south. Cruising down the almost empty motorway, Winnie felt like an old friend he hadn't seen in years, reunited on a new adventure. He thought about the excellent work Jake had done assisting with the engine's refurbishment.

Under a twinkling canvas of stars, Atticus relished the solitude. He was escaping from the hustle and bustle of folk coming and going at Barn Hill Farm, and as the night wore on it felt strangely good.

They stopped for a comfort break. Pulling on her lead, Ness had her nose to the ground and her tail wagged with excitement as she discovered a playground of new scents in the service area. Inside the camper, Atticus searched through the well-stocked cupboards for biscuits and taking a flask, poured piping hot coffee. Sitting comfortably on the sofa, he looked around. The interior light cast a comforting glow over the retro upholstery and wooden panelling, and he realised that the space was extremely cosy.

'What do you think, eh, Clara?' Atticus smiled and turned to Ness. 'We're going to enjoy this trip. Winnie will do us nicely.'

Draining his coffee and tossing a dog biscuit to Ness, Atticus carefully stored his items away, then returned to sit in the driver's seat with Ness strapped in alongside. He found Jake's gnome in his pocket and, with a smile, fixed it on the dashboard beside the satnav that Jake had insisted be installed.

'What shall we call him?' Atticus asked Ness as the dog sniffed the travelling gnome. 'How about Gonzalo the Globetrotter?'

Ness eyed Atticus, and with a nod, he confirmed the name. 'Gonzalo it is,' he said.

He tapped the dashboard compartment where the old wooden needle box was securely placed, and smiled, knowing that his wife's remaining ashes were accompanying him on his adventure, and Clara would be smiling too.

Glancing occasionally at the satnav and listening carefully to the spoken instructions, Atticus gripped the steering wheel as the road stretched ahead like a long, dark ribbon, and the miles slipped away beneath Winnie's wheels.

Leaving the motorway to arrive in Portsmouth with hours to spare before boarding the ferry, he drove along the seafront and parked the camper with a view overlooking the Solent. A roadside café lay ahead, and Atticus ordered two bacon rolls and a sausage for Ness.

'This is life,' Atticus sighed as he wound down the window. 'Smell the sea, Ness. We'll soon be sailing on the ocean.'

Having scoffed her sausage, Ness placed her head on Atticus's knee and began to thump her tail, sensing excitement in the salty air. As the sun began its slow ascent in the channel ahead, a massive ferry boat emerged from mist-shrouded waters. Its sleek hull sliced through the gentle waves, leaving a frothy wake in its path.

'That'll be us in a few hours,' Atticus said, lost in his thoughts as he gazed out to sea.

Piercing through the silence like a gunshot, the shrill ringtone of Atticus's phone shattered his calm. Jerking upright, he removed the phone from his pocket and saw Mungo's name on the screen.

He took a deep breath and nodded to Ness. 'Here goes...' Atticus said and poked the screen with a suspicious finger. It was a FaceTime call, and he tried to remember Jake's instructions.

'What the HELL are you doing?' Mungo's face yelled from the screen.

'Morning, Mungo.' Atticus wondered why he could only see his own nose yet hear Mungo loud and clear.

'WHERE in God's name are you?' Mungo ranted. 'Dad! Tilt the phone – I can only see your eyebrows.'

'Well, I was enjoying a quiet parking space by the sea in Portsmouth.'

There was a silence, and Atticus knew Mungo was digesting his words.

'Hello?' Atticus said, holding his breath as he waited. He fumbled with the screen and blinked hard. A random filter had given him cat's ears.

'I'm still here,' Mungo replied. 'For goodness' sake, sort your phone out!'

Atticus wondered if his son was counting to ten before he continued, and sure enough, within seconds, as Atticus corrected his settings and Mungo's face appeared on the screen, his son set to again.

'I cannot believe that you furtively disappear in the middle of the night without so much as a hint of discussion about your proposed trip!' Mungo snapped. 'You leave a curt note under the door in the office that simply reads...'

Atticus heard a rustle of paper.

'*Off to Spain. Don't worry about me. Love Dad. Contact number below.*'

Atticus thought about the note. Mungo had a point; it wasn't his finest move. 'You would have talked me out of it,' he reasoned.

'Of course, I bloody well would!' Mungo yelled. 'The idea is crazy! You could be killed in that ancient camper. She's not fit to travel across countries with an old man at the wheel.'

An old man at the wheel! Atticus digested Mungo's comment.

Mungo continued to yell, but Atticus wasn't listening and held the phone away.

Don't let the old man in... Clara's voice whispered

through the open window, and Atticus returned to the phone.

'Now, Mungo,' Atticus began, 'calm down.'

'How the hell can I—'

But Atticus interrupted, 'This is why I didn't tell you. I knew you'd kick off and create a fuss.'

'A FUSS?'

'Aye, exactly. But this is one occasion where I won't give in.' Atticus felt his muscles tense. 'I gave in to all your ideas about the farm and even gave up my precious Herdwick sheep,' he paused. 'But this is the one time where I get to choose what I want to do with the rest of my life.'

'But I saved the farm! You would have gone under without all the changes,' Mungo spluttered.

'Well, that we'll never know.'

'You know damn well that if...' Mungo began to shout again.

'Stop it!' Atticus raised his hand as though the act would silence Mungo. 'I'm not changing my mind, so unless you want to wish me a bon voyage and a happy holiday, I suggest you leave me alone.'

He tapped furiously to exit FaceTime but inadvertently turned on a voice filter. 'I do not understand your concern, human child...' a robot voice said.

Moments passed in silence before Atticus spoke again. 'Hello?' he said. 'Mungo, are you there?'

But Mungo had disconnected the call.

With a heavy heart, Atticus turned to Ness and picked up Jake's carefully compiled folder. Determined not to let Mungo ruin his trip, he resolved to become more familiar with his iPhone. Opening the folder, he began to study Jake and Arthur's concise instructions.

As Ness nestled her head on his knee, Atticus said, 'Well, that's that, old lass.' He reached out to gently stroke her head. 'It's just you and me now, and whatever unfolds beyond that wide-open sea.'

In rural Ireland, the sky was heavy with dark clouds, casting a foreboding pallor over the landscape as a relentless downpour soaked everything in its path. Mary had completed the school run and, with four damp and grumpy kids safely deposited, now drove along the coastal road that led to Kindale Golf and Wellness Retreat. Shrouded in mist, the countryside was deserted, with only the occasional brave soul venturing out.

Rain ricocheted off the windscreen of her Range Rover like bullets as Mary carefully negotiated muddy potholes and thought about the day ahead. Aware that Roisin, her cleaner, was hard at work at Belvedere House, Mary had no desire to return home and get in the way of the woman's overactive Dyson or make endless cups of tea. Instead, Mary was heading to the gym.

Roisin had been with the family since they moved to Belvedere House several years ago. She had a full diary with cleaning bookings at all the larger houses and ran her business, Roisin's Shamrock Shine, with her two daughters. Mary was conscious of never using the term 'cleaner' when Roisin was within earshot, knowing that the fussy, self-important woman preferred the more favourable 'Environmental Services Provider'. Roisin was a gossip of the highest order, and had it not been for the fact that her work was first-class, Mary would have ditched Roisin's Shamrock Shine some time ago. But, if Mary wanted to catch up on any goings-on in Kindale, Roisin was a mouthpiece worthy of a plate of chocolate biscuits and several cups of strong tea, as she shared generous titbits of spicy scandal.

This morning, however, Mary had more important things on her mind than a juicy gossip with Roisin. Over breakfast, with the kids fighting over Coco Pops and Rice Crispies, Conor, running late, was in a hurry to leave for work. Drinking the fresh fruit smoothie Mary had made, he'd informed her that he wouldn't be home for dinner that evening.

'Has something important come up?' Mary asked.

'It's the land deal. There's a dinner tonight at the country club. All the planning committee will be there, along with the builder who's bought the land.'

'Are wives not invited?' Mary asked as she watched Conor abandon his empty glass on the table.

'It's not that sort of dinner,' he replied.

Mary wondered what sort of dinner it was as she picked up his glass and carried it to the dishwasher. Turning to Conor to straighten his lapel, she asked him when he would be home.

'I have no idea, so don't wait up.' He paused to pick up a leather document case and stared at Mary. 'Your leggings are getting tight,' he said. 'Wouldn't a longer shirt be better if you go out?'

Mary felt her face flush and grabbed the hem of her top to tug the fabric over her tummy. It was the first time in months that Conor had commented on anything Mary wore. There was nothing she'd like more than to be tummy-tucked, groomed, and dressed in a smart suit and at the cut and thrust of their business. But instead, she shook her head. She was about to tell him that if he had to look after four highly demanding children, each a whirlwind who left chaos in their wake, he wouldn't have time to worry about a slowly expanding waistline. But before she could reply, Conor was all over the kids, covering them with kisses and telling them to be good and work hard at school that day. He left the kitchen before their sticky fingers could stain his immaculate suit.

Mary stared at Conor's retreating back.

She hadn't mentioned the shirt incident from the previous day, and with the evidence washed away, she wondered if she'd imagined it. Mary's gnawing sense of doubt about her husband's fidelity niggled at her, and despite her search for signs of betrayal, she knew that Conor was too busy with his job. Had she asked him, he would probably have explained away the scent, saying it had occurred accidentally, exchanged in a friendly embrace with a co-worker.

Mary felt that her own inadequacy had fuelled her paranoia. She'd let her weight increase, and it was her own fault if Conor didn't pay any attention to the often-fraught mum she'd become. *God, how she missed her former working life!* Tightening her fists, Mary followed Conor through the house. He stepped back as he opened the front door, almost colliding with her.

To his surprise, Roisin stood on the doorstep.

'Good morning, Mr Murphy,' Roisin beamed. 'I didn't expect to bump into you again so soon?' She raised a pencilled eyebrow.

Conor gave Roisin a curt nod and then turned to Mary. 'Goodbye, darling,' he said. 'Enjoy your day.'

As Mary drove her vehicle through the gates of Kindale Golf and Wellness Retreat, she wondered what Roisin had meant about meeting Conor 'so soon'. He always left the house before Roisin's arrival. Still, Mary reasoned as she parked and reached for her gym bag, Roisin was probably working at a property Conor was selling, and their paths had crossed there.

Mary held an umbrella, battling against a strong gust and rods of steely rain. As her trainers crunched across the gravel, she wished she still worked in the office with Conor, in the business he'd started and encouraged her to join. Mary missed the magic of negotiating sales and dealing with the public. But four children had put paid to that. She had been an integral part of the early days when they were establishing the fledgling business, setting up systems and charming clients, building trust. Murphy's Auctioneers had soon become an essential and popular agency in the area, and Conor and Mary were a glamorous young couple on everyone's party invitation list. These days, Mary couldn't remember the last time they'd had a night out together on the town.

The clear glass doors of the retreat glided back, and Mary was greeted by a subtle blend of essential oils that filled the air like a gentle caress. How tempting it would be to book a massage and escape from her everyday life for an hour to ease the tension out of her muscles. But, remembering Conor's comment, Mary deposited her damp umbrella, patted her stomach, and headed for the torture chamber – otherwise known as the gym.

As she reached the changing room, her phone began to ring. Hoping Conor had changed his mind and invited her to the dinner that evening, Mary tore into her bag to grab her mobile.

'Hello?' she said and held the phone to her ear.

'DEAR GOD, MARY, were you in on it too?' an angry voice bellowed, without any introduction or courtesies.

'Hello... Mungo?' Mary frowned. *What on earth was Mungo banging on about?* 'What's wrong? You sound upset.'

'UPSET?' Mungo yelled. 'I'm absolutely furious.'

'Calm down,' Mary said, looking around for a quiet corner to take the call. Perching on a bench at the far end of the changing room, Mary gripped the phone. 'Now, what's happened?'

'It's Dad,' Mungo stated. 'The old fool has set off in the camper and is in Portsmouth with the dog, waiting to board a ferry to Spain. Did you know?'

'I had no idea.' Mary's eyes were wide, and she began to punch the air without realising her actions. *So, he'd done it.*

Her dad was off on an exciting adventure! 'Well, I don't see what's so wrong with that,' she replied.

'WHAT?' Mungo was shouting now. 'He's driving thousands of miles in a vintage vehicle that should have been put out to grass years ago! For heaven's sake, Mary, Dad's never even been abroad!'

Mary could sense Mungo's exasperation. 'I'm sure he's very organised,' she said. 'I can't for one moment think that he'd attempt such a journey without planning and discussing it with Arthur.'

'Not just Arthur,' Mungo sneered. 'Jake must have had a hand in this too.'

Mary visualised her brother tapping his desk with tense fingers as he worked out how to get to the bottom of things. Her nephew needed to take cover. Mungo was bound to suss Jake out.

'He's only doing what Mum would have wanted him to do,' Mary said. 'Don't you remember that they'd planned a holiday to Spain?'

'Via an airplane and a creditable taxi service, not at the wheel of a vehicle held together with duct tape and dreams. He was talking like a robot when I spoke to him.' Mungo's voice was tight with frustration.

'Ah, he'll be getting used to the settings on his phone,' Mary nodded.

But as Mary made herself comfortable for the duration of Mungo's rant, she had no doubt that Atticus, Arthur, and Jake had carefully planned the trip. It amused her to think of the trio entrenching themselves in the barn. While sorting out Winnie's engine, Jake would have shown

Atticus the wonders of the internet, and Mary knew that it would have opened her father's eyes to endless possibilities.

At last! He was regaining his life.

Mungo was deliberating his issues with Atticus and the business, arguing that their father had now admitted he had simply given in to all the changes he'd instigated.

Mary rolled her eyes. She decided she'd had enough. If Mungo couldn't be happy about the situation, he must learn to live with it. Right now, she had far more critical things to consider than Atticus sipping sangria in the sunshine and making new friends. She had to make inroads on her waistline and regain the shape she enjoyed when she married Conor.

'Mungo, I have to go,' Mary said. 'Perhaps we can discuss this again when you've had time to think about things.'

'But you can't...' Mungo stuttered.

Oh yes, I can! Mary thought, and with a polite goodbye, she disconnected the call.

Chapter Ten

As the sun descended over the coastal town of Portsmouth, Atticus drove Winnie onto the Brittany Ferry *Galicia*, under the dying light of the day. Constantly checking his mirrors, he took great care to follow the instructions from attendants in high-vis jackets as he warily negotiated the camper onto the car deck and parked tightly alongside motorhomes, cars, and caravans.

'Phew, we made it,' Atticus said to Ness, breathing a sigh of relief as he sat back to watch passengers pile out of their vehicles, gathering overnight bags for the crossing. Ness perked up as she heard barks and yips, her tail wagging gently.

'You're not the only canine traveller,' Atticus said, hooking a lead on Ness's collar. 'And I'm afraid you have to wear this.' He slipped a muzzle from a side pocket on the dog. Raising a paw, Ness tried to unhook the mouthguard but stopped when Atticus tapped her on the head. 'It won't be for long, but it's a rule when you board,' he said.

Climbing out of Winnie, Atticus picked up his pre-packed rucksack and, taking care to lock Winnie, followed the crowd heading out of the car deck and onto the ship. After passing through customs, he'd received his boarding card and cabin number. Atticus was pleased that he'd successfully checked Ness in as well, managing the complicated paperwork and microchip check. He silently thanked Arthur and Jake for their research on travelling with an animal.

The pet-friendly cabin was comfortable and spacious, with two berths and an ensuite bathroom. 'We even have a porthole,' Atticus mused as he stared out at the dark silhouettes of buildings lining the harbour.

As the engines rumbled to life and the ship glided away from land, Atticus wandered around the decks, leaving Ness in the cabin. Beneath his feet, he felt a gentle sway as the ferry gained momentum, and the lights from the shore became a distant blur. The scent of the sea and the sound of the waves lapping against the hull had been soothing, and Atticus, who'd been anxious after his angry exchange with Mungo, felt his worries slowly sliding away.

Here he was! At last able to chart his own course.

So, Clara, this is what travelling abroad feels like, Atticus thought as he sat in the bar a short while later and ordered a pint. There was a buzz of activity all around him as passengers explored the ship's amenities and settled into their seats.

Atticus toyed with visiting one of the many restaurants and having a snack. But he'd enjoyed fish and chips with Ness that afternoon and needed no further refreshment.

He'd noted a film showing in the cinema and, soon to start, a cabaret act in the theatre. Promising himself a stroll around the luxurious duty-free shops, Atticus was in awe of all the entertainment and the many facilities available to make the journey comfortable. With a full day ahead tomorrow and another night at sea, Atticus would have nothing to do but explore, and he intended to make the most of his onboard stay.

Draining his pint, Atticus checked his watch. Having travelled through the night, he yawned, realised he was tired, and decided to go to bed. But Ness would need exercise and a comfort break before they turned in.

On the doggie deck, Atticus again thought of Mungo and wished his son had seen sense. Gripping Ness's lead as she tugged in pursuit of a tail-wagging Westie, he wondered if things would ever be right between them. But Atticus knew that Mungo, when vexed, was as stubborn as his father and dismissing the thought, he decided that as soon as he arrived at his destination, he would get in touch with Mary. His daughter, no doubt delighted, would know what to do and laugh joyfully at the thought of her dad off on an adventure.

As his head hit the pillow, Atticus's last thoughts were of sunshine and sandy beaches. He remembered the website for the Spanish campsite and visualised strolling along the shores of the Mediterranean with the sea as a calm, mesmerising canvas. In moments, all thoughts of his row with Mungo had gone, and with Ness snoring beside him, Atticus fell into a deep and peaceful sleep.

Thirty-two hours later, as the *Galicia* docked in Santander, a pale-faced Atticus sat on the car deck behind Winnie's wheel, waiting to disembark. He wondered if he was going to throw up again and prayed that the dry toast he'd managed to eat at breakfast had settled in his stomach.

The sailing, which had begun innocuously as the ferry departed, soon became a nightmare for Atticus, who was unaware of an impending storm. As they ventured south to leave the English Channel and head along the coast of France, Atticus was woken by the sound of waves crashing against the vessel. Determined to ignore the elements, he'd gripped a pillow over his head and tried to sleep. But a curious feeling in the pit of his stomach had begun, and feeling queasy, Atticus sat up.

'Oh, Ness...' he murmured as he gripped the side of the bed and raced to the bathroom. 'I shouldn't have had greasy fish and chips for tea.'

As the ship entered the Bay of Biscay, it mirrored Atticus's stomach, pitching and rolling. Gigantic waves created swells, rising then falling with relentless fury. The storm was vicious throughout the following day, and over the public address system piped into the cabins, the ship's purser advised passengers not to move around the ship for their own safety.

'Huh!' Atticus said to Ness as he raced to the bathroom again. 'Walking about is as likely as a pig flying!'

Finally, after an eternity, the storm began to relent. The

wind subsided, and the waves became calm. Relieved passengers emerged from their sheltered corners to enjoy a pleasant evening and a good night's sleep. But Atticus wasn't taking any chances. Other than venturing out of his cabin to walk the dog, he lay on his bed, restlessly drowsing and counting the hours until they arrived in Santander. His stomach had received a battering, and he needed to calm it down.

When the purser announced that the Galicia would dock that morning at eight o'clock and their arrival was imminent, Atticus, dressed and ready for the onward journey, slipped out of the cabin to walk on the doggie deck with Ness. With clear weather and good visibility, as they entered the bay of Santander, another dog owner greeted them.

'Ey up!' The man's accent was broad, and with a smile, he pointed out a lighthouse sitting on top of the cliffs. Informing Atticus that it was called Cabo Mayor after the cliffs it was perched on, he then indicated the Palacio de la Magdalena. 'Aye, the impressive palace is an iconic Spanish landmark,' he added.

The man introduced himself as Martin from Yorkshire. His dog, a Westie named Fred, made friends with Ness, while Martin told Atticus that he was heading to his apartment in Benidorm with his partner.

They chatted for some time, and Martin explained the benefits of Benidorm and why he liked living there. 'It's a popular resort on the Costa Blanca with a right good climate, lovely beaches, and great entertainment and nightlife,' he said in his Yorkshire tone.

Martin was insistent that Atticus visit. Wanting to

know all about Atticus's plans, he nodded with approval when Atticus explained that he was heading to Guardamar, south of Alicante, and that it was his first time abroad.

'Benidorm isn't far away, about a two-hour drive.' Martin handed Atticus a business card. 'Come to the Starlight Show Bar and make sure you ask for me. I run the club with my partner.'

As Atticus fastened Ness's safety strap and joined Winnie to the line of vehicles leaving the ship, he thought that Martin had seemed a friendly type and decided that he might make a trip to Benidorm. He remembered that Arthur and Jake had included Benidorm on Atticus's 'Places to Visit' schedule in the folder, adding a note that it was a popular resort for British holidaymakers. 'Perhaps we'll have a drive there one day,' Atticus said as he negotiated Winnie slowly down a ramp.

Overhead, the cry of seagulls mingled with the bustle of port activity, and the warmth of an October sun and bright blue skies greeted the new arrivals as port officials took them smoothly through the customs checking area. Atticus felt nervous as he drove on the right-hand side of the road and, once again, whispered thanks to Arthur and Jake for setting up the satnav, which had seamlessly picked up Spanish GPS signals and mapped out the route. With the early start and the torturous sea journey behind them, six hundred miles of open road lay ahead.

Atticus began to feel better. He sucked on an Uncle Joe's mint ball, which soothed his stomach, and thought of the upcoming itinerary, carefully planned with Arthur and

Jake's help. They'd all spent hours studying a map book, deciding that Winnie's top speed would only manage at most three hundred miles daily. Atticus must be sure to have plenty of stops for coffee and food – and not to forget Ness, as the old dog would need her comfort breaks too.

As they left the port and started the journey, the satnav instructed, 'At the roundabout, take the second exit onto S-20 heading to Salida Ciudad.'

Atticus smiled. *Driving abroad was easy,* he told himself. *Clara, we're on our way!*

Thanks to the wonders of satellite navigation, he could sit back, listen to instructions, and enjoy the journey. Noting that the mileage was now in kilometres, he glanced at Gonzalo, still perched on the dashboard. The little gnome moved to the vehicle's motion and appeared to be nodding his head. Atticus reached out to straighten Gonzalo's walking stick and the flag that announced, 'Adventure Awaits!'. And as the satnav instructed Atticus to merge onto the A-67 and head towards Burgos, he said, 'I certainly hope so, Gonzalo.'

Leaving Santander behind, Atticus settled into the journey. The coastal scenery transitioned to lush green hills and peaks, and he began to enjoy the road winding through the Cantabrian Mountains, which offered stunning views of forests and valleys.

'It reminds me a little of home,' Atticus told Ness, remembering the fells surrounding Barn Hill Farm. 'But I wouldn't like to be up here in winter,' he added, noting tall snow poles every few metres.

Occasionally, oncoming vehicles flashed their headlights, and the drivers held up a hand. Atticus was puzzled. There was no mention of this in his folder, and he wondered if it was some sort of Spanish road etiquette they'd missed.

It wasn't until he'd pulled into a picnic area that he began to understand.

A motorhome with German plates flashed its lights, slowed down, and the driver lowered his window. 'Very good wheels!' the driver called out. 'I like your Westie, an iconic German brand,' he added, and with a cheery wave, he drove on.

'Ah, it's Winnie they're appreciating,' Atticus muttered as he poured coffee from his flask and gave Ness a biscuit. He made a mental note to reciprocate whenever he saw a vehicle he admired.

Moving on, Atticus remembered that Arthur had told him to make time for sightseeing. Arthur had studied maps online and made notes for him on places worth visiting. There would be many historic towns and villages along the way, and with this in mind, Atticus took a detour. Following signs to the heart of Burgos, he found a car park beside the River Arlanzón, where a riverside walk allowed him to admire the town's landmarks.

In the town square, he stood with Ness and gazed around at the meeting place where visitors and locals alike enjoyed the lively atmosphere.

'Let's have a coffee,' he said to Ness, and moments later,

Atticus sat at a table and stared at a menu. He hadn't a clue what to ask for, as images of blood sausage and suckling lamb lay alongside dishes suggesting cheese and various rice concoctions.

A waiter approached, and Atticus cleared his throat. 'A café con leche, por favor,' he said. As the waiter disappeared, Atticus grinned. His practice with Jake on basic Spanish had paid off, and he could confidently order his favourite milky coffee.

'I think we've cracked it,' Atticus murmured as the waiter returned with his drink. He unwrapped the complimentary biscuit and handed it to Ness.

Strolling through the town along narrow medieval streets, Atticus felt the warmth of the sun and tilted his hat to avoid the glare as he passed museums and theatres, sensing centuries of history all around him. When he reached the Cathedral of St. Mary of Burgos, Atticus stopped to study the architectural masterpiece. Had Ness not been with him, he would have stepped inside and lit a candle for Clara. But unsure of Spanish rules about church-visiting Collies and unwilling to leave Ness behind, he sat on a nearby bench and looked up at the soaring spire and intricate façade.

'Hey, Clara, just look at me now,' Atticus whispered. Ness lay her head on his knee, and he absently stroked the dog's silky fur. 'The old man is out and about.'

On their walk back to the camper, Atticus was struck by the smell of freshly baked bread. Looking ahead, he saw a sign that read 'Panadería'. Deciding that it must be a bakery, he was delighted to find an open window displaying a mouth-watering array of crusty baguettes and rustic loaves.

A woman greeted Atticus. 'Hola,' she called out.

'Oh, er... Hola.' Atticus tapped his hat in acknowledgement and pointed to a soft, pale loaf.

'Pan de leche?' The woman smiled and wrapped the milky-coloured bread into a paper bag.

'Aye, er... right, and I'll also have dos of those, por favor.' He held up two fingers, then reached for a handful of euros as she added the chicken-filled pastries he'd pointed at to the carrier.

'Empanadas,' the woman said, 'very good, you enjoy.'

'I'm sure I will,' Atticus said, touching his hat. 'Buen día,' he grinned.

'Gracias. Adiós, handsome cowboy,' she laughed.

Atticus was surprised by the comment and decided that the Spanish were a friendly bunch and perhaps the lady sensed repeat business.

Back at the camper, he sat with Ness and munched on the empanadas. 'These *are* good,' he said as he bit into the delicious, savoury pastry, while Ness licked up flaky crumbs from the floor. After tidying up the debris, he stretched his legs in the sunshine and made ready to set off again. A motorhome, with several bikes strapped to the rear, drove past, and the driver tooted his horn.

'Très bien, camper!' a French voice called out. 'Like a big, fat canary!'

Atticus gave a curt nod as he cranked Winnie's engine to life, and they got back on the highway. He wasn't sure he appreciated his precious vehicle being compared to a big, fat canary. Still, he soon forgot the comment as the open road before him offered stunning views of vast farmlands, while Winnie chugged along.

Atticus passed mile after mile of vineyards and olive groves, occasionally pulling over to photograph points of interest. He was grateful that Jake had insisted on the latest version of the iPhone. The camera was excellent, and Atticus was amazed at how simple it was to use.

Jake had set up an Instagram account for him, calling it @thetravellinggrandad. The boy had shown Atticus how to upload photos using hashtags, explaining that it was a way of keeping in touch. Jake and Arthur had followed the account so they could see the photos and enjoy the journey, too. Atticus thought having a virtual photo album was a splendid idea. In his day, it had been film on a reel that you took to Boots the Chemist to be developed into pictures, which Clara would then glue into the pages of a glossy album.

This newfangled phone saved all that bother.

Standing on a grassy verge, he pointed his phone at a giant iron billboard standing over fourteen metres tall. The impressive structure depicted a massive black bull. Jake had a whole page dedicated to the bull in the travel folder and Atticus knew that approximately ninety-two similar bulls were positioned on hilltops or alongside roadways throughout Spain. Jake, intrigued by their existence, had told Atticus to photograph as many as he could find. Consulting the folder, Atticus learnt that the El Toro de Osborne – the Osborne Bull – had been created in 1956 to advertise brandy and had since become a national emblem.

'Gotcha!' Atticus said as he took several images.

As the day wore on, Atticus decided to break up the journey with an overnight stop before they reached Madrid. Having had little sleep on the ferry, he was feeling tired. He'd noted signs for 'Area de Servicio' and chose one with plenty of parking space. Atticus edged Winnie by a grassy verge between two articulated trucks. A café served hot food, and he tucked into a dish named 'Cocido Madrileña', which resembled a hearty stew. The meal was delicious and a perfect choice. Wiping the plate clean with a chunk of crusty bread, Atticus licked his lips.

With a full stomach and feeling weary, Atticus took Ness for her last stroll of the day. Heading back to Winnie, he noted that her round headlights gleamed like a pair of eager eyes, and her fender seemed to curve upwards in a grin. 'Hello, old girl,' he said and smiled with pleasure at his motorised companion.

Deciding to message Jake and let his grandson know all was well, he pulled out the camper's sofa and lay down on the bed, snuggling under a soft, downy duvet with Ness curled into his back. To the rumble of distant traffic, the world outside Winnie faded away. A sigh escaped from Atticus's lips while Ness's paws twitched in her dreams.

In moments, The Travelling Grandad and his dog drifted into a deep and satisfying sleep.

Chapter Eleven

In his bedroom on the second floor of Barn Hill farmhouse, Jake sat at a desk in one corner and studied his laptop screen. His Instagram account was open, and as he scrolled through a page of new images, a call came in on his phone.

'Is that you?' Arthur whispered.

'Hello, Uncle Arthur,' Jake replied. 'Yes, it's me. Who else were you expecting?'

'I wasn't sure. Word on the grapevine is that you've been grounded?'

'Yep, I'm only let out of my room to go to school. Grounded for a whole week.'

'That's a bit harsh, lad. Your dad must be very cross.'

'He's raging. He won't let me service the caravan site and refuses to let me near Grandad's Little Grey Fergie.'

'Maybe he thinks you'll do a disappearing act to Spain,' Arthur chuckled.

'I would if I could, although it might be slow going on a tractor.'

'What have you told him?'

'The truth,' Jake sighed. 'It's better that dad knows we did as much research as possible before Grandad set off.'

'Aye, that makes sense.'

'Perhaps he'll believe Grandad is safe in Winnie and is going to have a brilliant holiday.'

'It's hard to say – Mungo can be difficult,' Arthur said. 'He's probably upset because he knew nothing about it.'

'Well, that's his problem, not mine,' Jake huffed. A scowl etched deeply across his face, and his lips pursed in a tight line.

'Have you seen the Instagram account?' Arthur asked.

'Yes, I'm looking at it now.' Jake stared at the screen where the account for @thetravellinggrandad displayed a dozen new images. 'He's got a photograph of one of the bulls!' Jake was suddenly brighter. 'Have you seen it?'

'Yes, and Ness is sitting by the bull's hoof. She looks tiny,' Arthur laughed.

'He messaged tonight to say that motorhomes keep tooting him and flashing their lights.'

'Ah, the international sign of approval,' Arthur said, sounding pleased. 'In recognition of a fine vintage vehicle.'

'Grandad said that a French man told him Winnie was like a big, fat canary.'

'Bloody cheek, she's a beauty...'

'He went sightseeing in Burgos. I'm surprised; I didn't think Grandad was into ancient buildings,' Jake said, staring at images of Burgos Cathedral that Atticus had uploaded to his Instagram feed, which he'd labelled: #Unesco #WorldHeritageSite #Burgos. He'd even included a smiling selfie on the bridge by the River Arlanzón and added the hashtag #thetravellinggrandad.

'There are lots of hashtags. How does he know about them?' Arthur asked.

'He thinks they mean that just you and I will see the photos as soon as he uploads them.'

'Doesn't he know about followers?'

'No, we never got that far. It was becoming confusing for Grandad, like an information overload.'

'Ah, I see.' In truth, Arthur didn't see at all and only knew about Instagram from Jake's instructions. Social media was as puzzling to Arthur as the Rubik's Cube.

'Does Aunty Shirley know you're online?'

'No, I'm hiding in the shed. Shirley's not a fan of t'internet and thinks it will lead me into bad ways.'

'Like following Grandad to Spain?' Jake chuckled.

'Maybe.' Arthur chuckled. 'Shirley heard about his disappearance at her WI meeting tonight.'

'So soon?'

'Aye, some nosy parker with insomnia was curtain twitching when we drove through the village and recognised Atticus at Winnie's wheel.'

'Winnie *is* very noticeable.'

'The gossip has spread around the village like a disease.'

'Dad won't like that...'

There was a knock and Jake swivelled to stare at his bedroom door.

'Jake? Have you done your homework?' Mungo called out. 'Let me in.'

'I have to go, Uncle Arthur. Dad's making a racket,' Jake whispered.

'Catch you tomorrow, be good!' Arthur disconnected the call.

'Jake, let me in!' Mungo repeated.

'Keep your hair on, Dad. I'm coming,' Jake replied, and with a sigh, went to open the door.

At the service area in Spain, Atticus had woken early to the sound of engines roaring. The smell of diesel was strong, and for a moment, he wondered where he was. But Ness reminded him by moving to the window and twitching back the curtain with her nose. She began to bark as the trucks beside Winnie roared into life and set off on their onward journey.

'It's time we were up,' Atticus said and rubbed his eyes. He gave Ness a pat as she shot past him, tail wagging and tongue lolling, before sitting by the camper's door. 'Aye, hang on a mo. Let me get my trousers on...'

In the café where he had dined the previous evening, Atticus chose a dish that looked like an omelette, labelled 'Tortilla Española'. With two cups of strong coffee and a buttered baguette, the breakfast was the perfect start to his day. Afterward, he purchased a crusty loaf, a slab of pale-yellow cheese, a jar of local honey, and four litres of water, storing the items carefully in Winnie.

'That'll see us through the day,' he told Ness as they set off and Winnie hit the road again.

The sky was dark and cloudy, and with busy motorways ahead, Atticus hoped that it wouldn't rain. Jake had set the satnav to circumnavigate the vast city of Madrid, and already, with huge trucks careering past, vibrations shook Winnie's bodywork and Atticus felt hesitant about the drive. He wasn't confident the old camper's wipers would cope if there was a deluge.

Jake had explained that toll roads carried less traffic, as motorists paid for the benefit of their use. As the first toll booth came into sight, Atticus slowed down and nervously approached the barrier.

His grandson had installed a clever device called a Bipandgo on Winnie's windscreen, which was electronically recognised at a toll booth, allowing the driver to sail through without stopping to pay.

'Oh, please open,' Atticus prayed, hoping that Jake had installed it correctly. Wide-eyed with Ness, they crept into the lane. In his right-hand-drive vehicle, it would be a nightmare to get out and run around the vehicle to pay as a queue built up behind them.

But, to Jake's credit, the barrier smoothly lifted, and they drove through.

'Yes! That gadget is worth every penny.' Atticus gave an ecstatic fist pump, and Ness woofed. 'It charges your credit card at the end of each month,' he explained to his excited dog. 'Genius, eh? The modern gizmos that are available today,' he added, shaking his head.

As they headed south again, the satnav indicated that

they would arrive at their destination by mid-afternoon. But with several stops planned for Ness and a bite to eat, Atticus knew it would be much later. Leaving the outskirts of Madrid far behind, the muddy sky cleared as the sun came out. He gazed out at agricultural fields and the occasional small town in the distance, pleased that he'd chosen this route. Jake had suggested a more extended drive, sight-seeing through France over several days before crossing the border into Spain, south of Perpignan. But Arthur had advised that a shorter journey with Winnie might, on this occasion, be sensible. Despite the horrible ferry crossing, Atticus had to agree.

Miles of olive groves and vineyards whizzed by, and as they passed through the region of Castilla-La Mancha, Atticus noted a tourist information sign for the Castle of Belmonte.

'There's a castle perched on every hilltop,' he muttered to Ness.

Whenever Atticus saw a structure of the Osborne Bull, he stopped and took a photograph. The massive bull amused him, and he chuckled as he wondered if the Lake District Tourist Board might do something similar with Herdwick sheep in Cumbria.

On the edge of the town of Consuegra, he picnicked on bread and cheese with Ness, and while reading through the information in his folder, he learnt that the windmills scattered all over the area were immortalised in Miguel de Cervantes' *Don Quixote*, a novel he'd read at school.

'Fancy that,' Atticus mused as he studied the massive sails.

Passing through the province of Albacete, Atticus saw that the landscape had become more rugged, leaving the lush, fertile plains behind him. A mountainous terrain lay in the distance. But sometime later, when signs for Alicante began to appear, a glimpse of the Mediterranean came into view. Atticus gazed as a golden glow lit up the sky, and the sun started to dip towards the horizon. Ness stirred from her slumber and, as though sensing the journey had reached its final leg, she began to look out of the window.

'Not too far now,' Atticus said and followed the satnav's directions to bypass Alicante.

The vast city sprawled out before him, and Atticus hoped he wouldn't get lost. But end-of-day traffic was manic, with cars, motorcycles, and buses weaving in and out of lanes. A background of honking horns seemed to be the Spanish drivers' way of communicating and fearing that some of the noise was directed at him, Atticus tried hard to stay on the right road. Soon, though, he realised he was lost as the satnav screen changed crazily to update the route.

On the dashboard, Gonzalo the Gnome's head nodded to one side.

'Aye, you're right. I'll head to the coast,' Atticus told Gonzalo. 'If we keep to the sea on our left, we can't go wrong.'

Sure enough, with the Castle of Santa Bárbara perched high on Alicante's hilltop now behind them, the satnav corrected itself, and with traffic easing, Atticus drove Winnie south. 'Thirty-eight kilometres!' Atticus happily announced, before quickly converting the distance. 'Only twenty-three miles to go.'

The coastal road became single-lane traffic, meandering along an even plane. In a convoy, with a slow but steady speed, Atticus stared at the landscape that would soon become familiar.

'Would you just look at that...' he said in awe to Ness.

Large salt flats lay on either side of the road next to vast stacks of pure-white salt. Further on, the flats became lakes, and as the daylight softened, it cast a pink and silver hue on the water. Flocks of flamingos waded through the shallows, and with long stick-like legs, they moved with effortless grace, vibrant pink feathers catching the light. Each step of their delicate feet created ripples and Atticus was mesmerised.

Seeing a layby ahead, he slowed Winnie into a space. With Ness on her lead, they crossed the road and walked along a narrow boardwalk parallel to a lake.

'This is so beautiful,' Atticus whispered, beginning to take photos as reeds rustled in the warm evening breeze and water gently lapped against the shore. Herons took flight against the fading light, their giant wings a hypnotic beat as they soared above, and waterfowl mingled with the flamingos, their silhouettes reflected like a mirage.

It was an awe-inspiring sight, giving Atticus time to pause, and be thankful to Jake and Arthur for giving him the courage to come on this journey. With a happy sigh, he returned to Winnie, and they set off again.

Fifteen minutes later, the satnav announced that they had reached their destination.

'We must be here,' Atticus said to Ness as she leaned her head out of the window, breathing in the salty air. A large roundabout lay ahead and taking care to negotiate the correct side of the road, Atticus found himself travelling in circles. 'I can't see any signs?' he called out in frustration.

But as an entrance to the right appeared, Ness began to bark, and Gonzalo's head dipped in that direction. 'Alright, have it your way,' Atticus said and took the narrow road.

As they got halfway down, a large sign suddenly appeared.

Bienvenida – Willkommen – Bienvenue –
Welcome
Solma Vacaciones
The Home of Happy Campers

'Well, old girl,' Atticus said, stretching out a hand to rub Ness's head as he slowly negotiated Winnie onto the site. 'We made it, and here we are. This will be our home for the duration.'

Chapter Twelve

Atticus drove Winnie through the gates of the campsite, where a barrier prevented them from going further. Parking in a nearby space, he told Ness to stay while he went to check in. Reaching for his folder and placing his hat firmly, he strode toward a doorway marked 'Reception'. Behind a long counter, a woman wearing square-framed glasses, with dark black hair cut into a helmet style, studied a computer.

Atticus stepped forward. 'Good evening, er... Buenas noches.'

'Sí?' The woman's eyes didn't leave the screen.

'Do you speak English?' Atticus asked.

'Sí,' she replied.

'Then I'd like to check in.'

'Passport.' The woman held out her hand.

Atticus reached into his folder and waited while she confirmed his passport details. Making no eye contact, she stood and handed him two sheets of paper.

'Pitch number thirteen. Read these rules. The barrier has Automatic Number Plate Recognition. Study the map and follow the road,' she said briskly. A phone rang, and, turning away, she answered the call and began to speak rapidly in Spanish.

Atticus was baffled as he walked back to Winnie. *Welcome to Spain!* he thought as he cranked up the engine and drove slowly toward the barrier.

A little while later, he drove past the reception area for the fourth time. Atticus stopped and, in frustration, stared at the printed map again. 'I'm struggling to work this out,' he muttered to Ness. 'I've no idea where our pitch is.'

Reluctant to return and ask the woman for further directions, he was about to get out and walk around the site when a woman knocked on the window.

'Are you lost, dear?' she asked.

Grateful to hear a friendly English voice, Atticus wound the window down. 'Yes, I've just arrived and can't find my pitch.'

The middle-aged woman's skin was the colour of a conker, and she was dressed in a lime-green kaftan, her vibrant orange hair piled into a top knot.

'Let me help. I don't expect you'll get much assistance from our friendly receptionist.' She walked to the passenger side of Winnie and, to Atticus's surprise, opened the door. 'I'm Cheryl,' she announced as she climbed in. She placed a huge carrier bag, clanking with bottles, on the seat and looked around. 'Oh, this is lovely – a vintage camper. What do you call her?'

'Winnie,' Atticus said.

'Winne the Westfalia,' she nodded, then stared at Atticus. 'And you must be the Rhinestone Cowboy?'

Conscious of his old Stetson hat and comfortable hide boots, gifted from Mary following her holiday to Dallas, Atticus was bemused. The bandana knotted around his neck was for comfort, and the leather waistcoat an extra layer over his checked cotton shirt. He hadn't considered the outfit he'd chosen to travel in to be anything other than practical. *It must be the hat,* Atticus thought.

'I'm Atticus, and my dog is called Ness,' he said.

'Pleased to meet you, Atticus.' Ness placed her head on Cheryl's shoulder and sniffed.

'Sorry about Ness,' Atticus said.

'I like dogs,' Cheryl replied, tickling Ness's chin. 'There are a lot on the site; she'll soon settle in.'

'So, do you know where pitch thirteen is?'

'Yes, of course, they remove the plaque because folk think its unlucky,' Cheryl grinned. 'Fire Winnie up and take the third turning on the left.'

They moved slowly past spacious hardstanding pitches, separated by hedges and trees, where motorhomes and caravans were carefully positioned to maximise space. Awnings of all shapes and sizes created additional living spaces and were adorned with colourful lights, garden ornaments, and outdoor seating. Pet owners strolled with their furry companions, pausing to stare at the bright yellow camper. Upon recognising the woman in the passenger seat, they held up their hands and waved.

A man called out, '*Goedeavond!*'

'They're a friendly lot,' Cheryl said, 'especially the Dutch.' She waved at the man. 'Now look, we're here, the last pitch on the left.' She pointed to an ample empty space. 'Number thirteen, lucky for you because you're near the shower block, and me and Ruby are right around the corner.'

'Well, thanks for your help,' Atticus said.

'I'm not done yet. Let me get out, and I'll guide you back. You need to be parked over the drain, next to the water and electricity posts, which you'll never see at this time of night.'

Grabbing the heavy, clanking carrier, Cheryl slammed Winnie's door shut, then indicated with her hands and bellowed instructions. As he gratefully manoeuvred into position, Atticus wondered if she worked at the site – Cheryl was clearly used to directing new arrivals.

'Steady as you go!' she called out, slapping Winnie's rear when she was happy with the position. 'That'll do nicely,' she said as Atticus and Ness joined her and stood together to study his parking skills.

'That's great, I'll get settled,' Atticus began. 'Thanks again for all your help.'

'It's too dark to set up now, and I expect you've had a long journey.' Cheryl gave Atticus no choice. Thrusting the carrier into his free hand and taking his elbow, she began to guide him away. 'Ruby and I are having a barbecue with a few friends, so you and Ness must come and join us.'

'But I can't possibly...' Atticus lurched under the weight of a dozen heavy bottles, chinking in his hand.

'Nonsense. You must be hungry, and there are no strangers here. Everyone helps each other.' Cheryl brushed aside his protests.

'I'd better lock up,' he began.

'Oh, everything is as safe as houses.' Cheryl flapped her hand and, linking his free arm, they set off with Ness in tow.

Atticus stared at vacationers sitting outside under awnings. The evening was still warm, and most were dressed casually in shorts, sandals, and T-shirts, sipping drinks as they chatted and watched the world go by.

Cheryl appeared to know everyone.

'Good evening, Heinrich, say hello to Helga for me!' she called out to an elderly man who sat beside a vast motorhome.

Atticus's jaw dropped. The vehicle was the size of a double-decker bus!

'Hello Stefan, mind how you go with the Soberano!' Cheryl nodded to a half-empty bottle on the table, where a dark-skinned man sat with a cat on his knee. Turning to Atticus, she whispered, 'He doesn't know what day it is after a few glasses of brandy and thinks the pussy is his reincarnated wife. Best to steer clear at this time of night if you want to avoid a seance.'

She turned a corner, and to Atticus's surprise, two rows of wooden chalets lined a central path ahead of them. Spreading out from the balcony of the first chalet, a noisy group was gathered. Many were standing, but most were sitting on lightweight, portable chairs. The area was lit with rainbow-coloured fairy lights and lanterns, and a delicious savoury aroma drifted through the still night air.

A voice from behind a barbecue called out, 'She's back from her supermarket sweep and she's got the sangria and found a cowboy!'

Cheers went up, and relieved of the carrier, Atticus found a pint glass being thrust into his hand. A tall man with skin the colour of night held out a jug of wine and began to pour.

'What is this drink?' Atticus asked as he tasted the sweet red liquid, which had slices of orange, apple, and pineapple floating on top.

'Sangria, my friend,' the man said with a heavy Dutch accent. 'A Spanish drink.'

'It's very nice,' Atticus said. After the drive, he was thirsty, and the sangria tasted like refreshing lemonade.

'You must have more.' The man refilled Atticus's glass. 'I'm Erik from Holland, by the way,' he said with a half-smile, before moving away.

Atticus thought Erik had a striking look. Athletic and handsome, with perfect teeth and a smooth bald head, he was the kind of person who naturally attracted attention.

Looking around for Ness, Atticus spotted her sitting by the barbecue. As though appearing in an obedience class at Crufts, the old dog, her eyes fixed on the grilled sausages, was on her best behaviour. She rolled over on cue, played dead, thumped her tail, then held up a paw to shake several hands, soon finding herself rewarded.

Knowing that he'd likely be cleaning up after the

greedy dog all night, Atticus stepped in. Clipping a lead to her collar, he pulled Ness to one side.

Cheryl, with an arm around the barbecue chef, turned when she saw him. 'Here he is,' she smiled. 'Atticus, our new neighbour.'

The person with Cheryl, wearing a polo shirt and shorts, had cropped hair, grey at the sides, and a nose and ears pierced with studs and rings. A snake tattoo coiled around their neck, and more tattoos featuring animals continued along well-muscled arms and legs.

'Good evening,' Atticus said and held out his hand.

'Hello, I'm pleased to meet you.'

Atticus tried not to wince as the hand crunched his own.

'This is my Ruby,' Cheryl said and planted a kiss, narrowly missing a nose ring.

'Oh, hi, er, hello...' Atticus shook Ruby's hand.

'How long are you here for?' Ruby asked. She picked up a fork and tossed chunks of steak on a hot grill, alongside marinated chicken and fat juicy sausages.

'I'm not sure, a few weeks at least.' Atticus stared at the food and realised that his stomach was rumbling. It seemed a long time since his bread and cheese picnic.

'Travelling alone?' Ruby carefully turned the browning meat.

'Yes, despite my family thinking I'm out of my mind.'

'Your family doesn't approve?' Cheryl was curious.

'My son, Mungo, thinks that an old codger like me shouldn't stray far from home, and this trip in a vintage camper is crazy.'

'A crazy cowboy.' Cheryl smiled. 'Does your son think you're spending his inheritance?'

Atticus grinned at Cheryl's directness and decided that he liked her. 'He thinks that an old man like me isn't safe to be travelling on his own.'

'What tosh, eh Ruby?' Cheryl nudged Ruby's arm again. 'You're never too old to set another goal or dream a new dream.'

'Or take a nap halfway through both,' Ruby laughed.

'He thinks I'm old enough to know better than gadding about in a foreign country,' Atticus said.

'Ah, but you're *young* enough to know better!' Cheryl observed.

'You look hungry,' Ruby said, and taking a plate, loaded it with meat and handed it to Atticus. Spearing a cold sausage, she winked at Ness, who gobbled the offering before Atticus had time to tug her back.

'Help yourself to salads and sides.' Ruby waved her fork in the direction of a loaded table, where Atticus could see other guests tucking in.

'You must let me contribute to this,' he said, his mouth watering as he contemplated the delicious meal.

'Nah, don't be daft,' Ruby said, giving him a gentle fist bump. 'We'll all be round at yours tomorrow,' she added with a grin.

Atticus gulped. He hadn't expected to make new friends so early on in his holiday and wondered how on earth he would cope with Winnie's basic cooking facilities if a crowd turned up.

'Only joking,' Ruby laughed. 'Don't look so terrified.'

Erik returned and seeing Atticus's empty glass, slapped him on the back and reached out to refill it. 'Drink up, enjoy!'

The thirst-quenching sangria was delicious. 'Don't mind if I do,' Atticus said. He gripped his plate and meandered over to the table, where Cheryl pulled out a chair for him.

Someone had picked up a guitar and begun to play, and Atticus noticed several ukuleles lined up by the decking.

'Park yourself down here, next to me,' Cheryl said. 'Then tell us all about yourself. We haven't had a new face on the site for a while, and everyone wants to get to know you.'

'Yah!' a woman called out, followed by calls of 'Ja bitte!' and 'Willkommen!'

'They're all happy to meet you,' Cheryl said, piling tangy bean salad on her plate and patting Atticus's arm. 'You'll soon get to know us,' she smiled. 'Nights like this are called speed-dating the neighbourhood.'

Atticus had never heard of speed-dating and had no idea what Cheryl meant. He wondered if it was some sort of 'gossip grapevine' – an expression Clara used for keeping up with things in the village. But as the night wore on and he continued to down glasses of sangria, while Erik circled with brandy, Atticus soon got to know everyone.

Several people picked up their ukuleles and began to play, and someone produced a drum. It turned into an international singsong, and delighted to be included, Atticus joined in whenever he could.

Falling fully clothed into bed hours later, his head was

spinning as he gave Ness a tipsy grin and nestled her into his arm. 'That's what you call fast-tracking friendship...' Atticus muttered. 'I think I'm going to like it here.'

In moments, Atticus Arnott, the Cumbrian Cowboy, was out for the count as he fell into a deep and delightful sleep.

Chapter Thirteen

After damp weather all week, Saturday morning in Kindale was fine and sunny. Mary dropped Finn off for a football game, hoping the team would play on the club's Astroturf. There were no shower facilities at the club and playing on the rain-soaked field would mean Finn returned like a mud ball and despite wrapping him in a bin liner, the car would need to be valeted.

Fortunately, car valeting was an additional service offered by Roisin's Shamrock Shine. Roisin's brother Ruari, who was not only the most handsome man in Kindale but also a dab-hand with a chamois, ran the valeting amenity. Mary wasn't precious about her vehicle but as Conor insisted that she keep it in pristine condition, she never hesitated to engage Roisin's Shamrock Shine whenever her vehicle needed cleaning. Ruari, known locally as Romeo Ruari, was effusive with his flirting and flattery and, in only five minutes, could make Mary feel twenty-one again.

Ruari's daughter, Ola, was the same age as Declan, and

Mary occasionally ran into him at school events. Since parting from his wife, the divorced Ruari had become the undisputed heartthrob of Kindale. With his dark, handsome looks and shoulders broad enough to carry a week's worth of shopping, Mary knew that his smile could melt the frost off the town's coldest women. Mary's friend Una often muttered that *'Half the females in the town would throw themselves under a bus for him...'* and Mary's nosy neighbour had been caught straightening her cardigan and peering down the drive whenever Ruari was bent over Mary's Range Rover, engaged in a buff and polish.

But as she made a mental note to book her vehicle in for a valet, Mary smiled. She had no doubt that Ruari wouldn't be on the open market for long and was as likely to stay single as a tray of Helen's scones at the Eden craft fair. Already, there was a queue of women tripping in and out of Gaelic Glow, emerging with plumped lips and fresh highlights before cornering Ruari with a well-timed apple crumble or a casserole piled so high with dumplings it was almost a marriage proposal.

Mary remembered that she'd not spoken to Mungo, who was probably sulking that she'd abruptly ended their call and, knowing her brother, the sulk could last for days. Still, she'd sent a text to Jake, who told her he was grounded, but that he'd heard from his grandad and so far, the trip was going to plan. Reminding herself that she must ask Jake for her dad's mobile number, Mary hoped that Atticus was enjoying himself.

As Mary drove through the colourful streets of Kindale, where the houses and shops were painted in bright shades, she thought of Conor, who was at work and had left the house early. After the dinner at the golf club, she'd asked him if his meeting had been successful, and he told her that things may eventually go in his favour, but he didn't want to say more for fear of jinxing things. It was an unusual comment, as they generally shared all things work-related. With Conor so preoccupied, Mary hoped the deal would close soon so he could have more time for her and the kids.

Caitlin was child-minding Declan that morning, and Maeve, glued to Instagram, was looking for makeup tricks to make her the most desirable female at the school's '80s themed disco that evening. The sixth year had come up with a charity event to raise money for a proposed allotment. With Caitlin on the allotment committee and Maeve suddenly deciding that she was adopting a plant-based regime, Mary knew that the girls were keen to go.

To Mary's surprise, Conor had suggested that after dropping the girls off, they go for a quiet drink in Kindale. Mary, who'd arranged babysitting for Finn and Declan, was looking forward to an unexpected date night with her husband, and with time to spare – while Finn dreamt of premiership football and raced around the pitch – she was now on her way to Gaelic Glow for a facial, followed by a shampoo and blow-dry.

'I shall look like the belle of the ball,' Mary assured herself as she found a parking space outside the salon. 'Well, half-decent, at least, in the dimly lit Salty Dog Inn.'

As Mary settled herself on the comfortable bed in the therapy room, she let her thoughts wander as a beautician applied lotions to her skin.

So far, the diet Mary had begun earlier in the week was progressing. That evening, she planned to wear the gorgeous designer jeans she'd bought last Christmas and never fit into because they were too tight. The couple of pounds she'd lost had made a difference, and the jeans now zipped up. Mary contemplated digging out her Lycra knickers for added shape but knew she'd be unlikely to sit down comfortably. And what if Conor felt amorous when they got home? Beige Bounce Buster Briefs were hardly a turn-on.

'Anything planned for the weekend?' The beautician asked as she pummelled exfoliator into Mary's cheeks.

'A date night with my husband,' Mary replied. As she felt her face grow hot, she wondered if the beautician was using an industrial sander.

'A date night?' the beautician asked, holding a rotating device to scrape exfoliator from Mary's skin. 'Imagine that – romance is still in the air, even after all these years and four kids.'

'Yes, we like to keep our marriage alive.'

'Most marriages fall flat after the third baby, especially when the pounds pile on.'

Mary felt the slight and wished the busybody beautician would keep her nose out of things. Had Mary not been assured that the facial would make her look ten years younger, she might be giving the Gaelic Glow gossip a mouthful.

Determined to ignore any further conversation and relax into the treatment, Mary feigned sleep, letting out a barely audible snore. It did the trick, and soon the beautician worked in silence. As Mary drifted away, she thought of her week and the session she'd put in at the gym. It hadn't been terribly successful.

Only fifteen minutes in, feeling hot and sweaty from the treadmill, she'd moved to an upright bike, tuning the monitor to daytime TV, and began to gently peddle. A woman on *Good Morning Ireland* was moaning about her husband, Hubert, who'd left her to join a reclusive cult. Engrossed in the programme and wondering how Hubert was coping with the five wives he'd gained since joining the cult, Mary didn't look up when someone straddled the bike beside her and began to cycle as though competing in an event.

As the programme ended, a helpline number for an adultery hotline appeared on Mary's screen, and she heard a voice call out.

'Making a note of the number?'

Mary spun around and, to her horror, saw that the Lycra-clad figure beside her was none other than Lucinda Darby. Standing out like a pearl amongst stones, Lucinda seemed out of place in her sleek workout gear. Mary tugged on her baggy old top and wished she'd worn more fashionable leggings. Lucinda's unmistakably high-end, form-fitting top screamed 'designer', the expensive moisture-wicking fabric contouring her figure into flawless proportions. Luxurious leggings hugged Lucinda's lean limbs.

Mary ignored the catty comment and grabbed her towel. Wiping perspiration from her sweaty brow, she took a drink from her water bottle and, with a forced smile, greeted Lucinda. 'I thought you'd be hard at work in the office at this time of day,' Mary said.

Lucinda touched her immaculate hair. Expertly styled, it framed a face wearing minimal makeup, save for her glossy red lips.

'Not all of us have the luxury of being a stay-at-home housewife,' Lucinda purred. 'I've had a successful week and can allow myself a couple of hours of leisure.'

Stay-at-home housewife? Did this woman know what it took to bring up four boisterous kids and run Belvedere House? Mary stared at Lucinda and decided that Conor couldn't possibly have feelings for this stuck-up cow with her acidic tongue. Mary resisted the urge to tilt her water bottle and shower Lucinda's glossy head. Instead, she smiled and said, 'That's nice. Business must be good?'

'Oh, it gets better every day,' Lucinda replied, swinging her body off the bike. 'Will you be coming to our next Ladies' Lunch Club?'

'I wouldn't miss it for the world,' Mary said and wondered how she could get out of it.

'Excellent. We need to discuss our contribution to the Kindale Christmas Fair. I think we should make a little more effort this year.' She tilted her head and studied Mary. 'Don't you?'

Mary watched Lucinda move away and place her bony bottom on the seat of a rowing machine. As her toned arms stretched and pulled, Mary thought of the event Lucinda had referred to.

Their Ladies' Lunch Club supported the annual charity fair at Christmas by running a tombola stall. Gathering prizes had become a competitive affair, as the ladies outdid each other by calling in favours for alcohol hampers, luxury chocolates, aromatic candles, and gorgeous gifts. Last year, Mary, who'd forgotten all about her contribution with the run-up to Christmas and multiple school events to worry over, had searched the house and, at the last minute, donated an out-of-date box of biscuits and a wilting plant. It hadn't helped that the mulled wine stall was next to the tombola, and being such a frosty December day, Mary had overindulged to keep warm and ease her boredom. When Lucinda arrived at the stall to do her shift, she had found Mary three sheets to the wind, empty glass in hand, stuffing her face with mince pies. Lucinda's piercing gaze and sharp tongue had sobered Mary up in minutes, but the memory of letting the ladies down was etched deep.

This year, I must try harder! Mary vowed.

The beautician had finished the facial and was spraying a mist that smelt like dead roses over Mary's face. 'All done, Cinderella,' she said. 'You can go to the ball.'

'It will be the Salty Dog Inn, in truth,' Mary said, opening her eyes and sitting up.

'Isn't that great? I'm sure you'll have a lovely evening. You look ten years younger,' the beautician lied, handing Mary a little bag of complimentary samples. She thanked her for the booking, then left the room, leaving her client to dress.

'Guess who wants a large tip when I settle the bill?' Mary muttered as she studied her newly toned face and peered into the goodie bag.

A little while later, Mary stepped out of the salon.

She was pleased that there was no breeze to ruffle her beautifully blow-dried locks, and with luck, the style would hold for the evening. But as she drove to the football club, Mary groaned. A group of boys were huddled in the car park, and Mary had no idea which was Finn. The motley crew was covered in mud, as though they'd just emerged from a battle in the trenches. Once embellished with bright logos and numbers, their jerseys were now covered in layers of grime.

'Hiya, Mam!' Finn came forward, his face streaked with sweat and dirt. His shorts, saggy and heavy with the weight of damp soil, were a testament to his tackles and slides across the pitch. 'I scored the winning goal!' he said, eyes alight.

'Well, that's great,' Mary remarked as she jumped out of the Range Rover to retrieve towels from the back. 'I'm so proud of you,' she added, enveloping Finn in thick cotton and thrusting his boots into a plastic bag. She winced as Finn climbed into the back seat. He spread himself out, and Mary watched as flakes of mud and grass clung to the soft leather upholstery and pale cream carpet.

Conor will have a fit! she thought and started the engine.

But as she listened to Finn's excited chatter while they drove away from the club, Mary smiled. It was a good job she had Romeo Ruari on speed dial.

Chapter Fourteen

Morning had broken at the Solma Vacaciones Camp Site, and as vacationers went about their early chores, there was no sign of life on pitch number thirteen. Winnie's windows were closed, and the curtains were firmly shut.

Inside the camper, there was a lingering odour of the night before. Ness opened one eye and sniffed. If the old dog could talk, she'd announce that the air smelt of stale alcohol – sour and unpleasant – and with each gentle snore from the lump on the bed, she knew that it was coming from Atticus. Thrusting her nose forward and lifting a paw, Ness poked and prodded. When Atticus sighed and appeared to be coming back from the dead, Ness jumped up and began to lick his face.

'Aw...no! Leave off!' Atticus groaned. He reached out to push the dog away, but Ness was relentless, and with no chance of turning over and returning to the deep sleep he'd been enjoying, Atticus sat up.

He noted that the duvet was tossed to one side and realised he was still fully clothed.

'Eh? How did that happen?' Atticus scratched his head and tried to think back to the night before. He vaguely remembered linking arms with Cheryl and Ruby after the barbecue had ended as they walked him back to Winnie. 'I must have fallen asleep,' he muttered to himself, pulling back the curtains. Light flooded into the camper, and Atticus squinted. Ness was pawing at the door, and with a sigh, he knew it was time to get up. Reaching for her lead as she raced out, Atticus picked up his hat and stumbled out of the camper.

'Right, Ness, let's get you walked,' he said.

Yawning wide and shaking his shoulders to bring life to his bones, Atticus stepped away from his pitch and set off.

An hour or so later, Atticus was wide awake. After two days on the road, the hot shower and shave in the shared amenities made him feel brand new. Now, wearing clean clothes, he'd connected Winnie to all the services and was delighted to find that she had running water – properly draining away – and electricity from the on-site supply.

Taking a folding chair out of the storage space, Atticus sat in the sunshine and drank from a water bottle. He had an unusual thirst that morning as he ate the last of his bread, which he layered with the remains of the cheese, and wondered how much alcohol had been in the sangria.

He decided that he must send a text to Mary to let her

know that all was well. Reaching for his phone, Atticus began to type.

> All gud in suny Spain. Camp site neat.
> Hope u r ok.

Atticus didn't like the informality of abbreviated messages but as Jake had insisted, to keep up with the kids, he needed to know their online language. Happy with his communication, he pressed send.

Ness had finished her doggie biscuits and Atticus tossed her a crust. 'It's time to get the awning sorted,' he said as she gobbled it down. Placing the chair on one side, Atticus gathered a heavy canvas bag and deposited it beside a box of tools.

'Need a hand?' a man called out, and Atticus turned to see Erik stepping onto the pitch. Wearing shorts, sliders, and a vest, Erik was a picture of vitality. His dark skin glistened with a healthy sheen, accentuating the contours of his muscles and Atticus wondered how many hours a day Erik spent in a gym. A body like that required hard work and dedication.

'Aye, that would be great, if you don't mind.'

'This is a fine vintage camper,' Erik said and poked his nose inside.

Atticus wished he'd made the bed and tidied it into a sofa, but Erik seemed unperturbed as he looked around.

'A 1985 Westfalia, one point nine litre?' Erik asked and flicked open Winnie's bonnet to study inside. 'A water-cooled, manual engine,' he nodded. 'Simple, reliable, and low maintenance.'

'Yes, she's well-suited for leisurely travel.'

'Have you had the vehicle from new?'

'I certainly have,' Atticus said, running his hand over the smooth yellow paintwork. He omitted to tell Erik that Winnie had stood neglected for so many years. 'Do you have a caravan or motorhome?' Atticus asked.

'A motorhome,' Erik answered. 'Come and see it sometime. Pitch two hundred.'

The two men began to assemble Winnie's awning over a metal frame, and in no time at all, additional accommodation was created. Complete with flooring and windows, it had a zippered doorway with curtains that tied back. Inside, two collapsible chairs, a picnic table, and space for Ness's bed made the awning feel cosy.

'That's grand,' Atticus said as Erik hammered the last peg and secured the guy rope to the ground.

'Your Spanish home,' Erik smiled. He ran his fingers over his smooth head and stood back with Atticus to admire their handiwork. The vintage awning, sourced on eBay, was colourful with yellow and red panels, and together with Winnie, it made for a bright and cheerful sight.

'Can I offer you a drink?' Atticus asked Erik. 'I only have coffee or water. I need to go shopping for supplies.'

'No, my friend. I'm fine, but thank you. On Saturday mornings, most of us go to the market, where we shop and socialise.' Erik glanced at a watch on his wrist. 'I'm going to cycle there, so I may see you later.'

Atticus watched Erik walk away. He was sure his timepiece was a Rolex, studded with gemstones and glinting like gold. Despite Erik's casual appearance, Atticus knew that the jewelled item was probably worth a fortune.

Gathering his tools, Atticus was preoccupied when a vehicle drew up alongside his pitch and a voice called out, 'Cooee, cowboy!' Spinning around, Atticus saw Cheryl leaning out of the window of a brand-new, bright red Fiat 500. With Ruby at the convertible's wheel, the two women were beaming from ear to ear.

'Saddle up!' Cheryl said. 'We're taking you to the market!'

Remembering that Erik had mentioned the Saturday custom, Atticus replied, 'Okay, let me get my hat.'

'Bring Ness too,' Cheryl added as Ruby revved the engine.

Minutes later, Atticus squeezed into the rear of the Fiat with Ness sitting alongside. As they pulled away from his pitch, Ruby admired the awning. 'It's like a Punch and Judy portable theatre,' she laughed. 'I hope you'll be giving us a show later.'

As they drove through the campsite, Cheryl, keen for Atticus to get his bearings, gave a running commentary. 'On the right are the outdoor pools,' she began. 'The water isn't heated, but on a hot day, it's refreshing. Further along, you'll see the gym, spa, and heated indoor pool.'

Atticus was impressed when Cheryl pointed out a supermarket, a hair salon, and a children's play area.

'Sometimes, on weekends and holidays, the site fills with Spanish families who hire the chalets. The kids run wild and are up all night,' Cheryl explained, as Atticus noted swings, slides, and a large trampoline.

'Do you play tennis?' Ruby asked and pointed to courts alongside the outdoor gym equipment, as well as a putting green and bowling area.

'No, I'm afraid not.'

'You'll have to sort yourself out with a bike,' Cheryl said. 'It's the only way to get around if you haven't a car and don't want to disassemble Winnie.'

Atticus thought Cheryl made a good point and noted a sign that read 'Bikes for Hire' on a shop near the reception.

Circling the site again, Ruby slowed as they kerb-crawled past a sizeable open-air bar with a stage. 'There's nightly entertainment here,' she said, 'and you'll also find another bar, café, and restaurant.'

Atticus was staggered as he took it all in. He knew that the site had decent facilities from the website, but what he now saw was beyond his expectations. Remembering to keep Jake and Arthur up to date, he reached for his phone and began to take photos.

'Selfies?' Cheryl asked.

'I'm taking pictures for my grandson,' Atticus said. 'I promised to send them to him, as he wants to keep a record of my holiday.'

'Sensible grandson,' Cheryl said. 'But let's give him a true flavour of life at Solma Vacaciones.' She reached for Atticus's phone, checked his number, and then stored it on her own phone.

Taking it back, Atticus felt his mobile vibrate.

His eyes widened as Cheryl AirDropped images from the night before. Atticus appeared to be at the heart of the party, and, with his cheeks flushed with pleasure, he pressed 'Save'. Then, adding hashtags as Jake had instructed, he began to upload them to Instagram for Jake and Arthur.

'I trust they like the photos,' Atticus muttered as he pressed 'Share', hoping he wasn't boring his grandson and best friend.

Pulling away from the campsite, Ruby reached the junction that had confused Atticus the day before. She pointed out a long building set back from the road.

'That's Nancy's, and there's always a warm welcome if you call in,' Ruby called out. 'Especially for cowboys,' she added, watching Atticus in the rear-view mirror.

Atticus thought the building looked like a motel and wondered if Nancy was a friend of Ruby and Cheryl's. Suddenly, Ruby put her foot down, and as the pedal hit the metal, a rush of wind from all directions hit Atticus, perched in the back. The little Fiat picked up speed as it careered around corners, and its tyres screeched on the road.

Ruby's wild ride was terrifying, and Atticus closed his eyes.

Ness, sitting beside him, held her head high, her ears flapping in the breeze, and Atticus hoped she wouldn't be blown off the seat. He visualised a slower mode of transport and, circling an arm around his dog, remembered the bike hire shop at the campsite. He wondered if he could hire an extension trailer for Ness.

'It's the first thing I'll do when we get back,' Atticus said anxiously under his breath.

Chapter Fifteen

When Atticus felt the Fiat's motion slow and realised that they must be close to the market, he opened his eyes. Sure enough, Ruby was slotting neatly into a parking space, and as she cut the engine, Cheryl clambered out and held the door. Relieved to be in one piece and not splattered over a verge, Atticus forced a smile and gave a nod of thanks as Ness hopped out ahead of him.

'Our first stop is for a drink and a bite to eat,' Cheryl said as they set off.

Atticus walked with Ness, and Ruby and Cheryl held hands as they negotiated a narrow path crossing a tree-lined park. As they reached the market, he could hear people laughing and chatting, and his eyes widened at the sight of hundreds of stalls coming alive with the hustle and bustle of vendors and visitors vying for bargains. Atticus felt a sense of excitement and wondered what lay ahead.

'This beats Kendal market on a wet and windy Saturday,' he said as he was met by a kaleidoscope of colour and aromas.

In the brilliant sunshine, the market was a hive of activity, with shoppers weaving their way through the narrow aisles. The air was filled with the sweet scent of ripe fruits and the pungent aroma of spices, and Atticus took photographs as people of all nationalities inspected goods and haggled with vendors, filling their bags with fresh produce.

He'd never seen anything like it.

Goods of every description were displayed. Clothing hung on hangers or was piled on tables alongside electrical goods, handcrafted pottery, jewellery, and artwork. Snippets of conversation in Spanish, French, German, and Dutch fascinated Atticus as everyone shared the communal experience of shopping outdoors. Open-air cafés were crowded, and delicious smells filled the air. Stalls selling local cheese and cured meats were bustling as vendors called out prices and enticed passers-by with samples.

'This way,' Cheryl said, taking his arm. She led Atticus through the crowds to a quieter corner, where a path was lined with vibrant flowers and the sound of music filled the air. 'We like it here at La Tasca,' she said, guiding him to the bar.

Atticus looked at tables and chairs positioned under the shade of overhanging trees in a small square and noted a group of musicians gathered nearby.

Ruby commandeered three seats, and as Atticus sat down, she picked up a menu and asked, 'Are you hungry? We normally have tapas at this time of day.'

'I'll have whatever you are having,' Atticus replied. 'This is on me,' he added as Cheryl and Ruby studied the menu, deciding what to eat.

Ruby disappeared to the bar to order their food and Atticus turned to Cheryl. 'We didn't get a chance to chat about you last night,' he said. 'Will you tell me what brought you and Ruby to Spain?' He removed his hat and took a handkerchief from his pocket to wipe his hot brow as Ness placed her head on his knee.

'I used to have a place out here,' Cheryl began, 'in the days when I was married.' She looked thoughtful. 'My old man and I ran a bar in Quesada, on the main street. It was busy, and I worked my backside off, beginning with breakfasts for the expats in the morning, right through to bingo and karaoke at night.' She paused, a hint of nostalgia in her eyes.

'That sounds like hard work.' Atticus frowned.

'It was backbreaking, to be honest,' Cheryl sighed. 'But we made decent money and sensibly bought a property, then applied for Spanish citizenship.'

'But things didn't work out with your husband?'

'Nope, there were too many sweeties in the sweetie shop for my Steve.'

'I'm sorry to hear that.'

'Don't waste your tears.' Cheryl smiled. 'By then, Ruby had come to work for us and was a dab hand at the stove. I loved the fact that she made my life so much easier.'

'And would I be right in thinking that you came to love Ruby too?'

'Got it in one, Cowboy,' Cheryl smiled. 'Ruby was travelling around, trying to find herself. She'd just come out, so to speak, and we hit it off from the moment we met.'

Atticus chuckled. 'Sounds like quite the adventure.'

'Oh, it was,' Cheryl agreed, her eyes sparkling with fond memories. 'We've been on quite a journey together, Ruby and I.'

'What happened to the bar?'

'Steve's still running it. He paid me off and shacked up with one of the waitresses.'

Atticus laughed. He looked at Cheryl and decided he'd never met anyone like her. In her sixties, she was a woman with a warm smile and a twinkle in her eye. Wearing white shorts and a halter top to show off her nut-brown tan covering her ample body, Cheryl was larger than life and as open as any book he'd ever read. Atticus instinctively knew she was a woman with a heart of gold.

'We spend some of the year back home at Ruby's house in Halifax,' Cheryl said. 'Ruby was a mental health nurse, but we're both retired now, and we fill our days doing voluntary work at the local hospice and helping to run their charity shop.' She dug a folding fan out of her bag and began to wave it in front of her face. 'It's heating up,' she said, then continued, 'When we're here, we both put a shift in at Steve's bar if he's short of staff.'

'And you stay in a chalet at Solma Vacaciones?'

'Yes, the management let us have a long-term let. Honestly, the site has everything we could want.'

'Aye, I can see that.' Atticus thought of all the amenities he'd been shown earlier.

'It's close to the beach and the town of Guardamar. We must take you there; you'll enjoy it.'

'I'd like that.' Atticus nodded, his heart warmed by Cheryl's thoughtfulness. 'I'm so pleased that I met you, Cheryl. You've been very kind to me.'

'Ah, getaway with you.' Cheryl patted his arm. 'I expect you've got a story to tell too?'

'Not really,' Atticus said. 'My life has been very simple. I ran a sheep farm in Cumbria and was married to my Clara for a very long time.' He paused and eased the heavy fabric of his shirt away from his perspiring skin. 'Part of this trip is to honour Clara. We'd planned a lavish Spanish holiday to celebrate our special wedding anniversary.'

Cheryl nodded. 'But she passed before you could make the trip together.'

'Yes,' Atticus said, his voice tinged with sorrow. 'But I brought a part of her with me.' He turned to Cheryl with a small smile. 'She's in a box, in the front compartment of Winnie.'

Cheryl's face lit up, and she clapped her hands. 'How wonderful! Then you must have a lovely celebration and scatter her ashes in the sea – the same waters you both would have swum in.'

'That's exactly what I'll do.' Atticus nodded. 'When she died a few years ago, I was heartbroken. I'm afraid I let things slip at the farm until my son, Mungo, stepped in.'

'Your son kept the business going?' Cheryl leaned forward, her head tilted to one side.

'Well, he completely transformed it and it's now a fancy farm shop, café, and caravan site.'

'It sounds successful?'

'It is, but I haven't a clue about my son's newfangled ideas, and I'm afraid I became a bit of a hermit until I recently discovered Winnie in an old barn. My grandson helped me get her back on the road.'

'Mungo doesn't approve?'

'Nope, he thinks I'm off my rocker.'

'A few cards short of a full deck?'

Atticus laughed. 'A few screws loose too, I think.'

'But you're enjoying your trip, aren't you?' Cheryl squinted in the sunshine as she studied Atticus's face.

'I'm having a great time. The journey was a joy, and meeting you and Ruby has been the icing on my cake.'

'Well, don't listen to Mungo for now.' Cheryl gripped his hand. 'You enjoy every minute and don't let anyone tell you what they think you should do.'

'Thank you,' Atticus said and smiled at Cheryl as he returned her grip.

Wiping his brow again, he wished he'd worn something cooler. He hadn't bargained for such warm weather at this time of year. Feeling hot and sticky, Atticus rolled up the sleeves of his heavy cotton shirt and felt the dampness on his skin as perspiration accumulated. Even his moleskin trousers clung to his legs.

Ruby returned with a bowl of water for Ness and patted the dog as she greedily began to drink. Taking a seat, Ruby looked at Atticus. 'You look uncomfortable,' she said. 'While we're at the market, it might be a good idea if you got kitted out with some lighter-weight clothes.'

'That's a great idea!' Cheryl clapped. 'We know just the right vendors to go to, eh, Ruby?'

'Yep, just call us "Bargain Brits Abroad" when you want the best deal,' Ruby grinned and reached out to stroke Cheryl's face. In return, Cheryl leaned forward and kissed her.

Atticus was caught off guard. He'd never witnessed affection so openly displayed between two women who were clearly loving partners. It didn't shock him, quite the opposite, in fact. He felt a warm glow. Love for another was a splendid thing, and his own life felt empty without it. Watching Cheryl and Ruby seemed to highlight his own loneliness.

A waitress arrived with a jug of sangria, which Ruby poured. Dishes of tapas followed, and soon, the table was covered with tasty treats.

'Photo opportunity!' Cheryl held out her phone and began to snap.

'Cheers,' Ruby said, holding her glass to toast Atticus. 'Here's to making a new friend.'

They chinked glasses and Atticus swallowed. 'I think sangria is going to be my new friend, too.'

As the musicians played, Atticus sampled the delights of tapas. He tasted his first mouthful of garlic shrimp, seasoned with chilli, and dipped crusty bread into warm olive oil. Splitting the bread, he passed a chunk to Ness.

'Try this,' Ruby urged, forking thinly sliced ham onto his plate. 'It's made from acorn-fed Iberian pigs, which are prized for their rich flavour.'

As the soft meat melted on his tongue, Atticus closed

his eyes and thought he'd never tasted anything so delicious. Next, Cheryl spooned spicy chorizo onto his plate. The peppery sausage had a fiery flavour that made his eyes water. 'By heck, that's got a kick!' he gasped.

When the jug of sangria was empty and the tapas dishes were clean, Cheryl sat back and rubbed her tummy. 'I feel better for that,' she said. 'Now, before shopping, should we finish with a coffee?'

'Cracking idea,' Ruby said as a server approached the table. 'Tres cafés Belmonte, por favor,' she said.

Atticus wondered what Ruby had ordered. Jake hadn't included more than a *café con leche* in his list of essential Spanish phrases. He was intrigued when a small glass cup, with a layer of creamy condensed milk at the bottom and topped with strong coffee, was placed before him.

'Get your laughing gear around this,' Cheryl said. 'It will set you up for your shopping expedition.'

Atticus took a swig of the coffee and almost choked as a considerable measure of brandy hit the back of his throat. But as a sweet hit filtered through the shot of espresso, he licked his lips. *The café Belmonte was delicious!*

'Fancy another?' Ruby smiled.

'Why not...'

Atticus sighed with pleasure as his hand gently stroked the top of Ness's head. Feeling mellow from the brandy, he felt like time had suddenly slowed. Sitting here in the sunshine, listening to music, and experiencing new tastes, he could hardly believe that he'd only been in Spain for three days. Despite the heat, Atticus felt like he'd been wrapped in a cosy blanket on a chilly winter evening and was grateful for the simple pleasure of good company with two new friends.

Suddenly, Cheryl stood. 'Come on, cowboy,' she said. 'We need to source some bargains before the market shuts up for the day.'

Atticus settled the bill, and with Ness pulling ahead, he found himself linked by Cheryl and Ruby. 'Lead on,' he replied, placing his hat on his head. 'I am entirely in your capable hands.'

At Barn Hill Farm, Jake was fed up. Saturday was stretching out like the longest day ever, and with two more days of being grounded, his bedroom walls felt like they were closing in on him. At least he'd been able to go to school during the week, but as soon as he got off the bus and arrived home, Mungo had been at the door waiting for him.

'Bedroom,' his dad commanded and pointed towards the stairs.

Dragging his rucksack and cursing under his breath, Jake stomped off to his room. 'Why do I have to have the most unreasonable parent in the world?' he grumbled and threw himself down on his bed. He'd only been trying to help his grandad. If his dad couldn't see that things were suddenly looking up for Atticus because of his and Arthur's help, then his dad was a miserable old git who didn't deserve Jake as a son.

Jake sat at his desk and stared out of the window.

He could see the farm shop and café, where weekend visitors were milling around. Over at the campsite, there wasn't an empty pitch, and Jake yearned to be out on the Little Grey Fergie, servicing the site and helping new campers settle in or assisting anyone who needed a hand. He wondered what his grandad was up to and if campsites in Spain lived up to their reputation. Did Solma Vacaciones really have the amazing swimming pools he'd viewed on the website, and was it really *so* close to a long, sandy beach?

Swivelling in his chair, Jake turned to his laptop, his fingers poised over the keyboard. He hadn't checked the @thetravellinggrandad account on Instagram that day. Atticus's previous photos of his journey and the giant bulls had been interesting, but today, Jake hoped there might be something showing the campsite.

Opening the account, Jake scanned the page.

At first, his expression remained neutral as he realised there were scores more images to view. But as the content of the photos came into focus, Jake's eyes widened, and his eyebrows arched as he leaned in closer to absorb every pixelated detail. Without realising he was smiling, Jake suddenly began to laugh. 'Oh, Grandad,' he giggled and fist-bumped the air.

Reaching for his phone, Jake dialled Uncle Arthur's number.

''Ello?' Arthur answered. 'Who is this?'

'It's me, Uncle Arthur,' Jake said excitedly. 'Who else would be calling your mobile?'

'Well, I'm certain Julia Roberts has been trying to get through; she's gagging to have an affair with me.'

'Julia who?' Jake was puzzled.

'Never mind, lad,' Arthur sighed. 'Have you had word from abroad?'

'Nothing from Grandad, but have you seen his Instagram account today?'

'I haven't. In truth, I'm in the pub.'

'Uncle Arthur, you've never seen anything like it!' Jake gasped, keen to share his newfound knowledge. 'Grandad is having a blast.'

'Eh? What do you mean?'

'He's been partying, and there are all sorts of people in the photos, and...' Jake trailed off as his eyes fell on an image of a person covered in tattoos, linking her arm with Atticus. 'Wow...' Jake breathed. 'Just look at those piercings...'

'Piercings? Atticus has got piercings?' Arthur sounded confused.

'Crikey!' Jake exclaimed. 'These tattoos look like a zoo!'

'He's had a zoo tattoo?' Arthur was aghast.

'No... Listen.' Jake shook his head, remembering Arthur's old Nokia, despite urging him to upgrade to a smartphone. 'You need to go home to your computer. Get on to the Instagram account I set up for you and see what he's up to and...' Jake suddenly stopped. His jaw dropped, and he sat back, his eyes falling on the number of Atticus's followers.

'What's up? Are you there?' Arthur sounded anxious.

'Bloody hell...' Jake breathed.

'Now, you know you shouldn't swear,' Arthur remarked.

'Grandad has nearly five thousand followers!' Jake gasped.

'Eh? I thought only you and I followed him?'

'You're as bad as Grandad,' Jake said, exasperated. 'When you use hashtags, it doesn't give you exclusivity; it allows people to search for that hashtag, and if they like what they see, they'll start following the account.'

'Oh, is that so?'

'Yes. I knew Grandad didn't understand,' Jake sighed. 'He thinks only you and I will see the photos.'

'Do you mean he's going global?' The light was slowly dawning in the back room of The Black Bull's snug.

'I'll say,' Jake giggled. 'The Travelling Grandad is becoming an internet sensation.' Atticus's hashtags had created visibility, and Jake scrutinised the descriptions. 'He's used all these: *#party #tattoos #laterlife #travel #upall-night #sangria #piercings*.'

Jake laughed and smiled again as he saw *#VWCamper* and *#WinnietheWestie* – even his cousin Maeve had reshared the images and started to follow the account. The surprise he'd felt calmed into joy as Jake devoured comments from the new followers.

'Living your best life!' @oldbeforemytime

'This boomer knows best!' @BoomersAreBest

'Grandpa's snaps are hotter than the sun.' @sweet73

'This is how retirement is really done!' @69and-holding

'Age is just a number!' @ageisjustanumber100

'Warning: This influencer may cause severe envy.' @IwishIWasYou

'Influencer?' Jake stared at the messages. 'Grandad is a hero!' He began to laugh again. His grandfather, @thetravellinggrandad, had achieved in forty-eight hours something Maeve had spent the last two years trying to accomplish.

'Are you still there?' Arthur asked.

'Yes, sorry, but I'm going to go because I want to call Aunty Mary,' Jake said.

'Do we need to call your Grandad?'

Jake could hear Arthur gulp the last of his pint.

'No, I don't think so. It's doubtful that he'll even answer his phone.'

'Why is that?' Arthur sounded curious.

'By the look of things, he's having far too much fun.'

Chapter Sixteen

At Belvedere House, the Murphy family was running late. Finn, unhappy to be left at home with his younger brother and under the care of a babysitter, whined that it wasn't fair that he couldn't join Mary and Conor at the pub.

'But we always come out with you,' Finn said petulantly, kicking the end of the bed in Mary and Conor's bedroom while Mary tried to get into her jeans.

'Exactly,' Mary puffed as she sucked in her stomach and held her breath, easing the zip into place. 'You and your brother and sisters are *always* with us, and your dad and I want an evening on our own.'

'I hate you,' Finn mumbled, crossing his arms and scowling as he shuffled across the room. At the door, he paused, then turned and stuck out his tongue.

'Finn Murphy!' Mary yelled and swept out her arm, but the boy had slammed the door and disappeared before she had time to catch him.

'Kids,' Mary sighed. 'I'm ready to throttle the lot of them.'

Knowing that he would be left behind too, Declan had refused to eat his tea earlier that evening.

'Don't like it,' he whinged and poked at his favourite chicken nuggets with a finger.

When Mary told him that if he didn't want to eat, she'd take his tea away, Declan's tears began dramatically, streaming down his face until he started to scream, throwing his teddy across the room. At that moment, Conor entered the kitchen, returning from the golf club. Witnessing all hell breaking out and ducking to avoid the teddy, he did a U-turn. Caitlin, too, had refused to eat, stating that she'd have a takeaway later with the allotment committee.

Maeve pulled a face, and Mary heard her berate her sister: 'Takeaway? I don't know how you can indulge in a greasy, calorie-laden concoction dripping with fat and sodium.'

Mary thought the comment was a bit catty, coming from someone who'd just devoured salad leaves and quinoa and was edging longingly towards the biscuit tin. A large tikka masala would work wonders for Maeve's diet.

'And I don't know how you can eat like a rabbit,' Caitlin snapped back. 'Plant-based food is hardly human.'

'Girls, will you stop squabbling and get ready, or we'll all be late.' Mary cleared the table and, reaching into the freezer, handed red-eyed Declan an ice cream. Anything to stop him from crying and allow her to get ready.

Now, as she fluffed out her hair and applied a coat of

glossy lipstick, Mary studied her reflection. The jeans were a little tight, but they gave her bum a lift, and the pretty lacy top with a low neck flattered her cleavage and hid her tum. *Not bad!* she thought.

Mary could hear Conor yelling from the bottom of the stairs, urging her to hurry up or the girls would be late for their school disco. She rolled her eyes. Conor – without the need to clean up after the kids, iron clothes for two lazy teens, pacify a five-year-old, and stop Finn from banging his football against the patio windows – had taken a leisurely shower, dressed, and had time to sip a cold beer.

'Coming!' Mary called out and picked up her bag to hurry from the room. 'So much for joint parenting...' she muttered to herself.

Finn and Declan were curled up in front of the TV in the playroom with their babysitter, munching on biscuits and sweets, when Mary finally left the house to drop Maeve and Caitlin off at the school disco, with Conor in the passenger seat.

'The car looks spotless.' Conor observed as he strapped himself in. 'You've been busy.'

'There was an incident with Finn's football kit earlier,' Mary replied as she drove off the driveway. 'You know how wet it's been all week, and Finn was covered in mud.'

For some reason, Mary felt reluctant to tell Conor that Ruari had been round like a shot when he'd received her call. There was something wild yet attractive about the man, with his shoulder-length curls, strong shoulders, and the fluid grace of his body as he moved. Leaning into the vehicle's interior, the fabric of his T-shirt emphasised his toned torso, and in Mary's fantasy, she ran her fingers over Ruari's chiselled muscles as he cleaned every particle of mud from every nook and cranny, including the plush carpet and the crevices between the seats. She watched his strong hands grip a portable vacuum cleaner and imagined them gripping herself.

Stop this! Mary admonished with a quick shake of her head to prevent her thoughts wandering further. But unable to resist, she remembered Ruari as he sauntered around her Range Rover to inspect the job, then casually asked if Mary had any areas that needed special attention. The comment made her blush, and her embarrassment increased when it was time to settle. Ruari turned to Mary and, with a slow grin told her she was like a well-oiled machine and gave a cheeky wink. Fumbling for cash, Mary had generously over-tipped and told herself he'd been referring to the vehicle.

Now, as Conor sat silently beside her, she certainly wasn't going to mention the incident. Conor always said that Ruari was trouble. But maybe, Mary pondered as she drove the Range Rover onto the school road, in her fantasies, a little trouble wouldn't be the worst thing.

They arrived at the school, and Mary opened her window to call out as the girls scrambled from the car. 'Be here at the door at ten o'clock sharp,' she instructed. 'If not, we'll come in and get you.'

'Oh, Mam, don't you dare.' Two horrified faces stared back.

Mary closed her window and took one last look at Caitlin, who wore a modest button-up shirt with stirrup pants. Maeve, the rebel, favoured an '80s punk-rock look, and Mary winced at her youngest daughter's short leather skirt, ripped fishnet tights, and acid-washed vest.

'You wouldn't go into the disco and drag them out in front of their friends, would you?' Conor asked as he watched other parents deposit their offspring at the school gates. For the '80s-night, retro vibes appeared to be popular, with giggling girls dressed in high-waisted jeans and crop tops, while others wore off-the-shoulder blouses, channelling classic '80s style.

'You bet I would, I can't imagine what Maeve will be getting up to.'

'It would be most embarrassing.'

As Mary drove away, she wondered who would be the most embarrassed: Conor or the girls? She wished Conor would ease up and not be such a stuffed shirt. And why couldn't he be more hands-on? A bit more help would be appreciated, instead of the perpetual excuse that he was too busy with work.

But Mary also thought that Conor was preoccupied and as she pulled into the Salty Dog Inn's car park, she felt pleased that there were a couple of hours of conversation ahead that might iron out a few relationship wrinkles.

Crossing the car park, Mary reached out to take Conor's hand and noted that he barely glanced at her as her fingers curled into his own. As they stepped into the pub the air was thick with the chatter of patrons occupying every nook and cranny. Conor eased his way to the bar, and as he ordered a pint and a sparkling mineral water for Mary, she heard him speak to the landlord.

'Saturday nights used to be quiet here. Is there something I've missed?'

'You need to keep up, Conor Murphy. We've got live music now at the weekends and an open mic.'

Unable to find a seat, Mary and Conor huddled together as the strains of Irish music struck up from a band on a corner stage. It was a hive of activity, and despite the dim lighting, the pub was humming with happy drinkers in the warmth of good company and a well-poured pint.

'This is nice.' Mary leaned into Conor, trying to catch his attention over the sound of a fiddle and a piercing penny whistle.

'If you like this sort of thing,' Conor replied.

Mary remembered Conor's suggestion was for a quiet drink and wondered if he was regretting his decision to bring her here. She was about to suggest they move somewhere more peaceful when she felt her phone vibrate. Mungo was calling. Mary remembered that she'd missed an earlier call from Jake and wondered if something had happened to Atticus. Feeling slightly panicked, she mouthed the word 'Mungo' and indicated to Conor that she was going outside to take the call. Conor made a gesture of exasperation and turned away.

Moving quickly across the car park, Mary told Mungo to hang on. Deciding to sit down, she unlocked her car and climbed in. 'That's better,' Mary said. 'I'm all ears. Now, how are you, Mungo?'

There was a pause before her brother began to speak, and Mary wondered if he was collecting his thoughts. 'Have you heard from Dad?' Mungo asked.

Mary thought of the text she'd received that morning.

> All gud in suny Spain. Camp site neat.
> Hope u r ok.

Atticus had been short with his words, and she'd been surprised by the abbreviations, but she knew he would have received lessons from Jake.

'Yes, he texted me today, and I replied that I hoped he was enjoying his holiday.'

'Enjoying his holiday,' Mungo calmly repeated her words.

'Is there something wrong with that?' Mary asked.

'Have you looked at Instagram lately?'

'Mungo, I barely have time to talk to my husband, let alone spend hours on social media.'

'Well, you might want to rethink that.'

'Why?'

'Have a look at @thetravellinggrandad.'

'Hang on...' Mary said, and, turning her phone to loud-speaker, opened the Instagram app. 'The... travelling... grandad.' Mary typed.

As the page appeared, Mary hadn't a clue what she was supposed to be looking at. She flicked through photos of Atticus with flamingos and a giant hoarding of a black bull.

But as Mary stared at a group of colourful, suntanned people, she could see them having a high old time at a barbecue. A woman with vibrant orange hair piled into a top knot and wearing a lime-green kaftan had her arms around her father, who was wearing the cowboy hat she'd gifted him. On the other side of them, a tattooed lady, covered in piercings, was linking Atticus's arm.

Mary began to laugh, her eyes wide as she saw Ness sitting on a fold-up chair with a massive sausage in her mouth. Another image showed her father in a conga line, dancing along a lantern-lit pathway.

'You think it's funny?' Mungo asked.

'Is it really our dad?' Mary asked, stifling another giggle.

'Oh, there's more. Keep going, turn to the video feed.'

Mary pressed play, and to the background music from several ukuleles, a guitar, and a drum, Atticus took centre stage as he duetted *Islands in the Stream* with the orange-haired woman. He held a glass of sangria in his hand and, to cheers, downed the drink in one as the song ended.

'I think it's absolutely wonderful,' Mary laughed. 'He's finally come out of his comfort zone and is enjoying himself.'

She continued to scroll through images of a brightly coloured awning and a tall, athletic man, wearing a huge gold watch which dazzled against his dark skin, smiling as he posed with Atticus in a selfie beside Winnie. Her Dad was clearly making new friends, but somewhat faster than she'd ever imagined.

'But he's seventy years old, in a strange place with

people who might take advantage!' Mungo's voice was raised, and Mary sighed, knowing she was in for an argument.

'Did you know that he has over six thousand followers, all of the boomer generation, from all over the world? And the numbers seem to be increasing,' Mungo droned on.

Mary did indeed know now and was fascinated by the hundreds of comments Atticus was receiving. *Fancy that!* Her dad was going viral – just wait until she told Maeve!

'Well, that has to be a good thing, right?' Mary was puzzled.

'I hardly think it will do the family business any good if people see the head of it drunk as a skunk, on a permanent bender with a crowd who look as though they're performing in a circus.'

Mary sighed. What was wrong with her brother, and when had he become such an old man? She thought of their mother and her infamous words: *Don't let the old man in.* Mungo had let the old man in long before his time, but in Spain, Atticus seemed hell-bent on letting the old man out!

'Listen to me, Mungo. Will you just get over yourself?' Mary said. 'Dad is clearly enjoying himself. Can't you be pleased that he's having a great holiday?'

'I knew you'd stick up for him.'

'Yes, I damn well will. And for Jake.' Mary felt cross now. 'I hear you've grounded him, and for the life of me, I cannot see why.'

'Because he went behind my back.'

'Oh, stop it!' Mary's tone was sharp. 'Jake was helping

his grandad. He knew Atticus was going on this journey, with or without anyone's approval, and had the good sense and kindness to do everything he could to ensure that his grandad was safe.'

'He should have told me!'

'What? And have you do everything you could to put an end to it? I don't think so,' Mary sighed. 'You can be very controlling sometimes.'

She thought of the farm and how much Atticus had wanted to continue with his sheep, but she knew that Mungo had talked their dad out of it. Undoubtedly, it had been for the best, but she remembered how heartbroken Atticus had been when the last of the Herdwick herd was sold.

'Well, I can see that it's a waste of time talking to you,' Mungo said. 'But all I can say is that I refuse to take any responsibility when Dad drops down dead.'

Mary gasped. She was shocked by the venom in Mungo's voice. Feeling unable to carry on with the conversation, she spoke softly. 'I'm sorry that you feel that way...' She paused, waiting for Mungo to say more, but only silence followed. 'And now, I am going to end the call,' Mary added.

She hung up and, for a few moments, sat and thought about Mungo's words. Then, picking up her phone again, she tapped out a text to Atticus.

> Hi Dad. Hope you're having a great holiday and meeting lots of new people. I am enjoying your photos on Instagram. Keep well and safe and speak soon. Love Mary xx

When Mary returned to the pub, she noted that Conor was several drinks in. He'd found a table, and empty glasses lay before him. His pint was gone, replaced by a large whisky, which he held in one hand while speaking on his phone with the other.

There was a break in the music, and as Mary sat down, she asked her husband who he was talking to.

'Just checking on the kids,' he replied, quickly hanging up and thrusting the phone into his pocket.

Mary frowned. She wasn't aware that he had the babysitter's number, but if he was, at last, having some input with the children's welfare, she wouldn't question him.

'Are they okay?' Mary asked.

'Of course, glued to the TV,' he replied. 'Is Mungo alright?'

Mary thought she detected a slight slur in Conor's words and realised that she'd been away too long. This wasn't how she'd planned the night. Conor was hopeless after a few drinks, and although he was a pleasant drunk, he tended to fall asleep.

Mary began to tell Conor about the call, but as the music struck up again, she could see that he wasn't interested and was now singing along with the group.

Mary picked up her glass and sipped the sparkling

water. It tasted warm and flat. *Exactly how I feel,* she thought to herself.

Conor was on his feet, joining in with a rowdy chorus. As Mary stood too, she suddenly felt the button pop on her jeans, and her stomach burst over the top.

So much for her date night!

Chapter Seventeen

Atticus was settling into a routine, and as his first week in Spain came to a close, he found that he was enjoying the leisurely pace of life. Waking early, as light trickled through Winnie's curtains, he pulled on shorts from a selection he'd acquired at the market, added a T-shirt, and slipped into comfortable sandals. Ness shook her head to rouse herself, rose with a gentle stretch, and needed no encouragement to accompany Atticus on his first walk of the morning. The days had rolled by, and Atticus was only aware that it was Saturday again because Cheryl and Ruby had reminded him that they would be going to the market for their tapas lunch if he chose to accompany them.

Now, as Atticus stood in the shower block and leisurely shaved, he thought about home. The fells in autumn would look lovely, but with winter approaching, the weather would soon change – a time when his arthritis would start to niggle, and his joints would become stiff. He thought of the damp winter months that never seemed to affect business at the farm and knew that the tills in the farm shop and café would be ringing loudly. With any luck, it would put a smile on his son's face, Atticus reflected as he walked back to Winnie. He knew that his exploits enraged Mungo and hadn't heard a word from the farm, other than Jake's daily texts informing his grandad that Mungo was a numpty. Thankfully, Jake was no longer grounded.

Feeling disinclined to make a call and receive another ear-bashing from Mungo, Atticus grabbed his hat and set off. Ness, walking to heel on her lead and with a happy wag of her tail, was the perfect example of a well-behaved dog – unlike some of the animals Atticus had encountered on the site. It amazed him that a variety of creatures travelled with the campers. He'd seen birds in cages, dogs of all shapes and sizes, and every variety of cat. A Swiss couple nearby had even built an enclosure for their rabbit, and it was allowed to roam freely.

'Good morning!' Atticus called out to a Dutch couple heading to the spa for an early swim. With towels rolled under their arms and wearing a brief bikini and trunks, Atticus wondered what folk back home would think if he paraded about in almost nothing.

Averting his eyes from skin that told of a life well lived, Atticus decided that older bodies looked far better covered up. He'd discussed this with Cheryl the previous day when they sat under a shady umbrella and drank coffee beside the open-air pool.

Cheryl, wearing a baby-pink tankini, listened to his comment, and eloquently replied that true beauty didn't lie in the perfection of youth but in the depth of character that came with age.

Atticus did a double take and wondered if she'd read that somewhere, but acknowledging that she had a point, he wasn't convinced as he watched ancient bodies bounce up and down in an energetic aqua aerobics class. Waist-deep and moving to the rhythm of lively music, the water rose and fell like a tsunami. At the same time, an enthusiastic young Spanish instructor named Sophia, wearing a minuscule bright red one-piece, spurred the elderly swimmers on.

'Sí! Hagámoslo!' Sophia yelled as she danced by the side of the pool, kicking her legs and waving her arms. 'Let's do this! Get moving, my senior squad!'

Atticus thought that if some of the senior squad moved any more energetically, they would end up in the nearest accident and emergency department, and Sophia might be sued. Still, he'd kept his thoughts to himself as he helped Cheryl to her feet and eased her into the children's pool.

'Are you joining in with the class?' he'd asked.

'Not likely,' Cheryl replied. 'I'm going to catch a few rays.'

Cheryl waded across the pool, where large synthetic animals formed slides and rides. Ignoring the notices that stated, 'No child over twelve allowed on the rides', she straddled an inflatable hippo and sat down. 'Come in, the water's lovely!' she called out.

Atticus smiled as he remembered Cheryl topping up her tan, her head thrown back and arms outstretched. Her spandex-encased body sprawled across the hippo.

'It's a grand life,' he said to Ness as they went through the site and headed to the track leading to the beach at La Marina.

Once off her lead, Ness ran ahead, sensing new smells in the reedy vegetation that sprang from the edge of the River Segura, running adjacent to the track. Fishermen looked up and called out a greeting as they cast their lines into the muddy-coloured water.

'Hola,' Atticus replied, thinking that local folk were as friendly as those back home. 'Buenos días!'

He stopped to stare at grey herons wading in the shallows. With their long legs and necks, the majestic birds fascinated Atticus. Entering a wooded area, he saw Great Cormorants perched on tree branches, their sleek black plumage forming dark silhouettes against the brightness of the sky. When the birds took flight, Atticus thought of the miles of windswept coastlines and tumultuous seas that their vast wings soared over.

'Nature is amazing,' he said to Ness.

When they reached the beach, Ness began to excitedly run around in circles and Atticus grinned. The old dog wasn't the only one experiencing a new lease of life.

He slipped off his sandals and paddled in the waves lapping against the shore. The soft, golden sand stretched as far as his eye could see, curving into a bay where the whitewashed buildings of the town of Santa Pola glistened in the early-morning sunshine. Enjoying the warm, salty water on his toes, he thought about the climate and how everyone here agreed that the area, combined with the laid-back atmosphere and healthy cuisine, was the ideal place to reduce stress and enjoy mental well-being. No wonder so many retired folks spent most of the winter on the Costas. *How Clara would have enjoyed it!*

Atticus tilted his hat and scanned the beach. Halfway along, there was a café at the end of a row of old fishermen's cottages. Erik had mentioned that the café served great food, and at this time of day, a breakfast menu was chalked on a board. It might be something Atticus enjoyed, as it offered English food.

Atticus had the café in mind as he strolled past a sign pronouncing 'Naturist Area', noting with relief that there were no unclothed bodies. 'I think we'll have a treat and indulge in a full English,' he told Ness as he brushed sand from his toes, slipped into his sandals, and clipped on her lead.

Taking the steps to the café, Atticus saw that it was busy, but he found a table that overlooked the bay. Placing his hat down, he studied the menu and waited to be served.

Gazing out to sea, Atticus saw the shimmering waters of the Mediterranean in the distance, and he was fascinated by dark shapes dotted along the horizon. Erik had told him that these were mussel beds and explained that the vital ecosystem was a haven for various marine species, which supported a thriving fishing industry. Erik himself owned a fishing boat and, for a modest rent, supported a local family who might otherwise have been unable to fish. The father and son used traditional methods – trammel nets and longlines – to harvest not only mussels but also a variety of other seafood. Erik admired their commitment to sustainability, knowing their careful practices would help preserve the region's fishing culture for years to come.

Atticus thought about his own principles for farming methods. Intrigued, he considered taking a guided tour of the beds during his holiday.

He was so preoccupied that he didn't notice a woman standing beside his table, a notepad in her hand. But when he felt Ness's wet nose bump his leg, he jerked his head and turned. For a moment, the café chatter blended into the background, and time seemed to stand still.

'It's a great view, isn't it?' the woman smiled. 'I'm Britta, your server. What can I get for you?'

Momentarily frozen, Atticus's breath caught in his throat. 'Yes... A g-great view.' He stared at Britta, captivated by her beauty.

Britta smiled and Atticus was mesmerised. Her skin reminded him of melted caramel, and he wanted to reach out and touch the soft blonde hair that gathered loosely into a clip, with wispy tendrils escaping. He couldn't help but be enchanted by the curve of her lips, the dimples in her cheeks, and the way her cornflower-blue eyes stared down at him.

'Are you alright?' Britta asked. 'Can I get you some water?'

'Y... yes, that would be grand,' Atticus stuttered.

'Anything else?'

'Aye, I'll have a café con leche and a full house.'

'Full house?' Britta tilted her head.

'Oh, sorry. Where I come from, it means an English breakfast with everything,' Atticus replied.

'Okay, and would your dog like some water too?'

Atticus looked down at Ness and saw the dog staring at Britta with the same fascination as his own.

'Water? Sorry, water, yes. Ness would like that.'

He watched as Britta walked away. Her body moved gracefully as she stopped to take orders or clear glasses from tables. Britta's voice, with a slight hint of an accent, was music to his ears. As Atticus tore his eyes from the kitchen where she'd disappeared, he wondered what on earth had just happened.

One minute, he was sitting calmly, taking in the beauty of the beach, but the next, he was stumbling like a schoolboy blinded by his first crush.

'I need to pull myself together,' Atticus said to Ness.

Coughing to clear his throat, he sat up and determined not to be so foolish. Men of his age didn't fall in love at first sight, nor second or third. In fact, it was unlikely to ever happen at all. And why would he entertain such thoughts? He was happy just as he was, with no one to report to or worry about other than himself, the dog, and their temporary way of life.

And there was Clara. *What on earth would his wife think?*

It was some time before Britta returned with Ness's water and his breakfast order, which enabled Atticus to control his emotions.

'Sorry it took so long,' she said, placing his breakfast before him. 'The café is busy today. Can I get you anything else?' she asked, leaning down to pat Ness.

Atticus was about to say that he was fine and had everything he needed, but Clara's voice suddenly whispered in his ear.

Let the old man out! Ask her out!

Atticus stared into Britta's eyes and suddenly felt foolish. Of course he couldn't ask this woman out; he didn't even know her.

'More toast or coffee?' Britta asked.

Enough! You've faced worse things than asking a woman out!

'Will you have a drink or a meal with me?' Atticus blurted out.

Britta took a step back and he saw that she was surprised.

'I don't think so...' Britta said.

'No, of course not.' Atticus shook his head. He felt stupid. What on earth had possessed him to ask such a question? A woman like this would never glance his way – she was younger than him, Atticus guessed, maybe fifty or so.

'I don't know you,' she said.

'But you will get to know me if you come out with me.' Atticus swallowed. What the hell was he doing, making such a fool of himself? Clutching at straws, he bumbled on, 'I am staying at Solma Vacaciones, and I'm from England. I live on a farm.'

'Oh,' Britta replied.

'My name is Atticus Arnott and...' Atticus dried up. What was the use? Britta probably had a boyfriend, husband, or partner like Cheryl and Ruby.

'Atticus?'

'Aye... Terrible name, but I'm stuck with it.'

'I think it's a good name,' Britta said with a smile, before moving away to continue taking orders.

'Well, Clara, I messed that up,' Atticus mumbled and felt a flush creep across his face.

What on earth was he thinking? Britta must get asked out all the time, and she'd never look at someone like him. He began to eat his breakfast, despite his appetite disappearing, and, forking a sausage, handed it to Ness.

When his plate was almost empty, Atticus pushed it away and drained the last of his coffee. As he prepared to leave, Britta appeared, placed his bill down, and began to clear the table.

'I am free later tomorrow after my lunchtime shift,' she said. 'You could call for me at about four o'clock?' Britta smiled. 'I live in the cottage a little further down. It's called Casita del Mar – the little sea cottage.'

'Casita... del... Mar?' Atticus slowly repeated the words.

'Yes.'

'You mean... you'll have a bite to eat with me?'

'Yes.'

'Aye. Great. I'll be there.'

'See you tomorrow, cowboy,' Britta laughed, nodding at his hat on the table before turning away.

Stunned, Atticus fumbled for euros as he watched her move away. He looked down at Ness. 'What's going on?' he whispered. 'Oh, hell, Ness, what on earth have I done?'

Britta watched Atticus leave the café. As he descended the steps to the beach, he paused to remove his sandals and unclip the dog from its lead. She hesitated. She could still call after him, say she was sorry, that she'd remembered another engagement – a harmless excuse, an easy way out. But something about him made her linger. His eyes were kind, his smile disarmingly warm. When she accepted his invitation, she'd seen genuine surprise and pleasure on his face. It had been so long since a man had looked at her without an unsettling feeling lurking beneath his interest.

But doubt gnawed at her. *Should she take a chance?*

Britta wasn't reckless or impulsive; she liked the predictability of her quiet life. And yet... what would be the harm in spending a couple of hours with Atticus? She exhaled, forcing herself to ignore her caution. It was just a bite to eat and conversation. A better way to pass the time than sitting on the patio of her cottage, staring at an empty canvas and willing inspiration to strike.

'Yes,' she whispered, turning away from the beach and moving to clear debris from a table. 'Perhaps I *will* take a chance.'

Chapter Eighteen

In the back room of The Black Bull, Arthur sat in the snug, nursing a beer. It was cold outside, and the first chill of winter was making itself felt as wind and rain whipped over the Cumbrian hills, with an early frost threatening for the weekend. Inside the pub, log fires crackled, knives and forks clunked, and with the smell of home-cooked food from the plates of lunchtime diners, Arthur felt cocooned in a cosy world.

'Have you heard from The Travelling Grandad this past week?' Reg asked as he ran a cloth over the bar and straightened a beer mat.

'Yes, as a matter of fact, I have,' Arthur nodded and drained his glass.

'We're enjoying his daily Instagram posts,' Reg laughed. 'He's becoming quite the celebrity.'

'Aye, who'd have guessed...'

Arthur had never imagined that Atticus would take so many photos and was amazed that his friend was becoming a dab hand with the camera. His images were almost artistic, with inspirational shots of enticing beaches, stunning sunsets, colourful Mediterranean food, and characters from all walks of life. He'd even mastered the art of a short video, and they packed quite a punch.

'It just goes to show that you don't have to be young to have fun,' Reg remarked as he took Arthur's glass and slowly poured him another pint of frothy beer. 'Atticus is gaining quite an audience. He's made me think about a winter holiday in the sun.'

Arthur nodded as Reg wandered away. He thought about Atticus's frequent updates which hashtagged the names of the places he visited. High-profile travel accounts were sharing his posts and @thetravellinggrandad was turning into a travelogue for pensioners seeking fun in the sun. Atticus's fans were increasing daily. Even The Black Bull Domino League had taken an interest, with Tuesday night's 'Fives & Threes' delayed as players discussed The Travelling Grandad's latest exploits.

But what surprised Arthur the most was something from an earlier phone call with his friend.

Arthur had been in his shed at the bottom of the garden at Shirlarth Cottage, stacking garden pots and planters. He began to wrap Shirley's impressive collection of garden gnomes for their winter storage, and enjoyed packing away her pint-sized protectors, which multiplied every year. Arthur loathed the gnomes; the gaudy statues scared the living daylights out of him. No longer limited to gardening, Shirley's collection included nautical gnomes in sailor outfits, sporty gnomes in athletic attire, and gourmet gnomes carrying baskets of vegetables. To his horror, a collection of three-foot Zen gnomes had arrived that summer, posed in a variety of yoga stances. Arthur wasn't familiar with the 'downward dog' and thought that no self-respecting gnome should be either. As he considered taking a hammer to Serenity Sam and Zen Master Ted, his phone rang.

'Hello, who is this?' Arthur said, holding his Nokia to his ear.

'It's me, Atticus.'

'Ah, The Travelling Grandad,' Arthur sighed with pleasure. He pulled out his old rocker to make himself comfortable and placed Peaceful Pete on his knee. 'How's life on the Costas?' he asked, beginning to rock as he eagerly awaited news of Atticus's adventures. He closed his eyes to imagine the sun, sea, and warm salty air – a million miles away from the grey skies, wind, and rain outside the shed window.

'Well, a surprising thing happened to me at the beach this morning,' Atticus began.

Arthur imagined a group of flamenco dancers performing an impromptu dance on the sand, or a pod of dolphins swimming close to the shore. Perhaps a hot air balloon had drifted off course and made an emergency landing nearby.

Arthur visualised many scenarios and smiled as he waited for his friend's revelation.

'I've met a woman, and I've asked her for a date.'

Arthur's eyes bulged and his mouth dropped open. Gripping his phone, he jerked up, sending Peaceful Pete to the floor. Arthur was unaware of a dull thud, followed by the sound of ceramics shattering, as Peaceful Pete landed on the Zen family, creating destruction that would break Shirley's heart. His pulse was racing, and he tried to digest Atticus's words.

'What did you say... old mate... I think I misheard you?' Arthur struggled to find the right words.

'Her name is Britta, and she's beautiful. I'm taking her out tomorrow.'

'Britta...' Arthur repeated. Shirley had a gnome named Britta, who wore a floppy hat and a patchwork tunic with a leather belt cinching her bulging waist. The image wasn't appealing.

'I think she might be Danish or maybe Dutch. She has a trace of an accent,' Atticus explained.

'You don't know where she's from?'

'I didn't speak to her for long. I'd just ordered my breakfast.'

Arthur sat up. He leaned forward, cradling the phone, bushy eyebrows furrowed as his wellingtons crunched on the broken pottery. *I'd just ordered my breakfast...* Arthur struggled to take it all in.

'Aye, she didn't know what a full house was, and I had to explain,' Atticus chuckled.

Arthur listened to his friend, his mind grappling with the suddenness of it all.

'Britta made a fuss of Ness and fetched her a water bowl.'

Arthur drew back his head, his voice filled with confusion. 'And that short exchange with a stranger developed into a date?'

'It didn't develop,' Atticus said. 'It hit me like a thunderbolt!' His voice was animated. 'I knew that if I didn't ask her then and there, I'd never have the courage to do so.' Atticus paused. 'And there was something else,' he added.

'Eh? What was that?'

'Clara told me to do it.'

'I see,' Arthur said, not seeing at all. *Now his friend was hearing voices!*

'But I think she's younger than me,' Atticus remarked, 'maybe in her fifties.'

As Atticus began to discuss where to take Britta for their date, Arthur shook his head and sat back. *His friend was dating a foreign woman who was several years younger.*

Beginning to rock again, Arthur sighed as he listened to his friend babble on.

Reg tapped on the bar and pulled Arthur out of his trance. 'You look like you could use a stiff drink,' he said. 'Is everything alright, Arthur?'

'Aye, sorry. I was miles away.'

'Wishing you were in sunnier climes with Atticus?'

'Yes, something like that.' Arthur was thoughtful. He'd decided not to mention Atticus's news, hoping it would fade away with the Spanish tide.

Arthur couldn't help but feel a mix of emotions – happiness for his friend, but also a tinge of envy. His golden years with Shirley were decidedly dim, the light having gone out decades ago.

'Give him our best regards when you next speak to him,' Reg continued. 'The pub's Senior Socials Club wants to know if he'll be their speaker when he gets back; they've all got The Travelling Grandad bug.' Reg reached up to an optic and poured Arthur a large whisky. 'Everyone's started Instagram accounts to follow him.'

Arthur wondered what the pub's pensioners would make of Atticus's latest news, soon to hit social media. More worryingly was Mungo's reaction. Arthur downed his whisky and thought of the explosion that would shatter the peace at Barn Hill Farm when The Travelling Grandad shared love letters from the Costas and captivating date nights. Mungo would have a fit and probably think Britta's attraction to Atticus was financial.

But as Arthur finished his drink, gathered his coat, and reached for his bob hat and scarf, he knew he had far more pressing problems. There was a gnome crisis at Gnome-Sweet-Gnome, and Arthur urgently needed to confer with Jake to find a gnome-emergency repair shop.

'See you soon!' Arthur called out to Reg. He secured his bob hat, and with a wave of his mitten-clad hand, braced himself not only for the wild weather but also for the tricky challenges with Shirley at Gn'Home.

Saturday lunchtime at the local Spanish market was once again a bustling hive of activity. The charming little café,

La Tasca, was busy with locals and tourists crowded around tables and chairs, engaged in lively conversation.

Sheltering from the sun in the shade of overhanging trees, Atticus sat with Cheryl and Ruby as flamenco music floated across the square. Feeling the heat, Ness lay under the table, her tail lazily flicking at flies. The aroma of freshly brewed coffee from a nearby stall mingled with the sweet fragrance of churros dusted with cinnamon. Chatting idly, Cheryl sipped fresh orange juice, and Ruby held a glass of sangria, while Atticus enjoyed his café con leche. They'd ordered tostados, and as they waited for their brunch, Atticus suddenly felt compelled to speak. He needed advice and hoped that his new friends might help him.

'You're fidgety,' Cheryl said, adjusting huge sunglasses perched on her nose. She studied Atticus, who held his hat in his hand and twisted it round and round.

'Aye, sorry,' he replied, placing the hat to one side. 'I don't know who to ask, you see. I need some assistance.'

'We can help.' Cheryl reached out and patted his arm. 'What's bothering you?'

'Fire away,' Ruby instructed and pulled her chair closer.

'I was on the beach earlier and stopped to have a bite of breakfast,' Atticus began, 'and there was this person, well, lady, you know, a woman...'

'Yes, love, we know what one of those is,' Cheryl said.

'She was very nice and er...' Atticus stuttered, 'before I knew what I was doing, I asked her if she'd have a meal with me tomorrow.'

'Bulls eye!' Ruby took a swig of sangria.

'You don't hang about, do you?' Cheryl chuckled.

'To be honest, I'm staggered that I asked, and even more staggered that she agreed.' Atticus shrugged. He wondered if he should confide that Clara had spurred him on, but his friends might think he was going doolally. 'But now I haven't a clue where I might take her, and I hope you can help.'

'What's her name?' Cheryl asked.

'Britta. I think she may be Danish or perhaps—'

'—Dutch,' Ruby and Cheryl butted in, stopping Atticus mid-sentence. They exchanged glances.

'Do you know her?' he asked.

'Britta lives in one of the cottages on the beach,' Cheryl explained. 'Yes, we know her.'

'She's a very private person and keeps to herself,' Ruby added. 'We've met her when the café puts on a special event for the locals, such as Spanish music or folk festivals, which are popular here.'

'And we've chatted when we've had meals there or stopped by for a drink,' Cheryl said. She turned to Ruby. 'Do you remember her birthday?'

'Yes, the café did drinks and tapas for the staff and locals to celebrate Britta's sixtieth,' Ruby replied.

'Sixty?' Atticus raised his eyebrows. 'She looks much younger.'

Ruby sat back, her brow furrowed, and absently ran her fingers through her cropped hair while Cheryl pressed her lips together in a thoughtful line.

Minutes ticked by and Atticus wondered what they

were both thinking. *Had he done wrong in their eyes? Was dating at his age a crime?* Perhaps they thought he was punching above his weight.

'You think I've been foolish,' Atticus said. 'I hope I haven't annoyed you.'

'Oh, my dear.' Cheryl leapt up, and Atticus suddenly found himself engulfed by a hot, heaving bosom. 'A date! I think it's bloody marvellous.' She wrapped her arms around him and kissed the top of his head.

'Nice one.' Ruby smiled and grabbed his hand in a finger-crunching shake.

'We've never seen Britta with anyone,' Cheryl said. 'Not that I'm being nosy, but she doesn't appear to have a partner or anyone close.'

'We know of expats and locals who've asked her out, but she keeps to herself,' Ruby said. 'She likes to paint; you'll see some of her artwork in the café.'

'I've invited her to our barbecues,' Cheryl added, 'but she's never come to one.'

'Do you think a meal is too much?' Atticus asked. 'Perhaps I should have just asked her for a coffee or a drink.'

'Nah, she's a grown-up,' Ruby said. 'If things aren't going well, she can easily make an excuse and walk away. A meal is good.'

When their tostadas arrived, they all took a slice of crusty baguette topped with olive oil, juicy tomatoes, garlic, and melted Manchego cheese.

As they ate, they discussed 'The Date'.

Cheryl and Ruby debated restaurants. Given that it was a first date, they decided that casual beachside, open-air dining – and nowhere too formal – would set the tone for the couple to relax and get to know each other.

'*Casablanca*!' Cheryl and Ruby said and high-fived.

'It serves food all day, and the Sunday menu is good,' Cheryl confirmed with a nod as she licked tomato from the corner of her mouth and flicked crumbs from her ample chest.

Ruby began to give Atticus directions. The restaurant was in Guardamar, a ten-minute drive away. Atticus nodded. He realised he'd have to disconnect Winnie from the electricity and water, so she was ready for the road.

As though reading his mind, Cheryl said, 'You must take our car.'

'Oh, no. I couldn't possibly,' Atticus shook his head.

'Don't be silly, you can't be dismantling Winnie and have all that mither. Of course you can take the car, can't she, Ruby?'

Ruby, her mouth full, nodded and waved her hand as though the question needed no answer.

'You're insured, aren't you?' Cheryl asked.

'Yes,' Atticus nodded.

'Good, so that's all sorted,' Cheryl smiled. We're going to a poolside party at the site tomorrow, with live music and karaoke. We don't need the car.'

'You can have a practice drive on the way back so you get used to it,' Ruby suggested. 'In the meantime, shall we have a drink to celebrate The Date?'

Atticus watched as a pitcher of sangria magically appeared and Ruby poured three glasses. Taking only a sip, so he wasn't over the limit, he felt grateful to them for their kindness and laughed as they both called out, 'Here's to The Date!'

A little while later, Atticus eased into the driver's seat and drove the four of them away from the market and along the main road to Guardamar. Cheryl was perched in the back, with Ness on her knee.

'Smile!' she called out, and using a selfie stick, began to take photos of Atticus at the wheel, with the sun shining on the sparkling sea and the Spanish coastline making a splendid backdrop. 'Send these to the folks back home,' she added.

Minus his hat, Atticus felt the warm wind tousle his hair and the sun caress his skin. The nimble Fiat handled well, and he waved when he noticed passers-by smile as he zipped along. Casablanca was an easy restaurant to find, and Ruby's instructions were clear: keep the sea on the left, turn onto a service road, and follow it past blocks of beach-side houses and apartments. On the corner lay Casablanca, with open-air seating overlooking the sea.

'You can park on the opposite road,' Ruby said, and Atticus duly turned to check out the available space.

'I like this car,' he commented as they returned to Solma Vacaciones. 'It's very kind of you to let me use it.'

When they reached the site, Cheryl and Ruby said goodbye and headed off to relax at the poolside bar. As Atticus walked back to Winnie, with Ness trotting happily alongside, he thought how far away his lonely life in Cumbria now felt.

From the moment he'd found Winnie again, Atticus felt a surge of life as new plans began to take shape. Spain had become a healing process – a place where he could leave his sadness behind and embrace a new beginning. A heavy weight had been lifted, replaced by a feeling of rejuvenation. Clara was still in his thoughts, but he had to accept that she had gone, and he was lucky to have had so many good years with her. But now, that part of his life was over and there was nothing he could do about it. Knowing that Clara would have approved, he questioned why he hadn't embarked on this journey years ago, instead of lingering in the shadows of his past.

Atticus exchanged greetings with campers sitting outside, and as he walked by, he wondered what Britta was doing. *Was she still at work, or had she gone to her cottage?* Cheryl said Britta liked to paint, and he pictured her at an easel on a patio overlooking the beach.

Suddenly, Atticus began to panic. What on earth was he thinking? It was madness to consider taking a woman out for a meal at his age. He pulled out a chair and flopped down, his mind swirling with 'What ifs'.

What if he said something foolish?

What if Britta didn't find him interesting?

After all, he was just a humble sheep farmer who'd never ventured far from home. *What if Casablanca was too extravagant or perhaps not extravagant enough?* The self-doubt gnawed at him, making him feel unsure.

The doubts continued as he sat in the sun, and Ness sheltered under his chair. His palms felt clammy, and Atticus was restless as he realised, he didn't even have her number to take the coward's way out and text to cancel their meeting.

'I must keep busy,' he resolved, determined to push his doubts aside. 'If I stop thinking about her, it will be alright.' He took his phone from his pocket, downloaded Cheryl's photos, and uploaded them to his Instagram account. 'A few more shots for Jake and Arthur,' he muttered.

He read a text from Mary and smiled, pleased that she approved, as he knew she would. Reaching down to stroke Ness, Atticus remembered that he'd intended to hire a bike. Two-wheeled transport would enable him to get about without Winnie whenever needed.

'We'll wander up to the bike shop,' he told Ness, who began to thump her tail, sensing a walk. As they set off, Atticus couldn't help but think of Britta again. 'It's just a date,' he muttered to Ness. 'Nothing more than two people sharing conversation and a meal.'

But to Atticus, in that moment, it felt like the world's most daunting challenge.

Chapter Nineteen

Autumn mid-term in Kindale seemed to come around quickly this year, at least to Mary. It felt as though it had been only five minutes since they'd returned from Cumbria after the summer holidays, and soon, they would be turning the corner into Christmas and another break. Not that she minded. At Christmas, Conor always took the time off and was a big help with the kids – it was her favourite time of year. She'd wished he could have been with them during the last week of mid-term, but business was brisk in the estate agency world, and Conor had hardly been home.

Mary's week, meanwhile, had been manic.

With 'Mum's taxi' fully operational, she'd been fetching and carrying the kids from A to B and back again. Finn had been going to a football camp which involved skills development and training, culminating in a mini-league play-off where parents were obliged to attend.

Following the funds raised at the disco, Caitlin had been working on the school allotment. As Mary dropped her eldest off each day, she wondered how much lipstick, false eyelashes, and makeup was required to build raised garden borders. She suspected an attractive boy had caught Caitlin's eye and was likely involved in the project. Maeve, when not posing around the house and pouting into her phone to take selfies, wanted to be ferried into Kindale so she could 'hang out with her friends'. Limiting Maeve and her mate's mid-term rendezvous to four daylight hours, Mary prayed she could trust her youngest not to get up to mischief.

Declan celebrated his birthday that week, and at six – going on sixteen – he insisted that friends from his class be invited to a house party. Given the time of year, he wanted a Halloween theme, and Mary spent hours decorating Belvedere House with spooky decorations. The party would take place in the open-plan kitchen and lounge, and Mary found herself up to her ears in cobwebs, bats, and ghosts, which were suspended from the ceiling and covered every inch of spare wall.

Mary's friend Una had offered to help, but typical of the woman, Una – busy with her own family – was running late. Mary had confided in Una about her doubts regarding Conor, hoping for a sympathetic ear. But Una dismissed Mary's fears, telling her she was imagining things. 'Conor is about as likely to have an affair with Lucinda as a priest is to buy a round in a pub,' she'd said. Una added that Conor must embrace many colleagues during his working day, and it was a wonder he didn't come home smelling like the perfume counter in a chemist's shop.

'Are you sure it isn't from the air freshener in his car?' Una asked. 'He spends enough time in it; perhaps it's a new one, installed when the car was valeted.'

'On his shirt?' Mary stared at Una as though she were mad. 'And do you not think I know the difference between Thierry Mugler and a smelly dangler?' she asked.

Una giggled. 'Well, obviously,' she added, noting Mary's glare.

Removing the last tray of pumpkin-shaped cookies from the oven, Mary arranged them alongside bowls of candy, chocolate bars, and a cauldron of green, fruit-flavoured punch.

'Hey ho, it's a spooking we will go,' Mary sang.

Laying the food out buffet-style, Mary was proud of her efforts and nodded with approval as she tweaked the spider pizzas, witches' broomsticks, and mummy hotdogs onto platters, alongside Halloween cupcakes, crisps, and a graveyard dip. Knowing that the parents would curse her for returning their sugar-high six-year-olds at the end of the party, she wondered if it was too early for a glass of wine.

Insisting that everyone was prepared for the party, Mary yelled up the stairs. 'Finn, are you ready? Caitlin, have you dressed Declan? Maeve, come and give me a hand!'

'I hope you've catered for plant-based guests,' Maeve said upon entering the kitchen. Dressed as a princess and taking selfies, she turned to study the food.

Mary wasn't sure what part a princess might play at

Halloween, nor how many six-year-olds followed a plant-based diet. However, as she poured herself a large Chardonnay, she pointed to the fridge, where a pumpkin platter with veggies and fruit was chilling.

'Where are the monster eyeballs?' Maeve asked as she opened the fridge and gazed suspiciously at the platter.

'Get a life, Maeve,' Mary replied, taking a large sip of wine. 'I don't have time to peel dozens of grapes and fill them with cream cheese and chocolate chips.'

'You should be more like Grandad,' Maeve retorted.

'What do you mean?'

'Not so grumpy. Enjoy life and have fun.' Maeve reached for a carrot stick and began to munch. 'He's a Golden Insta Influencer now,' she said.

'A what?'

'Oh, Mam, keep up! Grandad has zillions of followers on Instagram because of his fun-filled posts,' she sighed. 'He's achieved in days what I could never do in years.'

'You mean like an Insta Gramps?'

Maeve gave Mary a look of disdain and, rolling her eyes, reached for another carrot stick.

They were suddenly distracted when mayhem descended, and Zombie Finn slid down the stairs, followed by Catlin, the vampire, and Declan, a mini werewolf.

With the party about to kick off, Mary checked her watch. She had a few minutes to change and hoped that Witchery Wanda, the storyteller-turned-magician she'd hired for the event, would be on time and keep the kids amused during the celebration.

'Caitlin,' Mary said as she headed for the stairs, 'pack

the party bags. Everything is on a shelf in the larder. Keep your brothers and sister in order, and make sure they don't touch any food!'

In her bedroom, Mary took another slurp of her wine. Conor had promised to finish work early and, hopefully, would be home soon to help. With no time for a shower and only minutes to change, Mary grabbed a dress hanging in her wardrobe. It was long, fitted, with a high neckline and sleeves that reached to the wrist. Mary hoped the black, silky fabric would flatter her ever-increasing figure. There had been no time for the gym that week.

She was wriggling into her Bounce Buster Briefs when her phone rang. Blindly reaching out, Mary held it to her ear.

'Have you seen what he's gone and done now?' Mungo sounded exasperated.

'Oh, hello, Mungo.' Mary's voice was high-pitched as she tugged up her briefs and wondered why the hell they were so named. *Giant Passion Killers That Give You Whiplash* would be more appropriate. 'I guess you're talking about Dad?'

'He's parading about in a brand-new, bright red Fiat 500 convertible!'

'Wow, good for him,' Mary breathed as she tugged the passion killers into place over her tum.

'Good for him?' Mungo exploded. 'If he's bought a car, he's spending recklessly and intends to stay in Spain!'

Mary slid into the dress and was pleasantly surprised it went on quite easily. *God Bless Bounce Buster Briefs and all who squeezed into them.* She began to brush her hair and apply dark, smudgy eyeshadow.

'Are you still there?' Mungo shouted.

'Yes, but I really don't know what you are worried about,' Mary replied as she smoothed blood-red gloss on her lips. 'Dad is obviously having a good time if he's uploading fun photos to Instagram.'

'Fun photos?' Mungo sounded incredulous. 'A pensioner riding about in a Noddy car is a fun photo?' He snorted. 'It's had over five hundred likes already. God knows what people must think.'

There was a pause, and when Mungo realised that Mary wasn't going to respond, he moaned, 'I don't know why I bother phoning. You always side with him and will never see the danger ahead.'

'Oh, Mungo,' Mary said, exasperated. 'You have no idea what danger is. Come here and host a Halloween party for two dozen hyper six-year-olds and their paranoid parents, and you'll soon see what living on the edge is all about.' Mary drained the last of her wine and, deciding to stay barefoot, left her bedroom and padded down the stairs.

'Don't hang up on me again,' Mungo sounded angry.

'Sorry, Bro,' Mary replied as the front doorbell rang, 'but Harry Potter and the Sorcerer's Apprentice have just arrived, plus a spaceship full of aliens.'

'What?'

'I have to go, I'll catch you later,' Mary said and flipped the phone into her pocket.

As she opened the door, her mouth dropped. Standing

on the step, dressed as James Bond and looking as handsome as a Hollywood hunk, was Ruari.

'The invite said, "Come as a Halloween or Superhero character",' he grinned. 'And with my ex-wife away, it's my weekend to have Orla, so I thought I'd oblige.' Ruari held the hand of his beautiful six-year-old daughter, who, like her outfit, was angelic. 'Single parents can scrub up,' he added, 'almost as well as you married ones.'

Mary was about to tell Ruari that he'd misunderstood the invitation, and that it was for children not parents. But the sight of so handsome a man made her think that it might be fun to have another adult at the party.

Ruari was studying Mary from head to toe. As his eyes levelled with her own, he said, 'You're looking magnificent, Morticia.'

Framed by thick, dark lashes, Ruari's cobalt blue eyes were as deep as the ocean, and as he stared into hers, Mary had an urge to dive in. Feeling flustered, she threw back the door and stepped to one side. She hadn't intended to dress as a member of The Addams Family, but took Ruari's comment as a compliment. She smiled at Orla and ushered her unexpected plus one in.

'Go through, Orla,' Mary said as the little girl, gripping a brightly wrapped gift, ran into the house. 'Declan is the werewolf crawling over the sofa,' she added.

'Nice place,' Ruari said as he strode ahead and walked over to the enormous glass doors that opened to the garden. 'You have a magnificent view.'

Mary thought her own view was as good as it got as she watched James Bond walk with purposeful steps, like a sculpted work of art brought to life. 'Help yourself to a drink,' she called out, tearing her eyes away from Ruari as the doorbell rang again. 'You'll probably need it.'

As Declan's guests arrived, a flood of mini-monsters, ghosts, and demons came tearing into the kitchen. Parents, eager to do the drop-off and disappear, waved from behind the wheels of their four-by-fours before driving off at speed. As Mary was about to close the door, a battered old van appeared and parked in front of the house.

'Oh heck,' Mary mumbled, 'Conor will have a fit when he sees a pile of junk littering his driveway.'

The driver, draped in tattered robes, climbed out and moved with a slow, deliberate gait. Strands of silver hair poked out from a hood, and as Mary stood mesmerised, a woman's face slowly appeared. Her watery eyes were set in a wrinkled face, and crooked fingers of one hand gripped a ragged bag, while the other reached out to take Mary's.

'Witchery Wanda?' Mary asked as she shook the woman's clammy skin.

'I am the keeper of ancient knowledge, here to entertain,' Wanda croaked and edged past Mary. 'Where are the children?'

'Go right on through.' Mary held out an arm. A shiver ran down her spine as the old crone ambled past. With a sudden panic, she wondered if she'd made the right choice of entertainment for the party.

But as Mary closed the door and turned to the children's screams of horror and delight, she was grateful that Wanda had at least left her broomstick behind.

Atticus and Ness arrived at the Solma Vacaciones bike shop, and their eyes were drawn to the sign that promised adventure: 'Bikes for Hire'. Despite the open door and a can of cola on the counter, the shop was eerily quiet. Atticus decided to head to the reception to see if anyone there might help.

To his dismay, the woman he'd encountered before, with square-framed glasses and helmet-style hair, sat silently, studying a computer behind the long counter.

'Hola,' Atticus began and stepped forward. Receiving no reply, he tried again. 'Buenas tardes, er, can you help me?'

'Sí.' The woman didn't look up.

'Yes? Good. I want to hire a bike.'

'Shop outside,' she replied, fingers clicking across a keyboard.

'Yes, I know. But there's no one there.'

'You wait.'

'How long?'

'Who knows.'

Atticus struggled to stay civil, but before he could respond, a phone rang. The woman grabbed the receiver and began to speak in loud, rapid Spanish. With a sigh, he turned and, with Ness by his side, walked away.

Outside in the sunshine, Atticus wandered over to a line of bikes and presumed that they were for hire. 'What do you think?' he asked Ness as the pair studied various shapes and sizes. He was about to reach for a bike that looked suitable when he heard a *ding-ding*.

A familiar voice broke the silence.

'Hola!' it called out, and Atticus looked up to see Sophia, the aqua aerobics instructor, heading towards him.

Pedalling a scooter, she wore the same minuscule red one-piece, teamed with a vibrant visor and trainers. Atticus smiled at her timely arrival.

'I sorry!' Sophia said and screeched to a stop. 'I work with my senior squad; they play bouncing balls today.'

Sophia thrust the scooter to one side and indicated that Atticus follow. As he fell into step behind her, her ample rear had a rhythm of its own. Barely covered by skimpy fabric, Atticus wondered what the senior squad's blood pressure made of Sophia's posterior during a bouncing ball game.

'You want cycle,' Sophia announced and pulled out a bike. 'Try this,' she said and adjusted her visor to watch Atticus tentatively climb on.

It had been years since Atticus had ridden a bike, and at first, he felt quite unsteady, but as he hesitatingly began to move forward, the knack of pedalling soon came back.

Ness began to bark as she ran alongside, and Sophia clapped her hands.

'Come back!' she called out. 'Now we find trailer for dog.'

Sophia insisted that if Atticus was going any distance, it wouldn't be safe for Ness to run alongside. Fifteen minutes later, lighter by a considerable amount of euros, Atticus placed his hat on his head and pedalled away with Ness, upright in a mesh pod attached to the back of his bike.

'This is life!' Atticus exclaimed. He was filled with joy as they sped along the site's paths, immersed in the simple pleasure of a bike ride. Ness, with her head held high and the wind tickling her ears, barked her approval from the rear.

Rounding a corner near the tennis courts, Atticus stared at the pitches as he rode by. They were several times bigger than his own, and his jaw almost dropped when he caught sight of pitch number two hundred.

A motorhome was positioned like a palace on wheels, a symphony of sleek lines and polished surfaces that glittered in the sunshine, inviting admiration from all who passed by. Beside it, in the middle of an open-air haven, Erik was stretched out on a lounger, beneath a vast umbrella.

Looking up, Erik shaded his eyes and, recognising Atticus, stood. 'Hello, my cowboy friend,' he called out. 'Come and have a drink.'

Erik was wearing the briefest Speedos Atticus had ever seen, and as he dismounted, releasing Ness from her pod, Atticus wondered if Erik shopped at the same store as Sophia. Erik's physique was sculpted, with defined muscles, and his broad shoulders tapered down to a narrow waist. With a chiselled chest and well-defined pecs, Erik commanded attention.

Opening the gate to the pitch, Atticus stepped onto soft, cushioned flooring. 'My goodness, Erik,' he began. 'This is quite a place you have here.'

'I'm glad you like it,' Erik said, walking over to a

canopied bar. 'Beer?' he asked, opening a fridge and holding up a chilled bottle.

'Perfect,' Atticus replied.

Atticus's eyes were wide as he studied a dancing area with a light show and a revolving disco ball. A nearby gym was well-equipped, and Atticus understood the convenience of having a home exercise area. Endless hours of physical dedication had contributed to Erik's fine physique. Beside the bar, an outdoor kitchen had every device a Michelin-starred chef might need.

'Do you like it?' Erik asked.

'Sensational,' Atticus smiled.

'Come, look,' Erik said, guiding Atticus up several steps.

Inside the motorhome, sumptuous furnishings and skilled craftsmanship unfolded into a series of rooms. Soft leather sofas enclosed the lounge, where panoramic windows added light. A wood-panelled corridor, containing storage, led to a state-of-the-art kitchen. In the softly carpeted ensuite bedroom, a king-sized bed was plumped high with plush pillows. But Atticus's breath was taken away when he stepped into the entertainment area, complete with a home theatre system, computers, gaming consoles, and a mini bar.

'My goodness,' Atticus exclaimed, astonished by what he saw.

'Take photos, make yourself at home,' Erik said and sat down.

'I've never seen anything like it.' Atticus said as he wandered around, enjoying selfies in the luxurious space.

'Do you still work?' Atticus asked, noting a work area with a desktop.

'Of course, I run my businesses remotely, and Spain is a good place for me to be.'

'That's convenient. What do you do?'

'Oh, this and that.' Erik smiled, giving nothing away. Changing the subject, he remarked, 'You have a bike now, it's good, we can cycle together. I can show you around.'

'I'd like that,' Atticus said. 'Do you cycle far?'

'Some days. But for distances, I take the car.'

'Car?'

'It's stored below.' Erik pointed to the floor, and Atticus nodded. Naturally, this magnificent beast would have storage, and Atticus imagined the lift and ramp system below.

'Tonight, we barbecue here. You must stay.' Erik stood and reached for Atticus's empty beer bottle.

'Well, that's kind of you to ask, but I must go to the supermarket and contribute.'

Erik shook his head. 'No, my friend, one day we will all come to you,' he said, 'and the restaurant here is delivering everything for me.'

As Erik disappeared to the bar, Atticus puffed out a breath. He tried to imagine the value of the motorhome and thought it must be worth a fortune. How fascinating it was to see such a different way of life. Atticus thought of Winnie and remembered Erik's kindness when erecting the awning. What ever must he have thought of Atticus's modest setup compared to his own?

But as Atticus sank deep into the luxurious sofa, he felt a sense of relief. The barbecue would take his mind off thoughts of The Date next day and his anxiety about Britta. He knew it would only be momentary, but in the meantime, at least he could relax and make himself useful by helping Erik with the cooking.

Atticus looked around and remembered Arthur once saying that money can't buy happiness. Atticus began to chuckle. His friend should consider purchasing a one-way ticket to Spain.

Chapter Twenty

Sunday at Belvedere House, the morning after the Halloween party from hell, Mary sat in her kitchen, idly wondering how she would get red paint off a brilliant white wall.

Strangely, her worry wasn't a big concern.

Neither was her anger toward Patrick, the child who'd produced a paint gun and, like a scene from a massacre, proceeded to pump paint over two dozen departing party-goers. Mary remembered the pleas of the parent of Paint-balling Patrick, who swore they thought the paint was washable and had no idea that her little darling would use the gift he'd brought for Declan.

Mary's hangover was pounding, and as she sipped her coffee, she winced and thought of the horror on the faces of parents arriving to pick up their offspring. Clutching party bags and riding sugar-fuelled highs, little feet hardly touching the ground, the mini-ghouls and monsters squealed as they dodged Patrick's parting shot and ran out of the house. She wondered how soon it would be before the bills for dry cleaning arrived. The house phone beeped with messages from horrified parents complaining about the liqueur chocolates in the party bags, and Mary cursed Caitlin for grabbing the first items that came to hand in the larder.

'Oh, sod it,' Mary muttered as she looked around at sticky surfaces and a crumb-filled floor. Having risen early to deal with most of the mess, Mary decided that Roisin could deal with it. She wandered over to the window and felt glad that she'd booked the Environmental Services Provider for that day.

Gazing out at her garden, where rain lashed, Mary felt as battered as the bushes and trees that swayed in an unrelenting southwest wind whipping over the headland from the Atlantic. More pressing problems than cleaning weighed her down, and these concerned Conor and Ruari.

The party had begun well, and the children enjoyed the food Mary had painstakingly prepared. Una turned up halfway through, breathless and full of apologies. She was dressed as a leprechaun in a glittery green outfit, carrying a massive bag containing enough sugary snacks to fuel a classroom riot.

'Do you still think Conor is having an affair with Lucinda?' Una asked as she lobbed sweets into the air like a chaotic piñata.

'Keep your voice down,' Mary hissed, glancing nervously at the children swarming around Una like seagulls after a chip.

'Ah, Mary, you've nothing to worry about. Conor is a

family man,' Una said. 'You think you have problems? Last week, I found a pair of knickers in Jimmy's coat pocket, but did I panic?' Una shook her head.

Mary clutched her chest. 'Oh, God, Una, what did you do?'

'I put them in my own coat pocket,' Una smirked, 'and am waiting to see if the eejit has the nerve to ask for them back...'

Settling in a circle surrounding Witchery Wanda, the children's eyes were wide as she performed a magic show, casting playful spells and performing tricks. They listened carefully to tales of friendly ghosts and haunted houses, before eagerly taking part in the Monster Freeze dance, standing like statues and prancing like monsters.

But it was the Halloween Twister where trouble began.

Declan insisted that the grown-ups play the game, and as the birthday boy for the day, Mary could hardly refuse her youngest. Una had refused to get involved and went into the garden for a smoke and the only other grown-up in the room was Ruari, who was keen to participate. As children spun the dial, calling out colours and body part combinations, Mary and Ruari stretched and contorted to reach the circles without falling over. Boundaries blurred as they navigated the slippery mat, and soon, they tumbled in a giggling tangle when Mary fell flat on her back, and Ruari landed on top of her.

It was at this moment that Conor arrived home.

Mary remembered moving Ruari's soft, curling locks from her face to see who was towering over them. Her dress had ridden up her thighs, where Ruari had fallen between them.

'What on earth?' Conor hissed as the two quickly parted. His eyes were stormy, and his face flushed. 'This is a children's game,' he added.

'Keep your cool,' Ruari said as he eased to his feet, straightened his jacket, and reached out to help Mary. 'The kids suggested it, and they've had a lot of fun.'

'Yes, Daddy!' Declan yelled, gripping his father's leg. 'You go next.'

'Not now,' Conor said. He turned to Witchery Wanda and told her to organise another game.

As Conor led Ruari toward a corner by the garden windows, a row soon ensued. Mary, perched behind a bookcase and unseen by the two men, heard Conor ask why Ruari was at the children's party. Ruari, angry at being insulted, retaliated by asking Conor why he spent so much time at Creek House when he had a beautiful wife at home.

Creek House.

Like a Monster Freeze dance participant, Mary froze like a statue. It took all her strength not to grab the cauldron of green punch and fling it at Conor.

Now, as she stared through the windows, where forceful gusts bent branches and trees swayed, she knew for sure that Conor had been spending time at Lucinda Darby's home.

Time when he said he'd been working.

She thought of their night at the Salty Dog Inn and the look of guilt on Conor's face as he ended a call. Mary suddenly realised that he'd been speaking to Lucinda and not the babysitter. There hadn't been an opportunity for discussion, and with too much to drink, Conor had fallen asleep as soon as they'd gotten home. In the days that followed, the kids were as demanding as ever, and Mary had felt too weary to pursue her misgivings.

Now, Witchery Wanda's departing words came back like a slap in the face. She'd reached for payment from Mary's hand, then leaned in and sang in her ear.

'Beware, for betrayal lurks in shadows deep,
where hearts now wander,
secrets they shall keep.'

Mary had wanted to tell Wanda to mind her own business and cut the witching out. But as she stood in her kitchen, still staring out at the garden, she replayed the night before, and the old woman's words rang true. Conor, furious about the game of Twister where she'd humiliated herself, had blamed Mary for the paint incident and for not being more attentive. He'd retreated to the playroom with the kids and told her he'd put them to bed. Unaware that she'd overheard his conversation with Ruari, he had suggested that Mary unwind in a bath. Taking a large glass of Chardonnay, Mary felt too exhausted and upset to discuss the state of her marriage with Conor in front of the kids. After a soak, she went to bed and fell into a fitful sleep.

Now, Mary looked at the wild beauty outside and sighed. She thought of calling Una, but her friend was unlikely to be out of bed at this time on a Sunday morning.

Mary wished the energy of the wind could revitalise her. Indeed, she should be racing up the stairs, demanding to know what her husband had been up to and sorting out their flawed life. But at that moment, she felt weary. Instead of being angry at Conor and his probable lies, her emotions were filled with sadness. Sadness for the closeness she'd once shared with her husband and the happy times they appeared to have lost. Sadness, too, for the way Ruari looked at her, with lust in his eyes, when it should have been Conor staring that way. Mary longed for loving arms to wrap around her and tell her everything was alright.

She slumped onto a chair and wrapped a blanket around her legs. As her family slept on, Mary reached for her phone. There was one person she might be able to talk to, and she had a sudden urge to speak to her dad. It was an hour ahead in Spain, and with luck, he would be up. But before she found his number, Mary turned to his Instagram page.

The Travelling Grandad was having the time of his life! New images showed Atticus driving around in a Fiat 500 convertible. Mary thought it suited him, unlike Mungo's comments about the Noddy car.

Mary gasped when she saw photos of Atticus on a bike, towing Ness in a trailer. 'How bloody brilliant!' She grinned. Atticus had caught the sun and wore shorts and a white T-shirt. Gone were his comfortable hide boots, and now, tanned toes peeped out of a pair of leather sandals.

Mary realised what a handsome man she had as a father. With a full head of hair, a toned body, and well-muscled limbs, years of farming had kept him in good shape. Clearly, the climate in Spain was suiting him.

'And he's out partying...' she breathed, shaking her head.

Atticus was at a barbecue, cooking steak and handing out fat sausages from a long-handled fork. In the many images, he was laughing and smiling with guests at the party, which appeared to be held in and around a palatial-style motor home.

Mary sat up. 'Oh, Dad, I am so happy for you,' she smiled.

Suddenly, footsteps sounded on the landing, and Mary pushed her phone to one side. The kids were up, and Conor, despite the wind and rain, would soon be off to his Sunday morning workout. There wasn't time to speak to Atticus, and as she stared at the gloomy weather, she knew she could hardly go pouring out her troubles to him. It would be so unfair when her dad was having such a good time.

'Mammy! Finn's got Teddy, and he's throwing him downstairs!' Declan screamed.

Mary took a deep breath and sighed. 'Coming,' she called out.

As she passed the front door, Roisin's Shamrock Shine pulled up, and in seconds, Roisin let herself in. 'I hear it was quite a party,' she commented as she marched past Mary, who was picking up Teddy from the bottom of the stairs.

Mary turned to watch Roisin, bucket and mop in hand, stomp into the kitchen.

'Jaysus, Mary, and Joseph!' Roisin exclaimed as she stared at the red colour on the wall. 'It's industrial cleaning you'll be wanting today.'

'I'm sorry about the paint, Roisin, but I know you'll do your best,' Mary said, and, thinking of the two-faced cow Lucinda, wondered mischievously if Roisin's many talents might include contract killing.

'Just as long as you know,' Roisin sighed as she reached for a bottle of heavy-duty cleaner and tugged thick rubber gloves onto her hands. 'It's triple-time on a Sunday!'

In the cosy shed at the back of the garden at Shirlarth Cottage, Jake stood at Arthur's workbench and stared at the collection of broken gnomes. Zen Master Ted was missing his head, and Serenity Sam was in pieces.

'You've made a right mess of things, Uncle Arthur,' Jake said as he took hold of Peaceful Pete and glued his arms to his torso. 'Does Aunty Shirley know that you've created a gnome-sized apocalypse?'

'Aye, very funny,' Arthur sighed. 'But if we can't get them back together, Shirley will be fuming like a teapot on turbo, and I'll be in the doghouse for weeks.' He sat on his rocker and watched as Jake got to work.

'I'm not sure I can do anything with Pete's chipped nose,' Jake said, looking puzzled as he studied the tools he'd set out for the gnome crisis.

'Blu-Tack any good?' Arthur asked. He produced a fluffy ball from his cardigan pocket. 'I always keep a piece on hand for emergencies.'

'I'll use a blob of Polyfilla and a dab of paint.'

'Good lad.' Arthur nodded.

Jake assembled a pointed hat in three pieces and reached for a tube of Gorilla Glue. 'This needs to set. Shall we call Grandad while we wait?'

'That's a good idea,' Arthur replied. Knowing that Atticus had a date that day and his friend would be on edge, a few friendly words from the folks back home might settle his nerves.

'Let's FaceTime,' Jake said excitedly. He pulled out his phone and, turning away from the bench, leaned close to Arthur.

Atticus answered after three rings.

'Hola, Grandad!' Jake called out. 'Can you see us?'

'Hello.' Atticus smiled from the screen. 'What are you two rascals up to?'

He squinted into the camera to see Arthur in his rocker, scarf and bob hat in place, while Jake, muffled into a duffle coat, stood before a shelf of broken garden gnomes.

'It's like an episode of *The Repair Shop* in Uncle Arthur's shed,' Jake said. 'He's broken lots of Aunty Shirley's gnomes.'

Atticus began to laugh. 'Ouch, someone's in trouble. You must have been gnome'ing around, Arthur. Is Jake helping you gnome them back together?'

'Aye, hilarious. Two comedians to contend with,'

Arthur grumbled. 'We're working hard while you're messing around in the sun.'

'I'm not messing around. I've been out with Ness, and now we're tidying the pitch. There's lots of dust and leaves to brush up in the morning.'

Arthur and Jake could see Atticus leaning on a broom.

'I thought you'd be getting ready for your date,' Arthur said.

'Date?' Jake looked from the screen to Arthur and back again. 'Grandad has a date?'

'Yep, I'll let him explain.'

'Well, it's nothing to get excited about—' Atticus began, but Jake interrupted.

'—I left a list of online Spanish dating sites in the folder,' Jake said. 'I knew you'd try them out.' He punched the air. 'Was it "*Romance Arrugado*" or "*Amor Anejado*"?'

'Eh?' Arthur looked puzzled.

'"Wrinkled Romance" or "Aged Love",' Jake explained.

'Neither, actually. It's someone who works in a café where I had breakfast.'

'Wow, the Spanish are so cool, employing pensioners.' Jake grinned.

Atticus laughed. 'She's a bit younger than me, and she's Dutch.'

'A kitten queen!' Jake exclaimed.

'What?' Arthur and Atticus were baffled.

'You know, like a bunny babe or a junior jewel. A much younger girlfriend.'

'Listen, Jake,' Atticus began, 'she's not a girlfriend, just someone I got talking to and who's agreed to a meal with me. We'll sit by the sea and have a chat. That's all.'

'I can't wait to tell Dad that you have a girlfriend,' Jake continued, ignoring Atticus's explanation. 'If you get married, will the wedding be in Spain?'

'It would be better if the happy couple came back to Cumbria,' Arthur joined in. 'The Black Bull is a perfect venue.'

'Aye, and you could line the garden with wedding gnomes in dapper suits, bow ties, and top hats.' Atticus narrowed his eyes. 'Your Shirley would enjoy decking them out with banners and bouquets.'

'Now you're getting into the spirit of things,' Arthur laughed.

'Imagine the hits it will get on Instagram,' Jake said thoughtfully. 'Your followers will love it.'

'What followers?' Atticus asked.

'The people who see all your posts.'

'*People*? I thought only you and Arthur saw my photos.'

'Oh, Grandad, you need to keep up.' Jake shook his mop of hair. 'You have more than ten thousand followers tuning in to see where and what you are doing – The Travelling Grandad is inspiring people. You're showing the world that age isn't important when it comes to following a dream.'

'*What*? All those folk know what I am doing?'

'Yes, and they're loving it.'

'Bloody hell.' Atticus looked stunned and began to rub his chin.

'I hate to interrupt this fascinating conversation on life,

love, and how to inspire sun-seeking pensioners,' Arthur chipped in, 'but there's a box of broken gnomes waiting to be mended, and our Shirley is on the warpath, heading this way with my lunchtime sandwich.'

'Aunty Shirley will go crazy if she sees what's happened to Serenity Sam,' Jake said. 'We'd better go, Grandad. Let us know how your date goes and remember to post lots of photos.' Jake reached for Peaceful Pete.

Arthur held the phone and tilted his head, then paused as he stared at his friend.

'On a serious note,' Arthur said, a smile crossing his face, 'enjoy yourself and remember, you only pass this way once.' Giving a thumbs-up, he concluded, 'What's meant for you won't go past you...'

Chapter Twenty-One

Sunday at Solma Vacaciones was always a busy day. Spanish families, vacationing for the weekend, were out in force by the chalets, where tables overflowing with food were shaded by pretty umbrellas lining the pathways. At the same time, children of all ages raced about on scooters and bikes and played games, their shouts and giggles loud as they ran around the garden area with boundless energy. In her chalet, Cheryl was ready to head off to the poolside party. She wore her baby-pink tankini under a voluminous silvery kaftan, and her eyes shone as Ruby emerged carrying a beach bag with books, suncream, and snacks.

'You look the dog's doodahs,' Cheryl said and gave Ruby a peck on the cheek.

Ruby, in white shorts and a black vest, reached for a cap and placed it on her head. 'Have you seen Atticus?' she asked.

'He just called to say he's on his way.' Cheryl dangled

car keys and stepped onto the decking. 'He's here now,' she smiled as Atticus approached.

Wearing pale chinos and a short-sleeved shirt that accentuated his broad shoulders, Atticus, in new leather deck shoes, walked towards them with Ness by his side.

'My, don't you look smart,' Cheryl said, studying both from top-to-toe. 'I like Ness's bandana,' she added.

'How are you feeling?' Ruby asked.

'Truthfully?' Atticus said, scratching his chin. 'Nervous,' he admitted, his voice tinged with apprehension.

'You'll be fine,' Ruby assured him and patted his arm. 'Remember to keep the conversation light and enjoy it.'

'Okay.'

'Drive carefully.' Cheryl smiled and leaned in to kiss Atticus on the cheek. 'If you get back early, come to the pool party,' she added.

Minutes later, Atticus sat behind the wheel of the Fiat. The top was down, and the sun was hot as he drove slowly through the site.

On his way to the pool party, Erik stopped when he saw Atticus. 'Enjoy your date!' he called out. Campers sitting in the sunshine raised their hands as Atticus went past, each with a friendly greeting. They were a tight-knit community and enjoyed exchanging friendly banter.

'You've still got it!'

'Smooth operator!'

'Charm her off her feet!'

'Go get 'em, tiger!'

Atticus shook his head as he heard their comments. 'Nothing gets past these folk,' he said, and thought of Cheryl and Ruby's gossip grapevine.

But as the road stretched ahead and the sun shone brightly, Atticus knew he couldn't be annoyed. Everyone seemed to have his best interests at heart, and it was impossible for him to feel down or sad in a place where the atmosphere was so cheerful. In this enclosed bubble, problems felt far away, along with the world's troubles. Atticus knew that these people had lived lives that may have been difficult, after all, everyone had problems to overcome. But here, they rewarded themselves with the little things that gave pleasure in later life.

'And why not?' he asked Ness. 'At our age, it's now or never and all about making the most of what we have left.'

He thought of his Instagram account. Atticus was staggered by the number of followers he had amassed, but after reading the comments and realising that his photos might inspire others of his age group to follow suit and have an adventure, he was keen to add more.

Turning off the main road, Atticus drove carefully along a track until he came to the beach. A row of ancient cottages, their walls weathered by the salty sea air, came into view, and he thought of the generations of fishermen who'd lived there. Not unlike that of a sheep farmer on the Cumbrian fells, their coastal life must have been relatively simple.

The cottages were rustic, built of sturdy stone and weather-beaten wood. Rusting metal blinds covered many doorways, and paint-peeling wooden shutters were secured with heavy padlocks.

Atticus checked his watch. He was early but decided to find Britta's cottage to avoid being late. He parked the Fiat, and Ness hopped out.

Britta had told him that she lived in a cottage named Casita del Mar. *The Cottage by the Sea.* But as Atticus searched along the row, he wondered if he'd got it wrong. These buildings looked derelict. Surely no one lived here.

He considered going to the café and asking there. Stepping onto the sand, Atticus kept the cottages on his right while Ness ran towards the sea. From this side, he saw that the row was separated by wooden rails and trellis. To his surprise, each cottage seemed to have its own personality, some decorated with fishing nets or weathered buoys, with driftwood and seashells alongside planters of ornamental grasses. All had an expansive terrace area and steps leading down to the beach.

Halfway along, bunting fluttered from the framework of a pastel-painted cottage, where lanterns were strung along old wooden beams. Standing beside an easel, with sun-kissed blonde hair cascading over her shoulders, Britta gazed at a canvas.

Atticus saw that her dress – a soft, floaty fabric – wrapped gently around her slim frame, accentuating her curves. The delicate fabric fell lightly across long legs, the skin, a golden hue, suggesting days spent under the warm embrace of the sun.

He was mesmerised. There was a sense of raw beauty about Britta that belied her years. Bathed in the glow of the late afternoon sun, with her gaze fixed on her work, she carried herself with the vitality of a much younger woman. As he stared, Atticus felt a forgotten desire stir. A feeling he hadn't experienced in a long time.

Suddenly, turning from the canvas and showing no surprise at his presence, Britta looked directly at Atticus. In that moment, their eyes met, and both began to smile.

In the distance, the waves rolled towards the shore, and the sky was a perfect blue. Atticus felt a profound connection, as though he had a fleeting glimpse of something magical happening – like the promise of a new beginning, a spark of romance in the air. It was a feeling he couldn't ignore, one that told him this was more than just a casual date.

Ness began to bark and pounded along the beach.

'You're early,' Britta called out. 'Please, let me welcome you to Casita del Mar.'

Any nerves he'd felt suddenly vanished, and with confidence, Atticus strode across the sand and climbed the steps as Ness skidded to a halt beside him. 'The dog?' he asked, reaching for Ness's collar.

'Oh, she's fine. I have water for her,' Britta said, moving away from the easel and placing a dish on the floor of the terrace. Ness began to drink thirstily, then, as though she'd been there a thousand times before, lay down on a rug and closed her eyes.

'This is lovely,' Atticus said, admiring the comfortable outdoor seating where cushions were scattered haphazardly over a sofa-like swing, suspended by thick ropes from the ceiling. A brick-built oven doubled as a barbecue, alongside two rattan chairs and a table tucked under the trellis. Atticus imagined relaxing there, having a bite to eat while admiring the glorious view.

Britta's easel stood in the middle of the terrace.

'May I?' he asked.

Britta shrugged. 'Yes, of course, it's not very good.'

The canvas she was working on depicted soft washes of watercolour that blended into shades of sand and sea. Atticus could see that it was the view from Britta's cottage. The landscape rose in the middle ground, curving into the bay, revealing a village of whitewashed houses with terracotta roofs. In the distance, the buildings of Santa Pola perched along a rocky promontory.

'I think it's excellent,' he said. 'It must be wonderful to create something so beautiful.'

'Your comment is kind,' Britta replied. 'But it's not finished, and I seem to have lost my mojo.'

'What do you mean?' Atticus asked.

'I haven't painted for some time; the inspiration seems to have deserted me.' Britta sighed.

'Maybe you're overthinking it?'

Britta gave a small laugh. 'I think if I stare at the canvas anymore, I'll end up throwing it in the sea.'

'No, never do that. Perhaps you need to put it to one side for a while.'

Britta changed the subject. 'Would you like a glass of lemonade? I made it this morning.'

'Yes, I'd love some.'

She moved into the cottage, but Atticus hesitated to follow.

'Come through,' Britta called out, 'glasses are on the shelf.' She waved a hand in the direction of a kitchen and then disappeared through a door to a cellar.

As Atticus looked around, he was amazed. Far from being a derelict wreck, as observed from the track side of the cottage, the interior was sophisticated. Modern elegance met coastal charm as natural light filtered through open windows. Spacious, with oversized sofas and armchairs, it was decorated in neutral shades of soft ivory, sandy beige, and muted blues. Cushions and throws added splashes of vibrant colour. The floor was polished marble, covered in pretty rugs, and carefully placed mirrors reflected light, adding to the sense of space. The focal point was a fireplace with a wood-burning stove, surrounded by custom-built shelving filled with books and decorative objects.

But it was the artwork on the walls that caught Atticus's eye.

A vibrant sunset brightened one corner, while a morning mist over the shoreline gave an ethereal glow in another. A brightly coloured beach scene depicted swimmers and surfers catching waves, and tumultuous dark clouds hovered over a stormy sea on a canvas above the fire.

Atticus turned to see Britta as she reappeared. Barefoot and softly padding towards the kitchen, she held a bowl. Opening the door to a small fridge, she reached for a jug and, finding two glasses, added ice from the bowl and began to pour.

'Oh, I'm so sorry,' Atticus said. 'You asked me to find glasses.'

'It's okay,' Britta said, placing the fresh lemonade in his hand. 'Welcome.'

Atticus sipped the drink and wasn't surprised to find it tasted delicious. 'You're very talented,' he said. 'And you have a lovely home.'

'It's not how it looks from outside, eh?'

'No, I have to admit that the exterior is deceiving.'

'Most of these cottages have been in families for generations and are used in the summer months, then locked up all winter,' Britta began to explain. 'The exteriors are deliberately shabby. It puts intruders off.'

'But the inside is wonderful,' Atticus said, his eyes raking around the room.

'Yes, there is a cellar of the same size, with a comfortable space, a bathroom, a larder, and storage.'

'And upstairs?'

'Two bedrooms and another bathroom.'

'How long have you lived here?'

'For a year,' Britta said, 'but it's not mine. I rent it.'

'I see. You've made it homely, and the owner must be delighted.'

'He never visits.' She shrugged. 'He lives in Madrid, and his family isn't interested in the property. They are wealthy, and this area isn't upmarket enough for their taste. They have villas further south in La Manga and Marbella.' Britta reached for the jug and refreshed his glass. 'But I think the cottage is quite special.'

'So do I,' Atticus agreed. He wanted to tell Britta that he thought she was special too, but, instead, he followed her to the terrace.

'In the summer, the beach is busy, and the weather is very hot.' Britta stared out at the coastline. 'I like it,' she added.

'And the winter?'

'The Spanish say it is cold in this area, but the temperature is perfect for me. I swim every day.'

'Goodness, it must be warm.'

'It can be.'

'But you are Dutch,' Atticus said. 'What brought you to Spain?'

'Are we going out to eat?' Britta asked. 'If so, I need to change.'

Atticus sensed that Britta had avoided his question and, hoping he hadn't upset her, quickly said, 'Yes, there is a restaurant in Guardamar that has been recommended, but please, there is no need to change; you look lovely.'

'You're kind,' she smiled. 'Okay, but perhaps I should find some sandals.'

Atticus helped Britta carry her easel into the lounge, and she locked the cottage.

Moments later, they were heading along the beach track that led to the main road. As they drove past, Atticus commented on the multiple motorhomes parked in the wide laybys.

'Is it always so busy?' he asked.

'Yes, mostly with Germans who are touring for the winter months. It's a well-known place, and they stay for a few days because it is free.'

'No charge at all?'

'What would they be paying for? There's only a tarmac space and a nearby beach – no facilities.'

'Why would anyone park an expensive vehicle in a layby when there are sites with facilities nearby?'

'Not all the vehicles are expensive,' Britta added. 'Some are quite modest and old.'

Atticus began to chuckle. 'Like me,' he said. 'I must introduce you to Winnie; she's modest and old, too.'

Britta spun around. 'Winnie? Your wife?' she asked.

'Oh, goodness, no. I'm a widower, and Winnie is my camper van. She's an old VW Westfalia with several decades under her bonnet,' he said.

Britta laughed. 'Winnie sounds wonderful. I want to meet her.'

'I hope that you will,' Atticus said.

She wants to meet Winnie! He resisted the urge to reach out and take Britta's hand.

Arriving in Guardamar, Atticus carefully parked where Ruby had advised, then hurried to open the passenger door. He clipped a lead on Ness's collar and indicated that the restaurant was just over the road, by the beach. As they began to walk, Britta took his arm.

Suddenly, Atticus felt ten feet tall. The sun shone, the sky was blue, and he was out with a beautiful woman! Cumbria and the lonely fells felt a long way off.

Chapter Twenty-Two

At Casablanca, a charming server showed them to a table overlooking the beach. It was perfect, and Atticus was pleased that he'd phoned ahead and made a reservation.

'This is lovely,' Britta smiled as she placed a napkin on her knee and picked up a menu. 'I might have the mussels. They're harvested locally and should be good,' she said as she studied the choice of seafood, salads, and pasta.

Atticus was struggling not to stare. Britta's eyes were the most captivating shade of blue, and he almost had to pinch himself as he decided what he'd have to eat. They ordered a jug of sangria, and it arrived with a basket of oven-warm rolls, sides of aioli, and finely chopped tomatoes marinated with herbs.

'The food is delicious,' Atticus said as he copied Britta, spreading aioli on the bread and topping it with a spoonful of tomato. 'What is it?'

'Aioli is garlic, olive oil, and egg yolks. I often make it,' she explained. 'A Mediterranean diet is simple.'

'It's certainly very different from the stodge we eat at home,' Atticus remarked, thinking of the thick stews and pies he'd grown up with.

'In Holland, we eat a lot of dairy and bread, with cheese and meat,' Britta explained and sipped her sangria. 'Stamppot is popular too.'

'Stamppot?'

'It's made with mashed potato, vegetables, and smoked sausage.'

'Stamppot sounds delicious,' Atticus smiled. 'Your English is excellent. Did you learn it at school?'

'Yes, English is taught as a second language, and we are exposed to English media, with music, TV, and movies.' Britta's voice was soft, and Atticus liked that there was a trace of an accent.

'It makes me feel inadequate.' Atticus shook his head. 'I've never had any reason to learn languages, but I'm trying to learn a little Spanish.'

'I speak some Spanish. It's not too hard.'

Their appetisers arrived, and as they shared a dish of warm mussels in a white wine sauce, Atticus told Britta about his home and family.

'I never wanted the farm to change,' he said, 'but I lost all interest after Clara died, and Mungo seemed to take over.'

'Tell me about your wife.'

Atticus spoke of Clara, their happy marriage, and how he'd been in a rut for a long time after her death.

'You loved each other very much,' Britta smiled.

'Yes... we did.' Atticus suddenly felt guilty. He was discussing his marriage with a stranger and hoped that Clara would approve of his actions.

'But your son – he has done something good?' Britta asked. 'The farm is successful with all the changes, and this is best for the family?'

'Yes, I suppose it is, but I struggle with change.'

'But you are here. You have changed your life, and embarked on a great adventure by coming to the sunshine in another country. Was this such a hard thing to do?'

'No, when you put it like that, I suppose not, once I'd set my mind to it.'

'So, your family are happy now, and all is well.'

'Well, not all my family.' Atticus sighed and pushed his empty plate to one side. 'Mungo thinks I'm mad and have lost my marbles.'

'Your marbles are missing?' Britta looked puzzled. 'Is this a game?'

'No, sorry,' Atticus laughed. 'It's a silly English expression that means I've lost my mind.'

'Mungo is cross?'

'Yes, he thinks I am behaving badly here.'

'And are you?'

'No, I don't think so.' Atticus shook his head. 'I'm enjoying meeting new people and seeing different places. At the site, everyone is very friendly, and they ask me to their pitches for drinks and food.'

'That is good, but how does Mungo know what you do here?'

'Oh, he's seen my Instagram account.' Atticus reached out and poured more sangria into their glasses.

Britta thanked the server as the dishes were cleared. 'I don't have Instagram,' she said, 'but I know what it is. Please explain what you have done.'

'I foolishly thought that only my grandson Jake and my best friend Arthur had access to the account,' Atticus began. 'Jake set it up for me and called my account 'The Travelling Grandad'. Now, I realise that anyone can see my posts, and I seem to have gathered many followers.'

'What fun!' Britta clapped her hands. 'You have a collection of cyber friends!'

'Aye, something like that.'

Their main course arrived, and Britta spooned colourful salad, prawns, and spicy potatoes onto their plates, alongside lightly grilled halibut in a buttery sauce.

Deciding that he was talking too much, Atticus asked Britta about her life. She told him she had worked at the café for almost a year since arriving in Spain and finding the cottage. It suited her to have a modest income from the café, which allowed her time to paint on the rare occasion that inspiration struck.

'Have you family?' Atticus asked as he munched on the last of the potatoes.

'I was married,' she replied. 'I have no children.'

'You're a free spirit. Were you married for long?'

'Yes, too long. My husband wasn't a good man, and he...' Britta had finished her meal and dabbed at her mouth with her napkin. She thanked the server as the table was cleared. 'Let me say that he dominated me, and I had to get away.'

'I'm sorry to hear that,' Atticus said, not wanting to pry too deeply. 'Tell me about your art. Have you always painted?'

'I hadn't painted for years before I came here,' Britta said. 'It was a passion when I was younger, but life got in the way.'

'Do you want to talk about it?'

'Well, there's not much to tell.' Britta dismissed an offer of dessert and nodded when Atticus ordered coffee before continuing. 'I grew up on a farm in the countryside around Utrecht. We farmed wheat, barley, and maize. It was a smallholding, and, as an only child, my parents wanted me to marry a boy from a neighbouring farm.'

'But you wanted to paint?'

'Yes, and I worked hard to gain a place at the Rijksakademie, a renowned institution in Amsterdam that supports emerging artists through a residency program.' Their coffee arrived, and Britta smiled when she tasted the café Belmonte. 'I like this.'

'Me too,' Atticus agreed. 'But what did you do when you finished the program?'

'I was told I had talent and was even offered studio space in Amsterdam, close to the gallery where I'd managed to get a job.' Britta sighed. 'My parents objected; they didn't want me to work in the big city and they asked me to come home.' She continued, 'I went against them, and I loved my job and being with creatives, immersed in the art world. Every day was exciting, and I had the freedom to paint alongside others in the studio. But when my mother announced that she was dying, I had no choice but to return.'

'So, your mother died?'

'Oh no.' Britta shook her head and gazed thoughtfully out to the sea. 'Not for a long time, but she took to her bed to keep me there.'

Atticus struggled to fathom why a young, talented girl would stay in an environment she disliked when her dreams lay elsewhere. He thought of Mary and knew that wild horses would never have prevented his daughter from following her dream when she decided to stay in Ireland and marry Conor. As a parent, he would never have stopped her from doing so.

'You wonder why I stayed?' Britta asked, and when Atticus nodded, she continued. 'The boy on the neighbouring farm began to call, and soon we were dating. He said that if we married, he would let me paint to my heart's content.'

'So that pleased both you and your parents?'

'Not exactly. My mother had anxiety, an illness. She was, how do you say... hypo...chond...?'

'Hypochondriac,' Atticus helped.

'Yes, that. Then she really did become ill, and I nursed her until she died. My father seemed to give up on life. He died not long after.' Britta shrugged.

Atticus thought of his own circumstances and how he'd given up when Clara died. Listening to Britta, he silently thanked Mary, Jake, and Arthur for shaking him out of his self-imposed shell. Remembering his earlier guilt, he began to feel that Clara *would* approve of Britta now that he was getting to know her.

'I'm so sorry for the loss of your parents, but if you married, were you happy?'

Britta smiled. 'Well, I married the boy, and our farms became one.'

'Ah, and there wasn't a happy ending?' Atticus was anxious to hear about her husband.

Britta looked away and stared out at the sea again with a slight tilt of her head. Her gaze was unwavering, as though she was weighing up her answer. In the silence that enveloped them, neither spoke.

But suddenly, her expression softened, and her eyes swivelled to meet his own. She reached out, and her warm fingers stroked his. 'The happy ending?' she repeated, a gentle smile playing on her lips. 'That's a story for another day.'

Helping Britta into the car and securing Ness in the back seat, Atticus began the drive back to Britta's cottage.

'It's not too late,' Britta said as Atticus parked carefully. 'Would you like a nightcap before you return to the campsite?'

'Well, if you're sure...' he hesitated. 'That would be great.'

The evening air was warm as they walked toward the cottage. Britta removed her sandals as they stepped onto the beach, and Ness ran ahead. On the terrace, she lit the candles in the lanterns, and their light reflected pretty patterns on the whitewashed walls.

'Take a seat.' Britta smiled and pointed to the swing.

As they nestled into the soft cushions, they watched the moon, low in the sky, shimmer over the calm sea.

'I love sitting here, watching the beach at night,' Britta said as she sipped brandy and gazed out at a fishing boat, its distant light twinkling like a star against the backdrop of the oncoming darkness.

'It feels like time has stood still,' Atticus whispered. He felt like he hadn't a care in the world as he gently swayed with Britta beside him. Sated by excellent food and conversation, the effects of the brandy were mellowing.

'I wish I could bottle this moment,' he said, and as Britta lifted his arm and snuggled close, a tear welled in his eye and slid slowly down his cheek.

'What's wrong?' Britta whispered, placing a finger on the tear. 'Are you upset?'

Suddenly, feeling brave, Atticus kissed the top of her head.

'I haven't felt this happy for a very long time,' he replied. 'Perhaps I'm just a foolish old man.'

He turned to stare into her eyes, and when her lips touched his own, the kiss spoke volumes without a single word. Britta's touch was a light caress – intimate yet tender. When their eyes locked, Atticus felt as if he'd discovered a hidden treasure.

Was this the beginning of something beautiful? he asked himself.

Was it possible for him to feel such emotion later in life?

When they parted, Atticus stood up, reluctant to go but unwilling to outstay his welcome. His mind raced, but he smiled with relief when he felt Britta slip a note into his pocket.

'Take this,' she said. 'Call me.'

Britta watched as the man and dog descended the steps, their figures swallowed by the night.

The evening had been easy in a way she hadn't known in years. Being in the company of Atticus – talking and laughing – had been the most enjoyable few hours she could remember. For once, she hadn't felt like she was always glancing over her shoulder, waiting for something to go wrong.

As she turned to gather the empty glasses and blow out the candles, her heart gave a little lurch. *Could she really feel this way about someone she'd just met? And more importantly, could she allow herself to?* She'd given Atticus her number, hoping he would call, but a familiar unease hung thick in the air, as though the devil was dancing in the shadows at her door.

'Stop it!' she admonished as she secured the bolts into place. 'You're safe now. Don't let the past spoil the future.'

But as Britta climbed the stairs, the shadows stretched long across the whitewashed walls. No matter how much she told herself otherwise, she couldn't shake the feeling that some doors, once opened, never truly closed.

Chapter Twenty-Three

Life for Mary had become miserable. With the constant worry of Conor's potential affair, each morning started with a heavy heart as she forced a smile for the kids and began her daily routine. With persistent doubt and suspicion, Mary felt insecure as she searched for clues of his infidelity. Ordinary tasks were no longer straightforward, and she was on a mission, checking pockets and examining every item of Conor's clothing before tackling the mountain of washing and ironing produced by a family of six.

When Conor left for work, she stared as his car disappeared from the driveway, wondering where he was going and who he might be with. Was he phoning Lucinda to wish her good morning and whisper secret endearments?

The hours stretched endlessly, broken by occasional calls to Una, who told Mary to quell her anxiety and reassured her that she was probably just being silly. Una was convinced that Conor would never do anything to jeopardise his family and business, despite Mary's fears. But Mary knew that Una was wrapped up in her own life, with a husband who spent too much time in the pub and a household full of stroppy teenagers.

Mary's only friend appeared to be the cake tin.

'If I gorge any more, I'll have to file for a restraining order,' she told herself each time the tin lured her closer.

Other than Una, Mary's circle of friends no longer felt close, and with the kids occupying most of her time, she'd drifted away over recent months. At the Ladies' Lunch Club, any confidences she might share with the others, or requests for their emotional help, would go from classified to front-page news in a flash, and soon filter through to Lucinda. Mary felt low and didn't want to discuss her feelings, knowing that juicy gossip among the ladies was an Olympic sport.

With the kids at school and Mum's taxi hard at work, Mary felt as though the world was going on without her. Everyone was submerged in their own lives while she drowned in hers. Days had passed since the Halloween party, but Ruari's comment remained a persistent itch.

The thought of her husband spending time at Creek House refused to go away. Any attempt to discuss the subject with Conor was met with eye-rolling and a heavy sigh, as though she were the most tiresome person alive.

'Mary, for God's sake, why do you go on and on?' Conor snapped one afternoon when he'd called home to collect his golf clubs.

'I can't help it,' she persisted, her throat tight. 'You're

never at home, and I heard Ruari say that he saw you at Lucinda's home.'

'Hah! You know what they say about eavesdropping, and you've completely misinterpreted that conversation.' Conor stomped around the kitchen, his hands thrust deep in his pockets. 'You're like a desperate detective,' he said, his voice sharp with irritation. 'Yes, it's true. I *once* visited Creek House to collect paperwork for a property being co-sold by our businesses. And guess what? Your troublemaking friend was valeting one of Lucinda's cars. Ruari is not to be trusted, and you are a fool to listen to anything he says!'

Conor bristled with barely contained anger and Mary winced as he slammed the kitchen door behind him. The walls shook and the sting of his words cut deep, leaving her feeling humiliated.

It was clear to Mary now that Conor saw her as nothing more than a foolish, insecure woman. '*Don't you see how busy I am providing for this family?*' he would ask. '*Don't you understand how tired I am after a long day, with my remaining energy spent on the children?*'

Later that evening, as they prepared for bed, Conor had said surely she had better things to do than mistrust her husband, that he only ever had his family's best interests at heart.

He always had all the answers, and with no hard evidence to challenge him, Mary found herself giving in once again.

At night, if they made love, she was aware of the physical closeness they shared in the moment, but every touch felt tainted by betrayal. *Was his affection genuine, or was it merely a cover-up to conceal his affair?* Her trust was crumbling, and suspicion enveloped her in a cloud of confusion.

That morning, as she stood alone in the house, Mary wondered where her marriage was heading. After breakfast, she followed Conor into the hallway and queried when he'd be home. Unable to stop herself, she asked if his meetings would be held at Creek House that day – and whether the lovely Lucinda would be in attendance.

She regretted the words as soon as they left her lips.

Conor sighed and scowled. 'You can't let it go, can you?' he'd said as he shrugged his arms into a cashmere coat and picked up his document case. 'You are obsessed with something that simply isn't true.' He shook his head and issued a parting shot. 'For your information, I shall be in the office all day. If you spent as much time on yourself as you do doubting me, I'd have the wife I married – not the cumbersome woman you've become.'

Cumbersome? Bullseye! Conor had hit his target, and Mary cringed as the door slammed behind him.

'What's dad getting his boxers in a bunch for?' Caitlin asked as she joined Mary in the hall. 'He's always got a bee in his bonnet these days,' she added, reaching into the cloakroom to find her coat.

'Oh, it's nothing, just work,' Mary replied. 'Your dad has a lot on.'

Pasting on a smile, she returned to the kitchen to chivvy Maeve, Finn, and Declan. 'Come on, you lot,' Mary said, reaching for bags and lunch boxes. 'You're going to be late for school.'

The clock in the kitchen at Belvedere House inched towards noon. Mary raced through her chores and now stood by the patio windows, staring out at a kaleidoscope of autumn colours, where trees swayed in the chilly breeze. Their amber and gold leaves fell lightly to the ground. Mary could almost smell the salty tang of the sea drifting over the Old Head of Kindale in the distance. It had carried into the garden, where the large lawn was enclosed by rustic stone walls, and clusters of late-blooming flowers peeped out from deep borders, their petals proud, as though reluctant to bid farewell to the fading year.

How beautiful it is, Mary thought as she slouched against the glass.

She remembered the pleasure she'd shared with Conor when the house had been built, and they'd painstakingly planned their garden. In one corner, Conor had designed a play area for the children, with a treehouse perched above a swing hanging from an oak tree, alongside a slide and climbing frame. Opposite lay beds of roses, and Mary thought of the multiple blooms in summer as bees buzzed from flower to flower. Benches were placed in sunny spots, and comfortable garden furniture sat beneath winter covers.

Suddenly, the wind lashed with a sharp gust, and a branch scratched across the window. It caught Mary off guard, as though alerting her to the reality of her situation.

'Pull yourself together!' Mary chided herself. Thrusting out her chin, she drew herself up to full height, then placed her hands on her hips. *Are you really prepared to give this all up?*

If Conor *was* telling the truth, she conceded, she vowed at that moment to believe him. There had to be trust in their relationship.

Turning away from the garden, Mary suddenly decided that she would surprise Conor. With the kids at school, the daily mountain of laundry chugging in the machine, dinner prepared, and an hour or two to spare before the school run, she realised it had been months since they'd had lunch together – he'd told her he would be in the office all day.

If Conor said nothing was going on with Lucinda, Mary thought as she raced around pulling a picnic lunch together, *she had to believe him and get on with 'making the most of their marriage'* – words that Una had repeatedly spoken. Una had told Mary that it was futile to feel sorry for herself and that she should be putting in the effort to make things work instead.

Roisin was due at any time, and Mary wanted to avoid her. If Ruari let slip the incident at Declan's party, she didn't want to face any awkward questions. Gossip was Roisin's original social network, which she spread while going about her cleaning duties.

Hurrying upstairs, Mary stood in front of a mirror and studied her waistline. Her leggings did little to flatten the tummy, which seemed to have risen faster than the balloons at Declan's party. Still, as she examined her face, Mary thought that the rest of her wasn't so bad. Her hair was silky and thick, with rich curls that flattered. Thanks to the glycolic acid oxygen peel by the beautician at Gaelic Glow, which promised to resurface and brighten, her skin shone.

The peel had shed more layers of skin than a snake, and her current glow was almost youthful in a certain light.

She chose the most flattering outfit she could find: designer jeans, a navy T-shirt, and a white jacket edged in faux fur. Leather ankle boots and a matching bag topped it off. As she stared at her reflection, Mary touched her cheeks as if to smooth away the traces of too many restless nights and glasses of wine.

'I could carry my shopping in those bags,' she muttered, pulling a face as she stroked another layer of concealer over the dark circles beneath her eyes. Adding bright lipstick, a spray of perfume, and fluffing out her hair, she raced down the stairs.

'Rats!' Mary exclaimed, almost tripping over Roisin, who was kneeling in the hallway. 'You're early.' Mary felt the woman's eyes study her from head to toe.

'Are you going out?' Roisin asked, stating the obvious as she ran a feather duster along a skirting board and nodded to the picnic basket by the door.

'Yes,' Mary said, picking up her car keys. 'If you could give Finn's room an extra going over today,' she added, knowing that the nine-year-old's chaotic kingdom was a masterpiece of messiness. It would take more than a duster to bring order to Finn's untidiness.

'If you really think it's necessary,' Roisin scowled.

'I do.' Mary forced a smile, grrabbed her basket, and opened the front door. 'I've left your money on the kitchen table,' she said. 'Enjoy your day.'

Chapter Twenty-Four

Murphy's Auctioneers was in the centre of Kindale. Amidst the quaint streets and historic charm, the modern estate agency was a beacon of contemporary sophistication.

We've come a long way, Mary thought as she parked in a reserved space and reached for the picnic basket. She stared at the sleek glass frontage and remembered the days when they'd had little more than cupboard space squeezed between a butcher and an ironmonger. Happy days when each new listing felt like a trophy and a sale as though they'd struck gold. With Mary glued to the phone, chasing every lead, and Conor dreaming up inventive ways of marketing his fledgling business, they'd been like kids in a candy shop, excited by everything that ended up on their books.

Although Conor had started the business in his sole name, Mary had often thought it would be advisable to have her name on the paperwork too. Mungo, always worried about the future, had urged her to make it official to protect her and the children should anything happen. Conor had laughed off Mungo's suggestion, assuring Mary that if he were to suddenly die, she'd get the lot as his wife. But family life had since taken over, and as she'd eased away from work, Mary had forgotten all about Mungo's concern.

Four children were a full-time job.

As she opened the door and stepped into the office, Mary was distracted by the warm glow of designer lighting. It illuminated the reception area and the modern furnishings, which provided both style and comfort. She looked around at the space she'd so carefully redesigned shortly before Finn was born. It was wearing well. High-tech interactive screens showcased virtual tours and 3D images of each property listing, allowing clients to immerse themselves in homes without needing to step inside.

The girl on reception was new. Mary didn't recognise her and wondered when this young face had joined the company, and why Conor hadn't mentioned that Linda – a lovely woman who'd been with them for years – had moved on.

'Good morning, can I help you?' the girl asked.

'I'm here to see my husband,' Mary replied, then began making her way toward Conor's office, which lay at the top of an open-plan staircase, behind a glass door. She waved at the staff working behind low partitions, who looked up with expressions filled with curiosity.

'I beg your pardon?' the girl asked, appearing puzzled and chasing after her.

'I'm Mary Murphy, Conor's wife. I'm sorry, but I don't know your name.'

'Oh...' the girl hesitated, then began fiddling with her necklace. 'I'm afraid Mr Murphy is in a meeting and can't be disturbed.'

'Don't worry, whatever your name is, he'll disturb his meeting for me.'

Mary swept up the stairs, and when she reached the door, she carefully balanced her basket and turned the handle. Stepping cautiously so as not to surprise her husband and his client, she opened the door and walked in.

To her surprise, Conor's office was empty. *The meeting must have finished,* Mary thought, just as she heard the sound of a sink flushing. Conor was in the bathroom.

Placing her basket on a chair, she began to unpack its contents onto the corner of his desk. She smiled as she unwrapped his favourite cheesy quiche and a pot of caramelised onions.

Just then, Mary heard the bathroom door open and turned to greet her husband. 'Surprise!' she called out.

The sight that greeted her was not that of an overworked husband, harried from a meeting, but a red-faced Lucinda, her blouse half undone as she zipped up the side of her skirt. Taking a step back, Lucinda almost fell into Conor, who was buttoning his cotton Oxford shirt.

'Oh,' Lucinda said, an eyebrow raised and an amused smirk crossing her ruby-red lips. 'I didn't realise we'd ordered room service.'

Mary wasn't clear on her exact words as she flung caramelised onions over her enemy's immaculate hair.

Conor raced forward, and despite his acrobatic twists and turns, he couldn't avoid the impact of a whole cheesy quiche, which landed slapstick-style on his open-mouthed face. Unable to speak, he began to choke on Mary's perfect pastry.

Mary followed up her dramatic display of culinary vengeance with two tubs of creamy coleslaw, which caught both cheaters in the chest. Grabbing more food projectiles, Mary's aim was sharp. Conor, ungluing cheese from his eyes, hurriedly bustled Lucinda back into the bathroom and locked the door.

'There's your room service!' Mary yelled as she landed a custard slice on the door's smooth wooden surface and watched a sluggish trail of thick, creamy rivulets descend.

Conor's words sang like a chorus in her head as she theatrically swept past *whatever-her-name-is* from reception, who now stood alongside a group of highly bemused staff assembled on the stairs.

'*You are obsessed with something that simply isn't true*,' he'd lied.

As Mary ran down the stairs past the staff and marched out of the office, she thought she heard a ripple of applause and one or two cries of 'Bravo!'

Did they all know? she questioned, thrusting her car into gear and racing away from the building. A cyclone of emotion was whirling through Mary's body, unleashing a fury that threatened to blind her as she tried to focus on the road and stay calm. Her heart was pounding, each beat a punch as a tidal wave of anger crashed over her.

'How bloody dare he!' she screamed when Kindale

began to fade, and the coast road lay ahead. 'Lies and more bloody lies!' Mary's resentment bubbled in her throat, and for a moment, she thought she might be sick. She dialled Una's number, desperate to talk to her friend but the call went to voicemail and Mary hung up.

A beach came into view, and biting her lip to stem tears, Mary turned off the road and pulled into a space overlooking the sea. Silencing the engine, her hands trembled as she bunched them into fists, the nails dagger-like on her skin.

'You are a lying, deceiving husband,' Mary muttered, staring out to sea. 'Conor, you're a coward!'

Her humiliation was complete as the discovery hit her like a freight train, and she wondered what the hell she was going to do. They had four kids who were about to find out that their home life was broken, and their daddy didn't want Mummy anymore.

'Oh God,' Mary cried. *How on earth was she to live with the shame?* But the most profound pain was that Conor didn't love her, and he'd repeatedly lied.

His love was now for Lucinda.

Mary stepped out of the car and began to walk along the windswept shore. A squall whipped her hair into a mess that mirrored her feelings, and salty spray stung her cheeks. Tears blurred her vision as she tried to make sense of the betrayal that had shattered her world. At that moment, she had no one to turn to and longed for Atticus's strong arms to wrap her in his warm, fatherly embrace and tell her that it would all be alright.

But her dad was in another country, embarking on a

new phase. How could she burden him when he'd only just gotten his mojo back? She couldn't talk to Mungo and knew that her brother had little time for Conor and would probably race over the water, ready to kill his unfaithful brother-in-law. And that would serve no purpose other than to cause distress for the kids.

This was one battle she had to solve on her own.

Mary shivered and turned away from the sea. She felt cold all over and rubbed at her arms. Somehow, she had to find the strength to chart a new course, but at that moment, as her phone began to ring, all Mary wanted to do was curl up in a ball and sob. Reaching into her pocket, she stared at the screen.

Conor.

'Go to hell!' Mary yelled, then pressed disconnect.

Ahead, waves crashed, and Mary was tempted to move forward and keep walking. To let her body be carried by the sea's deep current, away from the pain. Like the turmoil of the water, her emotions were all over the place, but Mary knew that she had to face the situation and somehow emerge still standing.

Resisting the urge to lash out and kick at the pebbles on the beach, Mary screamed into the wind. 'Damn you, Conor. I gave up my career to have your children, and in return, I get a husband who treats me like a housekeeper and a pile of laundry that never bloody ends!'

Mary folded her arms and thought of the time when she'd been a woman running a business with a title that didn't involve the word 'mammy'. She'd swapped the cut and thrust of commerce for toddler tantrums and ungrateful teens.

Reaching down to pick up a pebble, Mary hurled it into the sea.

A sharp gust almost knocked her sideways, and staggering, she cursed. 'I may have given up my career and my waistline, but just you bloody wait, Conor Murphy!' she yelled. 'You might not appreciate me, but I won't go down without a fight!'

Mary closed her eyes as spray dampened her skin, and her children's faces appeared. Her four beating hearts were waiting for their mammy, and suddenly, Mary knew that life had to carry on. Unlike their father, she wouldn't let them down.

'I can do this,' Mary told herself, repeating the words as she opened her eyes. Biting her lip and flexing her fingers, she drew in a deep breath and breathed out very slowly.

Turning away from the rhythmic crash of waves, Mary climbed into her car.

It was almost time to pick the kids up from their schools, and if she didn't put her foot down, she'd be late. Glancing in the mirror, she attempted to straighten her hair. Somehow, she mustn't appear upset. Reaching for her lipstick, she smoothed the gloss evenly. The kids mustn't know that anything was wrong. She needed time to think about their future and was determined that she wouldn't let her children down.

'Not like my scumbag, pig of a husband!' she whispered. Sitting upright, Mary gripped the wheel tightly and set off.

Chapter Twenty-Five

A new week began at Solma Vacaciones. With the sun rising above caravans and motorhomes, there was a gentle rustle of palm trees and the chirping of birds as campers lifted their sleepy heads and set about their day. The housekeeping team was riding on buggies stacked high with cleaning products and tools, ready to freshen the facilities. They called out cheery good mornings to the campers out early, walking their dogs, jogging, or simply enjoying the freshness of the morning. In the supermarket, the aroma of freshly baked bread and pastries drifted over the site, encouraging guests to purchase crusty breakfast baguettes and buttery croissants.

Atticus, back from his preamble with Ness, had already brushed the overnight fallen leaves and windblown sand from his pitch. Now he was making a start on Winnie's windows, and when he was confident that they gleamed as brightly as her bodywork, he set to work on the awning, wiping down the table and chairs.

'Cooee!' a voice called. 'Someone's up early!' In a fluffy dressing gown with old-fashioned rollers tucked under a plastic cap covering her hair, Cheryl shuffled towards the awning in pink fluffy mules.

Atticus smiled as she approached.

'Couldn't you sleep, or didn't you come home?' Cheryl asked. She pulled out a chair and plopped her body down without waiting to be asked.

'Good morning,' Atticus said. 'Good to see you, can I tempt you with a coffee?'

'Yes, that would be lovely, and you can tell me all about your date.' Cheryl loosened the belt on her gown, revealing a shortie nightie and, kicking off her mules, stretched out her plump legs. Ness lay down beside her, and she gently stroked the dog's head. 'I take it that things went well?' She raised an eyebrow as Atticus handed her a mug of milky coffee. 'You didn't come back to the pool party, and it went on till very late.'

'I had a great time,' Atticus said, sitting down, too. 'Casablanca was the perfect choice, so thanks to you and Ruby for the recommendation.' He took a sip of coffee. 'We even went for a paddle on the beach after our meal. The car was great, and I enjoyed driving it.'

'Yes, yes.' Cheryl rolled her eyes. 'But how did you get on with Britta?'

'She's lovely,' he replied. 'Very special.'

'I don't know, you men!' Cheryl tapped her fingers on the table. 'It's like pulling teeth.' She sat forward. 'Tell me what her home is like, what you talked about, and if you're seeing her again. Ruby and I want all the gossip.'

Atticus felt like a teenager being interrogated by his mother. Cheryl's rollers began to bounce, and he smiled as the cap slipped over her forehead. Deciding to put her out of her misery, he began.

'Her home is comfortable,' he said.

'Those cottages don't look like much from the outside.'

'No, they don't, but inside it's a complete contrast, and I liked it.' Atticus remembered the artwork and tasteful furnishings and described Britta's home in detail.

'What's her background?' Cheryl asked. 'Married? Kids?'

'She's been married and there are no children, and she grew up on a farm near Utrecht.'

'Sounds a bit of a mystery, but then folk come to Spain for all sorts of reasons, not always because of the weather.' Cheryl drained her coffee and slipped her shoulders out of her gown. 'Phew, it's warming up already. My head thinks it's in a sauna,' she said, pulling off her plastic cap. 'Have you made another date?'

Atticus leaned back in his chair. He stretched out his legs and smiled, his expression almost smug. 'Yes,' he said, 'I *will* be seeing her again.'

The memory of Britta was like a warm, comforting hug – a feeling he wanted to cling to. Wriggling his fingers in his pocket, he felt her folded note and wondered when he should call her. He knew she was working that morning. *Should he wait until her shift ended, or would that seem too eager?* He had no idea how these things played out and didn't want to bombard Britta and seem overly keen.

'You look like the cat that's got the cream,' Cheryl said. 'I take it that you had a late night?'

'Not too late.' Atticus reached for his coffee. *Should he tell Cheryl how he felt and perhaps ask for her advice?* But before he could voice his uncertainty, he felt Cheryl gently pat his arm.

'I think Cupid has fired a rocket launcher,' she chuckled. 'Your face says it all – and now you haven't a clue how to handle things?'

Atticus breathed a sigh of relief. He stared at Cheryl and saw that she had a knowing gleam in her eye.

'It was just the same when I fell for Ruby,' Cheryl said. 'Never mind any of that slow-burner stuff. When the arrow strikes, there's little you can do about it.'

'I can't tell you how happy I am,' Atticus said. 'But I almost feel guilty for feeling this way.'

'Guilty about your wife?' Cheryl asked.

'Yes, in truth, guilty that I can feel happy again when Clara had her happiness cut short.'

'You mustn't feel guilty for being happy,' Cheryl shrugged. 'Love is a self-indulgent thing. If Clara was anything like the woman you say she was, I know she would be happy for you and urge you on.'

'But what if Britta doesn't feel the same way?'

'Now you're adding hurdles when the path is currently clear. I'd say she is probably smiling at the customers in the café this morning just as much as you are sitting here smiling at me.'

Atticus stared at Cheryl. She'd voiced his exact feelings

about Britta. *Was it so obvious? Did he wear a sign that announced his newfound joy?*

'But what do I do now? I've no experience. It's been decades since I dated, and I feel like a teenager again.' Atticus frowned. 'I don't want to get this wrong.'

Cheryl nodded. 'Why not drop her a text in a bit and say you had a lovely evening?' she suggested. 'Ask if she might be around if you give her a call later?'

'Okay, good idea.'

But before Atticus could reach for his phone, Cheryl patted his arm again.

'A word of advice,' she said. 'Be a bit guarded with Mungo. From what you've told us about your son and his thoughts on your trip, he might not be as thrilled as you are that you've suddenly fallen head over heels.'

'I don't care what Mungo thinks,' Atticus said.

'Aye, you say that now, but he is family after all,' Cheryl warned. 'Tread carefully, that's all I'm saying.'

Atticus was about to make more coffee when Erik appeared. He'd been on his usual morning run and was wearing jogging gear, with a towel resting on his athletic shoulders.

'Hey, Lover Boy!' Erik called out. 'How was your date?'

Erik leaned in to kiss Cheryl as Ness rolled over and held up a paw. With a smile, Erik rubbed the dog's tummy and then pulled up a chair.

Atticus wondered if the whole campsite would be stopping by to check on his love life, and seeing Erik make himself comfortable, he knew that the question couldn't be avoided.

'Coffee?' Atticus asked.

'Strong and black, just like me,' Erik replied, giving Cheryl a wink. 'Now let's hear all about it...'

In the office at Barn Hill Farm, Mungo stared at the Instagram account on his phone. The Travelling Grandad had clocked up considerably more followers – now over fifteen thousand. By the looks of things, comments were coming in thick and fast as the latest posts went viral.

'More from the Costas?' Ali cheerfully asked as she sat at her desk and watched her boss's expression change from curiosity to astonishment, then anger.

'I can't believe it,' Mungo said and shook his head, his eyes never leaving the screen. 'He's dining out with a woman and has posted a dozen selfie photos of a blonde sharing a bowl of mussels. He's even recorded a video of the two of them paddling in the sea.'

'Sounds like he's having a great time,' Ali commented, thinking that heading to Spain was the best possible move Atticus could have made. She wouldn't mind a bit of sun, sea, and whatever else Atticus was having.

'He's making a complete fool of himself,' Mungo said, slamming the phone down. 'This woman looks years younger and is bound to be after his money. Why on earth would she have reason to be with him?'

'To enjoy his company?' Ali asked, silently thinking that if an attractive silver fox like Atticus wanted to spend time with this woman, she would have to be insane or blind to turn him down.

But Mungo ignored the comment. 'God knows where he's picked her up from. I can't imagine what my mother would think.'

Ali was about to say Clara was probably punching the air with delight but knew that would only infuriate her boss. 'Maybe you should stop following him for a while?' Ali suggested.

'And see our inheritance whistle into a Spanish wind with some woman he's only known for five minutes?'

Ali stared at Mungo, who was immersed again in the images on his phone. *So that was what it was all about...* she thought. Mungo was worried about his inheritance. It wasn't the thought of his father enjoying himself so much as the possibility that Atticus might meet someone, fall in love, and even remarry.

Ali smiled. Stranger things have happened, and folk who find themselves single in the later years of their lives are often lonely and want to find a partner to share the final chapter. Being aware of the legalities surrounding the Arnott family, Ali knew that Atticus's name was on the business alongside Mungo and Mary, which encompassed the whole farm. If Atticus died, everything would go to his children, but if Atticus remarried, Ali knew that his share, by law, would go to his wife unless they had a premarital agreement. There was no current clause in the will to stop this, as no one ever envisaged Atticus remarrying.

Ali swivelled in her chair and turned to face her

computer. Mungo was still cursing his father, and Ali wondered why offspring never saw their parents as the rest of the world saw them. Mungo was preoccupied with his own life and business, and Ali knew that he thought Atticus was old, uninterested in their lives, and now, an embarrassment.

Over time, through conversations with Helen over coffee in the village or during evenings at the local Women's Institute, Ali had come to understand the depth of Atticus's devotion. Helen spoke of her father-in-law with fondness and admiration, knowing how tirelessly he must have worked to provide for his family and ensure they had a comfortable home and a good education. Ali wondered if Mungo ever thought of the grief that consumed Atticus when Clara died, and the unbearable loss when he parted with his precious herd.

What a shame Mungo doesn't stop and smell the roses, she thought. Only then would he see that his dad was happy, not a burden to his family, and enjoying his life for the first time in years.

The phone suddenly rang, and Ali picked it up. 'Barn Hill Farm, Ali speaking. How may I help you?' she said. But as she half-listened to the caller, she reached for a pen and made a note on her pad:

Open Instagram account today & follow The Travelling Grandad.

Chapter Twenty-Six

Three weeks had passed since Mary learnt the truth about Conor and his relationship with Lucinda. Three nightmare weeks, where Mary barely knew one day from another as she struggled to come to terms with her husband's infidelity while caring for her children.

Initially, after the office incident, Conor didn't come home. He'd told Mary to tell the children he was on a business trip, adding that he needed time to 'sort his head out'.

Mary thought that a good punch in the jaw might make Conor see some sense, but with his refusal to take her calls, she was at a loss as to what to do. When he returned a week later, he moved into the spare bedroom and wouldn't entertain any conversation with Mary – not even in whispers behind closed doors.

'You have to let me come to terms with things while I decide what I want,' Conor selfishly told her as they crept around the children, each trying to mask their feelings and not cause concern.

'You've had three bloody weeks!' Mary retorted. 'If you don't sort yourself out soon, I'll sit the kids down and tell them we're divorcing.'

'I promise I'll sort things out by Christmas,' was all Conor would say.

Turning away from an angry Mary, he buried himself in the TV and games room with the children whenever he was at home.

In truth, Mary barely knew what she wanted anymore. Conor had made a laughingstock of her at the office, and, for fear of gossip, she hadn't had the nerve to show her face at the Ladies' Lunch Club at the golf club. Preferring to keep well clear of the gym in case she ran into Lucinda, Mary didn't want the local paper to run a headline: '*Murdered with a Kettlebell!*' if they met. But the way she was feeling, nothing would have given Mary more pleasure than to throw a steel ball at Lucinda and wipe the smug smile off her face.

Una's suggestions varied from cutting up Conor's boxers and socks to placing a billboard in Kindale with Conor's image that read: *Missing! Conor 'Cheating' Murphy – If found, please return to reality!*

Mary was at a loss. *If Conor still wanted to be married, should he stay on the condition that he had nothing further to do with Lucinda? Did she want her marriage to work, and would she ever be able to trust Conor again?*

In her heart, Mary knew that she still loved him. *He was the father of her kids, for goodness' sake, but could she live with the shame? And would the children soon learn of their father's affair through the school grapevine? What if*

Conor really wanted out? What would she do then? Could she embrace being a part-time parent and sharing custody?

Mary felt certain Conor would fight to see his children as often as possible, but she knew that their parting would break the children's hearts. Declan and Finn were too young to have their little lives in turmoil, and Maeve and Caitlin's teenage hormones were like a roller coaster – up and down, unpredictable, intense, and at times overwhelming.

Putting her feelings aside, Mary couldn't imagine that Conor would do this to his children. *What was more important: life with Lucinda or his family?*

Mary could barely think straight. She changed her mind by the hour.

Cursing him one moment, then crying with grief for her loss the next. Days and nights merged into one as she kept busy, going through life's motions – running around after the kids, fetching and carrying them in the car, and turning up at events, sports matches, and after-school classes – while all the time her heart felt like it had cracked into a thousand unhappy pieces as her world turned upside down.

Large glasses of wine didn't help but, for a while, dulled her feelings, and Mary felt powerless as her self-control slipped away. Reaching constantly for the comfort of the biscuit tin, she survived on custard creams.

Most days, she thought of her dad, and when she had a spare moment, she curled up with a cosy blanket in her chair by the window to flick through his Instagram account, which now had over thirty thousand followers. He was always out and about, discovering and photographing the delights of Spain. The Travelling Grandad, an inspiration to so many, had become quite the travel guide.

One day, he might be perched on Mount Benacantil at Santa Bárbara Castle in Alicante, posting images of the historic fortress and panoramic views of the city and the Mediterranean Sea. The next, he could be at the fascinating Cuevas de los Rosales, making video reels of the hidden underground gem, a place that seems to be home to unique crafts and artists.

'You're quite the traveller,' Mary whispered.

Mary continued to study the photos and could see that a blonde woman often appeared in the images. *Had her dad fallen in love?* The woman was attractive and probably younger than Atticus by a few years.

'Don't get hurt, Dad,' Mary said, gently tracing his handsome face on the screen with her finger as he smiled into the lens.

Her brother's words rang loud in her ears. Only last night, Mungo had ranted and raved that their father was making a fool of himself and was being taken for a ride. 'If they weren't all careful, he'll make the mistake of marrying this minx, and where would the family be then?' In Mungo's estimation, it would all come to a sticky end.

In their text messages, Atticus told Mary that the woman was called Britta. She was Dutch and lived in a little cottage on the beach. Britta was a talented artist who worked in the beach café.

'Heavens, it sounds like a Netflix romcom,' Mary said

when they spoke. 'Struggling artist meets wealthy older man and falls in love.'

She'd laughed with her dad at the time, but on reflection, Mary realised that Atticus's situation was exactly as Mungo described: a younger, possibly impoverished woman stealing the heart of an older, well-off man. Mary didn't have the energy to argue with her brother, and since Mungo never asked, she hadn't told him about her marital problems with Conor either.

But *if* things worked out between her and Conor, Mungo need never know that her marriage was crumbling or that her whole world felt as though it were falling apart.

Forcing herself to be cheery when she spoke to her dad, she didn't want to burst the happiness bubble that Atticus was enjoying. If things with Britta did go suddenly wrong, there would be plenty of time for discussion when Mary knew what she was dealing with.

'I've enough problems of my own,' she sighed as she stared out the window. The garden was under assault from an oncoming storm, and once-vibrant plants were now bedraggled, their leaves strewn across the muddy path like confetti from a forgotten celebration. The overcast sky was as gloomy as Mary felt, and the howling wind seemed to echo her pain.

'Good luck, Dad,' she whispered, placing her phone in her pocket and casting her blanket aside in preparation for the school run. 'At least someone is having the time of their life.'

In the shed at the bottom of the garden at Shirlarth Cottage, Arthur, cosy in his bob hat and scarf, sat in his rocking chair beside a stack of carefully packed boxes. Standing nearby, with his laptop open on Atticus's Instagram page, Jake reached for a kettle and began to make tea. Outside, the wind howled, shaking the flimsy walls and sending shivers through the wooden planks. With each gust, the old shed creaked and groaned in protest, while rain beat against the roof.

'I feel like we're in a ship, navigating a stormy sea,' Jake said as he poured boiling water on tea bags in two chipped mugs. 'Each gust is trying to drown us.'

'You watch too much online nonsense,' Arthur replied. 'With your imagination, you should be writing books.' He nodded as Jake held up a bag of crusty sugar. 'Three lumps before the milk.'

Stirring his tea, Arthur smiled. He loved the smell of damp wood and earth, mingling with a faint scent of rusting metal and aged compost. He enjoyed the cosiness of his shed, where the power of nature outside could be observed from a safe distance.

'So, what's in all the boxes, and what do you want me to do?' Jake asked.

'You'll find Shirley's Christmas gnomes,' Arthur replied. 'It's time for the little folk to come out of hibernation and make a display on the driveway and in the porch.'

Jake lifted the top off a box and peered in. Removing a layer of newspaper, he winced when he caught sight of a line of pint-sized objects. 'What do you want me to do with them?' he asked, staring at mismatched outfits, bright red hats with oversized pom-poms, and clashing plaid shirts. Their rosy cheeks and glaring eyes looked scary, and Jake stepped back.

'Check 'em over for chips and cracks, and maybe perk one or two up with a touch of paint.'

Jake wasn't sure he wanted to fiddle about with the multiple stripy trousers and curled-up shoes that tinkled with bells. Still, he'd give the bushy beards a quick coat of white gloss and hope for the best.

As Jake got to work, Arthur reached for the laptop and began scrolling through Atticus's Instagram posts. 'What do these signs on his pictures mean?' he asked as he scowled at the array of symbols followed by names.

'Grandad is tagging places that he visits,' Jake said. He reached for a paintbrush and set to work on a faded beard surrounding an upturned nose.

'Eh?' Arthur looked puzzled. 'What's the point of that?' He stared at @alicante_city.

'If the place gets lots of hits, Grandad might get paid.'

'But he doesn't need any money?'

'He's probably doing it to bring business to the places he's visiting.'

'Decent of him,' Arthur agreed.

'Uncle Arthur,' – Jake paused in his painting – 'do you think Grandad has a girlfriend?'

'Yes, lad, of course he has,' Arthur nodded. 'You can see her in some of the photos.' Arthur thought of a recent call with Atticus, where he'd called his friend a dark horse and a lucky devil. 'Her name is Britta, and she's Dutch.'

'Dad says she's after Grandad's money; I overheard him

banging on to mum about it.' Jake finished the gnome's beard and went on to the next.

'You mustn't listen to other people's conversations, and if you have any questions, think about asking your grandad. He'll always give you a straight answer.'

'Alright. I suppose it *would* be okay to have a new grandma though.'

Arthur stared at the images of Britta and thought that his mate was currently the luckiest man in Spain. Life on the Costas was sunny and bright, unlike the damp, dark days and persistent Cumbrian chill that seeped into Arthur's bones and made him feel every day of his increasing years.

Turning to Jake, he asked, 'How are you getting on with Mistletoe Mike?'

'He's finished. I'm on Holly Harry, then Tinsel Tina and Jingle Julie...'

Arthur looked puzzled. 'I don't remember Tinsel Tina and Jingle Julie having beards?'

Jake smiled, a mischievous glint in his eye. 'They have now,' he replied.

Chapter Twenty-Seven

In what now seemed like the autumn of his life, Atticus felt an unexpected happiness, heightened by Britta. Their blossoming love was enhanced by journeys to new places, where together they felt the same wonder and excitement as they discovered the charm of Spain and the joy of companionship.

After several meetings, their relationship intensified.

'Would you like to stay tonight?' Britta asked one night after a long walk on the beach, her voice a whisper as her soft lips brushed his ear. As though a spell had been cast, Atticus nodded. *There was nowhere that he would rather be.*

Allowing himself to be guided by her lead, Britta led Atticus to her bedroom, where the subtle scent of her perfume lingered in the air. He'd only ever loved one woman and thought that had been for life, yet despite feeling vulnerable, he was excited and aroused.

Their lovemaking was slow and tender, and everything

he could have hoped for. Britta's body suggested an active lifestyle, and her curves were pronounced. Her skin felt as smooth as silk, despite the natural signs of ageing, and to Atticus, she was beautiful. But the skin across her thighs felt rougher, almost shiny, and when Atticus looked, he almost gasped as his eyes discovered raised scars – brown in colour, almost angry. The marks were so vivid they seemed to almost disfigure her upper legs.

'What happened?' he asked.

'I got burned.'

'But... how?'

'It's not important, I'm better now.' Britta touched his lips with her fingers as if to stop further questions and, with a contented sigh, closed her eyes.

As dawn broke, Atticus lay awake.

He felt concern about the scars and would ask her again when the time was right. But now, as Britta slept in his arms, her breath a peaceful rise and fall on his chest, she instilled a calmness he hadn't felt in years. Life, with all its twists and turns, had brought him to this moment, and the warmth of her body reminded him of the comfort of closeness with another being.

As he watched her sleep, he noticed small details: the way her hair fell across the pillow, the softness of her features, and the smile that hinted at a happy dream. Atticus felt the need to protect this woman, and the prospect of spending time with Britta filled him with a newfound sense of joy.

On Saturday mornings, they explored the bustling local market together and, after stocking up on provisions, sat with Cheryl and Ruby in the sunshine, enjoying tapas and sangria. The two women had welcomed Britta into their circle immediately, with the same warmth they had shown Atticus on his arrival at Solma Vacaciones, and Atticus treasured Cheryl and Ruby's friendship and support.

When Britta wasn't working, she walked with him along serene beaches, and they loved exploring, especially with Ness happily trotting alongside. Britta had rediscovered her mojo for art, making sketches of their discoveries. Later, with Atticus's encouragement, she used these sketches to inspire many paintings, which were now stacked heavily against a wall in the cottage.

One afternoon, Britta asked Atticus if she could sketch him beside Winnie. Taking a charcoal pencil, she sat in the sunshine with her drawing pad on her knee. Britta's gaze flickered between her work and Atticus, who now stood with Ness by his side. With her sleeves rolled to her elbows and her hair pinned messily, a few loose strands escaped, and Atticus longed to reach out and tuck them back.

'Keep still,' Britta laughed, tilting her head to study him with her artist's eye.

Winnie's door was open, revealing the cosy interior, and Atticus leaned casually against the side, one hand resting on his hip, the other absently ruffling Ness's soft fur.

'Can I see?' Atticus asked.

'Not until it's finished, and who knows when that might be?' Britta smiled, her fingers smudging a shadow onto the paper.

It was a simple moment, one filled with the quiet happiness found in each other's company.

Atticus had become obsessed with his Instagram account and enjoyed making videos to share his travels. Now that he understood the power of social media, he wanted others to be inspired and enjoy their later years, too. Judging by the reaction he received, his posts were doing their job. Each image or video received hundreds of comments and likes, and Britta laughingly told him that he was encouraging an influx of nomadic pensioners to make their way to Spain.

In Guardamar, Atticus was recognised as they strolled along the scenic promenade where soft sand gently sloped into the Mediterranean. They observed sun worshippers, toasting under the winter sun, wearing little more than a hat perched jauntily over thinning hair, a colourful swimsuit and sarong, or brightly patterned shorts.

Atticus had his photo taken with @BrightonBornBrian78, who'd rented an apartment for the winter after reading Atticus's posts. @EssexErnie insisted on a selfie and told The Travelling Grandad he was enjoying his newfound freedom after being inspired by Atticus and Winnie and that he had spent his life savings on a motorhome. Sue and Jill from Surrey, the @CamperVanCousins69, linked arms with Atticus and beamed at their selfie-stick camera, excited to say that they were thrilled to meet him and couldn't wait to share their post.

Atticus still couldn't believe how he'd come out of his shell.

His confidence surprised him, and never in a million years would he have expected to be doing the things he did. But his time with Britta was unhurried and he savoured each moment, storing the memories carefully for the days when he might not be so able. In quiet moments, relaxing on Britta's terrace and staring out to sea while she sat at her easel, he realised that he hadn't just found love but had rekindled a zest for life. He knew that Clara would be smiling down, delighted that Atticus no longer let the old man in. Each day felt like a new adventure, and each night spent in Britta's arms was a reminder that it was never too late to experience the magic of love. Even holding hands felt like all the riches in the world as they sat silently on the terrace swing and watched the ever-changing scene on the beach.

One afternoon, Atticus and Britta sat in quiet companionship, sipping wine as the sun dipped toward the horizon and the waves whispered to the shore.

Placing his glass down, Atticus turned to Britta.

'There's something I need to do,' he said, his voice low. 'Before Clara died, we talked endlessly about coming here together,' he paused, 'but the trip never happened.'

'Go on,' Britta encouraged, reaching out to take his hand.

'I… I brought some of her ashes with me to Spain.' Atticus swallowed. 'Because I never finished letting her go.'

Lacing her fingers through his own, Britta smiled. 'Then let's do it together,' she said.

Retrieving the old wooden box from Winnie, they both stepped onto the beach, the sand warm beneath their feet. The tide lapped as they reached the water's edge, and Atticus took a deep breath. With a reassuring squeeze of his shoulder, Britta nodded.

Holding the box, Atticus opened it, and with a gentle shake, the ashes swirled upwards as if carried by unseen hands. They both watched in silence until, suddenly, a light gust blew, shaping the ashes into a delicate heart that rose in the fading light.

'God bless you, Clara,' Atticus whispered, his voice thick with emotion. He stared in awe as the heart lingered above their heads before slowly dissolving on the dying breath of air.

Britta's eyes were wide as she moved towards him, their arms instinctively entwining. 'Now you've let her go,' she whispered. 'The sea will carry her home.'

Chapter Twenty-Eight

Atticus often spoke of his children and grandchildren, telling Britta about each one, and as he talked, he realised how special they all were.

'I have no children and would love to get to know yours,' Britta said. 'Children are a gift to be cherished.'

'I'd like you to meet them.'

'That would make me so happy.' Britta smiled.

One day, knowing that Britta wasn't working, Atticus announced that he had a surprise trip planned. She was to be ready at ten o'clock and to pack a swimsuit. With Winnie's awning safely removed, Atticus strapped Ness into her seat, and together in the camper, they headed for Casita del Mar.

As Winnie chugged happily through the lanes of Solma Vacaciones, the sun shone in the clear blue sky, and campers going about their day waved and smiled as Atticus drove past.

'Where are you off to?' Erik called out mid-workout in his outdoor gym.

Atticus pulled up by the pitch. 'We're going to Tabarca. What about you?' he replied.

'I have work to do and some local business to attend to,' Erik replied, wiping his perspiring brow. 'But we could catch up later?'

'That would be grand,' Atticus smiled, and revving Winnie's engine, went on his way.

The route to the cottage had become as familiar as the winding lanes at Barn Hill Farm back home. With Winnie's engine purring gently, Atticus drove slowly through the little town of La Marina, where outdoor cafés were lively with patrons sipping coffee and catching the gossip of the day. The track to the beach was bumpy, and as he carefully navigated, Atticus noticed many motorhomes still parked up in laybys, the sun-kissed occupants sitting outside chatting or heading to the sea for a swim.

'Guten Morgen!' Atticus called out as he recognised familiar faces from the café. Hands were raised in greeting, and smiles exchanged.

'You're right on time, as usual.' Britta smiled as she slung her bag into Winnie and inched Ness along the seat. 'Where are we going?'

'Today, my love, we're going to experience the magic of the island of Tabarca,' Atticus said. 'I hope you've packed your sketchbook.'

'Oh, I've always wanted to go there,' Britta said as she made herself comfortable and rested a hand on Atticus's leg. 'I can see the island from the cottage. It's only accessible by boat from Alicante or Santa Pola.'

'At this time of year, there are infrequent ferries,' he said. 'But I know one runs from Santa Pola today.'

'And we have perfect weather for the trip.' She reached out and gently stroked his cheek.

Atticus flicked Winnie into gear and turned to catch a glimpse of Britta. 'Almost as perfect as you,' he said with a smile.

A little while later, having navigated the narrow streets of the coastal town of Santa Pola, Atticus found a parking space for Winnie close to the harbourfront. With Ness trotting beside them, they headed hand in hand to the ferry booth at a hut on the quayside, where Atticus purchased their return tickets.

Britta wore a colourful cotton dress, and her hair was in a heavy plait between her shoulders. She held a floaty straw hat and wore jewelled sandals. Atticus began to take photos as she climbed the boarding steps to the boat. He grinned when Britta turned and waved with Ness beside her, the old dog's tail wagging excitedly. The sea was choppy, and a warm, salty spray dampened their skin as they sat on the upper deck and admired the passing scenery.

'In summer, the island is a popular tourist destination,' Atticus said. 'People head over here because the snorkelling and scuba diving are so good.'

'But is there much history?' Britta asked.

'I searched the internet and discovered that the island

was a haven for Barbary pirates until the eighteenth century.'

Britta stared at the land, which slowly became more apparent as the boat got closer. As sunlight danced on the waves, she could see the island's rugged coastline with rocky cliffs and hidden coves. Seabirds soared overhead as they approached the little harbour, where fishing boats bobbed like dancers, gracefully swaying, their colourful hulls painting the harbour with vibrant charm. 'It's lovely,' she said as Atticus helped her step from the boat to the quayside.

'Apparently, Tabarca is the smallest inhabited island in Spain,' he explained as they wandered along cobbled paths, past a restaurant and café, before walking beneath a stone archway leading to the village. The streets were narrow and lined with whitewashed buildings, where bougainvillea burst from window boxes beneath colourful wooden shutters.

An indent in a wall displayed a glass-fronted nativity scene, reminding the couple that Christmas wasn't far away.

'Will you still be here at Christmas?' Britta asked, staring at the religious figures gathered around a crib.

'Yes, I will.' Atticus squeezed her hand. 'I'd like to be with you if that's okay.'

When Britta turned, smiled, and stood on her toes to kiss him, he felt that his heart might burst.

'I'd like that very much,' she whispered.

They wandered from one end of the island to the other and soon learnt that significant construction had taken place when King Charles III of Spain sought to fortify and populate the island.

'These must be the defensive walls established by the king,' Atticus said, looking up from his guidebook. 'He was also responsible for the Church of St. Peter and St. Paul,' he added as they stood in front of a large stone building, whose wooden cross dominated the skyline.

'What a shame that the church is locked,' Britta said, turning away. 'I would have liked to look inside.'

'In 1760, a group of Genoese sailors who'd been rescued from the Tunisian town of Tabarka were resettled on the island,' Atticus continued. 'The island then became known as Nueva Tabarca.'

'New Tabarca.' Britta nodded. 'Wasn't it also a place for prisoners too?'

Atticus flicked through the guidebook. 'Yes, you're correct. In the nineteenth century, Tabarca served as a state prison.'

'Not too bad a place to be incarcerated.'

'I would be happy to be incarcerated anywhere with you, my love.' Atticus grinned. 'Now, what about finding somewhere to eat before we head back on the ferry?'

A little while later, they sat under a canopy outside a restaurant and sipped cold white wine while waiting for their meal. An old cat sprawled lazily on the pavement, basking in the sun's heat. It trained one eye on Ness, who, returning the cat's stare, softly growled from under the table, where she was secured on her lead.

Britta was drawing on her sketchpad, and as he stared, Atticus wondered if now was the moment to ask about the terrible scars on her legs. Placing his glass down, he took a deep breath and gripped his hands together.

'Britta, I have a question,' he began. 'Please tell me about your scars.'

Britta stopped, her pencil poised. Their eyes met, and with a sigh, she closed her pad. 'Yes, it is time for me to tell you. But the scars are not just on my skin – they are in my heart too, and have taken a long time to heal.' She reached out and took hold of Atticus's hand. 'You have helped me to heal.'

'Go on...'

'I want you to know that what I am about to tell you must never affect our relationship. You have helped me to become whole again and bury the past.'

'Nothing you tell me will ever alter the love I feel for you,' Atticus said.

'From the moment I met you in the café, I knew that you were the one for me.' Britta smiled and stroked his fingers. 'I love you very much.'

'So, tell me.'

'My husband, Daan, was cruel,' Britta began. 'He sensed that life on the farm wasn't for me, and although we were happy at first, as the years went by, I yearned for the freedom of my youth and to return to painting.'

'What happened?'

'When no babies came along, he called me names and gave insults, saying I was... how do you say... washed up... barren? Is that right?'

'Well, no, it's not right for him to say those things.'

'We had no children to work on the farm, no family to follow him, and he blamed me.'

'What happened?' Atticus's voice was low, and he squeezed Britta's hand.

'He hurt me whenever he could, made me scared; I couldn't get away.' Britta hung her head, her voice hardly a whisper. 'But I had a little money kept from housekeeping each week and began to save.'

'So, you left?'

'Well, not exactly. One day, he crept up on me and discovered where I hid the money. He was so angry that he reached for a kettle and threw it at me.'

'Boiling water?'

'Yes.'

Atticus felt bile rise in his throat, his anger intense. He took another deep breath and tried to stay calm. 'What happened then?'

'There was no choice. I ran out of the farm, and collapsed in the road in such pain... A neighbour passing in his truck saw me before Daan came out... I had to go to the hospital.' Britta's voice was hesitant. 'The neighbour took me, and while I was there, I told a nurse what Daan had done.'

'Was he arrested?'

'Yes, the *politie* took him away for questioning. I knew I didn't have much time, so I discharged myself. Then I returned to the farm, where I discovered his wallet and the key to a safe. I took enough money and valuables to make my escape.'

'And that's when you came to Spain?'

'I had to leave. He might only have been fined, and next time, he would have killed me. Daan didn't know I had applied for a passport using a post office address. I took trains until I got far away, to Alicante, and then, after a bus ride south, I rented a room in Guardamar until I found the cottage and got a job at the café.'

When their meal arrived, the server took great care to serve the house speciality, Caldero Tabarquino, a seafood stew made with onions, garlic, and tomatoes.

Atticus poured more wine and raised his glass to hers.

'Thank you for telling me,' he said. 'Now I know why it was so hard for you to talk about your life with a husband who should be locked away for life.' He took a drink, shook his head, then reached for her hand again. 'But I can promise you that as long as we are together, no harm will ever come to you.' Atticus smiled. 'Now let's celebrate our day with this delicious meal.'

The sun began to dip in the sky as they boarded the ferry to leave the island. Atticus put his arm around Britta, and she lay her head on his shoulder while Ness nestled against their legs. He thought about Britta's story and wondered how anyone could hurt a woman and be so cruel.

Thank God she had the strength and courage to get away from Daan and make a fresh start on her own, he thought, as the ferry glided across the now-calm waters.

The sky began to transform into a canvas of pinks and purples as the silhouettes of the approaching buildings of Santa Pola were softly illuminated by the sunset. The bustling waterfront area came into view, and as visitors disembarked at the pier, they were greeted by the sounds of evening life. Laughter, music, and the clinking of glasses welcomed sightseers strolling along the quayside.

'Thank you for a perfect day,' Britta said as Atticus helped her climb into Winnie. 'I will always remember our time on Tabarca.'

Atticus smiled as Winnie chugged to life. He drove away from the town and remembered that Erik had asked earlier if they might catch up that evening.

'The day isn't over just yet,' Atticus said as they headed to La Marina. 'Would you like to have drinks with Erik at Solma Vacaciones? I'm sure there will be others there, too.'

Britta gazed out at the salt lakes on either side of the road, where flamingos were gathered in the pink glow of the oncoming night. 'That sounds lovely,' she whispered. 'Just as long as I'm with you.'

Chapter Twenty-Nine

Mary no longer felt able to think straight. Another week had passed, and with Christmas only three weeks away, she began to prepare in a daze. Present buying was a blur, and despite asking the children to make their lists for Santa, she felt sure she'd missed something. Usually, she and Conor enjoyed the pleasure of deciding what gifts to surprise the kids with and planning their time together for the precious two weeks he always took off to spend with the family.

But this year, he'd told Mary to go ahead and sort everything out herself. 'Wasn't she capable of arranging the simplest of things?' he'd said. Unsure whether Conor would even be with them for the celebrations, Mary felt like a robot as she endeavoured to do her best.

But on the morning that the new month arrived, December brought in colder weather and when Mary dropped the children off at their schools, she decided to take herself off to the coast. To hell with the washing and ironing, and avoiding Roisin's enquiring eyes. Feeling flat and weary, she needed time on her own and hoped that the sea and a freezing Atlantic wind might knock some sense into her.

Mary drove along the road, passing the car park beside Garrets Beach, where vast stretches of sand were bordered by rugged cliffs near the Old Head of Kindale. She cut the engine and facing the sea, stared out at the crashing waves. The beach was popular with surfers, but it was empty at this time of day, save for a single dog walker. The bustling summer spot, where she often took the children for picnics or to play pitch and putt nearby, was wintry now, becoming shrouded in a moody sea mist that hung like a ghostly veil. Visibility was limited, but as she exited her car, Mary knew she would find her way if she kept to the shore.

Buttoning her quilted coat and wrapping a warm scarf around her neck, Mary turned when a vehicle suddenly appeared, the tyres of a familiar van crunching across the gravel as it pulled up beside her.

'Rats!' she murmured when Ruari opened the door. Wearing a thick woollen jacket and slipping his fingers into the pockets, he headed towards her. All she needed was Ruari's upbeat company on a day when she might debate drowning.

'Mary!' he called out. 'What the devil do you think you're doing out here on a day like this with the sea mist closing in?'

'Morning Ruari, and what the devil do you think you're doing following me to the beach?' she replied.

'I wasn't following you. I'm on my way to a client, but I

recognised your car from the road and knowing that you might not be in the best of moods, thought I'd stop by to prevent you from wandering into the Atlantic.'

The wind was playing havoc with Mary's hair, and as she brushed strands from her forehead, she stared at Ruari and wondered how on earth he knew she wasn't in the best of moods. But as she gazed into his sparkling eyes and saw his handsome face crease into a smile, Mary knew he was aware of her marital problems. Roisin's bush telegraph was doing the rounds, and Mary's escapade at Conor's office must now be front-page news.

'I'm going for a walk, and I didn't ask for company,' Mary said, locking her car and beginning to set off.

'Well, that's a shame, because I'm going for a walk too, and it looks like we're going in the same direction.'

Mary rolled her eyes. It was hopeless trying to argue with Ruari. He was a determined force, and as he stepped beside her, she felt his arm reach out and link with her own. The air was cold and damp, and tiny droplets of moisture from the mist clung to her skin as a sharp wind cut across their bodies. But Ruari's arm felt comforting, warm, and supportive, and she realised that other than cuddles with the kids, she'd missed the feel of another human during the long, lonely days since she'd confirmed Conor's affair.

'Now, why don't you tell me all about it?' Ruari said as he steered them over pebbles, carefully avoiding the frothy lace that came and went with the high tide.

'Tell you about what?' Mary played dumb, unsure of what she wanted to disclose to the brother of Kindale's biggest mouthpiece.

'You're the talk of the town with your airborne meals-on-wheels.' Ruari laughed. 'The Amateur Dramatic Society wants to book you for this year's pantomime.'

'Oh God, does everyone know?'

'The staff at the office of Murphy's Auctioneers have had a whip-round for a fancy Christmas hamper for you in the hope that you'll repeat the performance.'

'I made such a fool of Conor. He must be cursing me.' She shook her head, trying to rid herself of the image of Conor's acrobatic twists and turns as her cheesy quiche landed clown-like in his face. She remembered the open-mouthed expressions of the staff as they stood back to let her pass on the stairs.

Suddenly, Ruari stopped walking. He gripped Mary's arms and stared into her eyes. 'I can't believe what I'm hearing,' he said. 'Are you seriously saying that you feel *sorry* for Conor?'

'No, no... not really. I... I'm so confused I don't know what I am saying.'

'Okay, then it is time you voiced all this. Let it out,' Ruari urged. 'Who have you spoken to? Do you have a friend to confide in?'

'I haven't.' Mary hung her head. 'There's no one these days. Una is made away with her demanding family, and I seem to have lost touch with any genuine friendships. My time has been solely for the kids and Conor.'

'What about your family in Cumbria?'

'Oh, Mungo would jump with joy.' Mary shrugged. 'He's never really warmed to Conor, and would probably like me to return to the farm and help with the business. I know he's snowed under with it all.'

'What about Atticus?'

'My dad is having the time of his life in Spain. I think he's fallen in love, and I can't burst his bubble.'

'Good for your dad, but in the meantime, why don't we sit in the warmth of the car, and you can tell me all about it.'

Mary looked up, her brow furrowed, but as she searched Ruari's face for signs of a teasing grin, she saw only concern in his eyes.

'I'm your friend, Mary,' he said softly.

She held his gaze, surprised by the warmth in his words. Mary had known Ruari for years, ever since she'd first arrived in Kindale, a stranger to the close-knit town. Una often said that Ruari could charm the hens out of a hen coop and was hand-carved by angels. At the Ladies' Lunch Club, the women all drove well-valeted vehicles and compared notes with smirks and winks. But Mary felt sure that Ruari wasn't the type to leave a trail of broken hearts. Despite his teasing ways, he'd always been there, watching from the background of her busy life.

Taking her hand, Ruari rubbed her fingers to warm them, then opened the back of his van to produce a flask of hot coffee and a small tot of brandy.

'Essential valeting tools,' he smiled, and, reaching for a blanket, wrapped it carefully around her shoulders.

'Let's stay here,' Mary said. 'I like looking out at the sea, and the mist seems to be lifting.'

'Your wish is my command,' Ruari replied. Moments

later, he placed two foldaway chairs side by side, facing the sea.

The weather was changing, and the tide was on the turn. The wind dropped as low-hanging clouds over the water parted to reveal glimpses of pale winter sunlight.

'The beach is so beautiful,' Mary said as she sat watching seaweed drift along the high-tide mark and white-caps form on the surface of each outgoing wave.

'Almost as beautiful as you,' Ruari said as he stared out at the stark splendour of the scene. 'Conor is an idiot,' he added. 'What are you going to do about your marriage?'

Mary ignored Ruari's compliment. She felt as beautiful as a wet weekend in Galway.

'I've told him I'll give him time to decide what he wants to do, and he says he'll let me know by Christmas,' Mary reluctantly admitted. 'I suppose he's working out whether Lucinda is a better option than me.'

'So... you've given him until then to selfishly make his decision, and you'll go along with whatever he decides?' Ruari appeared incredulous as he turned to face her.

'I have no choice. If he comes back, it's better for the kids. They're too young to be separated from their father.'

Ruari sighed. 'Mary, I had you down as an intelligent woman,' he said. 'Can't you see that your kids are better off with one happy parent than two who don't like each other?'

'But...'

'But nothing! You might want Conor back now, but when you accept what he's done, you'll come to dislike his actions. You'll hate him and be unable to forgive him. You'll find it impossible to live together.'

'How can you be so sure?'

'When my wife had an affair, we tried to work things out, but I could never trust her. The doubt was always there.'

'*Your* wife had an affair?' Mary's mouth fell open in surprise.

'You thought I was the one with the roving eye?' Ruari smiled and shook his head. 'Most folk think the same, but I never looked at another woman in the years we were together. It broke my heart when we called it a day.'

Mary tried to digest Ruari's words.

'But...' she began. 'Conor is trying to decide if he loves Lucinda. Surely, he needs space to make his mind up?'

'Oh, Mary.' Ruari punched his head with his fist. 'I cannot believe that you are allowing Conor to make this decision on his own – about your future. What about you?' He stared hard at her. 'It's time for you to face the facts, and I guess it's down to me to give them to you.'

'What do you mean?' Mary was even more confused.

Inching his chair closer, Ruari poured coffee into a mug. Adding a tot of brandy, he gave the drink to Mary.

'Roisin is a terrible gossip, as you know,' he began. 'She cleans many houses and businesses in the area, including Creek House. Once a week, I go there to valet Lucinda's cars.'

'I know you've seen Conor at Creek House.'

'Yes. Often. And Roisin has seen them together too. This isn't a recent fling. They've been seeing each other for months.'

'*Months*?' Mary blinked slowly.

'Ever since that prime stretch of land came on the market across town.'

'The Land Deal,' Mary nodded in acknowledgement, her voice flat.

'As you know, Conor got the sale through and earned a handsome commission. But the builder who bought it? He was loyal to Darby's. Worked with Lucinda's father when they were starting out. Now that the planning application's been accepted, they're going to build multiple houses, and Darby's will handle the individual sales.'

'Those sales will be worth a fortune in commission,' Mary said. 'I hear the plans are for at least two hundred houses, with both starter and affordable homes.'

'The town planners have agreed the area needs them, and the services are in place. There are few available properties at the moment, and this will help with local growth and prosperity.'

'So, Conor's missing out on the sales of the century to Lucinda?' Mary asked, shaking her head.

Sipping her coffee, she wondered if this would have happened if she had still been involved in their business. After all, she knew the builder, Cillian McCarthy, from previous sales. He'd always been quite a flirt, but they'd gotten along well. Mary remembered Cillian thanking her for her efficiency and for making his job easy. Her prompt and seamless sales had eased his cash flow during a tough time.

The warmth of the hot drink, combined with the comforting touch of brandy, allowed Mary to ease deeper into her chair. She felt the tension that had tugged at her shoulders for weeks begin to partially ease.

'Well, possibly not...' Ruari was hesitant.

Mary sat up, the tension suddenly returning. 'What are you saying?' she asked.

'Conor wants to join forces with Darby's, create a joint agency with both names, and dominate the area. That way, he'll benefit from the builder's sales.'

'Oh, shite.' Mary bit her lip as comprehension dawned. 'Murphy's Auctioneers is in his name alone. He can do whatever he wants with it. I have no say.'

'That could be difficult for you.' Ruari frowned. 'But it's not just the property sales he's after. Conor wants to get his hands on Creek House, too.' Ruari glanced at Mary and then continued, 'Roisin has heard them talking. Conor's turned on all the charm and proposed to Lucinda. He's promised to divorce you if she agrees to marry him.'

'*What*?' Mary's mouth went slack, her eyes blinking in confusion.

'He's waiting for her to say yes... and she's enjoying keeping him waiting.'

'Oh, Conor!' Mary gasped. 'You bloody fool.'

Suddenly, everything dropped into place.

Mary had always known that Conor would give his eyeteeth to have his name on the deeds of Creek House. He'd told her multiple times that it was his dream property, a place he'd stared at from the other side of the Brandon River when fishing in the estuary as a small boy. He'd often told Mary that Creek House had been his inspiration for starting the business, somewhere to aspire to and own. It must have cut Conor to the core when Lucinda bought it from the bankrupt chef.

'She was probably sleeping with him...' Mary murmured.

'Who?' Ruari asked, his expression amused.

'Lucinda and the chef...'

'Oh, that drunken celebrity? She'd been shagging him for months when she got her hands on his deeds, for a pittance.' Ruari laughed.

'But I know from conversations at the Ladies' Lunch Club that Lucinda insists that husbands and lovers are precluded by written formalities from any part of her business or wealth,' Mary debated. 'In light of what you've told me, I feel certain she's playing Conor.' She turned to Ruari. 'What do you think?'

'I know for certain that she is,' he agreed. 'Roisin has heard her on the phone to her so-called friends, bragging about how she's "eased another poor simpering lamb from his marriage". It's how she gets her kicks. But Mary, Lucinda is angry that you made a fool of her in Conor's office and is determined to make sure you come off worse by destroying your marriage.'

'I can't be any worse off.'

'Well, I don't know what else she plans, but she's certainly one very unscrupulous lady who enjoys manipulating people. It's all a power game to her, and Conor has fallen for her spell.'

'If Conor can put property and Lucinda before his family, he's welcome to both.'

Mary stood up. Suddenly, she had an idea. Shrugging

off the blanket, she placed her empty mug on the chair. Like a Christmas miracle, she felt the weight of deceit and mistrust rapidly lift, replaced by an exhilarating sense of possibility.

What on earth was the point of hanging onto Conor? If he could prioritise his greed over his family, he wasn't worthy of Mary.

Neither was he deserving of their four beautiful children.

'Dear Lord, Ruari, where have I been these last few weeks?' Mary said and reached for Ruari's hand. 'I must have taken a paralysing potion that numbed my senses.'

'Shock is a strange emotion, Mary. It takes time to overcome. Now, you must accept what life throws at you and deal with it.'

'Well, I'm not letting life throw anything else unless it brings happiness and joy for me and the kids.'

'My goodness,' Ruari looked heavenward. 'Where's the thunderbolt you've been struck with? You've changed in an instant.' He clicked his fingers. 'One moment, I thought I'd be dragging you from the sea, and now it looks as if you could walk on it.'

'A painful revelation has turned into something empowering,' Mary explained. 'I thought it was because I was fat and frumpy that Conor had gone off me. I thought that as I aged, I'd a face only a mother could love and was no longer interesting or as glamorous as Lucinda, and that it was my fault that he'd strayed.'

'Oh, pleeeeaase...' Ruari rolled his eyes.

'No, hear me out,' Mary said, putting a finger on his

lips. 'Now that I know it's Conor's greed for property and wealth, I feel like I've suddenly been freed – as though it's not my fault, and I can stop blaming myself.'

'Halle...bloody...leulah!' Rory lifted Mary into his arms and spun her around.

'You, Romeo Ruari, have made me see the light!' Mary laughed, and when her feet touched the ground, she was inches from his face.

'Oh, Mary... Beautiful Mary,' Ruari whispered.

Before she could stop herself, Mary reached her fingers into Ruari's glorious, silky hair and, pulling his face towards her, kissed him. His lips were salty and the most delicious thing she'd tasted in years. Mary suddenly felt safe as his strong arms wrapped around her.

'Thank you,' she whispered and kissed him again.

They stood like two urgent lovers. For some moments, each devoured the other, both oblivious to the sound of the ocean and the caws of the gulls overhead.

'I have to go,' Mary said. 'I've got a lot to do.'

Reluctantly, she pulled away.

'Take care, beautiful Mary,' Ruari said.

He was sensible enough to know that no further words were needed. Mary's journey into the future was, for now, one that she needed to take on her own.

As Mary started the engine and drew away from the beach, she smiled as she saw Ruari staring and waving his hand. 'Thank you,' she whispered, and, spinning the car around, hurtled away to make plans for the rest of her life.

Chapter Thirty

On pitch number thirteen at Solma Vacaciones, there was no sign of life in Winnie, and her awning, with the sides pulled back, stood slightly askew. A table was covered with glasses, and several empty bottles and cans stood littered alongside.

'Cooee!' Cheryl called out as she placed a fluffy mule on the tarp covering Atticus's pitch, where the water-resistant canvas was covered with leaves and windblown sand. 'Anyone home?' she enquired, noting the debris scattered around. She wore her voluminous lime-green kaftan, which floated as she moved, and her vibrant orange hair, freshly curled, bounced on her deeply tanned shoulders.

Movement in the camper made Winnie rock as bodies stirred. Moments later, Ness jumped out, wagging her tail, delighted to see Cheryl.

'Hello, lovely,' Cheryl said and began to pat the dog. 'Where's the boss? Is he still asleep?'

'No, I'm here,' Atticus said, blinking against the light, following Ness into the sunshine.

'That was some party last night.' Cheryl grinned. 'I've come to check that you are still alive. Ruby's doing a fry-up if you fancy starting the day with a plateful of carbs.'

'That sounds wonderful,' Atticus replied and rubbed at his head with his hands. 'But first, I better clear this lot away,' he said, sighing when he saw the vestiges of the pop-up event that had occurred on his pitch when he'd arrived back from Tabarca with Britta.

'Is Britta still here?' Cheryl asked. 'Bring her too.'

'Thank you, she is, but has to be at work by lunchtime.'

'Then she'll want a restoring breakfast before she clocks on.' Cheryl smiled. 'That was some punch Erik made. I wonder what he put in it?'

'It packed a punch, that's for sure.' Atticus shook his head as he remembered the barrel of alcohol that Erik had turned up with, closely followed by most of the resident campers, who brought along musical instruments and chairs. The party that followed went on late into the night, and Atticus felt sure that dawn was rising when the last of the campers, in a noisy, multicultural conga line, staggered back to their mobile homes.

'Well, Ruby is helping out at Steve's bar today, and she can give Britta a lift to her cottage if it helps.'

'That's very kind, Cheryl.' Atticus smiled. 'Thank you.'

'Sort yourselves out, then come over,' Cheryl replied, gathering her kaftan as she headed off into the sunshine toward her chalet.

A little while later, having showered and refreshed

themselves, Britta and Atticus tidied the pitch. Britta dumped debris into a plastic sack while Atticus took a broom and swept away leaves and sand.

'I'm ready for some breakfast,' he said. 'I can't remember drinking a great deal, but whatever Erik gave us was very strong.'

'Yes, I agree,' Britta replied. As she knotted the sack of debris and placed it to one side, her phone began to ring. 'Hello?' Britta said, holding her mobile to her ear. 'Oh, Mr Rodrigues, how are you?'

Atticus stopped brushing and leaned on his broom. He didn't want to listen in on her conversation but was curious – he recognised the name. Mr Rodrigues was the owner of Casita del Mar.

'I see,' Britta said after a few moments. 'Well, thank you for letting me know.'

Atticus noticed that Britta was flustered. Her hand gripped the phone tightly, and her face had paled.

'Is everything alright?' he asked.

'Well, no, things aren't alright at all.' She gave a quick shake of her head.

'What's wrong, my love?' Placing the broom to one side, he moved towards Britta and put his hands on her shoulders. 'Has Mr Rodrigues upset you?'

Britta sighed and scraped a hand through her hair, tucking it behind her ear. 'He plans to sell the cottage,' she announced. 'He says it will sell quickly because those cottages by the beach never come on the open market and are very desirable.'

'Good heavens, that's a shock. Come and sit down,'

Atticus said and reached for a chair. 'But he must have given you plenty of notice, surely?'

'I have one month.' Britta sat down with a heavy sigh.

'Oh, I see.'

Turning her body, Britta shrugged. 'It's okay, I... I'll find somewhere else,' she stuttered.

But Atticus could see that her shoulders were tense, and her knuckles were white as she gripped her fingers.

'Yes, of course.' Atticus took hold of her hands. 'Try not to worry. You know I'll help you.'

Britta looked up. Tears were forming in the corners of her eyes. 'I love that little c...cottage,' she said as her cheeks became wet. 'It's my s...safe place.'

'Hey, come on. We'll find you a safe place again; don't get upset.'

'S...sorry, it's my problem; I will sort it,' Britta sniffed.

'Your problem is my problem,' Atticus said. 'Look at me.' Crouching down, he placed a finger under her chin and tilted her head until their eyes met. 'We'll sort this out, and everything will be fine, I promise.'

'Okay,' she sniffed and stroked his cheek.

Ness sat beside them and scratched at his leg with her paw.

'She says you can always come and live in Winnie,' Atticus joked and patted the dog's head. 'Winnie could be a travelling art gallery,' he added, then frowned. 'Well, that might not be the best solution, but please don't worry.' He reached for Britta's hand and kissed it. 'Let's go and get some breakfast.'

'Maybe Cheryl and Ruby will have an idea or know of somewhere,' Britta said.

'Maybe,' Atticus replied.

But as he placed his arm around Britta's shoulders and they made their way to their friend's chalet, Atticus could sense Britta's distress and felt anxious too. His mind was racing with the weight of what she'd just told him.

Britta was about to lose her home. The cottage she'd transformed was so cosy and suited her quiet way of life. *How could she replace such a perfect place*? There had to be a solution, a clause, or someone who could help. Britta needed someone to fight for her, and he knew that he couldn't stand by and let this happen.

Britta was upset and dabbed at her eyes. 'It will be alright. I'll have to figure something out,' she said bravely as they approached Cheryl's chalet.

But it wasn't alright to Atticus. 'Don't worry,' he said. 'We'll find a way.'

When Atticus left Britta and she went to work her shift at the café, he headed straight to find Erik at the campsite.

'Hah! My friend, have a beer!' Erik greeted him with a grin as Atticus stepped onto his pitch. Erik was in the middle of another workout, but unperturbed by the interruption. Noting the worry etched on Atticus's face, Erik paused. 'What's going on?' he asked.

'I need help,' Atticus said, twisting the cap from his beer. 'Britta must move from her cottage. Mr Rodrigues, her landlord, wants to sell it, and I don't know what to do. The place is perfect for her, and finding something like it would be impossible.'

Erik raised an eyebrow. 'Sit down.' He pulled out two chairs and motioned for Atticus to join him. 'I don't see the problem.'

Atticus sat, his brow furrowing. 'She's so upset, and I need to find a solution. Do you know Mr Rodrigues?' he asked.

'Never heard of him. Don't need to,' Erik replied with a casual shrug. He took a long drink and wiped his toned chest with a towel. 'It is simple,' he commented. Then, studying Atticus, Erik leaned back and announced, 'Buy the cottage.'

'Eh?' Atticus stared at Erik, bewildered.

'It's easy. If you love the woman, buy the place. Problem solved.'

Atticus blinked, his mind racing. 'But... how does a Brit go about buying a house here?'

Erik waved away his concerns. 'Yeah, I know there are difficulties for the British buyers with EU regulations, but if it helps, I'll buy it for you. We'll sort it out.'

Atticus stared at Erik, completely taken aback. He was astonished that his new friend had an instant solution and Britta's problem could be overcome. 'Well, I never thought...' he began.

'Can you afford it?' Erik's asked.

Atticus nodded. 'Er... Yes, I can.'

'Then it's settled. I'll take you to my legal guy, who handles all my Spanish business. He'll take care of everything.' Erik stood, slapping Atticus on the back. 'All good?' He held out his hand.

Atticus shook Erik's hand firmly, still trying to process the sudden turn of events. 'All good, I suppose,' he replied.

'Then we'll go to see my man straight away, but first, we celebrate with more beer.' Erik smiled and reached for another bottle.

In the heart of the town, where ornate architecture adorned a cluster of buildings, Erik and Atticus made their way to Resano Abogados de Propiedad. The property lawyer's offices were behind a solid wooden door, where a brass plaque proudly announced the business's name and the year it was established.

An elderly secretary, her greying hair scraped into a severe style, was dressed in black and greeted Erik with a warm smile.

In his office, Señor Resano puffed on a huge cigar.

They made themselves comfortable in deep leather armchairs, and Atticus looked around at the piles of old books, framed diplomas, and memorabilia that reflected the lawyer's many years of professional achievement. Distinguished by neatly combed silver hair, Señor Resano's face suggested a well-lived life. His tailored suit, complemented by a conservative tie, matched his old-fashioned waistcoat.

Atticus thought Señor Resano was as ancient as the building itself and wondered if he was in safe hands. But Erik reassured him that all would be well and that he could trust the man's legal expertise.

Señor Resano, however, was hesitant to act on Atticus's instructions.

'You are gifting a property to a woman you've only known for a few weeks?' Señor Resano questioned. He puffed furiously on his cigar and smoke billowed around them, swirling in chaotic circles. 'I have to ask if you think this decision is wise?'

Atticus waved his hand to disperse the dense blue clouds of smoke.

'I know that you think the relationship might not work and I might lose a great deal of money,' Atticus argued. 'But at my time of life, there is really little to lose and much to gain from making a deserving person happy.'

'If you insist. It is a generous thing to do.' Señor Resano shrugged. 'But,' he added cautiously, 'I must inform you that, given the current political situation, a Dutch national can purchase property here more easily than a British subject.'

One phone call later and Mr Rodrigues was delighted to find a buyer so soon after deciding to sell, with no need for agents. The price agreed upon was favourable to both parties.

'So that's settled,' Atticus said. 'Please complete the paperwork as quickly as you can, and I will arrange to have monies transferred.'

'It is a fine property,' the lawyer said, rising to his feet to shake Atticus by the hand. 'I have it on good authority that the area will be developed in time, and those cottages will be worth a great deal.'

'Please don't share that information with Mr Rodrigues.' Atticus smiled as he shook on the deal.

'I appreciate you fitting my friend into your busy schedule,' Erik thanked the lawyer. 'Your next visit to Nancy's will be on the house.'

As they left the building and stepped out of the fug and into the sunshine, Atticus, taking a deep breath of clean air, was puzzled. 'What did you mean,' he asked, 'the visit to "Nancy's" will be on the house?'

'It is a service I provide, but a service you haven't needed.' Erik shrugged. 'I own Nancy's. It is why I stay at Solma Vacaciones, to be close, yet not far away.' Turning to Atticus, he grinned. 'I have another Nancy's in Amsterdam too.'

'I know Nancy's, the motel-like building set back from the main road junction, by the track leading to Solma Vacaciones,' Atticus said. He remembered Ruby pointing out the building when he first arrived. 'What sort of service?'

'Nancy's is my business in Spain, and in Amsterdam it is located in the Singelgebied area of the city, which is known as the red-light district.'

'But what sort of business is it?' Atticus was persistent. But as he saw Erik smile, the penny soon dropped.

'Nancy's is a place for gentlemen to relax, spend time, and ease their frustrations.'

'Ah... A brothel.' Atticus nodded.

And as they began to walk away from the lawyer's offices, Atticus began to smile too.

Chapter Thirty-One

It was a busy Saturday lunchtime in The Black Bull, and Reg was run off his feet. A roaring fire crackled in the stone fireplace, and the scent of mulled wine, spiced with cinnamon and cloves, mingled with the hearty aroma of the tasty daily specials chalked up on the blackboard, which were selling fast. With only three weeks until Christmas, locals and visitors to the caravan site at Barn Hill Farm appeared to be celebrating early. Festive décor made the pub cosy, with twinkling fairy lights draped across the beams and garlands of holly and ivy adorning the walls. A Christmas tree stood in one corner, covered with shiny baubles.

In the backroom snug, Arthur sat with Jake. Dressed in a warm woollen sweater featuring a gnome-like snowman embroidered on the front, Arthur supped on a pint of real ale.

'I like your Christmas jumper, Uncle Arthur,' Jake said, sipping a Coke.

'Shirley knitted it and insists I wear it throughout December,' Arthur scowled. 'I feel a bit of a tit, to be honest.'

'Do you think Grandad will be celebrating Christmas in Spain?'

'Aye, there's no reason for him not to. But it might be different there.'

'I wish we could go to Spain to see him.'

'I have to agree that Christmas in the sun is appealing,' Arthur said and grimaced at the thought of another year of Shirley, sherry, and a tin of Quality Street while glued to the Royal speech.

'Do you think Grandad will be having a party?'

'By the look of his posts today, I would say that's a certainty.'

Arthur leaned over to study Jake's phone. The Travelling Grandad's Instagram page displayed a video of jolly, ukulele-playing pensioners dancing in a conga line around Winnie and in and out of the awning.

'I like the photos of the island he went to.' Jake thrust his hand into a bag of crisps and began to chomp his way through them. 'He's explained that pirates used to live there.'

Arthur stared at the multiple images of Tabarca, which looked like a beautiful place. He had to admit that the photos of Britta in a colourful cotton dress and floaty straw hat – wandering along the beach and sketching in a churchyard – were captivating. Atticus had an eye for creating balance and guiding followers toward a focal point. He chose unusual angles for buildings and viewpoints, capturing moments to tell a story and evoke curiosity. No wonder his followers increased daily.

'Is your dad still angry with him?' Arthur asked.

'Dad moans about everything these days. He thinks Grandad is making a fool of himself and that his head's been turned by a younger woman.' Jake licked cheese and onion flavour from his lips and opened a bag of knobbly, chilli-tasting nuts. 'He reckons she's only with Grandad for his money.'

Arthur grinned. He reckoned that spending time with Britta would be well worth parting with his pension and envied his friend. 'Is it busy at the farm?' he asked, fiddling with a beer mat on the polished wooden table.

'Crazy busy. Dad has taken on more staff, but he says that when I've finished my schoolwork, I've got to help in the shop on the weekends leading up to Christmas. That's in addition to maintaining the caravan site.'

'The money will come in handy, surely?'

'True.' Jake nodded.

'Well, before you get stuck into selling soda bread and Cumbrian fancies all afternoon, you can give me a hand with the gnomes.'

'What needs doing?'

'Your Aunty Shirley likes a display up the driveway with flashing fairy lights.' Arthur raised his glass and drained his pint. 'So, if you've finished your knobbly nuts, we should get going.'

'I bet they don't have gnomes in Spain,' Jake grumbled

as he reluctantly followed Arthur from the pub and tightened the toggles on his duffle coat against the bitter wind.

'Not like Cumbria, eh?' Arthur tucked his scarf into his snowman jumper, adjusted his bob hat and reached for his coat. 'It'll be Gnome-Sweet-Gnome at Shirlarth Cottage this Christmas,' he sighed.

In Kindale, Mary was feeling energised and had been busy putting her new plan into action over the past few days. Christmas events at the children's various schools took up much of her time, and when she wasn't sorting through new paperwork, she made a shepherd's outfit for Declan's nativity and turned Finn into an elf for his school play. Mary kept her eye on Maeve and Caitlin, who, when not doing homework, were occupied with youth club events and the upcoming Christmas disco. Maeve's plant-based diet appeared to have gone out of the window along with a boy she'd been hankering after.

'He's a knob,' she told her mother as she sat in the kitchen, eating a thick, juicy beef burger and staring at her Instagram account. 'I never really liked him, and now he's on Caitlin's allotment committee, bossing me about.'

Mary imagined Maeve helping out in the cold at the allotment, having a tantrum over frozen winter turnips or crying into frosty cabbages. She decided that Maeve was better off in the warmth of the cosy youth club.

'Grandad's having a blast,' Maeve said as she finished

her burger and scrolled through images of The Travelling Grandad. 'It's one long party at his pitch in Spain.'

'Has he still got lots of followers?' Mary asked.

'Zillions,' Maeve muttered and closed her phone.

Meanwhile, Finn and Declan were fighting as they ate their tea. They were squabbling over the last hot dog, while Caitlin, preoccupied, dipped a fry into ketchup.

'Come on, go and do your homework, and Declan, it's bath time,' Mary said as she cleared the table, and the kids began to disperse.

Caitlin pushed her plate to one side and turned to look at her mother. 'Mam,' she said, 'can I have a word?'

'Yes, love, what is it?' Mary asked as she stacked the dishwasher. Turning to face Caitlin, she had an inkling of what was coming.

Caitlin looked around. Seeing that the coast was clear and that her siblings were out of earshot, she said, 'There's a rumour at school that you and Dad are splitting up.'

Mary took a deep breath to steady herself, then pulled out a stool and sat beside Caitlin. She reached for her eldest daughter's hand. 'What are they saying?' she asked.

'That Dad is hooking up with Lucinda Darby, and you'll get a divorce.'

Caitlin's voice was shaky, and Mary could see that she was biting her lip.

'Is it true?' Caitlin asked.

Mary sighed. Trying to assure Caitlin that all was well seemed pointless. Telling her that Dad just needed a bit of time out while he sorted through his work problems wouldn't wash with her eldest child. The real problem was the state of their marriage, and Caitlin was astute enough to know that something was wrong and things amiss – parents in separate bedrooms, tiptoeing around each other.

'Your dad is going through a difficult time,' Mary began. She gently rubbed Caitlin's hand with her thumb, hoping to comfort her. 'He's not sure what he wants at the moment, so I'm giving him a bit of space.'

'You mean like he's having a mid-life crisis?'

Mary searched Caitlin's anxious eyes. Her brain was racing, searching for ways to soften the blow that Conor was a selfish, arrogant, greedy rat who seemed to have forgotten his vows and respect for his family.

'I guess you could call it that.' Mary smiled. 'He's just a bit confused and needs some time to think about his life, the business, and what he ultimately wants.'

'Is he having an affair with Lucinda Darby?'

Mary stared at her daughter and felt guilty. She was angry with Conor for his betrayal and for putting her in this position. She knew Caitlin would be torn with love for both parents and unsure of where her loyalties should lie. Mary was filled with a desire to protect the children but knew that she had to explain the situation to Caitlin in a way that was as gentle and age appropriate as possible.

'Truthfully, yes, I think he *is* spending time with Lucinda,' Mary said.

'But what about us?' Caitlin's face crumpled. 'Does it mean he doesn't love us anymore?'

Tears were in her eyes, and Mary reached out to wrap her daughter in her arms.

'Oh, my darling, of course not,' she said, kissing the top

of Caitlin's head and gently stroking her hair. 'Your daddy loves you all, and he always will – even if he decides that he might not live with us all the time.'

Caitlin sniffed. 'He's horrible, and not good enough for you!' She suddenly sat upright and pushed back on her stool.

'Sweetheart, I understand that you are angry. It's perfectly acceptable for you to feel that way if things at home are changing.'

As she held onto Caitlin's hands, Mary remembered Ruari's words: the kids would be better off with one happy parent than two who didn't like each other.

'If Dad and I decide to live separately, you will have two great homes to grow up in,' Mary said. 'You and your sister and brothers will always be our priority.'

'It's okay, I get it.' Caitlin shrugged. 'Aisling Bryne's parent split up last year, and she told me all about it.'

'Is she alright?' Mary's voice was soft.

'Yeah, she's spoiled rotten now. She says they overcompensate, but she loves it. If this is best for both of you, we'll figure out how to adjust.'

'You're being very grown up, and that means a lot to me,' Mary said. But as she spoke, she noticed that Caitlin suddenly looked down and a child-like pout had appeared.

'Has Lucinda got a swimming pool?' Caitlin asked.

'Indoor and out… and tennis courts,' Mary added.

'She's still a stick-thin witch.' Caitlin raised her head.

'I can't deny that.' Mary shrugged, deciding she'd gone over the top by turning Conor into a saint for his kids. However, there was no reason to protect the evil Lucinda.

'Dad must be crazy. You're beautiful.' Caitlin threw herself into Mary's arms.

Mary returned the hug and remembered Ruari telling her she was beautiful, too.

'I want you to be brave,' Mary said, taking hold of Caitlin's shoulders and looking her in the eye. 'Things might not be easy, but we will get through this, and everything will be fine.'

Caitlin nodded, reaching for her discarded plate. 'I just want you to be happy, even if that means not being together.' She picked up a cold French fry and began to nibble. 'Can I go watch a movie now?' she asked.

'Of course, you can,' Mary nodded. 'I love you, Caitlin Murphy.'

'And I love you too.' Caitlin kissed Mary on the cheek, then slipped off her stool and hurried out of the kitchen.

As Mary watched Caitlin go, she prayed they would get through the mess Conor had created and the kids would come out unscathed. But divorce was never easy and could scar young hearts for life. Now, knowing that the inevitable *would* happen, Mary vowed to do everything in her power to keep things as painless as possible for her children.

She was sure of one thing. There was no going back.

Ruari was right, and she knew she'd never be able to trust Conor again. If they stayed together, she would come to hate him for the harm he'd done. Apart, they might eventually end up as friends. Falling in love with someone else was one thing, but being so deceitful in trying to manipulate his way into the sale of houses on Cillian McCarthy's land and getting his hands on Creek House was another.

After all these years, Mary felt as though she didn't know her husband.

Picking up Caitlin's empty plate and returning it to the dishwasher, Mary added a tablet and pressed a switch. As the machine began to hiss and gurgle, she pushed up her sleeves and methodically cleaned the kitchen. Wiping down the surfaces, she thought about Ruari. She could almost taste him on her lips and feel his arms around her. Their kiss on the beach had been emotionally and physically uplifting, and Mary had suddenly felt sure of herself. As Ruari kept telling her, she felt beautiful too. To hell with Conor and his cruel comments about her weight. So, what if she was a size sixteen and her jeans were a little tight? She remembered a mantra she'd read in a Facebook post: 'Beauty in all forms dulls in a cowering wreck but shines in one who has confidence.'

And what to do about Ruari? Mary paused. *Was she to leave it on the beach, a stolen kiss that might not be repeated?* He'd called several times to check in on her, and yesterday, when she'd gone to pick up the kids from school, she'd found a gorgeous bouquet of flowers on the front doorstep. The card read, '*Hang on in there, Beautiful, you've got this x.*'

But as she flicked her cloth for the final shine, Mary smiled and knew there would be plenty of time to think of Ruari in the coming weeks. There was no rush.

Mary thought of her plan and smiled.

It had begun a few days earlier with a phone call, followed by a meeting, and after a visit to a solicitor's office, several hours on the internet.

She stood back to study a sparkling kitchen that even Roisin would be proud of and wondered what Conor was anticipating for Christmas that year. As she headed to the playroom to tear Declan away from Peppa Pig and take him upstairs for his bath, Mary knew that Conor's Christmas gift would contain a surprise he wasn't expecting.

Chapter Thirty-Two

On the Autopista del Mediterráneo, Winnie chugged along at a steady pace. With Atticus at the wheel and Britta sitting alongside him, Cheryl and Ruby sat comfortably in the back of the camper. The previous few days had been busy for Atticus. Having set out to solve Britta's problems, he'd decided they should celebrate with a few nights away. He remembered meeting Martin on the ferry to Spain, who'd insisted that Atticus visit Benidorm and include a visit to the Starlight Show Bar. Cheryl and Ruby jumped at the opportunity to join the trip to Spain's famous coastal resort.

'I'm very impressed with your Bipandgo!' Cheryl called out. 'It's a nice, big bip with plenty of go,' she chuckled as the device on Winnie's windscreen electronically lifted the toll booth barrier, and Atticus drove seamlessly through.

'This road, the AP-7, might have paying toll booths, but it's an easy, fast route,' Atticus said and eased into a lane to let speedier traffic go past.

'Does anyone fancy a snack?' Ruby asked and rummaged around in a picnic bag to find neatly wrapped sandwiches that she'd prepared earlier that morning.

'There's coffee and cake too, and we haven't forgotten Ness,' Cheryl added and handed a treat to the dog, strapped in beside them.

Britta was thoughtful as she stared out at the landscape ahead, which boasted rolling hills and the distant mountains of the Sierra de Bernia. 'It's good to have a break before the Christmas rush; the café has been busy.' She sipped from a beaker of coffee. 'Many people have arrived in La Marina for Christmas,' she added, her thoughts straying to the café. 'It's going to be hectic over the holidays...'

The day before, Britta had been decorating the café with festive decorations to welcome new arrivals – many of whom were retirees descending on the area for the Christmas break to escape the winter chills and spend a few weeks in warmer weather.

The call came while she was placing baubles on a tree and arranging a garland.

'Britta, phone for you!' The café manager's voice carried over the chatter of diners.

'A call?' Britta hesitated. No one ever called the café for her. If Atticus needed her, he'd use her mobile. Puzzled, she wiped her hands on her apron and made her way to the office.

'Hello?' she said as she picked up the receiver.

Silence.

Britta listened, straining against the quiet. There was no voice, but she knew that she wasn't alone on the line. She could hear it. Soft, steady breathing. Someone was there. Listening.

Her grip tightened. '*Hello*?' she repeated, sensing the tension.

Nothing. A chill iced her bones, unsettling the warmth she felt in the café as she slowly replaced the phone.

'Everything okay?' The manager gave her a questioning look.

Britta forced a smile, shaking off her discomfort. 'A wrong number,' she'd replied. But the unease clung like a shadow, and Britta gave herself a shake. *She was being ridiculous! It was obviously a misdial.*

There was nothing to worry about, she'd told herself as she returned to her work.

The miles sped along as they passed vineyards that stretched endlessly and citrus orchards heavy with fruit. Lush pine forests appeared, the greenery contrasting starkly with the bright sunny skies. Terracotta roofs and whitewashed buildings could be seen from quaint Spanish towns in the distance, surrounded by rural agricultural land.

North of Valencia, Atticus pulled into a service station. Cheryl needed a comfort break, so Ruby took Ness for a walk. As Atticus and Britta stretched their legs and stood by Winnie in the sunshine, Britta turned to Atticus and took hold of his hands.

'I can hardly believe what you've done for me,' she said. 'Your kindness means everything, and now I truly feel safe.' They watched Ruby circling the area with Ness, whose nose was glued to the grass, intent on every new smell. 'I still don't think that the cottage should be in my name,' Britta said.

'It makes the paperwork easier,' Atticus explained. 'And I want you to feel secure and not worry about ever losing your home.'

'But what about your children? What will they think?'

'Leave that to me.'

'I wish I could meet them. If they knew me, we might get to like each other, especially the grandchildren.'

'One day, my love, you will.'

'Please,' Britta tried again. 'Put the cottage in your name?'

But Atticus was firm. 'We've discussed this, and you know my reasons.' He reached out to embrace her. 'We haven't known each other for long, but at my age, I have to make the most of every day, and you make me so happy.'

'Then move into the cottage with me?'

'Would you like me to?'

'Of course!' Britta was emphatic. 'Why would you think otherwise?'

'Because I respect your freedom, your need to paint, and the fact that you may want time alone.'

'Have I not told you that I love you? How often do you need to hear it?'

'As often as you want to tell me.' He kissed her upturned face. 'And I love you too, my darling Britta,' he added. 'But I may have to return to Cumbria at certain times unless the EU regulations change.'

'Is there anything to stop me coming with you?'

'That's what I hoped you would say, and nothing would make me happier than to show you my Cumbrian home and for you to meet my family.'

'Then that's settled,' Britta beamed. 'We have much to look forward to.' She wrapped her arms around Atticus, and they kissed again.

'Oi! You two!' a voice called out. 'Get a room!'

Cheryl strolled towards them with takeaway bags of food, her smile wide. 'You're like love's young dream, the pair of you,' she said, shaking her head. 'Now, where's my Ruby and that daft dog of yours? I've got both of their favourite treats to see us through the rest of the journey.'

Atticus stared at the mountain of food Cheryl was loading into Winnie. 'We'll be there in an hour or so,' he said. 'You've enough to keep us going for days.'

They all looked up as Ruby and Ness came racing around a corner.

'Are we off?' Ruby asked and climbed into Winnie.

'Waggons roll!' Cheryl said and settled her bulk beside them. 'Next stop, the high-rise haven of the Costas!'

'Granny's party paradise!' Ruby joined in.

Atticus helped Britta to her seat then checked to make sure his friends were comfortable. 'What have you let me in for?' he asked as he secured Winnie's sliding door.

Cheryl and Ruby glanced at each other.

'What happens in Benidorm, stays in Benidorm!' Ruby called out.

Cheryl turned to Atticus, with a hint of mischief. 'Unless you post it on Instagram...'

Jake and Arthur stood in the shed at Shirlarth Cottage and studied multiple strings of fairy lights heaped in a tangle on the bench before them. The festive gnome display that adorned the driveway had suffered a blackout the night before when Arthur, having enjoyed too many pints at the pub, stumbled and became entangled in the wires on his way home.

'You could have been killed,' Jake frowned as he observed the blackened bulbs.

'I ruddy well electrocuted myself.' Arthur shook his head. 'I've never sobered up so quickly.' He winced as he thought of the thunderous sound of Shirley's wellingtons as she pounded down the drive when the house was plunged into darkness and the screen of *Gogglebox*, her favourite TV show, went blank. With the stark light of Shirley's torch flashing in his face and her accusing words drumming in his ears, Arthur had spent the night in their spare bedroom with only a candle for company.

'It's taken me ages to fix the fuses this morning, but the electricity has been restored,' Arthur mumbled. 'Along with my marriage,' he added with a sigh.

'We've got our work cut out with this lot,' Jake said,

reaching for a box of spare bulbs. 'Good job you ordered in bulk.'

'Aye, well, Mistletoe Mike and Tinsel Tina can wait to light up the night,' Arthur grumbled and turned to reach for the kettle. 'I'm parched, and this cold weather is playing havoc with my arthritis. Let's have a cuppa before we crack on and see what your grandad is up to in sunny Spain.'

Jake beamed as he watched Arthur reach for a biscuit tin, revealing a hidden stash of chocolate Hobnobs. Taking his laptop, he searched for Atticus's Instagram page and, grabbing a biscuit, began to scroll through.

Comfortable in his rocker with a mug of builder's tea, Arthur dunked a Hobnob and gazed at the screen. 'By heck, he's been on a bus to Benidorm,' Arthur chuckled as he watched a reel of Atticus and three smiling women gripping the rail of a fast-moving coach. They were surrounded by beach-clad holidaymakers staring out at spectacular views of the Mediterranean, where yachts and sailboats dotted the sea.

'There are more motorised scooters than on the seafront at Morecambe,' Arthur noted as he studied a busy Benidorm street filled with market stalls and street performers, where bar owners encouraged the crowds to sample the delights of happy hour.

'Looks like they found a pub.' Jake bit into his biscuit. 'Grandad is eating fish and chips.'

'Very nice too,' Arthur said as he studied the way Atticus had one arm wrapped protectively around Britta.

'Crikey, Dad will explode when he sees this.' Jake's eyes were wide as he scrolled through another reel of a nightclub called the Starlight Show Bar. Atticus was on stage, surrounded by glitzy drag artists and a dancing dog.

'Ah... the queen of country,' Arthur breathed and smiled nostalgically as he studied a look-alike Dolly Parton.

Atticus was handed a mic, and together with Dolly, they began a duet before the reel ended.

Two women appeared in another image, and as Jake flipped through, he dipped his chin to peer at Cheryl and Ruby. 'Are they kissing?' he asked.

'Aye, it looks that way.' Arthur nodded and quietly thought that Atticus was the luckiest pensioner alive.

'It looks like they were all sleeping in Winnie,' Jake added as he continued to scroll. He recognised the familiar stripes of the awning but gobsmacked, he almost spat out his Hobnob as a reel began. It showed an inflatable bed slowly deflating, and the same two hysterical women as they untangled sheets and sank to the ground. Jake recognised Grandad's girlfriend, Britta, who held her hand to her mouth in surprise as Ness, leaping into the lens, scrambled away from the bed.

'Wow, they certainly know how to party...' Jake said.

'Looks like life is one long party on the Costas,' Arthur commented as he drained his tea and brushed crumbs from the snowman on his Christmas jumper.

'Shall I get started on the lights?' Jake asked and closed his laptop.

'Best get on with it, if we don't want World War Three to break out at this year's glimmering gnome-land.' Arthur sighed and wondered how long it would be before Shirley hammered on the door to remind him that the light would fade in an hour or two and her Gnomeville Wonderland must be illuminated in holiday cheer.

Arthur pulled his bob hat over his thinning hair and eased out of his chair. He wondered what Atticus was doing and knew that his friend was no doubt basking in the heat, perhaps on the beach with a bikini-clad Britta sunbathing beside him. He joined Jake at the bench and began to untangle lengths of wire and tease tiny bulbs out of lights that should have been permanently put out to pasture years ago. Arthur's sigh was heavy as he thought of Atticus and the lifestyle he was enjoying.

If only Arthur had the courage to follow in his friend's footsteps.

Chapter Thirty-Three

One week before Christmas, on a cold and crisp Saturday morning, Mary was full of vigour as she put her plans in place. Instead of her usual pre-festive lull in vitality as she raced around preparing for the big day, she felt energised. It was the day of the Christmas Fair in Kindale, and, committed to working the tombola stall for a couple of hours, Mary needed to get a move on and head into town.

The children were weary from end-of-school-term activities, with Finn and Declan immersed in pantomime preparations and nativity play rehearsals all week. Caitlin and Maeve's teenage hormones were drained by project deadlines, assessments, and extracurricular activities. With shorter days and colder weather, Mary felt that her offspring's energy and mood had dipped, and she was happy for them to be relaxing in front of a movie that Saturday morning. The siblings were snuggled close on the vast, comfy sofa, cosy in matching onesies, with their feet up while tucking into a tub of Celebrations chocolates.

'Now be good all of you, and Caitlin and Maeve look after your brothers,' Mary said. 'Roisin is here if you need anything at all, but I want you to behave and not give her any problems.'

'When's Daddy coming home?' Declan called out as he gripped his teddy.

'He'll be here when work is finished.' Mary ruffled Declan's hair and kissed his soft locks as Caitlin caught her eye.

Caitlin shrugged as Mary gave her shoulder a comforting squeeze.

Mary made sure she had her phone as she packed her bag and made a mental note to text Conor to remind him that he was on parenting duties after work. But she knew there was no need. Despite this agonising atmosphere between the two of them, Conor never let his children down in the spare hours he kept for them.

Busy dusting, Roisin looked up as Mary kissed all of the children goodbye. 'Don't worry, they'll be fine,' Roisin said. 'I'll keep an eye on them until you return. And I've got your number if we need you,' she smiled.

Mary did a double-take as she tightened a scarf and slipped her arms into her Barbour. Roisin's sharp retorts were no longer present, and recently, she'd gone out of her way to be helpful.

Sympathetic to Mary's situation and difficulties, Roisin patted Mary's arm. 'Get yourself off and enjoy your afternoon.'

As she drove away, Mary wondered if the whole of Kindale was following the Murphy marital breakdown, agog for news to feed the gossip grapevine. Mary knew that her elderly nosy neighbour, who hadn't moved faster than a snail since they'd lived at Belvedere House, now had a sprightly step, glancing at the drive and over the fence like an arthritic ninja whenever Murphy family members stepped outside. Una had told Mary that the Ladies' Lunch Club had a new topic for their chinwag, and 'Piecing Together the Murphy Drama' was weaving theories as intricate as a best-selling thriller.

Finding a space to park her car, Mary hurried through the town. As she passed Murphy's Auctioneers, she glanced through the window and caught the eye of *whatever-her-name-is* on reception. To Mary's surprise, the girl grinned and waved.

Mary wondered if Conor was in his office or warming his hands on roaring logs in the inglenook fireplace in the lounge at Creek House. Before he left early that morning, they'd exchanged heated words.

'Lovely morning, isn't it?' Conor had said.

He stood by the kitchen window, packing his briefcase, as Mary handed him a mug of tea.

'Oh, it's a perfect morning to be left hanging in the air, Conor,' Mary snapped, folding her arms. 'Nothing like dragging out your decision while your marriage is going down the drain.'

'Dear God, don't go on.' Conor rubbed his forehead. 'I told you. I'll have an answer by Christmas.'

'But *will* you?' Mary snorted. 'And what would you like

under the tree this year? A divorce or a frying pan to the head?'

'You're impossible.' Conor drained his tea, setting the mug down with a clatter. 'I'll be back at teatime to be with the kids.'

'Oh, is that right?' Mary shot back. 'Why not send me a note by pigeon post to remind me, as you don't communicate in any other way!'

Conor shook his head, then reached for his coat, and Mary remembered him leaving her standing alone, like a fool, as he strode out to his car without another word.

'Who the hell does he think I am to be kept waiting?' Mary muttered as she made her way to the market square. 'The doting little wife who will follow whatever her disloyal husband decides?' She balled her fingers in her gloves as she arrived with minutes to spare for her stint at the tombola stall.

Una, handing out tombola tickets, gave a thumbs-up when she saw Mary. Then, rolling her eyes, she nodded sideways to point out an elegant woman in a full-length white leather coat.

It was Lucinda, and she was handing out prizes.

'Good morning, Mary.' Lucinda glanced at her Chanel watch. 'You've made it on time; that has to be a first.'

Mary was determined not to bark back, but Lucinda had some nerve. Not only was she sleeping with Conor, but she brazened it out as though nothing was wrong.

'Happy Christmas.' Mary smiled at Lucinda. 'How's my husband's collection of unfulfilled promises working out for you?' Mary took her position at the stand as an elderly couple held up a winning tombola ticket. 'Did you manage to get the coleslaw stains out of your blouse?'

Lucinda glared as she handed the couple a box of scented bath cubes.

'I did wonder if the caramelised onions that I glued to your hair would alter the colour,' Mary continued. 'But apart from needing your roots touched up, I see that you managed to wash the mess out.'

Lucinda's hand flew to her head subconsciously, her fingers tracing the hairline.

The couple and Una joined two local ladies from the mulled wine and mince pie table, and leaned in. They looked encouragingly – from Mary to Lucinda – for the next comeback.

'Conor always said he liked cold leftovers,' Mary continued. She picked up a bottle of whisky and turned to look Lucinda up and down. 'It's good to see he wasn't exaggerating,' she said. Then, reaching out, Mary smiled at the couple and, to their amazement, handed them the whisky.

'You can't do that!' Lucinda cried out. 'Their ticket didn't end with the number five!'

'I can do anything I like,' Mary replied and tucked a box of luxury chocolates in the couple's shopping trolley. 'Happy Christmas,' she beamed.

'And to you,' the couple muttered and hurried away before the angry woman in white took back their stash.

'We'll run out of prizes if you carry on!' Lucinda's pale skin had reddened. Her aim was always for the tombola to raise the most money at the Christmas Fair.

Mary took a mulled wine from the adjacent table. She

raised the steaming mug and smiled as she saw a sudden fear in Lucinda's eyes.

'Is there anything else you want from me, besides my husband?' Mary asked. 'Perhaps you'd like to share this mulled wine?'

Lucinda stepped away from the stall. She was aware that the dark, sticky contents of Mary's mug might suddenly find themselves airborne, landing on the pure-white leather of her favourite coat.

'I need to go; my office is busy,' she countered. 'Do make sure you do the decent thing and make some money for our charity, rather than give everything away.'

'*I* do the decent thing?' Mary was incredulous. 'Oh, bog off, Lucinda!' she yelled.

Mary reached into her pocket to pay for the wine, but the ladies held up their hands. 'With our compliments,' they smiled as they watched Lucinda scuttle away. 'Would you like a couple of mince pies too?'

A little while later, Mary headed back to Belvedere House. Her exchange with Lucinda had left her feeling flat. Despite her plans, Mary yearned to put her enemy in her place and knew Lucinda thought she had the upper hand, dangling Conor like a puppet on a string.

It was a ridiculous situation, and one Mary could never have anticipated. Once again, she wondered if she'd ever really known her husband and questioned how he'd become so unrecognisable as the man she'd loved for many years, his ambition now more significant than his marriage.

Driving along the beach road, Mary lowered her window to take in the sharp, salty tang of the sea. As the bracing air circulated, her phone began to ring, and Mary pulled into the beach car park to answer the call.

'Hello, Dad,' she said, suddenly grateful to hear his voice.

'Hello, Love,' Atticus said. 'How are you?'

Mary was tempted to clear her throat and put on her most cheerful voice, but something in her father's tone suddenly softened her resolve. Closing her eyes, she realised that tears were sliding down her cheeks.

'Mary, are you there?'

'Yes, s...sorry, I'm here.'

'Are you crying? Mary, whatever is the matter?'

'Oh, you know, things aren't so great here,' she replied.

'My darling girl, whatever is wrong, tell me, and I'll make it better.'

Mary choked back a sob as the warm, comforting sound of unconditional love poured through the airwaves. 'It's okay, sweetheart,' Atticus said, 'just take your time.'

Mary did as she was told. Then, slowly, she explained her problem.

Her father listened patiently, and after she had given him all the facts, he asked if she'd made any decision about the future.

'Yes, I have, but I could do with your advice. I'm not sure if I'm doing the right thing.'

When Mary had outlined her proposal, she paid attention as Atticus added thoughts of his own.

'Would you like me to speak to Conor?' Atticus asked.

'No, Dad, it's okay. Now that you and I have talked, let's get on with my plans, as long as you're sure you're happy about it all.'

'You have my full backing.'

Mary felt much better, and wiping her eyes, she felt the tension ease as she stared at the sea. She'd told Atticus everything, beginning with Conor's longing for Creek House, his frustration at losing the new housing sales, and his determination to join forces with Lucinda – both at work *and* play. She spoke of her pain and anxiety as Conor agonisingly stalled on making up his mind about their future and waited instead for Lucinda to accept his proposal.

Mary even mentioned Ruari. She spoke about their friendship, his concern, and the reality check that Ruari had given her, which prompted the actions she was about to take.

'But are your feelings for him more than just friendship?' Atticus asked.

'I don't know,' Mary replied. 'I'm not emotionally equipped to think about that right now.' But as Mary talked, she told him that the feeling was incredibly good when she'd stood on the beach and kissed Ruari.

Atticus listened patiently. When he spoke, he was like a solid rock in a turbulent sea. His comforting words were the much-needed calm after the storm, and he agreed with Mary's decision, telling her he'd stand by and help with anything she needed.

How things had changed!

The reclusive man who'd grieved for so long was no

longer. Taking her mother's words to heart, Atticus hadn't let the old man in and, despite Mungo's misgivings, had set off on a great adventure, finding friends and love, and Mary needed to hear more.

'Now,' she said, 'you've listened to me rant, and I want to know all your news. Will you tell me what's happening with you and Britta and everything you've been up to?'

'You may be surprised,' Atticus laughed.

'Go on, shock me. I could do with gossip other than my own.'

'I've bought a cottage called Casita del Mar.'

'The Cottage by the Sea...' Mary breathed. Her eyes were wide as she listened to her dad explain.

'I've gifted it to Britta, and it's in her name. I want her to be secure and know that she will always have a roof over her head and a place she can call home.'

'But that's a wonderful thing to do.'

'Aye, well, I don't think your brother will think so.'

Mary heard Atticus sigh. 'Can I tell him?' she asked.

'No, it's my responsibility to let him know that his inheritance has just nose-dived by a considerable amount of euros.'

Mary began to chuckle and envisioned the scene in the farmhouse when Atticus broke the news. She didn't know the extent of Mungo's borrowings on the business, but this news wouldn't go down well. But it was her dad's own money to do with as he pleased, and if he chose not to leave it to his children, it was his affair.

'I think it's great, and you're moving in too. A home by the Mediterranean Sea. Mum would be so proud of you.'

'Aye, I think she probably would.'

Atticus explained that Britta loved to paint. He'd enjoyed taking her portfolio to a gallery in Alicante, who'd agreed to take some of her paintings. 'She's a typical creative,' Atticus said, 'talented, but always with a monkey on her shoulder telling her that she's not good enough.'

'Imposter syndrome. What a great thing that she's now got you to encourage her and promote her work,' Mary said. 'But tell me, what about the future? Do you think you might get married?'

'It's early days, and I am happy now that I know Britta has a permanent home, whatever happens to me.'

Mary turned the radio on as she ended the call and drove away from the beach. *The Brendan O'Conor Show* reminded Mary that Christmas was just around the corner and the countdown to the big day had begun. 'I've so much to do,' Mary muttered as the countryside whizzed by. Minutes later, she entered the gates of Belvedere House.

There was a festive atmosphere and Mary smiled as she noted the classic white fairy lights that she'd used to decorate the front of the building. She'd worked so hard to make everything perfect for Christmas, both inside and out. Evergreen garlands tied with tartan ribbons embellished the windows, a pretty wreath hung from the front door, and miniature Christmas trees stood on either side.

Mary parked in front of the house.

Knowing that Christmas was Conor's favourite time of the year, she'd worked tirelessly to ensure that their home looked its best. As she opened the front door and stepped into the hallway, Mary smiled as she gazed at a vast tree, topped with a crystal star. The tree was wrapped in twinkling lights, and delicate glass baubles hung from the branches. At the foot of the tree, pretty parcels contained the children's gifts to their father.

Mary hoped that Conor would appreciate how much care his family had taken in choosing his presents. Removing her coat and reaching for a hanger, she also hoped that, for his sake, he'd come to a decision about life with Lucinda. Conor was going through emotional turmoil too, and it wasn't a good place to be. Knowing that he'd promised Mary an answer by Christmas, she was thoughtful as her fingers adjusted a bauble on the tree.

In less than a week, Mary would find out.

Chapter Thirty-Four

First light appeared just before eight o'clock, and Britta was at her easel in the lounge at Casita del Mar, brush in hand, contemplating a canvas when Atticus announced that he would take Ness for a walk. Kissing her cheek, he handed Britta a coffee, then went out to the terrace and stared at the deserted beach, where the sky had begun to lighten with soft pastel hues and a hint of gold peeped above the horizon.

Skipping down the steps, Atticus went barefoot onto the cool sand. Untouched by the heat to come, the only footprints were those of early-morning seabirds, whose delicate tracks led to the water. Ness, nose to the ground, bounded ahead in pursuit. A gentle breeze stirred, and as Atticus inhaled deeply, he marvelled at the start of a new day and the picture-perfect world before him.

Atticus felt as though he'd won the lottery. Life with Britta was as good as it got.

Dipping his toes in the water, he smiled as he thought

about their trip to Benidorm and how they'd all fallen into a taxi after the evening at the Starlight Show Bar and returned to Winnie. Tired from the day's exertions, Cheryl and Ruby had climbed onto the inflatable bed, and Ness, keen to welcome everyone home, jumped on too. Suddenly, the bed had deflated, and the couple doubled over with laughter and fell to the floor.

'We need to get your claws cut, old girl,' Atticus said as he stood beside Ness and stared out to sea. 'And find a puncture repair kit,' he added, reminding himself that the perforated bed, lent by Erik, needed to be mended and returned.

As Ness ran ahead, rhythmic waves lapped at his feet, and occasionally, Atticus paused to study the treasures left by the tide. A seashell or unusual driftwood, a piece of sea glass; something that might please Britta. He thought of his children and hoped that Mary overcame her difficulties. He'd never imagined that her marriage would crumble and that Conor would behave as he had, but Atticus knew that nothing in life was certain.

He wondered how Mungo was coping with Christmas at the farm and hoped that business was good. A decent bank balance to cover the lean months of the new year might ease Mungo's financial anxieties and put his son in a better frame of mind. Not wishing to discuss the purchase of Casita del Mar with Mungo, Atticus had informed him in an email, burying the information amongst light conversation about the weather and the places he'd recently visited. He'd ended by wishing the family well and letting Mungo know that he'd deposited money into Mungo's personal account for family gifts at Christmas.

The sun cast long shadows under a misty blue sky as the beach came to life, and a jogger made their way towards Atticus.

'Buen día,' the handsome young man called out, his footprints leaving light impressions in the damp sand as he passed.

Two fishermen appeared. They carried rods and tackle boxes and prepared to take advantage of the early hours when fish were most active. Atticus was reminded of the fishing gnomes that lined the drive at Arthur's home in the summer. He thought of his friend and hoped that Arthur was surviving another cold winter, knowing that the chill wasn't good for Arthur's arthritis and caused him pain. If only Arthur could persuade Shirley to enjoy a warm winter break.

A paddle boarder was making their way toward the shore, silhouetted against the sparkling water, and as they got closer, Atticus began to laugh. The man was dressed in a Santa Claus outfit and raised his paddle in greeting.

'Feliz Navidad!' the paddle boarder called out.

'Happy Christmas!' Atticus replied and held up his hand to wave.

Atticus had almost reached the jetty that led to the marina in Guardamar. Glancing at his watch, he realised that he'd been walking for over an hour, and calling to Ness, they began their route back. Knowing that Britta would wonder where he'd got to, he reached for his phone and dialled her number. The phone rang out, and, puzzled,

Atticus thought that she must have forgotten to turn up the volume.

Hastening his pace, he began to walk quickly.

At Casita del Mar, Britta sat with her back to the beach and stared at her painting of Atticus and Ness standing beside Winnie. It was almost finished. The room was dimly lit, the only light from an arc lamp over the easel. Absently, she drained the last of her coffee. The drink was cold, and she realised that it was some time since Atticus had placed it in her hand, before setting off on a morning walk. Britta was determined to finish the section she was working on before he returned and discussed their day ahead.

Taking a long-handled brush, she leaned in to delicately dab at the canvas. To capture the soft fur of Ness's head, she used light brush strokes and dark shades, her mind absorbed by the task.

Highlighting the play of light and shadow, Britta was unaware of footsteps from the beach, nor did she hear a soft tread moving across the terrace. But as she sat upright, there was an unmistakable rustle from the curtain in the shadows of the doorway. She turned, a smile on her face, expecting to see Atticus.

But there was no one there. No handsome, smiling face nor Ness's cold, wet nose as she plodded across the marble floor to greet Britta.

A chill ran down Britta's spine. Her heart began to thud, and the familiar comfort of her surroundings felt suddenly overshadowed by an impending sense of dread.

She reached for her phone and seeing a missed call, realised that it was on silent.

'Who's there?' Britta called out.

Turning the brush in her hand, she ignored the trickle of dark paint that ran down her arm and dripped onto the fabric of her sarong. She stood motionless, her senses on high alert.

Then, after a moment, she dismissed the sound as a figment of her imagination and tutted as she stared at the stain on her sarong before returning to her easel. But suddenly, a chair scraped back on the terrace, and Britta turned again.

'Who's there? Atticus, is that you?'

A man stepped into the open doorway, and Britta gasped. With his back to the light, his ominous posture was tense, his shoulders slightly hunched, and his dark clothing blended with the shadows.

'Hello, Britta,' Daan said. 'I have finally found you.'

Britta screamed and recoiled in fear. Stumbling back, her phone fell from her hand, and she fell onto the easel. Daan lunged forward as the canvas tore beneath her.

'Stupid bitch,' he hissed. 'Did you really think that you'd get away from me?' He reached out and, grabbing Britta's arms, pulled her upright. 'It didn't take long for the folk back home to tell me they'd recognised you on your boyfriend's Instagram account.' Daan was inches from her face. 'What a fool he is to post photos of the café where you work. One call and I found you!'

His breath smelt of stale alcohol – hot and rank – and Britta recoiled.

'Where *is* The Travelling Grandad?' he mocked. 'Has the old man kicked the bucket?'

'Leave me alone!' Britta screamed again.

She could feel Daan's breath on her skin, and a primal terror gripped her heart. She knew that the man could hurt her, but the look in his hate-filled eyes suggested much worse. Britta kicked out with her bare feet, but Daan kicked back, bruising her shins and sending her spinning to the ground.

Britta curled into a foetal position and tried to make herself as small as possible as blows began to rain down. Every second felt like an eternity as Daan yelled and punched, his actions those of a madman, consumed by rage. Her mind was blurring, and unable to fight back, Britta knew her only defence was to scream and pray someone was in earshot. Summoning every ounce of her diminishing strength, Britta opened her mouth and screamed as loudly and as long as she could.

'Shut up, you stupid bitch,' Daan cursed and hit Britta again.

On the beach, the jogger who'd passed Atticus moments earlier thought he heard a cry. At first, it sounded like that of a gull, but as he got closer to a group of buildings, he realised that the sound was coming from inside one of the cottages. Taking a canister of alarm spray from the body belt at his waist, the jogger approached the steps of Casita del Mar and called out.

'Ey! *Qué está pasando*! What's going on!'

Tentatively, he held the can out, his thumb poised over the trigger. But before he could move any further, a tall man in dark clothing appeared on the cottage's terrace.

'What's happening in there?' the jogger called out again. 'I hear screams.'

The man had a wild glare in his eyes. Seeing the canister in the jogger's hand, he took one last look over his shoulder at the room behind him before thrusting forward and running down the steps. Pushing the jogger aside, he was unable to stop the alarm spray, which had already been activated. A spray of red paint, as though ejected from a gun, showered his face and clothing as he scrambled onto the beach and began running away.

Momentarily stunned, the jogger dropped the ringing alarm. Reaching to pick it up and holding it before him, he slowly ventured into the cottage.

Atticus was no further than five hundred yards from Casita del Mar when he heard a loud ringing noise. Instinctively, he knew something was wrong. His pace shifted into a run, with Ness bounding beside him. As the cottage came into sight, he saw a man stumbling down the steps, covered in a red substance, before running in the opposite direction.

'Oh, no!' Atticus wailed. 'Please, God, NO!'

Terror gripped his heart like icy fingers, and fear pulsed through his veins, fuelling his every stride as he raced toward the unknown. *Had an assailant harmed his precious Britta?* Sweat beaded on his forehead, and his muscles screamed with exertion, but overwhelmed by the need to protect her, he was unaware of any pain.

He reached the cottage, panic clawing at his throat. Taking the steps two at a time, Atticus flung himself into the room, where a man in jogging clothes crouched beside Britta, a phone held to his ear.

'Britta!' Atticus cried out.

The man held up his hand, and Atticus recognised him as the jogger who'd passed him on the beach.

'*La mujer ha sido atacada, necesitamos una ambulancia y la policía.*' The jogger spoke rapidly into the phone, then turned to Atticus who crouched beside Britta. 'She okay,' he said. 'I find her. I call ambulance and la policía.'

The jogger's English was broken, but Atticus instantly understood. He touched the man's shoulder and nodded his thanks. 'She's my girl,' Atticus said.

'It's okay, help come.'

Atticus took Britta's hand and gently stroked her face as she struggled to sit up. Her fingers shook uncontrollably, and her skin was unnaturally pale. 'It's alright, my darling,' Atticus whispered. 'I'm here. You're safe.'

The jogger moved away as Atticus gently lifted Britta into his arms and held her trembling body with great tenderness as Ness whimpered and lay down beside them. A dark stain marked Britta's sarong, and Atticus felt a wave of relief when he realised the stain was paint, not blood. But tears blurred his vision as he cradled her, his whole world narrowing to the fragile figure in his embrace. 'Who did this to you?' he asked.

Britta's body shuddered, and her fingers gripped Atticus's hand tighter. 'Daan,' she whispered. 'It was Daan... he... wants to... k-kill me...'

As Atticus waited for help, he whispered apologies and stroked her hair, urging her to feel his love and strength.

A siren wailed in the distance, growing louder, and moments later, paramedics hurried into the cottage. Britta was able to talk to the medical team, who told Atticus to move away while they examined her.

Atticus asked the jogger his name and learnt that the man was named Luis and lived in La Marina. He was returning from his morning jog when he heard a cry and saw a man running from the cottage.

'You've saved her life,' Atticus said as they stood on the terrace, and he took Luis's hand. 'I don't know how to thank you.'

'It's okay, she safe. Intruder is red now, la policía find him.' Luis grinned and showed Atticus his alarm.

Atticus was surprised as he took the small canister and studied it. Not only did the alarm give off an ear-splitting sound when activated, but it also released a burst of red paint that adhered to skin and clothing, marking the assailant and remaining impossible to remove for several days.

'Yes, I hope the police can find him,' Atticus said, thanking Luis again.

Atticus sat down. His heart was hammering, and he realised that he'd begun to feel shaky. It must be the shock, he thought. Ness was by his feet, and as she placed her head on his knee, he stroked her silky ears.

'I get water,' Luis said and disappeared into the kitchen.

Atticus reached for his phone and dialled Cheryl's number.

'Hello, cowboy,' Cheryl said brightly. 'Are you and Britta joining us for breakfast?'

Atticus explained what had happened and asked Cheryl if she would mind taking care of Ness for a while, as he would be going to the hospital with Britta.

Cheryl assessed the situation immediately, and with a reassuring voice, calmly told him that she and Ruby were on their way.

The police arrived just as Luis handed Atticus a glass of water, and suddenly, the situation was under control.

As Britta was lifted into the ambulance, Atticus climbed in beside her.

'I'm okay,' she said, smiling weakly.

'You *will* be okay,' Atticus told her. 'And I promise that what has happened will never happen to you again.'

Chapter Thirty-Five

Britta was kept in hospital overnight in Torrevieja for observation, but with no fractures, only shock and severe bruising, she was able to return to Casita del Mar the following day. Atticus was anxious that she might not want to return to her home, but he didn't have to worry. Britta was determined that Daan wouldn't ruin her newfound happiness and assured Atticus that she had every intention of carrying on with life precisely as before.

'I don't think he will come back,' she said as she lay resting in bed and held onto his hand. 'The police are looking for him, and with all the red paint on his face and clothing, he might not be too hard to find.'

Atticus was reluctant to tell Britta that he knew there wasn't a hope in hell that Daan would return. But when she was feeling completely recovered, he would give a reason for the confidence he felt and assure her that she could live safely in the knowledge that Daan was out of her life forever.

When Cheryl and Ruby arrived at the cottage soon after Atticus's call, Erik accompanied them. Cheryl took Atticus in hand and, after making a mug of hot sweet tea, told him that he had experienced a shock and needed to be checked at the hospital, too. Ruby, meanwhile, took charge of Ness. Erik spoke to the jogger and, after thanking him for all he'd done, assured the young man that there was a lifetime pass waiting for him on the door at Nancy's, should he ever wish to relax in friendly surroundings. Erik then spoke to the police and appeared to be on good terms with the officers.

To Atticus's surprise, Daan was found within hours, staying in an apartment in Guardamar. He was taken to a cell, and the police allowed Erik to visit him.

'You won't have any more trouble from him,' Erik told Atticus firmly. 'Tell Britta that she has nothing to worry about now.'

Atticus felt laden with guilt. He'd promised Britta that he would protect her, and he'd failed. But he instinctively knew that whatever had transpired in Daan's cell and whatever words had been spoken by Erik had ensured that Daan would never come near Britta again. Unwilling to push for further details, Atticus accepted Erik's comments and thanked his friend.

'It's nothing,' Erik said. 'In my line of work, I deal with this sort of thing all the time. There are some bad eggs out there.'

Britta had fallen asleep, and Atticus gently covered her with a blanket. Kissing her cheek, he made sure the blind in the bedroom was lowered to protect her from the sun, then went downstairs.

On the terrace, Cheryl sat on the swing. Ruby was walking along the shore, throwing a ball into the water for Ness to retrieve. Atticus joined Cheryl and heavily slumped onto a chair. Dark circles framed his eyes, and his shoulders sagged. His clothes, once neat, were now rumpled.

'You're exhausted,' Cheryl commented. She stood and poured from a pot on the table. 'Here, drink this,' she said, handing Atticus a mug.

'Sweet tea – the elixir for life's woes,' Atticus said, smiling.

'When the world feels heavy, sweet tea lightens the load.' Cheryl placed a hand on his shoulder. 'You've been up all night at the hospital. Why don't you take a shower, then go and snuggle up with Britta?'

'That sounds like a wonderful idea, but I have things that I need to do.'

'Like what?'

'Christmas is almost here. Do you remember when we discussed this?'

'Yes, I haven't forgotten, but there's nothing for you to worry your weary head about. Ruby and I will take care of everything.'

'But... I can't let you both...' Atticus began.

'Of course you can; that's what friends are for. And right now, the most important thing is your Britta.'

'What's that about Britta?' Ruby called out. She stood on the steps, a towel in her hand as she attempted to dry a wriggling Ness.

'I was just saying to Atticus that he needs to rest with Britta and leave all his Christmas arrangements to you and me,' Cheryl said.

'I quite agree.' Ruby marched onto the terrace and stood before Atticus. 'No arguments, and Ness will come with us too. She'll enjoy a little break.'

Atticus knew that arguing was useless, and Cheryl's suggestion was like music to his ears. Running a hand through his dishevelled hair, he leaned back, the chair creaking in response. Every ounce of his strength felt spent.

'Okay, I accept your help,' he said.

'Good man,' the two women replied. Taking an arm each, they hoisted Atticus from his chair and led him into the cottage.

'There's food in the fridge,' Cheryl called out from the kitchen as Ruby clipped a lead onto Ness and gathered up her biscuits.

'Sweet dreams!' they chorused.

It was the last day of school before the Christmas break, and Mary was like a whirlwind. She wondered why schools couldn't break up at least a week before Christmas to give parents time to prepare. With only four days to go before the big day, she had much to do.

She'd woken early and, dressing hurriedly, moved

through the house, her mind full of tasks. Conor wasn't home, but she could see that his bed had been slept in and remembered that he'd put the kids to bed the night before. He'd appeared relaxed and normal at school events, sitting next to Mary at Finn's pantomime and Declan's nativity, chatting with everyone as though their marriage was harmonious and happy. But Mary knew that the gossiping mums weren't fooled, and she'd overheard their whispered conversations from the row behind.

'*I hear they've been arguing non-stop, something about financial troubles?*'

'*Someone saw him leaving Creek House again last week, on his way to work.*'

The agony for Mary went on.

Making sure breakfast was on the table before the kids stumbled into the kitchen, sleepy-eyed but excited for their last day, Mary was gentle but firm as she shepherded them through the morning routine – brushing teeth, finding shoes, and packing lunches. As she bundled them into the car, Mary double-checked for backpacks.

'Does Santa have my list?' Declan asked. He sat beside Maeve, who was studying her phone, with his teddy gripped in his hand.

'Yes, my darling, Santa knows what you want,' Mary replied. 'And there is a big surprise for you all tomorrow, so I want you to be extra good.'

'Grandad hasn't posted anything for two days,' Maeve said, her thumb moving over her screen as she studied Instagram images.

'He's probably busy,' Mary replied.

Mary thought it was most unusual that Atticus hadn't uploaded any recent photos. Not a day had passed since his time in Spain when his followers hadn't been treated to an update. She made a mental note to call him after completing the day's many tasks.

With everyone safely at school, Mary drove home. In the kitchen, she made an extra-strong coffee. As she reached for her laptop and settled comfortably, her phone rang.

It was Mungo.

'Bit early for you, isn't it?' Mary asked and took a sip of her drink. Mungo was generally elbow-deep in paperwork at this time of day.

'Don't hang up on me.'

'It depends on what you have to say.'

'Dad has bought *that woman* a house.'

Mungo's tone was controlled, but Mary felt that her brother was about to lose it.

'I know. But it's not a house. It's a cottage on the beach.'

'*What*? You already know?' Mungo was furious.

'Yes, we spoke about it last week. The paperwork is with a lawyer, and Dad feels confident there won't be any legal hitches.'

'He told you, but informs me by email!'

'Dad probably doesn't want to be shouted at.' Mary rolled her eyes.

'He's not answering his phone.'

'Can you blame him? You're hardly the Christmas fairy, waving your wand with good cheer.'

'Don't you realise what this means?'

'Yes, Mungo, I'm not stupid.' Mary sighed. 'Dad might get married again, and we need to have a conversation with him about changing his will.'

'We can't let some money-grabbing floozy get hold of it all.' Mungo wasn't listening to his sister. 'First a house, next the farm.'

'Oh, for heaven's sake, get a grip and just listen to yourself.' Mary placed her coffee down and began to pace. 'Dad isn't stupid, and he'll never do anything to risk our financial future.'

'But he's lost his head. Women like that take advantage of doddering old men.'

Mary shook her head. She couldn't believe Mungo's naivety and wondered how Atticus would feel to be described as a doddering old man. Pinching her lips together, she decided to calm things down.

'I'll speak to Dad,' Mary began. 'Let me discuss the will and ensure he is clear in everything he does.'

'At least he might answer his phone to you,' Mungo grumbled, and Mary thought he sounded like a petulant child.

'Leave it with me, and I'll get back to you as soon as we've spoken,' Mary said. 'How's business, you must be run off your feet with the Christmas trade?'

'It's hectic; the locals are stocking up on last-minute purchases. But I think it will drop off tomorrow, and we'll close on Christmas Eve.'

'Good, then you'll have some time to spend with your family. I hope you're taking a decent break.'

'Yes, we don't open again till the New Year.'

'Perfect, and I hope Santa will put something lovely in your stocking, too.'

As Mary ended the call, she hoped that Mungo would relax. Her brother was tired, and he needed time off to be with his family and allow the tradition of Christmas to restore his energy.

She sighed, suddenly feeling tired, too. Reaching for her coffee, Mary took a long drink. The caffeine, like a bolt, cleared her fog, and she turned to her laptop to open her emails.

'It's you and me against the to-do list,' she muttered as she clicked on her printer. 'Let's make like Santa and get this sleigh on the road…'

The snug at The Black Bull was packed, and Arthur kept his elbows close to his sides as he sat in his corner, sipping a pint of ale. The air was thick with the scent of mulled wine, and patrons, bundled in festive sweaters, filled every nook and cranny. Arthur tutted as he stood to replenish his drink.

'I can hardly hear myself think in here today,' Arthur complained to Reg, who wore a Santa hat and moved deftly behind the bar.

'Be with you in a mo.' Reg was cheerful as he ladled mulled wine into glasses and poured steaming mugs of spiced cider.

'You should have an area reserved for your regulars,' Arthur chuntered as he watched Reg grasp the wooden handle of a beer tap and pull it skilfully towards him. The beer flowed into the glass with a frothy flourish, leaving a creamy head.

'Where's your Christmas cheer?' Reg grinned. 'You should enjoy the company, especially with your mate being so far away.' He handed the freshly poured pint to Arthur.

Arthur sighed as he returned to his seat. His Christmas cheer was currently taking a break, and it wouldn't return until Shirley's numerous friends and relatives had packed up and returned to their respective homes. Shirlarth Cottage had become a seasonal sanctuary for numerous waifs and strays and Arthur envisioned his Yuletide days being spent in his shed, when he wasn't busy washing dishes at the Christmas castaway camp.

'Uncle Arthur!' a voice called out.

Arthur looked up and was delighted to see Jake burst into the snug.

'Hey up.' Arthur smiled. 'This is a grand surprise. Now that you've finished school, I thought you'd be working at the farm.'

Jake pulled up a chair and squeezed in beside Arthur at his table.

'No, the caravan site is closed now till the new year,' Jake explained, 'and there's nothing for me to do in the shop.'

'Time on your hands, how lovely.' Arthur nodded. 'Have you heard from your Grandad?'

'Nope – he's gone off grid.'

'Eh?'

'SMS.'

'Ah.' Arthur nodded, clueless.

'Social Media Silence,' Jake explained. 'But it doesn't matter because I think I know how we can speak to him very soon.'

'It would be good to give him a Christmas surprise,' Arthur agreed. 'Shall we do that face thingy or hype?'

'FaceTime or Skype,' Jake corrected and scratched the back of his neck. 'No, listen.' He reached into his rucksack for his laptop and then placed it on the table. 'I've had an idea.'

'This should be good,' Arthur mused and drained his pint. 'Whenever you're ready, Reg,' he called out and held up his empty glass. 'I think I'm going to need it.'

Chapter Thirty-Six

It was Christmas Eve at Solma Vacaciones, and the site was buzzing with festive cheer. Campers, enjoying the atmosphere, had taken great pains decorating their pitches, and a multitude of colourful decorations added a jovial contrast to the natural surroundings. By the swimming pool, a Christmas market offered local crafts and Spanish delicacies, including cinnamon churros and tapas. Pretty decorations were displayed on tiny trees alongside hand-made ornaments. Expats and friends gathered, mingling with campers and exchanging multicultural greetings, while Christmas songs were sung by a group near the bar. Spanish families had arrived, setting up homes in caravans and chalets, placing tables in the gardens for communal outdoor eating.

In Cheryl and Ruby's chalet, Cheryl was busy ironing outfits. Erik was hosting a party that evening, and she wanted to look her best.

'I've just spoken to Erik,' she told Ruby, who'd taken Ness for a walk. 'All our arrangements are in place.'

'Is the transport he arranged on time?' Ruby asked.

'Yes, it's on its way to Alicante as we speak, and a later taxi is booked too.'

'Perfect,' Ruby said, rubbing Ness's head, reaching into the fridge for a cold beer. 'I've sorted the catering out with our friendly receptionist and am assured that it will be delivered on time to Erik's.'

'Have the cleaners finished next door?' Cheryl asked, watching Ruby lean out of the window to study the adjacent chalet.

'Looks like it,' Ruby replied.

'When you've finished your beer, let's get the place decorated.' Cheryl put the finishing touches on her outfit, smoothing the last creases.

'We'd better call Atticus and make sure all's well at his end!'

'I'm on it,' Cheryl said, reaching for her phone. As she waited for him to answer, she turned to Ruby and smiled. 'It's going to be a cracking Christmas.'

At Casita del Mar, Britta sat on the terrace with a paintbrush in her hand. Her easel, which was beyond repair, had been replaced by Erik.

'An early Christmas gift,' he'd explained when he carried the large frame into the cottage the day before.

Despite her painful bruises, she was determined to continue and finish her painting.

'I think you're doing too much,' Atticus said as he placed a glass of iced lemonade beside her. 'The doctor at the hospital said that you must rest.'

'I *have* been resting,' Britta said, smiling. 'And I've been in bed for twenty-four hours.'

'Do you think that you're up to the party tonight?'

'Yes, of course, the bruises will fade,' she said. 'My energy has returned, and now I know that Daan can't hurt me, my spirit feels strong, and I want to enjoy every moment with you.' Britta reached out to take his hand. 'This is our first Christmas together.'

'The first of many.' Atticus kissed her fingers.

He'd spoken to her about Daan and mentioned that, following Erik's intervention, he wouldn't be troubling her again. Britta had nodded. She understood and passed no comment.

'I am glad you're feeling better,' Atticus continued. 'I have a surprise for you at Solma Vacaciones.'

'I like surprises, but if you don't let me finish this painting, we won't be going anywhere,' Britta chided and kissed his fingers.

Atticus went to the terrace. It felt strange not to have Ness by his side; he missed the old dog but knew they'd be reunited soon and was grateful to his friends for stepping in and helping. Cheryl and Ruby were invaluable. Bringing food, supplying Arnica for Britta's bruises and herbal potions to help her sleep, they'd helped in more ways than he could have imagined.

Ensuring he rested too, they'd tidied the cottage, removing any trace of Daan's destruction. They even decorated it with festive cheer, draping pretty garlands and placing fairy lights around a Christmas tree, silently working away while Britta and Atticus slept.

Now, Atticus looked forward to the party and was pleased that Britta said she was up to it. He wondered what she'd make of his surprise and couldn't wait to share it. Glancing at his watch, he realised there were only six hours to go. Perhaps, when Britta finished her painting, they would swim in the sea. Britta had told him that saltwater works wonders on the body, cleansing and purifying with its natural minerals, which was why she took a daily bathe.

Sitting down on the steps of the cottage, Atticus stared at the empty beach.

Looking up, he saw a plane in the sky. Its metallic frame glinted in the sunlight, and from a distance, it appeared tiny but grew larger as it began its descent to Alicante airport. He smiled as he thought of the passengers on board, heading to Spain for Christmas.

What a Christmas this was going to be.

Chapter Thirty-Seven

Conor sat alone in his office, nursing his second whisky of the afternoon. He'd drunk a glass of champagne with his staff before sending them home, and there was an air of excitement amongst everyone as their Christmas holiday stretched out for two glorious weeks.

They couldn't wait to leave the offices of Murphy's Auctioneers to begin the celebrations. Conor was a generous employer at Christmas, providing fully paid holiday on top of their annual leave. This year, confident that a massive injection of commission was coming his way from the sales of the new properties being built on Cillian McCarthy's land, Conor had even added a bonus to their December pay packets.

But Conor wasn't feeling the tidings of comfort and joy that others were experiencing. Gripping his whisky glass, he moved to the window to stare out. A light flurry of snow was beginning to fall, and Christmas lights cast a colourful glow over the darkening streets of Kindale, where last-minute shoppers darted in and out of stores.

It was Christmas Eve, usually the time of year Conor enjoyed most.

He knocked back his drink and went into the bathroom. Turning on the tap, he splashed cold water over his eyes, then leaning heavily on the sink, stared at his reflection in the mirror. The face that stared back looked haunted, with an almost desperate look in his eyes. Dark circles suggested a sleepless night, and day-old stubble covered his jawline, giving him an unkempt appearance.

Conor Murphy, the dapper, successful auctioneer about town, had been dumped by his lover, Lucinda. She'd ended things abruptly, and her actions had left him reeling.

The thrill he'd sought outside his marriage – a flirtatious escape from the mundane at home – had vanished. Just as he was expecting an early Christmas gift in the form of Lucinda's acceptance of his marriage proposal and her agreement to merge their businesses, the rug had been well and truly pulled out from under his feet. He would never experience the pleasure of life at Creek House, nor would he benefit from the financial bonus that their combined businesses would bring.

At breakfast, with a diamond ring languishing in his pocket, he'd smiled as Lucinda suggested a Bucks Fizz. *This was the moment! She was going to say yes!*

'Darling,' Lucinda drawled as she picked up a crystal glass and brought it to her lips. 'I think that it's time you went back to your family.'

Conor thought that he'd misheard. But her next words

stripped him of the illusion he'd so carefully constructed. Lucinda's icy eyes and her declaration that she wanted nothing more to do with him were like a punch in the gut, rendering him senseless.

'I've met someone else, much younger than you,' she said. 'He's French, rich, virile, and the most handsome of men.' Lucinda smiled. 'Let's face it, things were getting a little tired and stale between us, with you dividing your time between me and your hordes of children.'

'But what about the business?' Conor's mouth was slack as he stared at Lucinda. 'You said we would align our interests and take the whole of Ireland's property market by storm.'

'Did I?' Lucinda stared at her polished nails. 'I must have forgotten.'

'Lucinda, you can't possibly mean what you are saying...' Conor stumbled on his words. He moved forward, his arms outstretched. 'We have something special; with our love and combined talent, there's nothing we can't achieve.'

Conor stared at his empty glass and replayed the scene in his head. He'd grovelled to Lucinda, and his face burnt with shame. Now he felt he didn't know her at all.

When she picked up her car keys, Lucinda left the kitchen before pausing by the door to retort, 'Post the house keys through the letterbox or leave them with Roisin on your way out.'

Conor had been tempted to pick up the bottle of champagne and fling it at the wall, but it was only the sight of Roisin leaning on a floor mop as she stood grinning on one side of the kitchen that stopped him. He hadn't just fallen from grace; he'd tripped, stumbled, and rolled down the whole flight of stairs, and Roisin would relish in spreading the news.

The irony of the situation wasn't lost on Conor as he reached for his coat and turned off the office lights. He'd thought he could juggle two lives, keeping Mary dangling while waiting for Lucinda to give him the green light. Now, his life felt precarious, and the thrill of the affair was gone.

Conor's tread on the stairs was heavy, and as he set the alarm and locked the front door, he realised what a complete and utter idiot he'd been. Why hadn't he seen through Lucinda? Was he so blinded to money, property, and wealth that he was oblivious to her playing him for a fool? He now realised that it was how she got her kicks as she moved from one man to another, destroying them in her wake.

But as Conor climbed into his car and the engine roared to life, he felt a sudden rush of relief that the life he'd so carelessly jeopardised was still waiting for him.

Thank God that Mary, his precious wife, had hung on.

It was Christmas Eve, and his children would be waiting for their daddy to come home. He would open champagne and tell Mary how much he loved her and what a fool he'd been. They would have a proper family Christmas like old times, and all his stupidity would be forgotten.

'Oh, Mary, what an arse I am,' Conor said as he tore away from the car park and headed home. 'My gorgeous, talented Mary, the mother of my kids, how patient you've been,' Conor mumbled, and as the sight of Belvedere House came into view, he almost cried out with relief. The building was festooned with Christmas decorations and looked as warm and enticing as any home in Ireland.

Mary's Range Rover was parked in its usual place on the drive, and Conor pulled up beside it. Hurrying from his car, he hurtled across the gravel, almost tripping over one of Finn's stray footballs, and wrenched the front door open. The Christmas tree that stood in the hallway sparkled with lights and dainty glass baubles. As Conor's eyes travelled down, he was delighted to see the piles of carefully wrapped parcels beneath.

'Mary, Love!' he called out. 'Maeve, Caitlin, Finn, Declan – Daddy's home!'

Chapter Thirty-Eight

The party at Erik's pitch was in full swing, and as the light faded, the disco ball above the dance floor spun slowly, catching the last of the sun and scattering rays over campers gyrating below. By the barbecue, Ruby took charge and, with a beer in her hand, tossed steaks, burgers, and sausages onto a flaming grill. Wearing a Christmas bandana, Ness sat beside her, the old dog patiently waiting for any offerings that might come her way.

A buffet was laid out under an awning, with the tables draped in red and gold cloth, all laden with Spanish cuisine catered from Solma Vacaciones's kitchens.

'This is "cochinillo",' Erik said to his guests. 'It's suckling pig, and it's delicious.' He munched on a slice of the tender meat with its crisp, golden skin.

Platters of thinly sliced Iberian ham were artfully arranged beside an assortment of Spanish cheeses, including Manchego, Mahón, and Cabrales. Large pans of paella, filled to the brim with saffron rice, tender chicken, and savoury chorizo, wafted a delicious aroma of garlic and spices into the warm evening air.

Tables and chairs had been laid out, and the ukulele-playing campers, wearing Santa hats, had already secured their spot. Members of staff from Solma Vacaciones had arrived, including Sophia, the bike-selling aerobics instructor. Dressed in her skimpy red one-piece, she'd added a mesh skirt and matching bolero. On her head, she wore a band with silver bobbles. Her glittery roller-skating trainers lit up as she grabbed Erik's hands and sashayed to the dance floor.

'Well, I never,' Cheryl said as she gazed at Erik and Sophia, who hip-hopped like no one was watching. 'I must get myself a pair of those trainers,' she said.

Cheryl was dressed in an emerald-green, full-length gown, and as the music changed to her earlier request, she looked around for Ruby.

Reminiscent of the TV show *Come Dancing*, before it morphed into the more modern *Strictly*, Cheryl's dress was a throwback from the '80s. Emerald green with a sweetheart neckline, the off-the-shoulder number fell into a bodice of sequins and a satin skirt. Ruby, handing over her barbecue tools to the Solma Vacaciones chef, looked dapper with slicked-back hair and a smart bowtie. She wore a tuxedo that matched her trousers, and, reaching for Cheryl's hand, they twirled like pros onto the dance floor, beginning their routine with a confident step. As they dipped and spun, everyone applauded. When the performance ended, whoops and whistles for more echoed around the pitch.

Atticus stepped out of a taxi and held the door open for Britta. He paid the driver and took Britta's hand as they began to walk past the reception area and followed the road that led to Erik's pitch. Spanish children dressed as elves and fairies whizzed by on scooters and bikes as parents sat in the fading light, drinking wine, and celebrating the start of the holidays.

'Feliz Navidad!' they called out as Atticus and Britta went by.

'I'm intrigued to know my surprise,' Britta said. She wore a long floaty dress, and her hair was pinned back with jewelled clips. Gripping Atticus's arm, Britta leaned heavily. Her bruised body still ached.

'You'll soon find out,' Atticus smiled. 'But I can hear music, the party must have started.'

As they approached the crowd gathered at Erik's pitch, the first person they saw was the receptionist from the campsite. Holding onto a fixed pole and swinging wildly around it, she ignored Atticus and Britta and, in rapid Spanish, garbled loudly into a mobile phone.

They looked at each other and laughed.

Getting closer, they sensed a delicious aroma from the barbecue and heard music from the disco. When Erik saw Atticus and Britta, he reached for the microphone and called, 'Everyone! Here's The Travelling Grandad and his beautiful partner!'

Atticus and Britta were greeted warmly, and guests held out their phones to take pictures with the man who'd put their campsite on the social media map. Ness began to bark and, sensing Atticus, bounded through the crowd to hurl herself onto her boss.

'Now then, old lass.' Atticus laughed. 'Settle down.' His face lit up as Ness wagged her tail and he ruffled her fur as the dog wriggled with delight.

Sophia glided forward and took hold of Britta's hands. 'I have a surprise from your man. You must close eyes!' she commanded.

Erik moved forward, and when Sophia told Britta to open her eyes, she gasped as she saw him manoeuvre a sleek tandem bicycle tied with a huge red bow.

'Oh, my goodness, is this my surprise?' Britta turned and stared at Atticus. She ran her fingers over the handlebars, admiring the craftsmanship.

Atticus reached out to ring the bell. 'I thought we could go on even more adventures together,' he said as Ness nuzzled his legs. 'Aye, you can come too.' He patted the dog's head.

'I love it.' Britta laughed. 'It's perfect.'

'Happy Christmas.' Atticus grinned and kissed Britta as she threw her arms around him.

'Come – eat, drink, and be merry,' Erik said, turning to all the guests. 'Feliz Navidad!' he called out. Circulating with a jug of sangria, he encouraged everyone to mingle as waiting staff produced trays of tapas in bite-sized portions.

Cheryl and Ruby greeted Atticus and Britta with hugs,

and as Ruby checked Britta's welfare, Cheryl took Atticus to one side.

'Whenever you're ready,' she whispered.

'No problems?'

'All gone to plan,' Cheryl said, smiling.

Atticus turned to Britta and took hold of her hand. 'I have one more surprise for you,' he said, and moving forward with Cheryl and Ruby behind them, Atticus walked to the edge of the pitch.

'But...' Britta began to protest. 'Please, you spoil me. No more gifts,' she pleaded.

But Atticus's heart had begun to thump, and he felt his breath catch in his throat. Turning Britta to face the path, he held onto her shoulders. '*Look...*' he whispered.

Strolling towards them with a grin as wide as the sky, came Mary. Holding hands, Maeve, Finn, Declan, and Caitlin walked on either side of their mum.

Atticus felt his eyes fill with tears, and a sudden surge of joy washed over him.

'Your family!' Britta gasped.

'Yes, my love.' Atticus struggled to contain the tidal wave of emotion as he felt Britta urge him forward.

'GRANDAD!' the children cried, running towards Atticus.

With open arms, he dropped to his knees to hug Finn and Declan, burying his face in their soft, sweet-smelling hair. His heart swelled with love as he reached out to embrace Caitlin and Maeve.

Looking up at Mary, who had tears in her eyes, he stood and wrapped his daughter in his arms. 'I knew you were coming, but I can't believe you're actually here,' he whispered, his voice choked with emotion.

'Oh, Dad, it's *so* good to see you.' Mary laughed and wiped her eyes. 'You have no idea what the last week has been like. I felt like a secret agent making all the plans.'

'Where are my manners!' Atticus held onto Mary's hand and turned. 'Now, you've already met with Cheryl and Ruby,' he said as more hugs were exchanged.

'These two lifesavers arranged a gorgeous chalet for us all, right next to their own,' Mary said. 'They've even decorated it for Christmas.'

'Mary, I want you to meet Britta,' Atticus said and touched Britta's shoulder.

Mary reached for Britta's hands as she moved forward. 'You're as beautiful as Dad described, and I am so happy to meet you,' Mary said.

For a moment, Britta was rooted to the spot. The acceptance in Mary's eyes was overwhelming. 'I... I'm...' Britta stuttered. 'So, so happy to meet you too. This is such a surprise; I had no idea.'

'Sorry for the onslaught,' Mary said, shrugging. 'I come with a ready-made family, I'm afraid.' She turned to her children. 'Kids, come and say hello to Grandad's lovely friend.'

Declan clung to his mother's leg, peeking out as Britta crouched down. 'Is that your teddy?' Britta asked softly. 'What's its name?'

Declan glanced up at Mary, and when she gave a reassuring smile, he replied, 'My teddy is called Teddy.'

'That's a great name,' Britta said, 'and you must be Declan. Your grandad has told me so much about you.'

Declan shifted his weight from one foot to the other. 'You can hold Teddy if you like.'

'I'd love to.' Britta held out her hand, and her smile grew as Declan parted with his precious teddy.

'Do you play football?' Finn asked Britta, as Mary swung Declan into her arms and handed him to Atticus.

'Er, no, but maybe you can teach me?' Britta replied.

'I like your dress,' Caitlin commented. 'Did you get it in Spain?'

'Can I take your photo?' Maeve had her phone in her hand and studied Britta. 'Do you eat meat?' she asked.

'Come on, kids,' Mary interrupted. 'Give Britta some space. There's plenty of time for all your questions.'

Gathering his family, Atticus held Declan and followed Cheryl and Ruby as they led the way back to the party, where Erik made a fuss as he organised the table and chairs. He'd met Mary and the children earlier, having arranged their transport from the airport.

'You didn't tell me that you had such a beautiful daughter,' Erik said to Atticus as he poured drinks and fussed around.

'You didn't tell me you had such a roving eye.' Atticus leaned in. 'Hands off, she's recently separated,' he added.

'Now that you are all here,' Erik said, 'I would like you to step into my home, where another surprise awaits you.'

'I don't think I can take any more.' Britta laughed as she linked arms with Cheryl and Ruby and followed Atticus and his family into Erik's motorhome.

'Cool,' Maeve said as she gazed at the luxurious camper, her camera in hand.

'Can we sleep here?' Finn asked as he climbed up the steps.

'Crikey, this is something else,' Mary breathed as they entered the lush space.

'Go through to the lounge!' Erik called out.

As Atticus stepped into the well-appointed sitting area, he almost dropped Declan to the floor. Side by side, wearing Christmas T-shirts featuring festive gnomes, sat Jake and Arthur.

'The Travelling Grandad!' Arthur called out. 'About time, too.' He grinned. 'Not that we've minded waiting in this parked-up piece of paradise.'

'Grandad!' Jake couldn't contain himself and leapt up to clamber barefoot over the sofa. 'We're here!'

'Good grief.' Atticus handed Declan to Mary. 'Do you want to give me a heart attack?' he asked as he embraced Jake and Arthur. 'How on earth have you two escaped?'

'Dad is having a fit,' Jake began. 'I left him a note to let him know that I was safe travelling with Uncle Arthur to Spain, and we got a very early flight out of Manchester this morning.'

'Oh hell, I wondered why I'd missed so many calls from Mungo.' Atticus was stunned and knew that he should have spoken to his son. 'But where did you fly to?'

'Alicante, of course,' Jake said. 'We didn't know that Aunty Mary was on the earlier flight but found out when Erik picked us up at the airport.'

'So, you are in on this too?' Atticus turned to Erik.

'The power of social media.' Erik smiled. 'So easy to make new friends and exchange messages.'

Atticus stared at Arthur. 'What on earth has Shirley got to say about you not being at Shirlarth Cottage for Christmas?' he asked.

'I doubt that she'll miss me.' Arthur adjusted the Santa hat that had dipped over one eye. 'She's up to her ears in gnome-land, with the usual house full of festive freeloaders who creep out of the woodwork at Christmas,' Arthur said, shrugging. 'But I left an explanatory note on the kitchen table beside Mistletoe Mike.'

'What did it say?'

'I told her it was me or the gnomes. I can no longer compete with a bunch of ceramic statues,' Arthur said. 'I wished her a happy Christmas and said I'd be back in the new year when I'd had time to consider my position.'

Jake said, 'I think the final straw came when Aunty Shirley wanted Uncle Arthur to wear a gnome outfit.'

'I found Mistletoe Mike sitting in my armchair when I got back from the pub.' Arthur shook his head. 'Shirley said the gnome was just keeping it warm, but I have my doubts.'

Atticus laughed. He could hardly believe that his best friend was relaxing before him. 'Where are you staying?' he asked.

'Why here, of course,' Erik chipped in. 'There is plenty of room for the boys.'

The 'boys' beamed as Erik handed them a beer and a Coke.

'Cool,' chorused Maeve and Caitlin.

'Aye, it's smashing having the accommodation that our

friend Erik has so generously offered,' Arthur said as he sipped his beer. 'For the price of the flights, you'd think the plane was made of solid gold.'

'We did travel last minute on Christmas Eve, Uncle Arthur,' Jake said, worried about the cost that Arthur had generously picked up.

'I'm not complaining, anything to get away from the gnomes. I'm convinced they were plotting against me.'

'So, everyone is happy?' Erik asked and looked at the guests gathered in his motorhome. 'Then let's celebrate,' he smiled. 'After all, it is Christmas, and I say, Feliz Navidad!'

'Feliz Navidad!' they all replied and, without further ado, began to enjoy the party.

Atticus stepped out of the motorhome and looked to the bar where Mary and Britta were chatting with Cheryl and Ruby, as though they'd known each other for years. Finn was kicking about a football with a Spanish elf, and Declan was holding hands with a pretty fairy, who also had a teddy. Maeve was wandering around taking photos, while Caitlin chatted to a young man whom Atticus recognised as the jogger, Luis, from the beach. Erik had the bonnet open on his motorhome, and Jake and Arthur were peering inside, their heads nodding as they studied the powerful engine.

If only Mungo and the rest of his family were here, Atticus thought and wondered if he would ever see eye to eye with his son. He knew that Mungo would be pleased that he'd instructed Señor Resano to prepare his new will.

Now, no matter what happened, his children would have their inheritance to do with as they pleased.

At that moment, the months of separation melted away, and Atticus realised that, together with his new friends and Britta, he was surrounded by people he loved. He vowed that, somehow, he would put things right with Mungo and make every effort going forward to be an important part of his family's lives.

Atticus hadn't let the old man in, and he was no longer a man adrift.

Chapter Thirty-Nine

Conor took off his coat and hung it in the closet in the hall. The familiar scent of home enveloped him, and he felt a surge of emotion as he tugged on the sleeves of his shirt and straightened the collar. Digging into his pocket, Conor felt the diamond ring he'd bought for Lucinda in its red leather box.

Perfect! Mary's Christmas gift was solved.

He took a deep breath and felt the weight of the past few weeks lift from his shoulders as he walked through the brightly lit hallway toward the kitchen door.

Mary would be baking, filling tins with mince pies and shortbreads, and preparing for the big day. Conor hoped that she'd made a trifle. It was his favourite dessert. Lucinda was the Duchess of Diets and on a perpetual quest for the perfect body, and Conor had gone along with her latest nutritional whims. Lucinda's kitchen at Creek House was like a chemistry lab, with packets of coloured powders and potions occupying every inch of cupboard space, and he didn't think his body could take another lemon juice cleanse.

How he'd longed for a slice of Mary's 'Death by Chocolate'!

Expecting to hear the clinking of dishes and the sounds of his children, Conor turned the handle, his heart racing with anticipation as he stepped into the kitchen, where the radio was on, and the room was filled with the sound of Christmas carols.

Conor looked around.

Oddly, the worktops were completely clear, and the kitchen was as neat as a pin. But there was no sign of Mary or the children. He wondered if they were watching TV and poked his head into the playroom, but other than tripping on yet another of Finn's discarded footballs, Conor could see no evidence of his family.

He raced to the foot of the stairs and called out, 'Mary! Are you there?'

There was no answer, and Conor wracked his brain to remember if the kids had any more Christmas activities. However, given the lateness of the day, it was unlikely. Mary had a calendar in the kitchen detailing each child's schedule. She'd often told him that it was a military operation to get everyone through their busy weeks. Heading to the notice board, he turned off the radio, and as he studied the calendar, he was surprised to see that the next two weeks were blank.

'What the hell?' Conor said.

As he reached into his pocket for his mobile to call Mary, he noticed a bottle of his favourite whisky by the kettle. She'd placed a glass alongside it, and propped up by the whisky was an envelope that simply read, *Conor*.

The only sound in the room was the soft hum of the refrigerator, and as Conor held the note, Mary's familiar handwriting felt like a ghost from happier times. Instinctively, Conor poured a large measure, took a sip, and then opened the envelope. He reached out to grip the granite surface of the counter and sat down.

The note was a two-page letter.

Hi Conor

If you are reading this, it will mean that you are briefly at home during Christmas, perhaps having a break from the festivities at Creek House. Christmas is a time that you've always spent with your family. Well, this year, things are a little different.

I've taken the kids to Spain, and we will be spending the holidays with Atticus.

I know that you will say I've gone behind your back, but had we discussed this, you would have stopped me, and I can't have our children getting upset any more than is necessary. They were confused and teary when I told them we wouldn't be with Daddy this Christmas. Still, you haven't been around much lately, and a plane ride and a week in the sun with swimming pools and entertainment soon swung in Spain's favour. I apologise for the extortionate expense of the flights and transfers from our joint account, but it is Christmas after all.

By now, Lucinda will have accepted your

proposal, and I hope that you raise a toast to yourselves in the comfort of Creek House. The last few weeks have been tough, knowing that you and I have no future together.

You have broken my heart, and I can't – and won't – allow it to be broken any further.

There are four beautiful Murphys who need our love and reassurance more than ever as we go through this difficult time. I have loved you from the moment we first met, but now, I think the modern expression is, 'I love you, but I'm not in love with you anymore.'

You are the father of our children, and I will never do anything to stop you from seeing them or being a part of their lives. But life, as you've planned with Lucinda, will be different for all of us.

I have consulted a lawyer and will remain in Belvedere House for the immediate future. Hence, nothing will disturb the children's routine. Murphy's Auctioneers is yours, and I want no part of the business, but you will contribute to the children. There is no point in lingering over paperwork, and I have filed for divorce. This will enable you to move forward swiftly with Lucinda.

A new, registered company has been set up in my name. Arnott's Auctioneers will begin trading in the new year, and as a courtesy, you should know that I have signed a contract with Cillian McCarthy to handle the sale of all the new houses he is building, following the land deal that you successfully negotiated. Cillian and I go back to the time when I worked with you. I helped him out, and now, he's helping me.

Please call whenever you like. The children will want to hear from you, and I hope you will spend time with them upon our return. The new arrangements must include them seeing you whenever suits. Caitlin can't wait to try the swimming pool at Creek House.

The children have left their gifts for you under the tree.

Good luck, Conor, and take care.

Mary.

Conor's hand trembled as he stared at Mary's words. '*Take care*' – no love, no kisses, just cold hard words. It was so final. In the past weeks when he thought she'd been giving him space, Mary had been beavering away, setting herself up for a life that he would have no part of.

Reaching for his whisky, Conor tossed back the drink. *How could she*? Mary had stitched him up and was making a life for herself with a new business that completely excluded Conor.

To hell with Cillian McCarthy too! *But at least Lucinda wouldn't be getting her greedy paws on that pot of business gold.*

Conor shook his head. He was dumbstruck by his wife's actions.

But he wasn't her husband anymore, was he? He'd forsaken that honour, and as much as he'd give anything to have her back, Conor knew that their relationship was over. *How he'd underestimated Mary!* Conor should have known that his bright, intelligent wife wouldn't be a walkover. And let's face it, he thought, Mary believes he has a new life with Lucinda.

A deep, aching sadness engulfed him and a pain in his chest felt as though a vital part of him had been ripped away. The letter was in his hand, now crumpled – like his life.

He tossed it to the counter, a silent testament to the end of a chapter he hadn't been ready to close.

'Oh, Mary,' Conor cried. 'What have I done?'

Chapter Forty

Atticus and Britta hosted Christmas Day at their home, Casita del Mar. The children helped Britta add more decorations to the Christmas tree and collected seashells from the shore. Britta added colourful items from her assortment of flotsam and jetsam, and Declan's face beamed as he added a starfish to the top.

With the lunchtime sun casting a glow across the sandy beach, Mary helped Atticus arrange a barbecue, beach chairs, and blankets. The café was open for drinks, and a local band set up on a small stage, entertaining with a mix of carols and upbeat tunes. People gathered with picnics, some dancing barefoot in the sand while others swayed to the music and children played games.

'I think you've found a little piece of heaven here,' Mary said to Atticus as she watched Jake and Finn play football with a group of Spanish boys.

'It's not a bad life, is it?' Atticus agreed as he stared at the shore where Arthur, trousers rolled up, was paddling.

'I'm going to start fishing on the boat Erik owns,' Atticus announced. 'Erik says the local man who rents it would appreciate a hand during the season, and I rather fancy trying my hand at harvesting the sea instead of herding the land.'

'That's a great idea, you'll enjoy keeping busy.'

'Aye, while we're here, we'll be spending time between Spain and Cumbria.'

'Britta is lovely. I'm so happy for you both,' Mary said as she watched the barbecue begin to flame. 'Thank goodness you were here when Daan tracked her down.'

'I wish I'd been with her when he broke in.'

Mary stared at her dad, relieved that he hadn't been at the cottage. A fight with Daan could have been fatal. 'But if Britta is still married to Daan,' she asked, 'won't he make a claim on the cottage if it's in her name?'

'She's applying for a quick divorce in Holland, and when both parties agree, it's only a matter of weeks,' Atticus explained, 'and it will take that long for the sale of the cottage to go through.'

'But why would Daan agree to a divorce?' Mary was puzzled.

'He'll agree,' Atticus said with certainty.

Atticus thought about Erik and the power of Erik's chat with Daan following his arrest. If Daan wanted to return to Utrecht upon his ultimate release from his forthcoming custodial sentence for the attack on Britta, avoiding any contact with her would ensure that he stayed alive to enjoy his remaining years.

Behind Erik's affable appearance was a man of iron will.

At Solma Vacaciones, there were rumours of Erik's involvement in the underworld, but given his laid-back attitude and kindness to all, no one dug too deep. Atticus knew that Erik could easily navigate both the social and the sinister sides of his life and felt grateful to have the Dutchman on his side.

Mary instinctively knew by Atticus's reply that Daan wouldn't resurface. 'But Daan found Britta through the photos on your Instagram account,' she said.

'Aye, well, that's the danger of social media.' Atticus frowned.

'What do you mean?'

'It's been fun being The Travelling Grandad, but I'm closing the account,' he replied.

'Why? You've encouraged a host of the later-life generation to set off on a great adventure, and your followers love your posts.'

'And that's where it ends.' Atticus was firm. 'I cannot put Britta or my family in jeopardy. Social media can have a dark side.' Atticus reached for a beer from a cooler and offered it to Mary before taking one for himself. 'There's trolls too, you know. Not everyone is happy about my travels.'

'How do you deal with that?'

'I don't reply to the comments, block the sender, and delete the posts.'

'I see your point.'

'But what about you? Divorce can take a terrible toll, and I know you're putting a brave face on things.'

'It's agony if I'm honest,' Mary said and felt Atticus's comforting hand on her shoulder. 'I spoke to Conor this morning, and things haven't turned out how he expected them to.'

'What do you mean?'

'Well, Lucinda has ended their relationship, and he's on his own at Belvedere House, which isn't a great deal of fun at Christmas.'

'But what did he expect?' Atticus gripped Mary's shoulders and turned her to face him. 'Conor didn't consider you when he had you dangling on a string all that time while he made up his mind. His children were low on his list of priorities, too.' He shook his head. 'I'm sorry, Mary, but I think he's got what he deserves.'

'I know that you're right,' Mary sighed. 'But when the children spoke to him today, they were enthusiastic and excited about everything in Spain. It must have been hard for him to hear.'

'Too bad.' Atticus shrugged.

'Caitlin wouldn't go to the phone, though. She refuses to speak to her daddy.'

'I wouldn't worry too much about Caitlin.' Atticus pointed to a young couple playing bat and ball on the beach. Caitlin was laughing with the jogger, whose name was Luis. 'She seems preoccupied to me,' he said, smiling.

'Well, we have a week here, and Conor has time off from work to be with the kids when we return. His office is closed for two weeks.'

'Then he can explain to them. Make sure he moves to one of the properties he rents out,' Atticus added.

'To be honest, letting him take over childcare for a few days will be good. If you remember, I have a new business kicking off in the new year.'

'How has that gone down?'

'Like a lead balloon.' Mary began to chuckle. 'When Conor stopped crying and pleading with me to change my mind, he suddenly remembered that I'm starting Arnott's Auctioneers.'

'I can't imagine that he was happy?'

'He was furious. In fact, he called me every name under the sun and accused me of sleeping with Cillian McCarthy.'

'The cheek!'

'He even added Ruari into the mix and said I must be sleeping with him too.' Mary sighed. She remembered Ruari's kiss, his gorgeous eyes and wonderful embrace, and almost wished she were.

'He's trying to find blame that might justify his actions.'

Mary linked her arm through Atticus's. 'An angry Conor is far easier to deal with than a crying Conor,' she said. 'I had no hesitation in ending the call while he ranted and raved. He won't have liked that.'

'I'm sure he didn't.' Atticus grinned.

'Have you spoken to Mungo?' Mary asked.

'I phoned to wish them a happy Christmas, but I'm afraid I woke him quite early this morning. Mungo wasn't exactly filled with Christmas cheer.'

'He'll be furious that Jake is here.'

'That was one of his grievances.'

'And the rest?'

'Where do I start...'

They both looked out to sea, where Arthur, who'd been chatting with a fisherman, was now heading up the beach. Dressed in his Santa hat and snowman jumper, he waved when he saw them.

'The barbecue is ready,' Atticus said, taking a long-handled fork.

'Do we have enough food?' Mary asked.

'Enough to feed an army,' Atticus replied. 'Erik sent us the buffet excess from last night and, as you can see, the cavalry has arrived.'

Trooping along the beach, arms laden with bags of food, came Cheryl and Ruby.

'Cooee!' Cheryl called out. 'Feliz Navidad!'

Cheryl was dressed as an elf, and her bright red-and-green costume hugged her frame. The bells on her shoes jingled with every step, and the bright red pom-pom on her hat matched her heavily rouged cheeks. Ruby, meanwhile, wore a more sedate outfit in stretchy brown Lycra, complete with bouncing antlers on her head.

'By heck, the gnomes have arrived!' Arthur panted as he joined them and looked anxiously around.

'Relax, my friend,' Atticus said, handing Arthur a beer. 'It's only Cheryl and Ruby.'

'Whew! For a moment, I thought Shirley had found me.'

'Happy Christmas!' Cheryl said and greeted them all. 'We thought we'd dress up as a treat for the kiddies.'

Atticus thought the kiddies might be traumatised at the sight of the two pensioners in their party wear, but he returned the greetings and handed his friends a beer.

'Erik and Sophia aren't far behind,' Cheryl said. 'They're rollerblading.'

In the distance, travelling in harmony along the boardwalk parallel to the beach, two figures dressed as Mr and Mrs Claus came into sight. Sophia, her lengthy hair cascading, wore a sequinned, fur-trimmed mini-dress that caught the light as she glided, followed by Erik in scarlet Speedos and a Santa hat. 'Feliz Navidad!' they called out.

'I wouldn't mind a pair of those Speedos,' Arthur said, wide-eyed.

'Grandad, can I get some rollerblades?' Jake asked and stared at Sophia as she joined them.

'Here, Jake, try these,' Erik said as he unbuckled his boots and gave them to Jake, then reached into the cooler for a beer. Moments later, Jake, gripping Sophia's hand, stumbled falteringly along the boardwalk.

'He'll soon get the hang of it,' Arthur mused as Jake tumbled head-over-heels onto the beach.

As night closed in, the terrace at Casita del Mar was a peaceful retreat, the air carrying the woody scent of a distant beach bonfire and the faint sound of waves lapping against the shore. Everyone had returned, tired but happy, to their accommodation. Atticus sat on the swing with

Britta, her head on his shoulder, eyes closed, as he remembered the bustling family Christmas Day.

Candles in lanterns flickered as he recalled the games they'd played with the children. Everyone joined in for beach cricket, and Atticus smiled when Cheryl collided with Arthur as they reached up to catch a ball.

'I've been elfed!' Arthur called out as he tumbled beneath Cheryl, and they fell onto the sand.

Atticus, encouraged by Britta, had gone for a dip and, once in the water, called out for everyone to dive in. The children squealed at first but soon began to enjoy the gentle waves. Mary, braving a bikini, produced a ball and, with Declan on her shoulders, threw it for everyone to catch.

The twilight blue of the night reflected the stars overhead, and Atticus watched their light bouncing off the sea's surface and thought of Mary and Mungo.

How he wished that Mary could find a partner who adored her. Her heart had been broken and her trust destroyed, but she deserved to be loved and appreciated. Any man in his right mind would snap her up.

On the other hand, Mungo lived in greyscale and seemed trapped in a cloud of gloom. How Atticus wished that his son could wake up and realise that the life he'd created was wonderful. His wife was a diamond, and he had two fantastic kids. The business would sustain them all, becoming a pot of gold at the end of Mungo's retirement rainbow.

But as Atticus stroked Britta's hair, he thought he was the luckiest man alive, and tonight was the end of a perfect day. Kissing her forehead, he gently closed his eyes and whispered, 'Feliz Navidad.'

Chapter Forty-One

Boxing Day at Solma Vacaciones was a time for the campers to get together and celebrate with an afternoon party around the pool. The management laid on a barbecue and buffet for their guests and with games for the children and activities for adults, the happy campers all joined in.

Sophia, wearing her bright red one-piece, was encouraging her senior squad to work off their Christmas excess in the pool. 'Sí! Hagámoslo!' she yelled, kicking her legs and waving her arms. 'Let's do it, get moving!'

Arthur, in a pair of Speedos borrowed from Erik, his Santa hat at a jaunty angle, was knee-deep in the water as he raised his leg and waved his arms. Atticus, comfortable on a nearby sunbed, prayed that Arthur wouldn't need 'gnome-ing' back together when he took the tumble that was imminent and ended up flat out in the pool.

'You've got this Aqua-Gnome!' Jake called out. 'Show the water who's boss, Uncle Arthur!'

'You're crushing it, Hydro-Hero,' Maeve joined in. She held her phone in her hand and was shooting an Instagram reel with the hashtags: '#PensionersPaddle at the #SeniorSplash'.

In the children's pool, Britta held Declan's hand and guided him to the slide on the hippo. She clapped her hands as he sped into the water. Nearby, Finn was enjoying a game of water volleyball with children from Spanish families.

'Where's Caitlin?' Mary asked as she joined Maeve.

'With lover-boy in the jacuzzi.' Maeve waved her hand to the side of the pool, where a smiling Caitlin sat in a bubbling inferno with Luis.

Sprawled out beside Atticus, Cheryl, in her tankini, smoothed suncream onto her legs. 'Want a squirt?' she asked. 'It's factor fifty and will stop your wrinkles.'

'It's a bit late for that.' Atticus tilted his hat.

Ruby appeared and throwing down her beach bag, stepped out of her denim dungarees and sat beside Cheryl. 'There are more folks arriving,' she said. 'I just saw a people carrier pulling up outside one of the chalets.'

'The more the merrier,' Cheryl said and held out her tube to Ruby. 'Be a love and do my back, would you?'

'Is Arthur alright? Ruby asked. She noticed a commotion at the pool where several members of the senior squad were gathered around Arthur.

'I think he's split his Speedos.' Atticus chuckled.

Hands reached for towels as Arthur, covering his modesty, was assisted from the water.

'You're a pool shark, Uncle Arthur,' Jake said and

helped him to a seat beside Atticus. 'That last leg kick was epic.'

'I've nearly sliced me unmentionables in two.' Arthur winced and clutched his towel to cover the gaping hole in Erik's designer swimwear. 'Have you got a needle and thread?'

'Anyone fancy a glass of sangria?' Ruby asked.

Hands shot up but Atticus tapped Jake and Maeve's down. 'They'll have a Coke,' he said as staff from the animation team, dressed in festive outfits, encouraged the children to the stage.

Mary went to help Ruby and carried a tray of drinks as they made their way back. The sun was fierce and Mary, squinting her eyes, wished she'd worn her sunglasses as she navigated her way.

'Oops!' she called out as she accidently bumped into a man who'd suddenly appeared before her. 'I'm so sorry, I can hardly see where I'm going.'

'Let me help you,' the man replied and held out his hands.

'O.M.G!' Mary screamed and almost dropped the tray.

Ruby, realising the danger, swooped low and caught it.

'MUNGO!' Mary gasped. 'What on earth?' She took a step back and squeezed her eyes shut then opened them to stare at the figure before her. 'Is it *really* you?'

'Yes, it's me.' Mungo laughed. 'We've just arrived. I asked the receptionist where you might be; she was quite offhand and garbled in Spanish. I couldn't understand her, but I thought I might find you all here by the pool.'

'WE?' Mary rubbed her eyes as if to reaffirm what she was seeing.

'Helen and Eliza are here too,' he said. 'Look, over there.'

Mungo pointed and Mary saw her sister-in-law and niece hugging Atticus and Jake.

'Well, I never.' Mary shook her head. Almost speechless, she linked her arm through her brother's. 'We'd better go and join them.'

Atticus was on his feet. At first, he thought he was imagining things. Was that really Helen and Eliza coming toward him? But as they got closer and ran to wrap him in a huge hug, he knew that their arrival was real.

'But where's Mungo?' Atticus asked.

'I'm here, Dad,' a voice behind him called out and Atticus turned to see Mungo and Mary.

Atticus glanced from one to the other. 'Did you know?' he asked Mary.

'Hadn't a clue – I'm as surprised as you,' Mary said, slowly recovering and beginning to grin.

Mungo reached out for his dad's hand. 'I'm sorry,' he simply said.

'Whatever for?' Atticus asked.

'For everything.' Mungo shrugged his shoulders. 'For not listening to you and being an overbearing father.' He glanced towards Jake. 'But most of all, for not appreciating my family. I've taken you all for granted and I'm truly sorry.'

'Well, that's...' Atticus was at a loss for words.

Britta held Declan, still carrying his teddy, and looked anxiously from Atticus to Mungo.

Mungo continued, 'You don't have to say anything, Dad. Just know that I think your great adventure to Spain is admirable. It took some guts, and I couldn't be happier that you've met someone and fallen in love.'

A little voice piped up and heads turned to stare at Declan.

'Uncle Mungo,' Declan said, 'do you know my new granny?'

Suddenly, the ice was broken, and everyone began to laugh. Atticus gave Mungo a bear hug and stood back to smile at his son.

Britta stepped forward and held out her free hand. 'Hello,' she said, 'I'm Britta.'

'Hello, Declan's new granny.' Mungo smiled. 'Ali insisted I take my family on holiday,' Mungo explained as questions rained upon him. 'She found us a Boxing Day flight to Alicante and told me she was perfectly capable of running the business for a week.'

'There was hardly anyone on the plane,' Eliza said excitedly, 'and I had a glass of champagne.'

Erik joined the party. He'd taken Ness for a walk on the beach and the old dog, recognising Mungo, wriggled her way into the crowd.

'Were my Speedos a bit snug?' Erik asked, his expression bemused as he stared at Arthur, now attired in Cheryl's voluminous green kaftan.

'Aye, you could say so,' Arthur replied.

Mary stood back and stared at the ever-increasing party. Unexpectedly, she felt exhausted. With weeks of little sleep and living on an emotional knife-edge she suddenly felt that she might collapse if she didn't take a moment for herself.

'Can you keep an eye on the kids?' Mary whispered to Atticus.

Atticus saw the look on Mary's face and nodded. 'Yes, love, of course. Why don't you go to the beach and stretch your legs? The kids are just fine.'

Mary gave a half-smile and turning away, she set off.

Matching the rhythm of the waves brushing against the shore, Mary's steps were slow as she began her solitary walk. The salty breeze tousled her hair, and she reached out to tuck it behind one ear. As she reached for her sunglasses, she stared at the wide expanse of the beach. The weight of recent events lingered heavily, and the decline of her marriage left Mary putting on a brave face for the kids, knowing there would be difficult days ahead as they came to terms with their parents' split. Overhead, seagulls cried, their calls echoing the unanswered questions in her mind.

Her longing for love emphasised her loneliness, but she thought of the texts she'd received from Ruari and smiled. Given half a chance, she'd jump into his bed and give in to his subtle invitations, but, Mary pondered, no man in his right mind would seriously look at a middle-aged woman with four demanding children. Lost in the complexity of her thoughts, Mary wandered along, her bare feet paddling in the water.

'How am I going to navigate through all of this?' she called out and stared up at the sky.

'I'll help you,' a voice replied, and Mary turned to see Atticus coming toward her.

'Dad!' Mary laughed and held out her arms.

Looking up, Mary and Atticus saw that a cluster of solitary stars had emerged. Like tiny gems, they twinkled and stood out in the still bright sky.

As father and daughter embraced on the shore, Mary spoke softly.

'Mum would be so proud of you.'

Epilogue

SIX MONTHS LATER...

Atticus and Britta were married in a simple ceremony on a bright and sunny day in the Parish of St. Lawrence. A carpet of wildflowers lined the path to the centuries-old church, and knee-high gnomes formed a guard of honour decked out in wedding attire. In a tuxedo, top hat, and tiny bowtie, Mistletoe Mike wore a monocle, while Tinsel Tina, transformed in a lacy dress, carried a minuscule bouquet.

'We did a cracking job,' Arthur told Jake. He'd arrived with Shirley on his arm, and they paused to admire her garden guardians. 'The little creatures have scrubbed up a treat.'

'I think we should go into production, Uncle Arthur,' Jake commented and remembered the hours spent in Arthur's shed with Polyfilla, a paintbrush, and an endless supply of tea.

Britta entered the church wearing a simple silk outfit that matched her cornflower blue eyes, and in her hands, she carried a bouquet of white roses. Close behind Britta came a trio of bridesmaids wearing outfits of their choice. Eliza and Caitlin were endearing in matching dresses and fur boleros, but Maeve, ever the rebel, favoured her '80s punk-rock look. She'd dug out her short leather skirt, ripped fishnet tights, and acid-washed vest once more.

In her emerald-green dress, Cheryl smiled at Maeve and whispered to Ruby, 'I wouldn't mind a get-up like that.'

'You've always looked good in leather,' Ruby, in a tailored suit, agreed.

Standing nervously by the altar, Atticus was accompanied by Mungo. 'She's here,' Mungo whispered and gave Atticus's shoulder a reassuring squeeze.

Sunlight filtered through the stained-glass windows as Britta came down the aisle, and Atticus thought she'd never looked more beautiful. Her divorce had been swift and now, surrounded by their loved ones, they exchanged their vows. When it was announced that the groom could kiss the bride, the congregation cheered.

Church bells rang as the happy couple emerged and were showered with confetti. Finn held onto Ness, who was decked out in a blue bandana, as the dog wriggled and thumped her tail. Erik, in a bespoke Savile Row suit, wore designer sunglasses, and his Rolex glinted in the sunshine. He stood with Ali, who blushed like a schoolgirl when he took her arm and walked her across the village green to The Black Bull, where Reg had laid on a reception.

The Senior Socials Club and the domino team were on their feet as the wedding party arrived at the pub, and the round of applause could be heard as far away as Barn Hill

Farm. Reg, dapper in a waistcoat, served champagne and congratulated the happy couple.

Mary stood at the back of the pub and watched the wedding guests, and she smiled as she saw her dad introduce his new wife to the locals.

For a moment, Mary thought of Conor.

Being with family had become vitally important to her estranged husband, and he endeavoured to be with his children at every opportunity. She was grateful that Conor was a good dad. It eased the pain of parting, and the children were adapting to their changed way of life. Even Caitlin had come around. She often spent time with Conor and his new girlfriend, and confided to Mary that Cindy, a hair stylist, was a lousy cook but a whizz with the scissors and the styling wand.

How useful, thought Mary as she admired Caitlin's new haircut. Caitlin, who spent hours on FaceTime with Luis, was these days, a much happier bunny.

Cillian McCarthy had been the first to tell Mary that Darby's had gone into receivership, and Lucinda, who hadn't been seen for weeks, was thought to be abroad. Creek House had unexpectedly gone on the market and Murphy's had been instructed for the sale.

When Conor called for the children one Saturday morning, Mary asked her ex-husband if he'd put in an offer. 'That ship has sailed,' Conor replied. 'Creek House was a dream that became a nightmare,' he added.

With the children's time divided between herself and

Conor, Mary concentrated on her business, which soon began to boom. She picked up sales that Darby's could no longer handle, and with the construction of Cillian's new houses underway, the future of Arnott's Auctioneers looked rosy.

The latest asset to her business was the handsome new agent who appeared to have the magic touch. With multiple sales and skilful negotiation, commissions racked up like a constantly ticking clock. Having sold his valeting business for a satisfying figure, Ruari was enjoying his new role.

'A glass of champagne?'

Mary turned to see Ruari beside her. *Goodness, he was easy on the eye!*

'You're miles away,' Ruari said, handing her the drink.

'Not really, I'm just thinking how lucky I am to have such a great family,' Mary said.

She caught the scent of his skin and felt the warmth of his arm as it snaked around her waist. Strangely, she'd lost weight without even trying, and her Bounce Buster Briefs were a thing of the past. Mary even enjoyed the Ladies' Lunch Club and discovered that the ladies were surprisingly supportive. To her amusement, she discovered that they disliked Lucinda too and were delighted when Una set them straight about the bitchiest member of their club.

Mary turned to Ruari and as she stared into his eyes, her heart almost skipped a beat. She'd no idea where this relationship was going but here, right now, she adored the man who was slowly rebuilding her broken heart.

Atticus turned to Britta. 'It's time to go, my love. Have you got all our paperwork?'

Britta tapped the bag on her shoulder. 'Ferry tickets to Santander and passports for you, me, and Ness, safely secured,' she said, smiling.

Guests, aware that departure was imminent, began to gather outside.

As Atticus and Britta made their way out of the pub, Jake ran ahead to give Winnie a final polish and ensure that the tin cans he'd attached to her rear bumper were secured. A 'Just Married' banner fluttered in Winnie's rear window.

Atticus secured Ness and helped Britta to her seat, then turned to thank everyone for their well-wishes.

'See you on the other side in Spain!' Cheryl and Ruby called out.

'Safe travels,' said Erik, his arm around Ali, who beamed and waved.

'Good luck, Dad.' Mungo smiled as he stood beside Helen. 'We'll be out to Spain again to see you both very soon.'

Atticus caught Mary's eye. Blowing her a kiss, he thought of the day Mary had marched him into the barn, and they'd discovered Winnie. It had marked the beginning of the rest of his life. He cranked Winnie's engine into gear and tooted her horn. To applause and cheers, Atticus and Britta set off for Spain.

As they drove away, Atticus looked up at a passing cloud and thought he saw the shape of Clara's smile.

'*Well done, my dearest,*' came a ghostly whisper, '*you didn't let the old man in.*'

Acknowledgments

This book was born from a simple kitchen table conversation when my hubby turned to me and asked, "How do you fancy spending our winters in Spain?" The idea of escaping Lancashire's cold, damp days for a place with warm sunshine and a gentler climate was too tempting to resist. So, the adventure began with Venus—our beloved home on wheels—and Fred, our Westie.

The excitement started in the planning and dreaming, long before we set off. And then, one freezing November day, it was time. Sailing from Portsmouth felt like the start of something special, though, like Atticus in this story, I'm not the best sailor—the Bay of Biscay certainly put me to the test! But a new world opened when we rolled onto dry and sunny Spanish land.

Our winter escape led us to a beautiful campsite on the Costa Blanca, a region famous for its golden beaches, lush pine forests, and a microclimate that feels like a warm hug. As we settled in, I couldn't help but be inspired by the fascinating people around me—of all nationalities, embracing their later years with energy, laughter, and a zest for life. And just like that, Atticus sprang to life in my imagination.

This journey reaffirmed what I've always believed: it's

never too late to fall in love, start fresh, or welcome happiness with open arms. After all, happiness has no deadline—it often finds us when we open our hearts to it.

I'd like to thank everyone I've met along the way who inspired me to write this story, with special gratitude to Bonnie Macleod for her invaluable expertise in refining the details and her brilliant editing.

I hope this story brings warmth and joy to your precious reading hours. Thank you for letting my characters into your world. And as the years go by, like Atticus, remember Clara's wise words:

"Don't let the old man in..."

Happy reading!

With love
Caroline

Join Caroline's newsletter for book news and giveaways:

www.carolinejamesauthor.co.uk/giveaway-and-newsletter

Also by Caroline James

The Cruise Club

The French Cookery School

The Cruise

The Spa Break

Hattie Goes to Hollywood

Boomerville at Ballymegille

The Best Boomerville Hotel

Coffee Tea the Gypsy & Me

Coffee Tea the Chef & Me

Coffee Tea the Caribbean & Me

Jungle Rock

Set sail on the Diamond Star for sunshine, romance – and just a little bit of mischief...

Cosy crime writer Carmen Cunningham is in trouble. Her inspiration has vanished, her deadline is looming, and her meddling elderly mother Betty consumes her every waking moment.

Hoping to revive her creativity, Carmen books a dream cruise, featuring workshops with her literary idol, Ruskin Reeve. It's the perfect plan – until Betty insists on tagging along...

Will the cruise reignite Carmen's writing muse or plunge her into the biggest plot twist of her life? Because, as she's about to find out, anything can happen at sea...

Available Now!

Printed in Dunstable, United Kingdom

66944991R00231